Parke Godwin

A Biography of William Cullen Bryant, With Extracts From His Private Correspondence

Vol. I

Parke Godwin

A Biography of William Cullen Bryant, With Extracts From His Private Correspondence

Vol. I

Reprint of the original, first published in 1883.

1st Edition 2023 | ISBN: 978-3-38510-599-7

Verlag (Publisher): Outlook Verlag GmbH, Zeilweg 44, 60439 Frankfurt, Deutschland
Vertretungsberechtigt (Authorized to represent): E. Roepke, Zeilweg 44, 60439 Frankfurt, Deutschland
Druck (Print): Books on Demand GmbH, In de Tarpen 42, 22848 Norderstedt, Deutschland

A BIOGRAPHY

OF

WILLIAM CULLEN BRYANT,

WITH

EXTRACTS FROM HIS PRIVATE CORRESPONDENCE.

BY

PARKE GODWIN.

IN TWO VOLUMES:

Volume First.

NEW YORK:
D. APPLETON AND COMPANY,
1, 3, AND 5 BOND STREET.
1883.

PREFACE.

SOME time after the death of Mr. Bryant, in 1878, his younger daughter, Miss Julia S. Bryant, to whom his papers were left, sent me copies of such of them as she supposed might be useful in the preparation of a memoir of his life. These consisted of letters written by him or to him, mostly of a private or domestic nature, and of a few unpublished or uncollected poems. Accompanying them were several scrap-books containing some of his editorial writings, and extracts of newspaper articles written about him at various times.

To these scanty materials I was able, through the kindness of their possessors, to add his letters to Arthur and John H. Bryant, his brothers, Gulian C. Verplanck, the Rev. Orville Dewey, Mr. John Bigelow, the Rev. R. C. Waterston, Miss Christiana and Miss Janet Gibson, of Edinburgh, Mr. H. W. Longfellow, Professor J. S. Thayer, of Cambridge, Miss J. Dewey, Mrs. L. M. S. Moulton, Mr. John H. Gourlie, Mr. R. H. Stoddard, and others—for which I return my thanks to such of them as are living, and to the heirs of such as have passed away.

Mr. Bryant, as the editor of a daily newspaper, was not

able to be a voluminous letter-writer. The letters he wrote were mostly on business, or in acknowledgment of others, and they were written at times when it was scarcely possible to engage in discussions of opinions or of the events of the day. Besides, his relations to his contemporaries were restricted, and, except with his intimate and life-long friend, Mr. Richard H. Dana, he cannot be said to have maintained any extensive correspondence. Nevertheless, out of the brief and familiar notes interchanged with his friends, I have been able to select many passages which, I trust, will be found of interest, either as illustrative of the times or of the writer's character. Whatever he said was gracefully said, and, either in the mode of expression or in the turn of the thought, was apt to contain something worthy of attention.

I will confess that I have been greatly embarrassed as to how I should treat the editorial part of his life, the more so as there are no models that I know of in English literature for work of the kind. The statesman by the measures he promotes, the soldier by his battles, the author by his books, and the artist by his works, furnishes certain stages, or, as the French say, *étapes*, or halting-places, in his career, which enables the biographer to mark the steps of his progress. But the life of the editor affords no such salient points. His labors consist of a series of incessant and innumerable blows, of the real influences of which it is hard to judge, except in a general way. It can only be told of him what he endeavored to do, and not what he actually did. Whatever effects he may have wrought on public opinion were wrought by indefinitely small increments, of the precise force and value of which we have no measure.

Mr. Bryant's editorial life extended over a period of more than fifty years. During that time he used his best abilities and exertions in affecting the sentiments and aims of his fellow-men : but to give a full account of his activity in this respect would be to write the history of his times as well as of his life, stretching the narrative into interminable volumes; and yet to omit all account of it would be to neglect a most important part of his usefulness. In this difficulty, I have adopted the method of taking it for granted that the reader is more or less familiar with the political history of the nation, and of referring to Mr. Bryant's position and efforts only in regard to its leading events. My desire, in every case, has been to estimate his services without any of the exaggeration to which I am, perhaps, unconsciously inclined by circumstances.

It has been thought advisable—to supplement this memoir and to preserve some permanent record of a singularly active and beneficent career—to add to these volumes a uniform edition of Mr. Bryant's more important writings, both in prose and poetry. It will comprise his Poems, his Orations and Addresses, some Sketches of Travel, and a volume of Miscellanies.

CONTENTS.

PAGE

devotion to freedom and equal rights ; his creed unpopular. His associate, William Leggett: Their intense and radical democracy ; uphold Jackson's administration. Proscriptions not condemned. Bryant's sympathy with revolutions and reforms: No great like of reformers. Poetry deserted, yet he gathers a volume ; sends a copy to Washington Irving in England ; letter to Irving.

CHAPTER FOURTEENTH.

A visit to Washington: The capital fifty years ago; glimpses of Old Hickory, Clay, Calhoun, Webster, etc. The poems in England : Irving's kindness ; notices of them in the reviews ; John Wilson ; notices of them at home ; letters to Dana on the subject. Versification : Advice to John H. Bryant on writing poetry. Edits "Tales of the Glauber Spa." Illinois in 1832. Captain Abraham Lincoln. The Bryant family pioneers of the State. The prairies. Cholera in New York. Residence in Hoboken. Mr. Bryant stays at his desk. Nullification condemned. Death of his friend Robert C. Sands.

CHAPTER FIFTEENTH.

Jackson's battle with the National Bank : Earnest support of the "Evening Post"; it alienates its mercantile clients; violent politics. A visit to Canada. Prologue to a play. Correspondence with Dana : Criticisms of one another's verses ; "The Robbers," a suppressed poem. A Boston edition of the poems published. Preparing to go abroad. Abolition mobs in New York.

CHAPTER SIXTEENTH.

Sails for Havre. Residence in France, Italy, and Germany ; Longfellow ; sudden recall home by Leggett's illness. Offered a dinner, which he declines. Affairs in New York. Miss Martineau. International copyright. Van Buren. Unpopularity of the journal, which rebukes the mob and defends the Abolitionists. Mr. Bryant meditates a removal to the West : Letters to his brother John on the subject.

CHAPTER SEVENTEENTH.

Jackson's "experiments on the currency." The question of corporations. Conspiracies and usury laws. Factitious prosperity. The "Even-

CONTENTS.

CHAPTER FIRST.

AN AUTOBIOGRAPHY OF MR. BRYANT'S EARLY LIFE.*

I HAVE friends who insist that I shall set down some notes of the events of my life, thinking that the narrative of certain parts of it may not be without interest or instruction. I suppose that as much as this may be said of the biography of almost any man if faithfully written. There is, however, one embarrassment with which I am met in undertaking this task. My memory does not, in general, retain minute particulars. Often when I desire to speak of what happened some years ago, or perhaps only some months, I find the attendant circumstances, some of which are perhaps desirable to be given for the sake of perspicuity, entirely beyond the reach of my recollection. If I could recover them, I might select from them what would give a lifelike air and an individual character to my story. When I compare what I am able to relate of my own life with the autobiographies of Franklin and some others, I find the poverty of my materials so apparent that I seriously distrust my power of engaging the attention of the reader. I have begun to write, however, and shall go on ; and, when a few sheets are filled, I shall be able to judge whether the manuscript shall be thrown into the fire or put by with the papers which I preserve.

* This was written in the year 1874-5.—G.

I was born in Cummington, in the State of Massachusetts, on the 3d of November, 1794, when that region was a new settlement. My father and mother then lived in a house, which stands no longer, near the center of the township, amid fields which have a steep slope to the north fork of the West-field River, a shallow stream, brawling over a bed of loose stones in a very narrow valley. A few old apple-trees mark the spot where the house stood, and opposite, on the other side of the way, is a graveyard, in which sleep some of those who came to Cummington while it was yet a forest, and hewed away the trees and were the first to till its fields.

My father, Dr. Peter Bryant, was a physician and sur-geon, who came to the place a young man from North Bridge-water, where he was born. He was fond of study and well read in his profession. As a surgeon he had a steady and firm hand and an accurate eye, and performed difficult operations with great nicety and dispatch. I remember to have heard Professor Eaton, of the Rensselaer School, in Troy, say that he was the most dexterous operator that he had seen handle the surgeon's knife. He was a pupil of Leprilète, a refugee from St. Domingo, educated in Paris, who settled in Norton, in the eastern part of Massachusetts, where he married the daughter of a plain farmer, and practiced as a surgical opera-tor with an extensive reputation. I remember having heard this anecdote of him. He was once on a visit to Taunton, when one of the ladies of the place, addressing the courteous and lively Frenchman, as he stood dressed according to his wont, with great elegance and precision, wearing ruffles at his wrists, said: "Do bring Mrs. Leprilète to Taunton; we will do everything in our power to make her visit agreeable." "Ah, madame," replied he, "you geev her leetle pork and beans; dot all she want."

My father delighted in poetry, and in his library were the works of most of the eminent English poets. He wrote verses himself, mostly humorous and satirical. He was not unskilled in Latin poetry, in which the odes of Horace were his favor-

ites. He was fond of music, played on the violin, and I remember hearing him say that he once made a bass viol—for
he was very ingenious in the use of tools—and played upon it.
He was of a mild and indulgent temper, somewhat silent—
though not hesitating in conversation, and never expatiated at
much length on any subject. His patients generally paid him
whatever they pleased, if ever so little, so that he could not by
any means be called a thriving man. In one respect he did
not stint himself; he always dressed well, and with a most
scrupulous neatness, his attire being that of a Boston gentleman, and he had a certain metropolitan air. In figure he was
square built, with muscular arms and legs, and in his prime
was possessed of great strength. He would take up a barrel
of cider and lift it into a cart over the wheel—a feat of which
he was not unwilling to speak. His life was a laborious one,
being obliged to make professional visits to persons living at
a distance, often in the most inclement weather. He always
made these journeys on horseback. The family was frequently disturbed at midnight, sometimes in the dead of winter or
in the midst of a furious storm, by a messenger from some
sick person who had put off sending for him until that un-
timely hour. Physicians say that the patient's desire to see
the doctor is very sure to increase with the lateness and un-
seasonableness of the hour.

I have been told by a farmer, a native of Cummington, that
he remembered with pleasure my father's polite manners, and
that he had always a bow and a kindly greeting for him when
he was a shy boy—a practice which he remarks that my father always followed, even toward the youngest.

My father took great interest in political questions. He
belonged to the party called Federalists, who at that time
were strong in Massachusetts, but in the Union at large were
a minority, and saw the Republic governed by their political
adversaries. He represented Cummington for several successive years in the Massachusetts Legislature, and was afterward a member of the State Senate.

My mother, Sarah Snell Bryant, was the daughter of Ebenezer Snell, of Cummington, one of the first settlers of the region in which I was born.   Concerning him I shall say more hereafter.   She was born in North Bridgewater, and was brought by her father when a little child to Cummington. She was tall, of an erect figure, and, until rather late in life, of an uncommonly youthful appearance.   She was a person of excellent practical sense, of a quick and sensitive moral judgment, and had no patience with any form of deceit or duplicity.   Her prompt condemnation of injustice, even in those instances in which it is tolerated by the world, made a strong impression upon me in early life, and if, in the discussion of public questions, I have in my riper age endeavored to keep in view the great rule of right without much regard to persons, it has been owing in a good degree to the force of her example, which taught me never to countenance a wrong because others did.   My mother was a careful economist, which the circumstances of her family compelled her to be, and by which she made some amends for my father's want of attention to the main chance.   She had a habit of keeping a diary, in which the simple occupations of the day and the occurrences in which the family or the neighborhood had an interest were briefly noted down.   Of the dates obtained from the diary I shall make some use in what I am about to write. I remember hearing her, while I was yet a child, speak contemptuously of Pope.   She read him, not without a certain admiration, but regarded him as the libeler of her sex in his " Epistle on the Characters of Women."

I was thought to be a precocious child.   On my first birthday there is a record that I could already go alone, and on the 28th of March, 1796, when but a few days more than sixteen months old, there is another record that I knew all the letters of the alphabet.   In both these instances it is probable that my mother, finding me rather docile, took pleasure in bringing me forward somewhat prematurely.   My elder brother, Austin, was more remarkable as an early scholar than myself. On the 28th of March, 1796, before the close of his third year, he began to read the Bible. On the 12th of April following, he had finished the book of Genesis, and on the 31st of March, 1797, before he had completed his fourth year, he had read the Scriptures through from beginning to end. I ought to be fond of church-going, for I began early, making my first appearance at church about the middle of my third year, though there is no note of how I behaved myself there.

In September, 1797, the family removed to Plainfield, but not so far from its first home as to be out of the circuit of my father's medical practice. Here, on the 7th day of February following, it is recorded in my mother's diary that I was ill, and the next day that I had a fever. I remember an incident of that illness. I was in bed, my father approached me with a lancet, and, taking my arm, pierced a vein at the meeting of the forearm and shoulder. As I felt the prick of the lancet I uttered a faint wail, which I seem even yet to hear as I write. Many years since—I can not say how many—I was told, by a person who lived near us at the time of which I am speaking, that my case was thought a doubtful one, and that my father and mother feared, to use his expression, "that they should not be able to raise me." * I have lately been to look at the site of that house. Nothing is left of it but the cellar and some portions of the chimney, among a thick growth of brambles. Not far from it is a deserted house, where there lived a neighbor, and beyond the house an old road no longer open

---

* Senator Dawes, whose uncle was a student in Dr. Bryant's office, in his Centennial Address at Cummington on June 26, 1879, says: " The poet was puny and very delicate in body, and of a painfully delicate nervous temperament. There seemed little promise that he would survive the casualties of early childhood. In after years, when he had become famous, those who had been medical students with his father when he was struggling for existence with the odds very much against him, delighted to tell of the cold baths they were ordered to give the infant poet in a spring near the house each early morning of the summer months, continuing the treatment, in spite of the outcries and protestations of their patient, so late into the autumn as sometimes to break the ice that skimmed the surface." This was doubtless the first application of hydropathy ever made in those parts.—G.

to the public, but given back to the fields from which it was taken. On each side of it are several square hollows, evidently the place of old cellars belonging to houses, showing that the neighborhood, now solitary, was not so formerly.

In May, 1798, our family removed again to the distance of about two miles, and occupied a house in Cummington. Not a trace of it now remains; the plow has passed over its site and leveled the earth where it stood, but immediately opposite are yet seen the hollow of an old cellar and the foundation stones of a house where there lived a neighbor. I remember it as then embowered among flourishing apple-trees, three or four of which, now in decay, the mere skeletons of trees, are yet standing. The whole region of hill country, which includes Cummington and the neighboring townships, shows tokens of having been, in the agricultural parts at least, much more populous than it now is. There are frequently to be met with, old cellars, remains of garden walls, clumps of exotic shrubs, tracks of old roads no longer open, here and there an abandoned house, still standing, and the remains of mills on the stream, where the dams have long since been swept away by the floods, showing that a gradual depopulation has been going on. Only in those townships where villages, of which there were none in my early days, have sprung up, is there any increase of population. The sod, at that time just reclaimed from forest, was exceedingly fertile; the cultivators were prosperous and growing rich. The soil is now exhausted; the fields which then yielded wheat and maize are turned into pastures and mowing lands; the plow is little used, and the land which once sufficed for two farms now barely answers for one.

From my new abode, before I had completed my fourth year, I was sent to the district school, but at first, as I infer from the minutes in my mother's diary, not with much regularity. I have no recollection of any irksomeness in studying my lessons or in the discipline of the school. I only recollect gathering spearmint by the brooks in company with my fel-

low-scholars, taking off my cap at their bidding in a light summer shower, that the rain might fall on my hair and make it
grow ; and that once I awoke from a sound nap to find myself
in the lap of the schoolmistress, and was vexed to be thus
treated like a baby.*

It was in this year that I received a severe kick from a
horse. I recollect it as clearly as if it were yesterday. A
lady, one of our neighbors, had called, and fastened the horse
on which she came to a little tree before our door. Some
chips, freshly cut from a log of wood, were lying about, and
my elder brother amused himself with throwing them at the
horse's heels to make him caper. I followed his example.
After a little while, my brother, thinking me too near the animal, called to me to come away ; but I paid no attention to
his warning. Suddenly the horse flung out his heels, one of
which struck me on the forehead and laid me flat. I was carried into the house, where my head was bandaged ; the scar
of the wound which I received remains on my forehead to this
day. Six days afterward, there is a record in my mother's
diary that I was unwell and was bled. The practice of letting
blood was then universal among physicians in that country.
After this occurrence, I remember going to school with a bandaged head.

In the house opposite to ours, in the family of a Mr. White,
lived Jane Robinson, an unmarried woman, an amazon in
strength and spirit, full-chested and large-armed, of whom I
have heard my mother relate this anecdote. There lived in
Plainfield a man named Colson, Chris. Colson he was generally called, who was said to be in the habit of beating his wife.
At a regimental review, then held every autumn, at which
were assembled the militia of several townships, and which
brought together great numbers of people, both men and
women, Jane Robinson headed a party of women, who took a

---

* The story in the family is that he was not merely "vexed," but almost frantic
with rage.—G.

rail from a fence, seized upon Colson, put him astride of it, held him on, carried him round the field, and dismissed him with an admonition to flog his wife no more. Jane Robinson afterward found a mate, but I venture to say that he never administered to her even what the English common law calls "moderate correction."

In April, 1799, when I was in my fifth year, our family went to live at the homestead of my grandfather on the mother's side, Ebenezer Snell, which I now possess, and which became my father's home for the rest of his lifetime. My grandfather Snell was, as I have already said, one of the early settlers of that region. He came to Cummington in about the year 1774, or perhaps a little earlier, while most of it yet lay in forest, chose a farm in a pleasant situation, with an easterly slope, just west of the one on which he lived at the time I came to him, and cut down the trees on the greater part of it, planted an orchard, and raised abundant crops of wheat, rye, and maize while yet the soil was unexhausted. As he grew richer he sent one of his sons, of whom he had two, to Dartmouth College, in New Hampshire, gave his farm to the other, and, purchasing the homestead east of it, built the house in which I passed my boyhood.

My grandfather Snell was descended from Thomas Snell, who came over to the Plymouth Colony from England, in what year I cannot make out; but it appears that he settled in Bridgewater in 1665, and is spoken of by Mitchell, in his History of Bridgewater, as probably the largest landholder there, since Snell's Plain and Snell's Meadows are still local names. His son Josiah married Anna Alden, a granddaughter of John Alden, who came over in the Mayflower with the first Pilgrims, and of Priscilla Mullins, celebrated by Longfellow in his poem. This Anna Alden was a grandmother of my grandfather Snell.

Squire Snell, as my grandfather was called in the neighborhood, for he was a Justice of the Peace, had some remarkable pleasantries of character. He owed very little to the schools, but he employed a good deal of his leisure in reading, mostly of religious books. The Calvinistic denomination has its subdivisions, and he belonged to the one founded by that subtle dialectitian, Dr. Samuel Hopkins, who at that time had many disciples in the New England churches, and who insisted that regeneration consists in the eradication of selfishness to such a degree that the true Christian should be willing to suffer eternal misery for the good of the whole universe. My grandfather was master of the argument, and not unfrequently discussed the dogma with those who could not receive it. He was habitually devout, and had family prayers morning and evening, such prayers as sixty or seventy years since were in vogue among the descendants of the Pilgrims, who culled from the Hebrew Scriptures the poetical expressions with which they abound, and used them liberally in their devotions. In this they followed the example of their ministers, who, however dry their services might be, were often poets in their extempore prayers. I have often, in my youth, heard from them prayers which were poems from beginning to end, mostly made up of sentences from the Old Testament writers. How often have I heard the supplication, "Let thy church arise and shine forth, fair as the moon, clear as the sun, beautiful as Tirzah, comely as Jerusalem, and terrible as an army with banners." One expression often in use was peculiarly impressive, and forcibly affected my childish imagination. "Let not our feet stumble on the dark mountains of eternal death." Then there was that prayer for revolution, handed down probably from the time of the Roundheads. "And wilt thou turn, and turn, and overturn, till he shall come whose right it is to reign, King of Nations, as now King of Saints?"

My grandfather Snell was not wanting in mother wit, and anecdotes of his clever sayings are still preserved in the neighborhood in which he lived. On one occasion a thrifty farmer, not remarkable for good manners, said to him:

"To-day I am going to kill the biggest hog in town."

"Hold, hold!" was my grandfather's answer, "don't talk of self-murder."

I remember one of the students of medicine in my father's office telling my grandfather of a controversy carried on in writing by two persons in Cummington on the nature of the soul.

"My uncle," said the student, "maintains that thought is the soul. He says the soul thinks; therefore thought is the soul."

"Poh, poh!" replied my grandfather, "the man spits, therefore the spittle is the man."

At one time in a town meeting, when a man who had committed some offence against the laws, for which he had not been prosecuted, became offensively noisy, he put him down by saying:

"Remember, sir, that the ears on your head belong to the county."

At that time corporal punishments were still inflicted by the courts, and for certain petty offences the ears of the transgressor were cropped. Flogging was also administered by constables on the sentence of a justice of the peace.

My grandfather once found that certain pieces of lumber intended by him for the runners of a sled, and called in that part of the country sled-crooks, had been taken without leave by a farmer living at no great distance. These timbers were valuable, being made from a tree the grain of which was curved so as to correspond with the curve required in the runners. The delinquent received notice that his offence was known, and that, if he wished to escape a prosecution, he must carry a bushel of rye to each of three poor widows living in the neighborhood, and tell her why he brought it. He was only too glad to comply with this condition.

My grandmother Snell, whose maiden name was Packard, was a descendant of Samuel Packard who came over from England in the ship Diligent of Ipswich, and settled in Hingham, Massachusetts, about the year 1738, whence he re-

moved to Bridgewater. The family were long-lived. I remember hearing her say that her grandmother lived to the
age of ninety-nine years. She was of a mild, affectionate nature, and cared tenderly for her grandchildren. I remember
that she often amused my elder brother and myself by drawing figures with chalk on the kitchen floor. One of these I
always viewed with particular interest, and sometimes teased
her to draw. It was a human figure, but with horns and clo-
ven feet and a long tail. She called it Old Crooktail; it was
evidently intended as a portrait of the Prince of Darkness.

My grandfather on the father's side was Dr. Philip Bryant,
of North Bridgewater in Massachusetts. He was a descendant of Stephen Bryant, who came over from England in the
infancy of the Plymouth Colony, and in 1643 was in Danbury,
whence in 1650 he removed to Plymouth. Dr. Philip Bryant was his great grandson. My grandfather Bryant studied
physic with Dr. Abiel Howard, of West Bridgewater, whose
daughter Silence he married. He had a large practice as a
physician, and, being an active, healthy man, of a calm temper
and wise conduct of life, he lived to a good old age, continuing to practice till very shortly before his death, which took
place in 1816, when he was in his eighty-fifth year. His wife,
my grandmother, and the mother of his nine children, died of
consumption, after a married life of twenty years, at the age
of thirty-nine. Several of her children—all the daughters, of
whom there were four—wrote verses. One of them, Ruth,
who died of consumption at the age of twenty-three, composed
poems which were then thought rather remarkable, and I remember a little manuscript volume of them copied by my
father in his beautiful handwriting.

My great grandfather, Dr. Abiel Howard, of West Bridgewater, was the first graduate of Harvard College from either
of the four Bridgewaters. He studied divinity and preached
awhile, but, finding himself inclined to the profession of medicine, he went through the ordinary course of study and became a physician. He was fond of poetry, wrote verses, some

of which I have seen in manuscript, and had a good library to which my father in his youth had free access, and where he indulged that fondness for study which continued through life.   Dr. Howard was the grandson of John Howard, who came over from England a very young man, and lived for some time in the family of Captain Miles Standish.   He was one of the earliest military officers in Bridgewater, and a man of much influence in the colony.   Dr. Howard was a man of irritable temper, but the irritation soon passed off.   A resident of West Bridgewater once told me that when a boy he was sent to call him to one of the family who was taken ill.   As soon as he delivered his message the Doctor exclaimed, " I can't go, and I won't go; I'm sick now," and flung himself into bed with his boots on.   After awhile he rose, mounted his horse, and visited the patient.

While living at the homestead, I went with my elder brother, Austin, to a district school, kept in a little house which then stood near by, on the bank of the rivulet that flows by the dwelling.   The education which we received here was of the humblest elementary kind, stopping at grammar, unless we include theology, as learned from the Westminster Catechism, which was our Saturday exercise.   I was an excellent, almost an infallible, speller, and ready in geography; but in the Catechism, not understanding the abstract terms, I made but little progress.   Our schoolmaster, who for many years was one of the neighbors, named Briggs, a kind and just man, believed in corporal punishment, and carried a birchen twig, with which he admonished those who were idle or at play by a smart stroke over the head.   It was somewhat amusing to see the delinquent cringe and writhe as the blow descended, but nobody dared to laugh.   I got few of these reprimands, being generally absorbed in my lessons.

When the scholars were let out at noon, we amused ourselves with building dams across the rivulet, and launching rafts made of old boards on the collected water ; and in winter, with sliding on the ice and building snow barricades, which we called forts, and, dividing the boys into two armies, and using snowballs for ammunition, we contended for the possession of these strongholds. I was one of their swiftest runners in the race, and not inexpert at playing ball, but, being of a slight frame, I did not distinguish myself in these sieges.

One of the scholars, a lad older than myself, sickened and died, and I went to his funeral. I well recollect the awe and silence of the occasion and the strangely pallid face of the dead. It was, I think, the first time that I ever looked upon such a sight.

The boys of the generation to which I belonged were brought up under a system of discipline which put a far greater distance between parents and their children than now exists. The parents seemed to think this necessary in order to secure obedience. They were believers in the old maxim that familiarity breeds contempt. My grandfather was a disciplinarian of the stricter sort, and I can hardly find words to express the awe in which I stood of him—an awe so great as almost to prevent anything like affection on my part, although he was in the main kind, and, certainly, never thought of being severe beyond what was necessary to maintain a proper degree of order in the family.

The other boys in that part of the country, my schoolmates and play-fellows, were educated on the same system. Yet there were at that time some indications that this very severe discipline was beginning to relax. With my father and mother I was on much easier terms than with my grandfather. If a favor was to be asked of my grandfather, it was asked with fear and trembling; the request was postponed to the last moment, and then made with hesitation and blushes and a confused utterance.*

One of the means of keeping the boys in order was a little bundle of birchen rods, bound together with a small cord, and

* This part of the autobiography (pp. 13-20), Mr. Bryant used in an article on The Boys of my Boyhood," which he contributed to the " St. Nicholas " magazine of December, 1876.—G.

generally suspended on a nail against the wall in the kitchen. This was esteemed as much a part of the necessary furniture as the crane that hung in the kitchen fire-place, or the shovel and tongs. It sometimes happened that the boy suffered the fate of the eagle in the fable, wounded by an arrow fledged with a feather from his own wing; in other words, the boy was made to gather the twigs intended for his own castigation.

It has never been quite clear to me why the birch was chosen above all other trees of the wood to yield its twigs for this purpose. The beech of our forests produces sprays as slender, as flexible, and as tough; and farmers, wherever the beech is common, cut its long and pliant branches for driving oxen. Yet the use of birchen rods for the correction of children is of very great antiquity. In his "Discourse on Forest Trees," written three hundred years ago, Evelyn speaks of birchen twigs as an implement of the schoolmaster; and Loudon, in his "Arboretum," goes further back. He says: "The birch has been used as the instrument of correction in schools from the earliest ages." The English poets of the last century make frequent mention of this use of birchen twigs; but in Loudon's time, whose book was published thirty years since, he remarks that the use of these rods, both in schools and private families, was fast passing away—a change on which the boys both of England and the United States may well be congratulated—for the birchen rod was, in my time, even more freely used in the school than in the household.

The chastisement which was thought so wholesome in the case of boys, was at that time administered, for petty crimes, to grown-up persons. About a mile from where I lived stood a public whipping-post, and I remember seeing a young fellow, of about eighteen years of age, upon whose back, by direction of a justice of the peace, forty lashes had just been laid, as the punishment for a theft which he had committed. His eyes were red, like those of one who had been crying, and I well remember the feeling of curiosity, mingled with pity and fear, with which I gazed on him. That, I think, was the last example of corporal punishment inflicted by law in that neighborhood. The whipping-post stood in its place for several years afterward, the memorial of a practice which had passed away.

The awe in which the boys of that time held their parents extended to all elderly persons, toward whom our behavior was more than merely respectful, for we all observed a hushed and subdued demeanor in their presence. Toward the ministers of the gospel this behavior was particularly marked. At that time, every township in Massachusetts had its minister, who was settled there for life, and when he once came among his people was understood to have entered into a connection with them scarcely less lasting than the marriage tie. The community in which he lived regarded him with great veneration, and the visits which from time to time he made to the district schools seemed to the boys important occasions, for which special preparation was made. When he came to visit the school which I attended, we all had on our Sunday clothes, and were ready for him with a few answers to the questions in the Westminster Catechism. He heard us recite our lessons, examined us in the Catechism, and then began a little address, which was the same on every occasion. He told us how much greater were the advantages of education which we enjoyed than those which had fallen to the lot of our parents, and exhorted us to make the best possible use of them, both for our own sakes and that of our parents, who were ready to make any sacrifice for us, even so far as to take the bread out of their own mouths to give us. I remember being disgusted with this illustration of parental kindness which I was obliged to listen to twice at least in every year.

The good man had, perhaps, less reason than he supposed to magnify the advantages of education enjoyed in the common schools at that time. Reading, spelling, writing and arithmetic, with a little grammar and a little geography, were all that was taught, and these by persons much less qualified, for the most part, than those who now give instruction. Those, however, who wished to proceed further took lessons from the graduates of the colleges, who were then much more numerous in proportion to the population than they now are.

The profound respect shown to the clergy in those days had this good effect—that wherever there was a large concourse of people, their presence prevented the occurrence of anything disorderly or unseemly. The minister, therefore, made it one of his duties to be present on those occasions which brought people together in any considerable numbers. His appearance had somewhat the effect which that of a policeman now has at a public assembly in one of our large towns. At that time there was in each township at least one company of militia, which was required to hold several meetings in the course of the year, and at these the minister was always present. The military parade, with the drums and fifes and other musical instruments, was a powerful attraction for the boys, who came from all parts of the neighborhood to the place at which the militia mustered. But on these occasions there was one respect in which the minister's presence proved but a slight restraint upon excess. There were then no temperance societies, no temperance lecturers held forth, no temperance tracts were ever distributed, nor temperance pledges given. It was, to be sure, esteemed a shame to get drunk; but, as long as they stopped short of this, people, almost without exception, drank grog and punch freely without much fear of a reproach from any quarter. Drunkenness, however, in that demure population, was not obstreperous, and the man who was overtaken by it was generally glad to slink out of sight.

I remember an instance of this kind. There had been a muster of a militia company on the church green for the election of one of its officers, and the person elected had treated the members of the company and all who were present to sweetened rum and water, carried to the green in pailfuls, with a tin cup to each pail for the convenience of drinking.

The afternoon was far spent, and I was going home with other boys, when we overtook a young man who had taken too much of the election toddy, and, in endeavoring to go quietly home, had got but a little way from the green, when he fell in a miry place, and was surrounded by three or four persons, who assisted in getting him on his legs again. The poor fellow seemed in great distress, and his new nankeen pantaloons, daubed with the mire of the road, and his dang- ling limbs, gave him a most wretched appearance. It was, I think, the first time I had ever seen a drunken man. As I approached to pass him by, some of the older boys said to me, "Do not go too near him, for if you smell a drunken man it will make you drunk." Of course, I kept at a good distance, but not out of hearing, for I remember hearing him lament his condition in these words: "Oh dear, I shall die!" "Oh dear, I wish I hadn't drinked any!" "Oh dear, what will my poor Betsy say?" What his poor Betsy said I never heard, but I saw him led off in the direction of his home, and I continued on my way with the other boys, impressed with a salutary horror of drunkenness and a fear of drunken men.

One of the entertainments of the boys of my time was what were called the "raisings," meaning the erection of the timber frames of houses or barns, to which the boards were to be afterward nailed. Here the minister made a point of being present, and hither the able-bodied men of the neighborhood, the young men especially, were summoned, and took part in the work with great alacrity. It was a spectacle for us next to that of a performer on the tight-rope, to see the young men walk steadily on the narrow footing of the beams at a great height from the ground, or as they stood to catch in their hands the wooden pins and the braces flung to them from below. They vied with one another in the dexterity and dar- ing with which they went through with the work, and, when the skeleton of the building was put together, some one among them generally capped the climax of fearless activity by standing on the ridge-pole with his head downward and his heels in the air. At that time, even the presence of the minister was no restraint upon the flow of milk punch and grog, which in some cases was taken to excess. The practice of calling the neighbors to these " raisings " is now discontinued in the rural neighborhoods; the carpenters provide their own workmen for the business of adjusting the timbers of the new building to one another, and there is no consumption of grog.

Another of the entertainments of rustic life was the making of maple sugar. This was a favorite frolic of the boys. The apparatus for the sugar camp was of a much ruder kind than is now used. The sap was brought in buckets from the wounded trees and poured into a great caldron which hung over a hot fire from a stout horizontal pole supported at each end by an upright stake planted in the ground. Since that time they have built in every maple grove a sugar house—a little building in which the process of making sugar is carried on with several ingenious contrivances unknown at that time, when everything was done in the open air.

From my father's door, in the latter part of March and the early part of April, we could see perhaps a dozen columns of smoke rising over the woods in different places where the work was going on. After the sap had been collected and boiled for three or four days, the time came when the thickening liquid was made to pass into the form of sugar. This was when the sirup had become of such a consistency that it would "feather"—that is to say, when a beechen twig, formed at the small end into a little loop, dipped into the hot sirup and blown upon by the breath, sent into the air a light, feathery film. The huge caldron was then lifted from the fire, and its contents were either dipped out and poured into molds, or stirred briskly till the sirup cooled and took the form of ordinary brown sugar in loose grains. This process was exceedingly interesting to the boys who came to watch its different stages and to try from time to time the sirup as it thickened.

In autumn, the task of stripping the husks from the ears

of Indian corn was made the occasion of social meetings, in which the boys took a special part. A farmer would appoint what was called "a husking," to which he invited his neighbors. The ears of maize in the husk, sometimes along with part of the stalk, were heaped on the barn floor. In the evening lanterns were brought, and, seated on piles of dry husks, the men and boys stripped the ears of their covering, and, breaking them from the stem with a sudden jerk, threw them into baskets placed for the purpose. It was often a merry time; the gossip of the neighborhood was talked over, stories were told, jests went round, and at the proper hour the assembly adjourned to the dwelling-house and were treated to pumpkin-pie and cider, which in that season had not been so long from the press as to have parted with its sweetness.

Quite as cheerful were the "apple-parings," which on autumn evenings brought together the young people of both sexes in little circles. The fruit of the orchards was pared and quartered and the core extracted, and a supply of apples in this state provided for making what was called "apple-sauce," a kind of preserve of which every family laid in a large quantity every year.

The cider-making season in autumn was somewhat correspondent to the vintage in the wine countries of Europe. Large tracts of land in New England were overshadowed by rows of apple-trees, and in the month of May a journey through that region was a journey through a wilderness of bloom. In the month of October the whole population was busy gathering apples under the trees, from which they fell in heavy showers as the branches were shaken by the strong arms of the farmers. The creak of the cider mill, turned by a horse moving in a circle, was heard in every neighborhood as one of the most common of rural sounds. The freshly pressed juice of the apples was most agreeable to boyish tastes, and the whole process of gathering the fruit and making the cider came in among the more laborious rural occupations in a way which diversified them pleasantly, and which made it seem a pastime. The time that was given to making cider, and the number of barrels made and stored in the cellars of the farm-houses, would now seem incredible. A hundred barrels to a single farm was no uncommon proportion, and the quantity swallowed by the men of that day led to the habits of intemperance which at length alarmed the more thoughtful part of the community, and gave occasion to the formation of temperance societies and the introduction of better habits.

From time to time the winter evenings, and occasionally a winter afternoon, brought the young people of the parish together in attendance upon a singing school. Some person who possessed more than common power of voice, and skill in modulating it, was employed to teach psalmody, and the boys were naturally attracted to his school as a recreation. It often happened that the teacher was an enthusiast in his vocation, and thundered forth the airs set down in the music books with a fervor that was contagious. A few of those who attempted to learn psalmody were told that they had no aptitude for the art, and were set aside, but that did not prevent their attendance as hearers of the others. In those days a set of tunes were in fashion mostly of New England origin, which have since been laid aside in obedience to a more fastidious taste. They were in quick time, sharply accented, the words clearly articulated, and often running into fugues, in which the bass, the tenor, and the treble chased each other from the middle to the end of the stanza. I recollect that some impatience was manifested when slower and graver airs of church music were introduced by the choir, and I wondered why the words should not be sung in the same time that they were pronounced in reading.

The streams which bickered through the narrow glens of the region in which I lived were much better stocked with trout in those days than now, for the country had been newly opened to settlement. The boys all were anglers. I confess to having felt a strong interest in that "sport," as I no longer call it. I have long since been weaned from the propensity of which I speak; but I have no doubt that the instinct which inclines so many to it, and some of them our grave divines, is a remnant of the original wild nature of man. Another "sport," to which the young men of the neighborhood sometimes admitted the elder boys, was the autumnal squirrel hunt. The young men formed themselves into two parties equal in numbers, and fixed a day for the shooting. The party which on that day brought down the greatest number of squirrels was declared the victor, and the contest ended with some sort of festivity in the evening.

I have not mentioned other sports and games of the boys of that day, such as wrestling, running, leaping, base-ball, and the like, for in these there was nothing to distinguish them from the same pastimes at the present day. There were no public lectures at that time on subjects of general interest; the profession of public lecturer was then unknown, and eminent men were not solicited, as they now are, to appear before audiences in distant parts of the country and gratify the curiosity of strangers by letting them hear the sound of their voices. But the men of those days were far more given to attendance on public worship than those who now occupy their places, and of course they took their boys with them. They were not satisfied with the morning and afternoon services, but each neighborhood held a third service of its own in the evening. Here some lay brother made a prayer, hymns were sung by those who were trained at the singing schools, a sermon was read from the works of some orthodox divine, and now and then a word of exhortation was addressed to the little assembly by some one who was more fluent in speech than the rest.

Every parish had its tything-men, two in number generally, whose business it was to maintain order in the church during divine service, and who sat with a stern countenance through the sermon, keeping a vigilant eye on the boys in the distant pews and in the galleries. Sometimes, when he detected two of them communicating with each other, he went to one of them, took him by the button, and, leading him away, seated him beside himself. His power extended to other delinquencies. He was directed by law to see that the Sabbath was not profaned by people wandering in the fields and angling in the brooks. At that time a law, no longer in force, directed that any person who absented himself unnecessarily from public worship for a certain length of time should pay a fine into the treasury of the county. I remember several persons of whom it was said that they had been compelled to pay this fine, but I do not remember any of them who went to church afterward.

In my ninth year I began to make verses, some of which were utter nonsense. My father ridiculed them, and endeavored to teach me to write only when I had something to say. A year or two later my grandfather gave me as an exercise the first chapter of the Book of Job to turn into verse. I put the whole narration into heroic couplets, one of which I remember, as the first draught.

> "His name was Job, evil he did eschew,
>   To him were born seven sons ; three daughters too."

My father did not allow this doggerel to stand, but I forget what I put in its place.* For this task I was rewarded with the small Spanish coin then called a ninepenny piece. I paraphrased afterwards the Hundred and Fourth Psalm. In

---

* Mr. Bryant had forgotten this ; but among his papers was found the following, which is probably a part of his amended version :

> "Job, good and just, in Uz had sojourned long,
>   He feared his God and shunned the way of wrong.
>   Three were his daughters, and his sons were seven,
>   And large the wealth bestowed on him by heaven.
>   Seven thousand sheep were in his pastures fed,
>   Three thousand camels by his train were led ;
>   For him the yoke a thousand oxen wore,
>   Five hundred she asses his burdens bore.
>   His household to a mighty host increased,
>   The greatest man was Job in all the East."   —G.

the spring of 1804, when I was ten years old, I composed a little poem, the subject of which was the description of the school, and which I declaimed on the schoolroom floor. It was afterward printed in the " Hampshire Gazette," the county newspaper published at Northampton. Meantime I wrote various lampoons on my schoolfellows and others, and when the great eclipse of the sun took place, in June, 1806, I celebrated the event in verse. I remember being told about this time that my father had said, " He will be ashamed of his verses when he is grown up." I could not then see why.*

---

* As many readers will, doubtless, be amused by this childish effort at the description of a great natural phenomenon, I append it :

" How awfully sublime and grand to see,
The lamp of Day wrap'ed in Obscurity.
To see the sun remove behind the moon,
And nightly darkness shroud the day at noon ;
The birds no longer feel his genial ray,
But cease to sing and sit upon the spray.
A solemn gloom and stillness spreads around,
Reigns in the air and broods o'er all the ground.
Once-smiling Nature wears another face,
The blooming meadow loses half its grace.
All things are silent save the chilling breeze,
That in low whispers rustles through the trees.
The stars break forth and stud the azure sky,
And larger planets meet the wondering eye.
Now busy man leaves off his toil to gaze,
And some are struck with horror and amaze,
Others of noble feelings more refin'd
Serenely view it with a tranquil mind.
See God's bright image strikingly portrayed
In each appearance which his power had made.
(Fixed in their hearts cool Meditation sate,
With uprais'd eye and thoughtful look sedate.)
Now burst the Sun from silence and from night,
Though few his beams, they shed a welcome light ;
And Nature's choir, enlivened by his rays,
Harmonious warble their Creator's praise.
The shades of darkness feel his potent ray,
Mine eye pursue them as they flee away ;

As soon as I was able to handle the lighter implements of agriculture I was employed in the summer season in farm work, under the tuition of my grandfather Snell, who taught me to plant and hoe corn and potatoes, to rake hay and reap wheat and oats with the sickle, for wheat was then raised in Cummington, and the machine called the cradle had not yet come into general use. In raking hay my grandfather put me before him, and, if I did not make speed enough to keep out of his way, the teeth of his rake touched my heels. I became tolerably expert in these occupations, but I never fully learned the use of the scythe, having left the farm before I had sufficient strength to wield it.

My health was rather delicate from infancy and easily disturbed. Sometimes the tasks of the farm were too great for my strength, and brought on a sick headache, which was relieved under my father's directions by taking a little soda dissolved in water. I was also subject to frequent and severe attacks of colic, which I discovered afterwards to have been caused by the use of pewter vessels for culinary purposes, which was then very common. When they were no longer used, I had no more of these attacks.

So my time passed in study, diversified with labor and recreation. In the long winter evenings and the stormy winter days I read, with my elder brother, books from my father's library—not a large one, but well chosen. I remember well the delight with which we welcomed the translation of the Iliad, by Pope, when it was brought into the house. I had met with passages from it before, and thought them the finest verses that ever were written. My brother and myself, in emulation of the ancient heroes, made for ourselves wooden shields, swords, and spears, and fashioned old hats in the

---

So from the greyhound flies the tim'rous hare,
Swift as a dart divides the yielding air."

This is inscribed in the boy's handwriting: "Written by W. C. Bryant, just after the great total Eclipse of the Sun, in the summer of the year 1806—in his twelfth year."—G.

shape of helmets, with plumes of tow, and in the barn, when nobody observed us, we fought the battles of the Greeks and Trojans over again. I was always from my earliest years a delighted observer of external nature—the splendors of a winter daybreak over the wide wastes of snow seen from our windows, the glories of the autumnal woods, the gloomy approaches of the thunderstorm, and its departure amid sunshine and rainbows, the return of spring, with its flowers, and the first snowfall of winter. The poets fostered this taste in me, and though at that time I rarely heard such things spoken of, it was none the less cherished in my secret mind. Meantime the school which I attended was removed to the distance of a mile and a quarter from our dwelling, and to it in winter we went often across the fields over the snow—when it was firm enough to bear us without breaking the glazed surface. Then the coming and going was a joyous pastime.

I cannot say, as some do, that I found my boyhood the happiest part of my life. I had more frequent ailments than afterward, my hopes were more feverish and impatient, and my disappointments were more acute. The restraints on my liberty of action, although meant for my good, were. irksome, and felt as fetters, that galled my spirit and gave it pain. After years, if their pleasures had not the same zest, were passed in more contentment, and, the more freedom of choice I had, the better, on the whole, I enjoyed life.

In those days the seasons of religious excitement, then sometimes called awakenings, but now revivals of religion, were of a more sensational character, so to speak, than at present. There occurred one of them about this time in Cummington and its neighborhood. The principal topic dwelt upon by the preachers and exhorters at these seasons was the doom of the wicked, which was set forth in the strongest terms that their rhetoric could supply. Prayer meetings and meetings for exhortation were held almost daily, especially in the winter time. The newly converted stood forth, and with passionate earnestness entreated their hearers to seize the op-

portunity of mercy, and flee from the wrath to come. I saw,
at this time, women falling to the floor, "struck down" under
conviction, as the phrase was, and lying for a time apparently
unconscious of everything that was passing around them. I
saw men wringing their hands in despair. In many instances
this state of depression was followed by a sudden revulsion of
feeling; a mood of gladness from which its subject dated his
new birth, and in which his heart overflowed with love to
God and to his fellow-creatures. He was then said to be
"brought out." A considerable number of admissions to the
church—our minister was of the Congregational denomination
—followed the revival. On these occasions were read the
"relations" of the candidates for admission, little manuscript
histories of their spiritual experience. Our pastor was prudent enough to wait a few months after a reputed conversion
before accepting the candidate as a church member, for it not
infrequently happened that relapses took place, and that those
who were reprobates before the awakening returned to their
old ways. Others remained constant to their new impressions.

In a community so religious I naturally acquired habits of
devotion. My mother and grandmother had taught me, as
soon as I could speak, the Lord's Prayer and other little petitions suited to childhood, and I may be said to have been nur-
tured on Watts' devout poems composed for children. The
prayer of the publican in the New Testament was often in my
mouth, and I heard every variety of prayer at the Sunday
evening services conducted by laymen in private houses. But
I varied in my private devotions from these models, in one
respect, namely, in supplicating, as I often did, that I might
receive the gift of poetic genius, and write verses that might
endure. I presented this petition in those early years with
great fervor, but after a time I discontinued the practice; I
can hardly say why. As a general rule, whatever I might
innocently wish I did not see why I should not ask; and I
was a firm believer in the efficacy of prayer. The Calvinistic
system of divinity I adopted, of course, as I heard nothing

else taught from the pulpit, and supposed it to be the accepted belief of the religious world.

In February, 1808, General Woodbridge, of Worthington, a place about four miles distant from our dwelling, died. He was a promising and popular lawyer, held in high esteem by the Federal party, to which he belonged, and was much lamented. My father suggested this event as a subject for a monody. I composed one beginning with these lines:

> "The word is given, the cruel arrow flies
> With death-foreboding aim, and Woodbridge dies.
> Lo! Hampshire's genius, bending o'er his bier,
> In silent sorrow heaves the sigh sincere;
> Loose to the wind her hair dishevelled flies
> And falling tear-drops glisten in her eyes."

The rest of the poem was very much like this. My father read it, and told me that it was nothing but tinsel and would not do. There were only four lines among all that I had written which he would allow to be tolerable.

About this time the animosity with which the two political parties—the Federalists and the Republicans, as they called themselves—regarded each other was at its height. There was scarcely anything too bad for each party to say of the other. My father was a Federalist, and his skill in his profession gave him great influence in Cummington and the neighboring country. Accordingly the Federalists had a considerable majority in Cummington, and by them he was elected for several successive years as their representative to the General Court or Legislature of the State of Massachusetts. I read the newspapers of the Federal party, and took a strong interest in political questions. Under Mr. Jefferson's administration, in consequence of our disputes with Great Britain, an embargo was laid in 1807 upon all the ports of our republic, which, by putting a stop to all foreign commerce, had a disastrous effect upon many private interests, and embittered the hatred with which the Federalists regarded their political adversaries, and particularly Mr. Jefferson. I had written some satirical lines apostrophizing the President, which my father saw, and, thinking well of them, encouraged me to write others in the same vein. This I did willingly, until the addition grew into a poem of several pages, in the midst of which the lines of which I have spoken took their place. The poem was published at Boston in 1808, in a little pamphlet entitled, "The Embargo; or, Sketches of the Times, A Satire; by a Youth of Thirteen." It had the honor of being kindly noticed in the "Monthly Anthology," a literary periodical published in Boston, which quoted from it the paragraph that had attracted my father's attention.

It was decided that I should receive a college education, and I was accordingly taken by my father to the house of my mother's brother, the Reverend Dr. Thomas Snell, in North Brookfield, to begin the study of Latin. My uncle was a man of fine personal appearance and great dignity of character and manner, the slightest expression of whose wish had all the force of command. He was a rigid moralist, who never held parley with wrong in any form, and was an enemy of every kind of equivocation. As a theologian he was trained in the school of Dr. Hopkins, which then, I think, included most of the country ministers of the Congregational Church in Massachusetts. My aunt, his wife, was a lady of graceful manners and gentle deportment. There were two children, of amiable dispositions, a son and a daughter, the son now a valued professor in Amherst College, and the daughter, now living in a Northwestern State, a lady scarce less remarkable, I am told, for dignity of manner, than her father. I had a little qualm of homesickness at first, but it soon passed away as I became interested in my studies, in which my progress was, I believe, more rapid than usual. I began with the Latin grammar, went through the Colloquies of Corderius, in which the words, for the ease of the learner, were arranged according to the English order, and then entered upon the New Testament in Latin. Once, while reciting my daily lesson to my uncle,

he happened to turn to a part of the volume several pages beyond where I had been studying. He read the text; I gave
the English translation correctly, answered all his questions
respecting the syntax, and applied the rules. He then perceived that the passage before him was not the one I had
studied, and, laying aside the book, immediately put me into
the Æneid of Virgil, which I found much more difficult, requiring all my attention.

While I was occupied with the Æneid, my father wrote to
me advising me to translate some portion of it into English
verse. Accordingly I made a rhymed translation of the narrative of a tempest in the first book and sent it to my father,
but got no commendation in return. I had aimed to be faithful to the original, but the lines were cramped and the phraseology clumsy. I wrote rather better when I had no original
to follow. Somebody showed me a piece of paper, with the
title "The Endless Knot," the representation of an intricate
knot in parallel lines, between which were written some home-
ly verses. I thought that I could write better ones, and, my
head being full of the ancient mythology, I composed these :

> So seemed the Cretan labyrinth of old,
> Maze within maze, in many a winding fold.
> Deep in those convoluted paths in vain
> The wretched captive sought the day again,
> But, lost and wearied with the devious way,
> Fell to the monster bull a helpless prey
> Till Ariadne lent the guiding thread
> That back to life the Athenian hero led.
> Thus, round and round, with intricate design,
> These snaky walks in endless mystery twine ;
> Yet here no danger lurks, no murderous power
> Waits the pale victim, ready to devour.
> Our hands in turn bestow the friendly clue ;
> Pursue our verse, our verse shall guide you through.

One day my uncle brought home a quarto volume, the
" Life of Sir William Jones," by Lord Teignmouth, which he

had borrowed, as I imagine, expressly for my reading. I read it with great interest, and was much impressed with the extensive scholarship and other literary accomplishments of Sir William. I am pretty sure that his example made me afterward more diligent in my studies, and I think also that it inclined me to the profession of the law which in due time I embraced. I recollect that a clergyman, from a neighboring parish, who came to exchange pulpits with my uncle, observing me occupied with the book, kindly said to me: "You have only to be as diligent in your studies as that great man was, and, in time, you may write as fine verses as he did."

In a closet of the room where I studied, I found a copy of Mrs. Radcliffe's "Romance of the Forest," which I began to read with an interest that grew stronger as I proceeded. My uncle found me with the book in my hands, and advised me not to go on with it. "These works," he said, "have an unwholesome influence. They are written in an interesting manner; they absorb the attention, and divert the mind from objects of greater importance." The book, however, was left within my reach. For some days I did not take it up, but my curiosity had been so strongly excited that I could not long refrain, and again began to read it. I was observed, and the book disappeared. When, not many years afterward, the "Romance of the Forest" came in my way, the first thing I did was to read it through.

While I was at my uncle's, in 1809, another edition of my poem, "The Embargo," was published at Boston. It had been revised and somewhat enlarged, and a few shorter poems were added.

I went through the Æneid in my Latin studies, and then mastered the Eclogues and the Georgics, after which my uncle put into my hands a volume of the select Orations of Cicero. While I was engaged with these, he once asked me which I liked better, Virgil or Cicero. I frankly gave the preference to Virgil, on which, without directly controverting my preference, he pointed out some of the excellences of Cicero's compositions, such as the solidity of the reflections, their application to the realities of life, and the constant reference of everything to the principles of justice.

I had occasionally a fellow-student or two who came to the house for the benefit of my uncle's instructions. Among these was Amasa Walker, since a professor in Oberlin College, and well known for his able works on political economy.

As the spring came on, I wandered about the fields and meadows, where I missed some of the early flowers of the highland country in which I was born, and admired others new to me. The hickory, the oak, and the chestnut trees, as they put forth their young leaves, were new acquaintances to me. As the summer came on, my attention was attracted to an elegant plant of the meadows—a wild lily—with whorls of leaves surrounding the stem. I watched impatiently the unfolding of its flower-buds, in hope that I might see it in bloom before I went back to Cummington, but in this I was disappointed.

While at my uncle's my constitution seemed to have undergone a favorable change. I had been subject, as I have already mentioned, to frequent and severe headaches, sometimes taking the form of sick headache, after eating gross food or taking immoderate exercise. These now left me entirely, and through a long life—I am now in my eightieth year—my head has never ached since. Though my health was delicate, the diseases of childhood—the measles, the mumps, and the whooping-cough—visited me lightly—the scarlet fever I never had. My father was one of the first to introduce vaccination in Western Massachusetts. I was made to take the infection, but, though the pustule was perfectly formed, I was scarcely indisposed in consequence.

In the beginning of July, 1809, having read through the volume of Cicero's Orations, I left the excellent family of my uncle, where I had been surrounded by the most wholesome influences and examples, and returned to Cummington, after an absence of just eight calendar months. I was welcomed by my four brothers and two sisters, all born before I went to North Brookfield—the youngest a boy two years old—and a lively house they made of it. They had all grown, of course, during my absence, but I well remember that, as much as they had grown, the house and its surroundings seemed to have diminished. The parlor, the kitchen, my father's office, all seemed to have shrunk from their former dimensions; the ceilings seemed lower, the fields around seemed of less extent, the trees less tall, and the little brook that ran near the house gurgled with a slenderer current.

I took my place with the haymakers on the farm,* and did, I believe, my part until the 28th of August, 1809, when I went to begin my studies in Greek with the Reverend Moses Hallock, in the neighboring township of Plainfield, where he was the minister. He was somewhat famous for preparing youths for college, and his house was called by some the bread and milk college, for the reason that bread and milk was a frequent dish at the good man's table. And a good man he really was, kind and gentle, and of the most scrupulous conscientiousness. "I value Mr. Hallock," my grandfather used to say, "his life is so exemplary." He was paid a dollar a week for my board and instruction. "I can afford it for that," he was in the habit of saying, "and it would not be honest to take more."

I committed to memory the declensions and the conjugations of the Greek tongue, with the rules of syntax, and then began reading the New Testament in Greek, taking first the Gospel of St. John. One of my fellow-students was Levi Parsons, afterward distinguished as a missionary in the East. He had not so good a verbal memory as I, and, as we two made a class, he frequently interrupted me to ask my help in the difficulties which he met with. I gave it for the first two or three days, but, the applications of this sort becoming rather frequent, I answered one of them with petulance. He went

---

* As the boy was not very strong, he often stopped in his labor to rest, when the grandfather used to taunt him with a "Well, Cullen, making varses again?"—G.

back to his place with a discouraged look; I saw him wiping
the tears from his eyes, and the next day it appeared that he
had given up for the time the study of Greek, and had gone
back to the Latin. I have never thought of my conduct in
that instance without a feeling of remorse.

I now went on alone, giving myself with my whole soul to
the study of Greek. I was early at my task in the morning,
and kept on until bed-time; at night I dreamed of Greek, and
my first thought in the morning was of my lesson for the day.
At the end of two calendar months I knew the Greek New
Testament from end to end almost as if it had been English,
and I returned to my home in Cummington, where a few
days afterward I completed my fifteenth year.

About this time occurred an event which I remember with
regret. My grandfather Snell had always been substantially
kind to me, and ready to forward any plan for my education,
but, when I did what in his judgment was wrong, he repri-
manded me with a harshness which was not so well judged as
it was probably deserved. I had committed some foolish
blunder, and he was chiding me with even more than his
usual severity; I turned and looked at him with a steady
gaze. "What are you staring at?" he asked. "Did you
never see me before?" "Yes," I answered; "I have seen
you many times before." He had never before heard a dis-
respectful word from my lips. He turned and moved away,
and never reproved me again in that manner, but never afterward seemed to interest himself so much as before in any matter that concerned me.

The next winter I was occupied with studies preparatory
to entering college, which for reasons of economy it was decided that I should do a year in advance, that is to say, as a
member of the Sophomore class. At this time I had no help
from a tutor, but in the spring I went again for two months
to Plainfield, and received from Mr. Hallock instructions in
mathematics. In the beginning of September, 1810, when the
annual Commencement of Williams College was at that time

held, I went with my father to Williamstown, passed an easy examination, and was admitted as a member of the Sophomore class. After the usual vacation I went again to Williamstown and began my college life.*

I found that kind of life on the whole agreeable, and formed pleasant relations with my fellow-students and instructors. There were two literary societies in the college, to one or the other of which every student belonged, the Philotechnian and Philologian, and, as my room-mate, John Avery, belonged to the Philotechnian, I was induced to join it. These societies had their literary exercises, in which I took a great interest.

My room-mate was a most worthy and well-principled person, several years older than myself, and I owed so much to his example and counsels that I have often regretted not having kept up a correspondence with him. He became in after life a minister of the Episcopal Church, and went to the Southern States, to Maryland, I think, whence, about the year 1835, he removed to Alabama, and died soon afterward. The students of Williams College were at that time mostly youths of a staid character, generally in narrow circumstances, who went to college with a serious intention to study, and prepare themselves for some of the learned professions, so that I have no college pranks to relate. The course of study in Williams College at that time was meagre and slight in comparison with what it now is. There was but one Professor, Chester Dewey, Professor of Mathematics and Natural Philosophy, a man of much merit, who had the charge of the Junior class. The President of the college, Dr. Fitch, superintended the studies of the Senior class, and the Sophomores and Freshmen were instructed by two tutors employed from year to year. I mastered the daily lessons given out to my class, and found much time for miscellaneous reading, for disputations, and for literary composition in prose and verse, in all of which I was thought to acquit myself with some credit. No attention was then paid to prosody, but I made an attempt to ac-

* October 9th.—G.

quaint myself with the prosody of the Latin language, and
tried some experiments in Latin verse which were clumsy
and uncouth enough.

Among my verses was a paraphrastic translation of Anacreon's ode on Spring. Moore's version of Anacreon's ode
was consulted, and my room-mate suggested that these translations should be shown to two members of the Junior class,
whom he named, and of whose judgment in literary matters
he thought highly, and that they, without knowing the authorship of either, should be asked to say which of the two
was the better. Both versions copied in the same hand were
accordingly laid before them by Avery. He came back to
me greatly pleased, and informed me that the two judges
had given the preference to my translation. He added that
they evidently supposed my translation to be that of Moore,
and spoke of the other in an encouraging manner as quite
creditable on the whole. He came away without undeceiv-
ing them.

My room-mate, for the sake of obtaining a more complete
education than the course of study at Williams then promised,
had resolved to leave the college and become matriculated at
Yale in New Haven. His example, and a like desire on my
part, induced me to write to my father for leave to take the
same step, to which he consented. Accordingly, in the year
1811, before the third term of my Sophomore year was ended,
I asked and obtained an honorable dismission from Williams
College,* and, going back to Cummington, began to prepare
myself for entering the Junior class at Yale.

I pursued my studies at home with some diligence and
without any guide save my books, but, when the time drew
near that I should apply for admission at Yale, my father told
me that his means did not allow him to maintain me at New
Haven, and that I must give up the idea of a full course of
college education. I have always thought this unfortunate
for me, since it left me but superficially acquainted with sev-

* May 8th.—G.

eral branches of education, which a college course would have
enabled me to master, and would have given me greater readiness in their application.   I regretted all my life afterward
that I had not remained at Williams, where, considering that
the expenses were less than at Yale, my father might have
been willing to support me till I should obtain the degree of
Bachelor of Arts.

While I was engaged in the studies of which I have spoken,
the medical library of my father being at hand, I read, in a
very desultory manner, of course, portions both of the more
formal treatises and of the periodicals, and became much interested in the medical art, though the hardships of a physician's life, as I saw in the case of my father, disinclined me
from making medicine my profession.   The science of chemistry had, not long before that time, been reformed and reduced by Lavoisier substantially to the system now received,
and provided with a new nomenclature.   By the aid of experiments performed in my father's office, with the chemical
agents which a country practitioner of medicine was obliged
to keep at home, I became a pretty good chemist as far as
the science, since that time vastly enlarged and extended, was
then carried.   I also acquired some knowledge of botany
from works in my father's library, in which the Linnæan system was explained and illustrated.   These readings and studies formed an agreeable relaxation, if I may so call it, from
my more laborious academic studies, but I have never regretted the time which I gave them.   Meantime, I read all the
poetry that came in my way.   I remember a lesson given me
in poetical composition by my father.   One day he took down
from the shelf in his office library Campbell's "Pleasures of
Hope," which I had read again and again until I had the most
of it by heart.   He opened at the passage which speaks of
Admiral Biron's wanderings in South America, and read it,
closing with the lines:

> "Till, led by thee o'er many a cliff sublime,
> He found a warmer world, a milder clime,

A home to rest, a shelter to defend,
Peace and repose, a Briton and a friend."

He then bade me and others who were present observe the tautology of these expressions, which was a serious blemish in the poems.

About this time my father brought home, I think from one of his visits to Boston, the "Remains of Henry Kirke White," which had been republished in this country. I read the poems with great eagerness, and so often that I had committed several of them to memory, particularly the ode to the Rosemary. The melancholy tone which prevails in them deepened the interest with which I read them, for about that time I had, as young poets are apt to have, a liking for poetry of a querulous cast. I remember reading, at this time, that remarkable poem, Blair's "Grave," and dwelling with great pleasure upon its finer passages. I had the opportunity of comparing it with a poem on a kindred subject, also in blank verse, that of Bishop Porteus on "Death," and of observing how much the verse of the obscure Scottish minister excelled in originality of thought and vigor of expression that of the English prelate. In my father's library I found a small, thin volume of the miscellaneous poems of Southey, to which he had not called my attention, containing some of the finest of Southey's shorter poems. I read it greedily. Cowper's poems had been in my hands from an early age, and I now passed from his shorter poems, which are generally mere rhymed prose, to his "Task," the finer passages of which supplied a form of blank verse that captivated my admiration.*

* Here the autobiography ends abruptly, and just at the time when the poet was going to tell us of the various influences under which his " Thanatopsis " was written. Why he stopped it is not known ; perhaps he found that his memory was failing him—although it is more likely that he became dissatisfied with the necessity his task imposed upon him, of thinking so much about himself—a practice to which he was always averse.—G.

CHAPTER SECOND.

THE PLACE AND TIME OF THE POET'S BIRTH.

I HAVE not been willing to break the simple and pleasant narrative we have just read by interjecting frequent notes; but, as the writer of it has allowed himself, through modesty or forgetfulness, to pass over many details that the public will naturally desire to see, I shall endeavor to supply them in a few supplementary chapters.*

If it be true, as Landor says,

> "We are what suns and winds and waters make us;
> The mountains are our sponsors, and the rills
> Fashion and win their nurseling with their smiles," †

some words ought to be devoted to the locality in which our poet had his birth and passed the days of his youth and earlier manhood.

The town of Cummington, where he first saw light, is a small hamlet, known to very few people, hidden away among the hills of Hampshire County, in the western part of the State of Massachusetts. It consists of several dwellings and stores, situated on the north fork of a stony-bedded little stream, called Westfield River, and of scattered outlying farmhouses that hang upon the slopes of the neighboring uplands. All the country round is mountainous, as indeed is the whole of western Massachusetts, comprising the four counties of Berkshire, Hampshire, Franklin, and Hampden.   An offshoot

---

* I am encouraged to adopt this method by the example of Mr. Lockhart, in his delightful biography of Sir Walter Scott. See "Memoirs of the Life of Scott," vol. i, Boston, 1849.

† "Hellenics," p. 274, London, 1847.

from the Green Mountains of Vermont, or, as the early Dutch settlers called them because of their wintry aspects, the Snow Mountains, it is like them also a spur of the great Appalachian chain that clasped the original republic. Its characteristics are those of a mountain country, but with peculiarities of its own. The hill-ranges, which sometimes reach an elevation of between two and three thousand feet, contain few single peaks standing out in solitary grandeur, although Graylock, Everett, Mettawampe, Holyoke, and Tom, the highest points, are objects of imposing magnitude. Nor are they huddled together, as we often see them in mountainous districts, making the depressions narrow and suffocating. They are

" Wide, wild, and open to the sky,"

and from almost any eminence the eye takes in a circle of broad and billowy masses that lose themselves in sublime distances.

Within the valleys are found all varieties of natural beauty: broad and grassy meadows, often gorgeous with flowers; tall and graceful trees, either single or in clumps or copses or forests; sheets of water that here nestle in pretty pools and there spread out in shining lakes; brooks that dimple and poise in open meads or under overhanging bushes, or noisy, impatient streams that make their way to the Connecticut River on one side, and to the Housatonic on the other, by which they are carried in more majestic currents to the sea.

This beautiful region, now largely covered by busy towns and thrifty villages, and nearly everywhere intersected by railroads, was, less than two hundred and fifty years since, an unbroken wilderness. The bear, the wolf, and the catamount were its almost exclusive possessors. Indians there were in plenty, but they affected the river bottoms mainly, and penetrated the higher thickets only in pursuit of game. To the newly come Pilgrims, who were a dot on the seacoasts, these mountains seemed a dark and terrible barrier, infested by savage beasts and wilder men, or by evil spirits, who burdened the winds with their howlings. It was thirty years

from the landing at Plymouth before they had erected plantations at Agawam, now Springfield, at Nonotuck, now Northampton, and at a few other places along the Connecticut River
—Northfield, Deerfield, Brookfield, and Hadley. The terrible
wars with the Indians, who desolated the settlements, left behind them a heritage of sombre traditions, followed up by
those of the horrors and cruelties of the old French war.

Long after civilization was established on the low grounds
and slopes of the hills, there was one broad tract of the mountains that lay in its original rudeness and solitude. This was
situated about midway of the two great valleys, many miles
from any of the towns, and at an elevation of two thousand
feet or more. The Indians called it the Pontoosuc Forest,
but on the maps of the colony it was only known as Districts
Number 1, 2, 3, 4, 5, and so on up to 10. It had been visited
to be surveyed, but no one lived there, and it was wholly inaccessible save by paths which each one made for himself.
The first recorded intelligence in regard to it, appears in the
year 1762, when the colony of Massachusetts was suffering
under the burdens of expense imposed on it by the Indian and
French and English wars, and caused the dim and shadowy
outskirts to be sold by public auction as a means of recruiting
its exhausted treasury. The division set down as Number
5, extending some eight or nine miles in one direction and
three or four in another, was purchased by a company of
twenty-six persons living at Concord. At the head of them
was a Colonel John Cuming, a Scotchman by descent if not by
birth, and a man of note and enterprise, who had been actively
engaged in the still recent Indian conflicts, and who was but
just returned from Indian captivity in Canada. What he or
any of his companions knew of the territory they had bought,
or what the motive of its acquisition was, does not now appear. " No white man was there to tell them of its climate,
its soil, its productions, its minerals, or its wealth, latent or
patent." * Only one, however, of the original owners ever

* Senator H. L. Dawes's Centennial Address, at Cummington, 1879.

occupied the place, and their names are not borne by those who were or are now among its inhabitants. They seem to have sent others to occupy for them.

It is characteristic of the times in which these wilds were sold, that a stipulation was entered in the contract of sale reserving a certain part of the land, with a settled income in rye "to be devoted to the support of a gospel minister," and another part for the maintenance of a public school which should be "free to all the people." At the very first meeting held in the settlement, which was not till 1771, eleven years from the time of the purchase, and five before the Declaration of Independence, the subject of "locating a meeting-house" was taken up with serious zeal and earnestness. But the settlers were found to be too few in number and too poor, to say nothing of their disagreements as to the proper locality, to warrant the erection of any public edifice, and the worship of the little community was carried on in houses of logs, where the swallows built their nests, and mingled their chirpings with a more nasal psalmody. It was not until the year 1793, one year before our poet was born, that the first church was erected on the hill-sides.

Yet, few as the settlers were, and remote from the centres of political life and activity, they did not escape the agitations of the outer world. That impatience of British oppression which had been stirring for some time in all the colonies, was felt alike on mountain and plain. The patriotic appeals of James Otis and others were heard as echoes among the hills. As early as 1774, before the soil of Concord was yet stained by the first blood shed in defence of popular rights, the little handful of emigrants to the mountains had appointed three of their principal citizens to be a committee of correspondence to keep the inhabitants informed of what was doing on the plains, and to provide 'powder and lead for any emergency.* On the 17th of June, 1776, Ebenezer Snell, Jr., an uncle of the poet, being in his father's cornfield, put his ear to the

* Centennial Address at Cummington, by H. L. Dawes, 1879.

ground and heard a cannonading far away, which proved to
be the onset at Bunker Hill.*   It was heard in a moral sense
all over the land.   This Eben Snell volunteered, and was
present at the surrender of Burgoyne at Saratoga.   All the
young men, indeed, who could be spared from the needful
labors of agriculture enlisted in the patriot army.   How many
went from Cummington into the service is not recorded; but
the names of ten of them, a large proportion for so small a
neighborhood, who afterward received a pension, are still
cherished in the grateful memories of their descendants; and
long after they had ceased to be, the stories of their devotion
and suffering, the romantic legends of Bunker Hill, Saratoga,
Bennington, and Yorktown, told by the lonely winter fire-
sides, kept alive in the hearts of the farmers and woodmen
the spirit which had brought about the independence of the
nation.   In truth, the youth of that generation were fed
upon tales of revolutionary prowess and endurance, and the
virtues and even the forms of the actors in the war assumed
in their eyes gigantic proportions; while the principles of
political liberty, for which they had contended and bled, became a kind of religious faith.

To this secluded District No. 5, with its few scattered habitations and utter poverty of social life, Mr. Ebenezer Snell,
called both Deacon and Squire, took his family just before the
outbreak of the Revolution (1774).†   A young physician of
Norton, Dr. Peter Bryant, seeking a place wherein to practice
his art, wandered into the same neighborhood many years
later; where, in course of time, he was smitten by the charms
of "sweet Sallie Snell," as he alliteratively expresses it in
verses still extant, and was married to her in 1792.   Their two
elder children, Austin and William Cullen, were born in a

* This story was lately told by a writer in the New York "Journal of Commerce," who heard it from Mr. Snell, then eighty years of age.

† Deacon Snell was, in 1784, and afterward, a representative in the General
Court, or Legislature, of the State, and also, for many years, a Judge of the Court
of Sessions—the County Court.

small frame house—the characteristic architecture of the frontier that follows the log-hut—on the top of a bleak hill some
two miles from the present village. For himself, Deacon
Snell procured a more commodious dwelling farther west,
now known as the Bryant Homestead. If he had been a poet
or a painter, he could not have chosen a more charming site.
From the cosy shelter of its newly-planted apple orchards, it
looked out upon an immense expanse of low and high lands.
The hills to the eastward rose one above another until the last
one met the sun in his coming ; and those on the west and
south extended their hands to old Graylock, " familiar with
forgotten years." In front ran the babbling brook, to be hereafter known as the Rivulet, through green meadows that descended, more or less precipitously, to the Westfield, whose
gentle murmurs, only heard in the stillness of night, broke
into a roar when the rains had swollen its current. Behind,
in solemn, interminable shade, stretched the primeval forests of beech, birch, ash, maple, and hemlock, of which the
readers of an " Inscription for the Entrance to a Wood" will
retain a vivid picture.

During the fairer season of the year, that is, from June into
October, the landscape here was all brightness and tranquil-
lity. The clearest of skies looked down upon waving fields of
singular beauty. The suns rose each morning as if it were
the dawn of a new creation, and they set each evening amid
the most dazzling effusions of color, and a profound silence,
unbroken save by woodland murmurs and the songs of birds.
In the autumn these vast billowy circles of forest blazed with
crimson, gold, and purple, whose brilliancy the most gorgeous
of Venetian painters would have envied; yet subdued by a
wreath of silver haze which made it soft, genial, and harmonious. It was a magnificence, however, that was short-lived, for
in a latitude so far toward the north the winter arrived early
and continued long, and while it lasted it was very intense. The
cold blasts cut to the marrow ; the trees not only lost their
leaves, but stalked out of the earth like the skeletons of trees;

all the birds were driven away, save the crow, the hawk, the
jay, the partridge, and the nuthatch, which have no melody in
their harsh screams and scolding shrieks; and, while the cattle
sought the shelter of barns and sheds, man clung to his fire-
side. In every direction the outlook was bleak and desolate; and, though the fancies of poets discern in the effects
wrought by the winds among the falling snowflakes *—when
the delicate sprays of the forests are glittering gems, the
massy trunks are encased in crystal, and the long-drawn aisles
of the wood-arches are amethyst and topaz—an architecture
that surpasses the richest arabesques and fretworks of Moor-
ish and Venetian genius, and to which no cathedral of the old
world is comparable—the conditions of life were extremely
severe. A soil for the most part reluctant or sterile was
scarcely compensated, in the minds of the husbandmen at
least, by—

> " The glory of the morn, the glow of eve,
> The beauty of the streams, and stars, and flowers."

In the midst of this lovely scenery the poet was born, and
at a time, too, not unworthy of passing remark. It was in
the second year of the second administration of Washington.
Our new political structure consisted as yet of only fifteen
States—Vermont and Kentucky having been added to the
original thirteen since the Revolution. Many of the Revolutionary heroes were still alive; the framers of the Federal Constitution were most of them in active political life;
the earnest contests of opinion, as to the character and direction to be given to the untried experiment of Democratic-
Republican government, were raging with great vehemence;
and it seemed yet undetermined, in spite of the hopes indulged
in by more sanguine temperaments, whether the glorious
inspirations which had sustained the patriotic mind through
the appalling difficulties of the war, and the no less appalling

---

* The New England poets, Bryant, Emerson, Whittier, and Lowell, have managed to get some of their most charming lines out of the snow-scenes of their home.

difficulties of the quasi-anarchy that followed it, should issue in a stable, compact, and vigorous polity, or in failure, disgrace, and ruin. These contests were complicated by events abroad, where a tempest of revolution had swept over France, and was threatening England as well as the nations of the Continent. The "black terror" was coming to an end, Robespierre and his accomplices had gone to the scaffold, but the Directory was still in power. French popular armies overran or menaced nearly all the ancient States. The British House of Commons was still ringing with the powerful eloquence of Burke, Fox, and Pitt, and the great man, destined to play a grander part than any one else in the coming drama, lately a lieutenant of artillery, who had just got his hand in at the petty siege of Toulon, was on his way to Italy, as General, to begin the most wonderful series of military exploits that history has ever recorded.

At that day no such thing as an American literature, in the proper sense of the word, existed. Fisher Ames, writing on the subject in 1801, says that, "excepting the writers of two able works on Politics,* we have no authors. Has our country produced one great original man of genius? † Is there one luminary in our firmament that shines with unborrowed rays?" As for poetry, he intimates that the Muses, like nightingales, are too delicate to cross the salt water, or sicken and mope without song if they do. ‡ But, as the political condition had recently undergone a great change, which was thought to be an improvement, the more buoyant minds of the era were hopeful of a literary dawn. A passage in the famous discourse which the eloquent Buckminster delivered eight years later, in 1809, before the Phi Beta Kappa Society of Cambridge, admits the fact of our sterility, but salves it with a prediction. "Our poets and historians," he said, "our critics and orators, the men of whom posterity are to stand in awe

* Jefferson and John Adams probably.
† He had forgotten Benjamin Franklin.
‡ "Life and Works of Fisher Ames," vol. ii, p. 428, Boston, 1854.

and by whom they are to be instructed, are yet to appear among us. But, if we are not mistaken in the signs of the times, the genius of our literature begins to show symptoms of vigor, and to meditate a bolder flight, and the generation which is to succeed us will be formed on better models and leave a brighter track." *

In Europe, the old spirit was visibly giving way to the new. Kant's three wonderful volumes of criticism were but recently from the press, and yet they had already moulded the acute and active German mind into new forms. Goethe had printed " Goetz of Berlichingen " and Schiller his " Robbers," and both were advancing to other and better work. In England the long reign of the Queen Anne's men was on the decline. Cowper, though he would write no more, had yet six years to live; Burns was singing a swan-song of departure; Scott was hunting up the old ballads of the Scottish borders; Byron was a boy at Harrow; Shelley was in his cradle, and Keats was not yet born; but the titanic Landor had issued his first book, and Wordsworth, Coleridge, and Southey were dreaming pantisocratic dreams of a golden age, not to be set agoing, as they fondly thought, in America, but in the pages of their own poetry, destined to revive

"—the melodious bursts that fill
The spacious time of great Elizabeth."

* " Sermons of J. S. Buckminster," Boston, 1829.

CHAPTER THIRD.

THE BRYANT FAMILY AND ANCESTORS.

NEITHER Mr. Bryant nor any of his kindred seems to have been possessed with what Southey calls the leaven of ancestral pride, or, at least, it did not work very powerfully in their blood. No one of them, so far as I am able to ascertain, ever took the pains to trace his family relationships among the records of the old world. Their curiosity in this respect stopped on the shores of the Atlantic. Though several of them, whose reports are before me, made inquiries as to their lineage, they were contented to go no further back than the days in which the Pilgrims were landed at Plymouth. What William the Conqueror and his followers are to the noble families of old England, the passengers by the Mayflower are to the noble families of New England; meaning the families that have nobly served their day and generation. They are the Eupatrids, or Founders, the only sources of distinction and honor. No Bryant was among these passengers; but, if we trace the family up through its degrees, we shall see that the poet had a triple title to Mayflower origin.*

---

* The following table of the generations upward furnishes, perhaps, all the information that may be required on this head :

I.—THE CHILDREN, BORN AT CUMMINGTON.

Austin Bryant, b. April 16, 1793 ; William Cullen, b. November 3, 1794 ; Cyrus, b. July 12, 1798 ; Sarah Snell, b. July, 1802 ; Peter Rush, afterward called Arthur, b. November 28, 1803 ; Charity Louisa, b. December 20, 1805 ; and John

The poet's mother was the daughter of Ebenezer Snell (see note III, 3 and 4), the fourth of the six children of Zachariah Snell and Abigail Hayward (IV, 5, 6), who was the youngest child of Joseph Hayward and Harriet Mitchell (V, 11, 12), and Mrs. Harriet (Mitchell) Hayward was the youngest daugh-

---

Howard, b. July 22, 1807. Of these seven children, only Arthur and John Howard are alive in 1882.

II.—THE PARENTS.

1st.
- (1.) Dr. PETER BRYANT, b. at North Bridgewater August 12, 1767; d. at Cummington March 19, 1820.
- (2.) SARAH SNELL, b. at North Bridgewater December 4, 1768; married 1792; d. at Princeton, Illinois, May 6, 1847.

III.—THE GRANDPARENTS.

1st.
- (1.) Dr. PHILIP BRYANT, b. 1731; d. 1816, aged 85.
- (2.) SILENCE HOWARD, b. 1738; married 1757; d.

2d.
- (3.) Col. EBENEZER SNELL, b. October 1, 1738; found dead in his bed August 16, 1813.
- (4.) SARAH PACKARD, b. September 10, 1737; married 1764; d.

IV.—THE GREAT GRANDPARENTS.

1st.
- (1.) ICHABOD BRYANT, b. 1702; d. 1759; lived at Rhancham, and thence moved to West Bridgewater.
- (2.) RUTH STAPLES; birth and date of marriage unknown.

2d.
- (3.) Dr. ABIEL HOWARD, b. November 6, 1704; d. 1777.
- (4.) SILENCE WASHBURN, b. 1713; married 1737; d. 1775.

3d.
- (5.) ZACHARIAH SNELL, b. March 17, 1704; d.
- (6.) ABIGAIL HAYWARD, b. August 3, 1702; married 1731.

4th.
- (7.) Capt. ABIEL PACKARD, b. April 29, 1699; d. 1774.
- (8.) SARAH AMES, b. January 23, 1702; married 1723; d. 1770.

V.—THE GREAT GREAT GRANDPARENTS.

1st.
- (1.) STEPHEN BRYANT, b. 1657.
- (2.) MEHITABEL ———, date of marriage unknown (1683 ?).

2d.
- (3.) FATHER of Ruth Staples unknown.
- (4.) MOTHER   "   "

3d.
- (5.) JONATHAN HOWARD,   ; d. 1739.
- (6.) SARAH DEANE, dates unknown.

4th.
- (7.) Capt. NEHEMIAH WASHBURN, b. 1685; d. 1748.
- (8.) JANE HOWARD, b. 1689; married 1713; d.

5th.
- (9.) JOSIAH SNELL.
- (10.) ANNA ALDEN, married 1699.

6th.
- (11.) JOSEPH HAYWARD.
- (12.) HARRIET MITCHELL.

ter of Experience Mitchell and Jane Cook. Now, this Jane (Cook) Mitchell was the third of the five children of Francis Cook and Esther his wife. Francis Cook and his son John came over as passengers in the Mayflower, landing at Plymouth December 22, 1620, while Mrs. Cook, who was a native of the Netherlands, came over in 1623 in the ship Anne, the third that made the voyage to Plymouth, accompanied by their three other children, Jacob, Jane, and Esther. Their fifth child, Mary, was born in Plymouth in 1626.*

7th. { (13.) ZACHEUS PACKARD, d. 1723, son of Samuel Packard, d. 1684, who came over in the Diligent of Ipswich, 1638.
(14.) SARAH HOWARD, dates unknown.

8th. { (15.) JOHN AMES, b. April 14, 1672 ; d. 1756.
(16.) SARAH WASHBURN, married January 12, 1697.

Stephen Bryant (see V, 1) was the son of another Stephen Bryant, who came from England in his youth in about 1632 ; was a town officer in Duxbury in 1644 ; removed to Plymouth, and was propounded as freeman in 1655; surveyor of highways in 1658, 1674, 1678. He married Abigail Shaw about 1645, who came over with her father, John Shaw, in 1632, and settled at Plymouth. From this couple the Bryants were descended.

Sarah Deane (V, 6) was the daughter of John Deane, a son of the first emigrant of the name, who came from near Taunton, in England, and settled at Taunton, in Massachusetts.

Jane Howard (V, 8) was the daughter of Capt. John Howard, who came from England, and lived at Duxbury in 1643.

Anna Alden (V, 10) was the daughter of John Alden, a son of the John Alden who came by the Mayflower.

Sarah Howard (V, 14) was the daughter of the first John Howard, born 1666, died 1750, and Mary Keith, daughter of the Rev. James Keith, of Aberdeen, Scotland.

Harriet Mitchell (V, 12) was the daughter of Experience Mitchell, who arrived in the Anne in 1623, and Jane Cook, a daughter of Francis Cook, a passenger by the Mayflower.

Sarah Washburn (V, 16) was a daughter of Elizabeth Mitchell and granddaughter of Experience Mitchell, just named.

* For these and other particulars I am indebted to Mr. Ellis Ames, of Canton, Mass., one of the Commissioners appointed by the Legislature in 1865 to compile a complete copy of the Statutes and Laws of the Province and State of Massachusetts Bay, from the time of the Province Charter to the adoption of the Federal Constitution. (Since published in nine volumes.) His researches have been minute and exhaustive.

Again: the poet's grandmother, *née* Sarah Packard, was the daughter of Capt. Abiel Packard and Sarah Ames (see IV, 7, 8), who was the daughter of John Ames and Sarah Washburn (V, 15, 16). Mrs. Sarah Washburn, wife of Mr. John Ames, was the youngest of the ten children of John Washburn and Elizabeth Mitchell, and Mrs. Elizabeth (Mitchell) Washburn was one of the eight children of Experience Mitchell and Jane Cook his wife; Mrs. Jane (Cook) Mitchell was the third of the five children of Francis and Esther Cook, already mentioned.

Again, and more important: Josiah Snell (V, 9), the grandfather of Ebenezer Snell, married Anna Alden, the daughter of John Alden, and a granddaughter of Capt. John Alden and Priscilla Mullins, whose story is so beautifully told in the poem by Longfellow.* Priscilla Mullins was the daughter of William Mullins, or Mollines, who, with his wife and two children, Joseph and Priscilla, and a servant named Robert Carter, came over in the Mayflower. William Mullins, the father, died in less than two months, viz., on the 21st of February, 1621, and his wife a few days before or after him, and his son, Joseph, and his servant, Robert Carter, died the same season; but the daughter, Priscilla Mullins, survived, married John Alden, and had eleven children, one of whom was John, the father of Anna, the wife of Josiah Snell,† the grandfather of Ebenezer Snell, who was the grandfather of William Cullen. Twice he ascends to Francis Cook, and once to the brave captain of history and romance.

The name Bryant, or Briant, would seem to be rather French than English, and is said to be prevalent still in Normandy; but the greater number of the names in our table are unquestionably English. A Scottish strain came in with the Rev. James Keith, a graduate of Aberdeen College, and for

---

* I cannot refer to this poem without remarking how much it adds to our interest in John and Priscilla to know that our two earliest and most eminent poets, Bryant and Longfellow, were descended from them.

† Authority of Mr. Ellis Ames, before cited (p. 49, note).

more than fifty years a minister at North Bridgewater, where the house he occupied still stands, and it may be supposed to have brought with it the proverbial intensity of the Scottish race, and "its double love of song and saintliness." But the stock, on the side of both parents, though it blossomed into no shining flowers, was a sturdy one, of vigorous sap and unusual tenacity of life.

"Our great grandfather, Ichabod Bryant," Mr. Arthur Bryant writes me, "was a man of gigantic size and strength. He would place his hands on the shoulders of any common man and crush him to the earth, in spite of his resistance. Our grandfather, Dr. Philip Bryant, lived to the age of eighty-five, and visited his patients till a fortnight before his death. A cousin of mine, who lived with him, and was grown up when he died, told me that he would mount a horse to the last with the greatest ease. Our father was a man of great muscular power, and used to perform feats of strength that no two ordinary men could accomplish. One of his greatest exploits, which seems incredible, but is well attested, was this: He accompanied two of his students of medicine to fish in a small lake of great depth which lies among the hills northwest of Cummington, and is the source of Westfield River. They went out upon the water in an old skiff, but their frail vessel soon broke asunder. The two students could not swim, and my father took them both and swam ashore with them. Our maternal grandfather was also uncommonly active and energetic; and, when our mother came to Illinois in 1835, she said, at the house of my brother Cyrus, that she used, when young, to mount a horse from the ground. He, affecting incredulity, remarked that he should like to see it done, when she, piqued by his apparent scepticism, added that, if a horse was brought to the door, she would do it again. A horse was saddled and brought to the door, and, though she was then sixty-seven years old, she performed the feat at once." *

* This vigor of race was sometimes shown in the collateral branches on the larger field of war. Seth Bryant, son of Ichabod, was at the capture of Louisburg in the old French war, was an orderly sergeant at Bunker Hill, and present also at the surrender of Cornwallis at Yorktown. Oliver and Daniel, sons of Philip Bryant, were both in the Revolutionary struggle, and the younger Philip Bryant was on board the Chesapeake in her action with the Shannon. A son of Stephen Bryant,

But, with all this strength, there was a taint of pulmonary weakness somewhere in the family, of which several of its members died, and which Dr. Bryant and two of his children inherited.

The greater part of the father's early life was a severe struggle against untoward circumstances. A paper in his handwriting, found within the last year or two by Mr. John H. Bryant, discloses many particulars of it, which he had never spoken of even to his children. It is evidently the fragment of a letter written to some friend who had consulted him in regard to his willingness to serve as Senator from the County of Hampshire in the General Court. It will be read, I think, with considerable interest.

"I have for some time been wishing to write to you upon a subject which you once mentioned to me, but a diffidence which I found it very difficult to overcome has till this time prevented my undertaking it. You, sir, are certainly so far acquainted with me as to be able to judge whether I have abilities to support the dignity of the office with honor to myself and my constituents. I do not affect that insensibility which would not prize the honor of representing so respectable a portion of my native State as the County of H——. Yet, if the last, I should be very sorry to be the least of the honorable Board. If my friends think that, by the exertion of such talents as I have, I can contribute something to the service of my country, I am willing under the great disadvantages that will attend my acceptance of the office, the sacrifices of personal interest, and the privations of domestic enjoyment, to consent to the nomination.

"I am sensible of the defects of my education, and have sought to supply them as far as industry and my limited means would permit. I had literally no attention paid to it from 8 to 14—the season when the mind is most susceptible and most easily impressed, and

---

and brother of Ichabod, William Bryant, who died in 1772, aged 88 years, has on his tombstone at Perth Amboy, N. J., that he made "fifty-five voyages between the ports of New York and London, and approved himself a faithful and fortunate commander." Julian E. Bryant, a nephew of the poet, served through our Civil War, rose to the rank of captain, and was drowned at Brazos, Texas, in 1865.

when it ought to receive the rudiments of knowledge. I was left with an uncle who, being an avaricious man, thought all time lost which was not employed agreeably to his frugal system of hoarding. I have often smarted under the lash for the time I had stolen to read such books as I could borrow in the neighborhood. During these years I never had a single day's schooling. I was so vexed at this treatment that I eventually ran away and refused to return. My father at this time had married a second wife. She proved to be a thrifty woman, and thought boys ought to be kept out of idleness—that no good could come of so much reading, and that some other employment was much more profitable. My father's farm was new; it wanted clearing and fencing. I was, therefore, kept closely at manual labor from this time till I was 20 years old, except about three months each winter during the four first winters, a part of which time I attended a grammar school and acquired some knowledge of writing, arithmetic, and the rudiments of Latin. At eighteen I was allowed the privilege of keeping school three months in the winter. By assiduous application I had at this time obtained a little knowledge of Greek, so that at nineteen I underwent an examination and was approbated as qualified to keep a grammar school. At twenty I commenced an open rebellion. My spirit could brook such management no longer. I have every reason to respect my father, and have no doubt he would have proceeded differently with his children had he not been too much influenced by the counsels and maxims of his wife. Finding, however, that I continued restive, I was permitted to enter myself as freshman at Cambridge. But from dread of the expense of a public education, or some other cause never explained to me, I was directed soon after to commence the study of medicine under the tuition of my father. With the avails of my school-keeping I purchased a few of the Latin and Greek classics, and in the mean time read Homer and Xenophon as well as I could without an instructor. I read also such history as a small circulating library established in the parish afforded, and as many medical books aside from my father's moderate library as I could procure by borrowing. My reading was mostly confined to antiquated books. With these helps and one year's instruction under a celebrated French surgeon, and attending a course of lectures with the medical professor at Cambridge, I was thought qualified at the age of twenty-three to enter upon the practice of my

profession. After this I continued two years with my father, performed all the drudgery of the business, and shared a small part of
the profits, no suitable vacancy presenting itself. At the age of
twenty-five, with my small stock of book-knowledge, without experience in the ways of the world, my whole property consisting of a
horse, a few books, and about twenty-five dollars worth of medicine,
I launched out into the wide world to begin business, and established
myself where I now reside. What happened during a two years' voyage to the East Indies, Isle of France, and Cape of Good Hope, is of
little consequence to this narrative. Suffice it to say that I returned
with more knowledge of men and things, but from several unlucky
incidents without having added anything to my property. I was
truly and literally poor."

The voyage referred to in this extract was undertaken by
Dr. Bryant in 1795, in the capacity of surgeon to a merchant vessel, in which he had also risked some small mercantile ventures. Unfortunately for his enterprise, the French
Directory just about that time, in retaliation of a similar outrage on neutral rights committed by Great Britain, had issued
an arbitrary decree against neutral ships destined to any of
the enemy's ports, which caused the vessel to be detained at
the Isle of France (Mauritius), where she was subsequently
confiscated, with all the property on board. Dr. Bryant was
compelled to remain on the island for more than a year, but
without wholly losing his time, as he practiced his art in the
French hospitals, and acquired a knowledge of the French
language. Some of the heavier hours of his exile he relieved
by pursuing the traces of the adventurous and susceptible
Bernardin de St. Pierre, who had visited the island a few
years before, and woven a spell of romance about its rustic
scenes and simple manners in the famous story of " Paul and
Virginia," which has brought tears to so many young eyes all
over the civilized world. On his return he stopped for a
while at the Cape of Good Hope, where he gathered books,
curiosities, instruments, and botanical specimens, all of which

were lost, with the rest of his luggage, by some accident that befell them when they were about to be landed at Salem.

It is a mere conjecture, but not an improbable one, that Dr. Bryant, while making acquaintance with the literature of France, should have acquired some of that freedom and independence of thought, which enabled him soon afterward to break away from the Calvinistic theology in which he had been bred. A personal sufferer under the odious despotism desolating France, and extending its sweep even to the oceans, he was not likely to become a very enthusiastic recipient of the French philosophy, in its applications either to religious or to political practice. On the contrary, he turned out a sturdy antagonist of those "French influences," which were supposed to be giving an infectious taint to our domestic modes of thinking. But a mind as open and inquisitive as his, could hardly have escaped some touches of a spirit which maddened nearly half the world. Be this as it may, it is certain that after his return, when he was chosen a delegate to the legislative assembly, he lent a willing ear to the new views of Christianity promulgated at Boston.

A great intellectual contest had been going on in the churches of New England ever since the middle of the previous century—an eddy of the mightier current that was bearing the civilized world away from its ancient anchorages, and launching it upon the open sea. From the dawn of speculative thought on this continent, some little independence of judgment had been exhibited by individuals, but the voices of dissent were like the pipings of solitary birds in the forests. They were not heard amid the roar of orthodox thunders. The flag of Calvinism was the only recognized standard of faith, and they who abandoned it or allowed it to be trailed in the dust, were thought to be traitors alike to their traditions and their God. Nor was the polemic confined to books and sermons. It absorbed the great body of the people, who discussed it in their wayside and household talks. Farmers and mechanics argued " of Providence, foreknowledge, will and

fate, fixed fate, free-will, foreknowledge absolute," as familiarly as Milton represents his more illustrious personages to
have done in the pre-Adamistic age.   Questions of State, too,
were mingled with questions of Church, and the debate was
often invigorated and inflamed by the incitements of political
as well as religious passions.

The battle was at its height when Dr. Bryant attended the
General Court for several successive sessions.   He began his
duties in 1806, continued them through the years 1808-'9-'12
and '13, and afterward as Senator in 1816-'18.   The eloquent
Buckminster was then at the summit of his power as a preacher, and the no less eloquent William Ellery Channing was
pouring forth those fervid and beautiful addresses which have
since won him a deathless name.   A Unitarian professor had
been appointed in Harvard University, and that seat of learning was destined soon to be wrested from the hands of its orthodox guardians, to become the nursery of a pronounced liberal religious sentiment.   Dr. Bryant listened attentively to
the innovators, subscribed to their publications, and carried
back to Western Massachusetts, where they had scarcely yet
penetrated, the general doctrines of the new school.

He does not seem to have neglected his professional duties
because of these alien political and religious engagements.
His practice widened, and his reputation as a learned and
skilful physician increased.   He wrote largely for medical
and other periodicals, was consulted by other physicians, and
attended regularly at the meetings of their societies, where he
became a prominent authority.   Even in his legislative capacity he endeavored to promote the interests of his profession,
and was instrumental in securing the passage of laws, intended
to raise the standard of medical education throughout the
State, which are still in force.   In his public as in his private
conduct he was distinguished for his strict and unswerving
integrity.   Men who knew him best honored him most ; and
to this day the traditions of his goodness and justice are carefully preserved among the descendants of his neighbors.   That

he should have consented to hide his fine endowments in the
obscurities of a small country practice is a proof of the modest
estimate that he put upon himself, and of his contentment
with other satisfactions than those that attend the pursuit of
riches and fame.

Mrs. SARAH SNELL BRYANT, the mother, was a woman of
less culture than her husband, but of vigorous understanding
and energetic character, and in every way worthy of his love
and confidence. Having gone to a new settlement when she
was only six years of age, she had enjoyed few of the advantages of education; but as Mr. John H. Bryant, her youngest
son, writes: " Amidst the hardships and privations incident to
a life in the forest, she grew up to a stately womanhood. Her
opportunities were necessarily limited, so far as schools and
books were concerned, but she made a creditable progress
in all the rudimentary branches of learning." Her household
activity and diligence would, in this later age of the world, be
considered something marvellous. In the days of general im-
poverishment after the war, the mother of the household did
nearly all her own domestic work. Factories there were none,
and, if there had been any, the roads were too rough to render
them of much avail. Each family had its own spinning-wheels
—a smaller one in the corner of the sitting-room, to which the
busy foot of the matron was applied in the long winter evenings, and a larger one in the hall or garret, where she could
walk back and forth with the spindle in her hands, and twist
the clean flax or tow into threads. It had also its loom for
the weaving of cloth, its carpet-frames, its candle-moulds, and
its dye-pots for the coloring of fabrics from the extracts of
various woods and weeds. Mrs. Bryant performed all these
labors. An idea of the amount of them is obtained from the
little diary, mentioned in the poet's narrative, in which she
registered what was done from day to day even in those pe-
riods which are most trying and exhaustive in a woman's life.
It is filled with such items as these: " Made Austin a coat ";
" Spun four skeins of tow "; " Spun thirty knots of linen ";

" Taught Cullen his letters"; "Made a pair of breeches";
"Wove four yards and went a-quilting"; "Made a dress for
the boy"; "Sewed on a shirt"; "Wove four yards and visited Mrs. ——"; "Washed and ironed"; "Spun and wove."
And so the simple record runs on, year after year.

"All this work our mother did," says Mr. John H. Bryant,
with pardonable pride, "looking after her young children,
feeding them and nursing them in sickness, teaching them
to read and write, which was faithfully attended to during their
earlier years, while she turned the wheel by the winter fire.
In those times many shifts and expedients of economy were
necessary to maintain an honorable independence, which are
rarely thought of in these days, even by the poorest people.
Not only was she industrious and persevering in ordinary labor, but she took a deep interest in public affairs, both national
and State, never neglecting any of her house duties, but visiting constantly, especially the sick, whom she nursed for days
and nights together. She exerted a considerable influence in
township and neighborhood improvements, such as schools,
roads, etc. It was through her persuasion with us boys that
the maple and other shade trees were planted around the
homestead and along the highways. Having observed something of the kind when on a journey, she resolved as soon as
she returned to have a similar work done at home. These
were the first trees set by the roadside in all that region,
where thousands have since been planted. She discouraged
all bad habits in her household, such as drinking, tobacco
chewing and smoking, and idleness and profanity. From this
last vice I believe all her children were entirely free, for if
any of them ever uttered an oath, I never heard of it. I
have often heard her exclaim, "Above all things, I abhor
drunkenness!" also, "Never be idle; always be doing something"; "If you are never idle, you will find time for everything." Dr. Johnson says: "It is a mortifying reflection to
think what we might have done, compared with what we
have done."

As there were no large schools in the vicinity, the children of this couple were mainly educated by the efforts of their parents. In the spring and summer the young men, as they grew to be old enough, took part in the labors of the farm, and the young women at all seasons in those of the household; but the long winter evenings were given by both to study. Dr. Bryant was something of a scholar, knowing the Greek, Latin, and French languages, and possessing, in addition to the largest medical library in those parts, a considerable number of the more important works of English literature, especially of the poets, having been himself addicted to making verses. Among these, according to a list which Mr. J. H. Bryant has furnished me from memory, were Hume, Gibbon, Rollin, Russell, Gillies, Plutarch, Shakespeare, Spenser, Milton, Dryden, Pope, Akenside, Goldsmith, Thompson, Burns, Cowper, Beattie, Falconer, Campbell (Pleasures of Hope), Hogg, Montgomery, Rodgers, Scott (Lord of the Isles), Byron (Lara, Bride of Abydos, and Corsair), Southey (Thalaba, and minor poems), and Wordsworth (Lyrical Ballads), and in other departments, Burke, Chesterfield, the Spectator, Fielding, Dr. Johnson, Dr. Adam Clark's Travels, Park's Travels, Disraeli's Curiosities of Literature, and Sismondi's Literature of the South of Europe. Besides the greater masters, Mr. Cullen Bryant tells us, "there were 'Sanford and Merton' and 'Little Jack'; there were 'Robinson Crusoe,' with its variations 'The Swiss Family Robinson' and 'The New Robinson Crusoe'; there were a Mrs. Trimmer's 'Knowledge of Nature' and Berquin's lively narratives and sketches, translated from the French; there were 'Philip Quarll' and Watts's 'Poems for Children,' Bunyan's 'Pilgrim's Progress' and Mrs. Barbauld's writings. Later we had Mrs. Edgeworth's 'Parent's Assistant' and 'Evenings at Home.'" They had also American versifiers in abundance, Freneau, Humphreys, Trumbull, Dwight, etc., whom it was the fashion to admire in Dr. Bryant's earlier days, but whom the children very soon ceased to read with pleasure.

That other New England families, particularly in the cities and towns, were more copiously and variously supplied with books, admits of no doubt, but few, I venture to say, living among the mountains could have made so good a show.*

Among these books there are two that, in the circumstances, are worthy of note—Shakespeare and Wordsworth. The Puritans and their descendants, down to a very recent time, were not accustomed to look with friendly eyes upon any of the playwrights. Dr. Channing tells us that, when he and Judge Story were students at Harvard, toward the last year of the last century, a few young men got together quietly for the purpose of reading Shakespeare's plays, as if it were something quite unwonted.† Indeed, Shakespeare, in those days, even in England, if read at all, was read rather for his interesting and dramatic stories than for the exquisite poetry in which they are embedded; and it is to be presumed that the Bryant children read him in that way. But as they advanced in years, Mr. Arthur Bryant informs me, their minds gradually opened to those higher qualities which English, guided by German, criticism, has since discovered in his pages. Wordsworth's Lyrical Ballads were first published in 1798 (a small volume of 210 pages), and a second edition, in two volumes, in 1800, from which a Philadelphia reprint was

---

* Mr. George Ticknor, writing of Boston, a principal city, and of one of its most wealthy and conspicuous families, in the years 1808–'11, says that in those days books "were by no means so accessible as they are now. Few, comparatively, were published in the United States, and, as it was the dreary period of the commercial restrictions that preceded the war of 1812 with England, still fewer were imported. Even good school-books were not easily obtained. A copy of Euripides in the original could not be bought in any bookseller's shop in New England, and was with difficulty borrowed. The best publications that appeared in Great Britain came to us slowly and were seldom reprinted. New books from the Continent hardly reached us at all. Men felt poor and anxious in those dark days, and literary indulgences, which have now become as necessary to us as our daily food, were luxuries enjoyed by few." — "Life of William Hickling Prescott." By George Ticknor. Boston: Ticknor & Fields, 1864. Page 9.

† "Memoirs of William Ellery Channing," vol. i. Boston, 1848.

made in 1802.* Dr. Bryant purchased a copy of them in Boston in 1810, and took them home, where they were read with no little admiration. The "Rime of the Ancient Mariner," and "Love," by an anonymous friend, which the book contained, were at first thought to be superior to the other pieces; but in time the principal poet took entire possession of their hearts.† It would thus seem that, while the great dispensers of British criticism were pouring out their unmeasured ridicule upon Wordsworth, he had found a small band of delighted appreciators in the backwoods of America. ‡

All the works, indeed, of this small library were kept for use, and not for ornament. The Doctor himself was so devoted a reader that he always carried some of them with him in his professional rounds, and, when he chanced to stop at a house where a new book of any value lay on the shelf or the table, he was soon lost in the perusal of it, sometimes forgetting alike his patients and his meals in the intensity of his interest, until reminded that he must break off if he wished to get home before nightfall. The mother was not so eager and liberal in her tastes, but she too managed, amid her many avocations, to attain a knowledge of the leading historians, of the best essayists, and of Pope and Cowper. As for the children, an aged lady who lived near by told me once that she never passed the Bryant house of a winter evening and looked into the windows without seeing three or four great hulks of boys stretched out, with their backs on the floor and their heads toward the birchwood fire, which was the only light, each one deeply immersed in his book. As they read, children-

---

* "Memoirs of William Wordsworth," vol. i, p. 176, note by Henry Reed. Boston: Ticknor, Reed & Fields, 1851.

† Cullen was then at school or college, and did not read the book till some time afterward.

‡ In 1814 Jeffrey allowed himself to speak of the Excursion as "a tissue of moral and devotional ravings," "a hubbub of strained raptures and fantastic sublimities." As late as 1822, Southey, in a letter to Landor, referred to "the duncery and malignity" with which Wordsworth was still assaulted.—Landor's Works, vol. i, p. 230.

like, without much discrimination, Pope was a great favorite with all of them, but particularly so with the father, who belonged to the generation for which he had written, and who shared in its opinion, expressed by no less a critic than Johnson, that Pope's verses were the acme of poetic excellence. The children preferred his Homer to his other works, the sounding and mellifluous couplets of which they found it easy to retain and to recite aloud. As they advanced in life and judgment, Pope was dethroned for other favorites, such as Spenser, whose stories of giants, knights, fairies, and fair ladies, told in the sweetest of numbers, are so apt, singly if not collectively, to captivate the fancy of the young.* Milton, the traditionary bard of the Puritans, is of too lofty a strain, generally, to commend himself to youth, so that Cowper's plainer sense, coupled with an equally fervent religiousness, rendered him a more familiar companion. Scott and Byron were read, as each of their works appeared, with much pleasure, yet with some dissent. When Wordsworth came, these "striplings of the hills," to use one of his own phrases, who knew nothing of the theories of poetry, which he paraded in his prefaces, speedily felt his charms. They found in his nice observations of nature, his simplicity of diction, his moral purity and elevation, truthful expressions of what had always been a part of their daily experience. The mountain scenery he describes so lovingly was lying in all its substantial features before them, and, as they climbed the hills or roamed the woods together declaiming his more impressive passages, they were enabled to attest his fidelity to real life, so far as it was known in their humble sphere.

Excepting what he was able to find in nature and in books, the companionships of our poet, in his childhood, were confined almost exclusively to the members of his own family. Their home was at a considerable remove from other habitations.

* Mr. Bryant once told me that he had read the "Faerie Queen" many times through.

Whatever sports they engaged in they were compelled to de-vise for themselves out of their heads or out of their reading. They had none of the advantages of great schools, of music, of art, of theatres, of social gatherings and games, and of visits to strange scenes and houses, which the youth of the present generation enjoy. Of public amusements there were none. Those rude rustic assemblages, which the autobiography speaks of—the sugar camps, the corn huskings, the house rais-ings, and the singing schools—were infrequent, and, at the best, could have possessed but little attractiveness for refined and youthful minds, and there was nothing in them or in any of their incidents to stir or expand the imagination or to kindle the best affections of the heart.

Nevertheless, there was one amusement the elder brothers were able to take together, which did not depend upon other company, and with the delights of which they were never sated. This was the exploration of the surrounding fields and forests, which presented attractions varying with the varying seasons of the year, but ever full and ever new. Day after day they scoured the depths of the woods, climbing the hills or descending into the ravines, until there was not a thicket, a precipice, a brooklet, or even a tree, with which they were not as well acquainted as they were with the objects of their own house. These rambles were not, of course, made merely for the sake of the scenery; boys, as I apprehend it, do not care much for scenery in itself, which they take in by the eye as unconsciously as they breathe the air. Their real objects when they go abroad, if they have any beyond the joys of mere physical exercise, are squirrels, birds' nests, wood-chucks, rabbits, and fruits and nuts in their seasons. Nature is only the background or adjunct of their sports, and mixes herself gradually with the substance of their minds, as the glow of health mixes with the blood of the body.*

* Wordsworth, in the Prelude, has finely illustrated the influence of what he calls "collateral objects and appearances" in impregnating and elevating the mind.—Po-etical Works, vol. vii, p. 30. Boston.

Our youngsters, like others, were alive to these special pursuits (although in later life Mr. Bryant evinced a vehement repugnance to all kinds of needless life-taking), and they coupled with them the higher pleasures of botanical research, which they had learned from their father, and of declaiming aloud what they had read, amid the silence and solitude of the fields. Cullen was particularly fond of composing his own little bits of verse, while wandering alone, and he refers to the practice in one of his earlier poems.*

This family, living so far from any considerable town, in a region almost inaccessible at the best of seasons, and for a greater part of the year buried in snow, enjoyed few opportunities of intercourse with the outside world. The post brought them newspapers and letters once a week, if the snow permitted; and all communication with the towns was made on horseback. Visitors of educated tastes and polished manners were only occasional. Dr. Bryant corresponded with men of note, and in his periodical visits at Northampton, to attend the meetings of the County Medical Society, he met many of the most accomplished members of his profession. He shared with them, also, the hospitalities of Judge Lyman's house, which was the resort of the most eminent and cultivated persons of the day—governors, senators, judges, lawyers, and literary men. Otherwise, his nearest friend, Mr. Samuel Howe, then a lawyer of local repute, and afterward Judge of the Court of Common Pleas and Professor of the Law School at Northampton, lived at a distance of four miles, in the little village of Worthington. Congenial tastes and rare elevation and purity of character rendered his society particularly agreeable to the Doctor.† Judges Howe and Lyman were men of the old school, as it is called, who retained the grand manner

---

* See the original poem as it appears in the note to Poetical Works, vol. i.
    "I cannot forget the high spells that enchanted."

† Judge Howe died in 1820. There is an article on his life and character in the "Christian Examiner," vol. v, No. 3. See also an address to the Suffolk bar by Chief Justice Parker. Boston: Nathan Hales, 1820.

of colonial times, uniting dignity and grace of deportment to fine intellectual endowments, wide reading, liberality of thought and act, and public spirit. They were, moreover, happily married to sisters, that were in every way worthy of their own excellences. Mr. Ralph Waldo Emerson says that he had never seen "so stately and naturally distinguished a pair as Judge and Mrs. Lyman. She was a queenly woman," he adds, "nobly formed, in perfect health, made for society, with flowing conversation, high spirits, and consummate ease."* Mrs. Howe, no less notable for force and cultivation of mind and for sweetness and beauty of life, became in later years the delight and ornament of her circle at Cambridge, where the fragrance of her graces and virtues still lingers.† These noble and accomplished people held Dr. Bryant in high esteem, always speaking of him as "the wise and learned Dr. Bryant," or, "the good and learned Dr. Bryant," whose "fellowship was always a great resource." Through their assistance, as well as on account of his own merits, he must have been introduced, when he went to Boston as a legislator, to many of the best men and women of the capital of the Commonwealth; but of this fact no record now remains. We only know, as the autobiography says, that he carried with him a metropolitan air, and that distinguished bearing which is derived from habitual intercourse with persons of culture and social eminence.

The isolation and retirement in which they lived defended the younger members of the family, no doubt, from vices and follies that are the result of contagious example, and preserved in them a simplicity of manner and taste which they never abandoned. But it left the impress also upon our poet of an austerity of deportment that he did not completely overcome

* "Private Memoirs of Mrs. Lyman." Cambridge, 1876.
† "Memoirs and Letters of Charles Sumner." Boston, 1877. Mrs. Lyman, I never knew personally, but Mrs. Howe, I have met at the house of her son-in-law, George S. Hillard, of Boston, and am able to confirm all that is said of her accomplishments and elevation of character.

in after life.   Up to the time of his going to college in his sixteenth year, it is doubtful whether he had seen anything at all
of the social world, outside of his immediate relatives and their
scattered neighbors.   It does not appear, by the diary, that he
was ever taken to Northampton by his father during the many
visits that were made to that place ; * and, if he had been, it is
not likely that the shy and modest boy, dressed in his mother's
homespun, would have been disposed to profit by the opportunities afforded him by its somewhat gay and polished society.
When he became a student of law at Bridgewater, he lamented
his want of those graceful and presentable qualities that are
acquired by commerce with men.   It must not be supposed,
however, that he was uncouth or awkward, as country yonkers
are apt to be ; for his native delicacy and refinement of fibre,
and the example of his father, saved him from every appearance
of rusticity.   He was merely sensitive and retiring, and often
fled from the encounter of strangers.   Once freed from the
constraints of their presence, he was instinctively courteous,
graceful, and easy.

---

* Mr. Congdon says (" Reminiscences of a Journalist," p. 33, Boston, Osgood &
Co., 1880) that Cullen was once brought to New Bedford by his father ; but that was
likely not until 1820.

CHAPTER FOURTH.

ALL the children of Dr. Bryant were practiced in reading verses, but Cullen took a livelier interest in them than the others, and at an earlier age. When he was but five years old, as the good mother delighted to inform her younger children, he used to clamber upon a high chair—formed of a one-leafed table, which, after having served for meals, was pushed back against the wall, as a seat—and preach. This preaching, as he called it, was the declamation of certain of Watts's Hymns, which he had learned at his mother's knee, or from hearing them repeated in the church and at prayer meetings. Those which he commonly selected are known by their first lines as, " Come, sound his praise abroad," " Now, in the heat of youthful blood," " Early, my God, without delay," " Life is the time to serve the Lord," and " Ere the blue heavens were spread abroad." The sentiment of these pieces is, for the most part, exceedingly sombre, and it is to be hoped that the child understood as little of them as the autobiography says he did of the darker parts of the Westminster Catechism. These displays were made freely enough before the family; but, if any strangers appeared, he was more bashful than a girl, and hid himself behind the first object he could find, even the rung of a chair.*

---

* I may here narrate an incident which shows the effect of what the scientists call Heredity. A few years ago, an old gentleman from New Orleans, whose name I have now forgotten, called at the house of his married daughter, where Mr. Bryant was then living, to see the poet, whom he had not seen since his childhood. As he entered the waiting-room, a grandson of Mr. Bryant—a little fellow of four or five

In his eighth year, as we learn from a letter,* he began to make verses of his own, and he continued to do so, according to the autobiography, in his ninth year. When he was ten years old, he was appointed to deliver an address at the school examination, which took place in the presence of the teacher, clergyman, deacons, selectmen, and visitors. This he wrote in heroic couplets, choosing for his theme the progress of knowledge in general, and of the school in particular, saluting, as he passed on, each class of his hearers with a graceful compliment. These verses were afterward printed in the newspaper of the county, the Hampshire "Gazette," of March 18, 1807, where they appear under the signature of C. B. They must have acquired more than a local repute, inasmuch as they became a stock piece for recitation in other schools. Only a few years since an elderly lady living in another part of the State enclosed them in a note to Mr. Bryant, saying that she had learned them as a little girl.† Other pieces of verse were sent anonymously to the paper about the same time, but they cannot now be identified.

His principal sources of inspiration were the political excitements of the times, so that he was a politician quite as soon as he was a poet; or, perhaps, it would be more correct to say that in childhood, as in later life, he was an active citizen. Never, perhaps, in our political history have the contentions of party been more violent and acrimonious than they were during the second administration of President Jefferson, and they were particularly violent and acrimonious in New England, where the free religious opinions of the President gave great offence to the Puritanic mind. It had become

years of age, who had been playing on the floor—instantly shot behind the leg of a table, where he tried to hide himself in perfect silence. "More than fifty years ago," said the visitor, "I entered Dr. Bryant's study, and a little chap with flaxen hair and flashing eyes did precisely the same thing, in the same manner in every respect. It was Cullen; and here he is again."

* Written in 1877 to Mr. George Stuart, Jr.

† On the back part of this note Mr. Bryant has written, "Some lines by a very little boy."

necessary for the United States, or it was thought to be necessary by the party in possession of the Federal government,
because of the English declaration of a continental blockade
in May of 1806, followed by the order in council of November, 1807, which had provoked the retaliatory decree of Napoleon at Berlin in November, 1806, and at Milan in December, 1807, to take action against these arbitrary and outrageous
violations of the rights of neutrality. The doctrine of non-
intercourse or of non-importation, which had been a favorite
one in the early stages of the Revolution, and which, during
the administration of Washington, had been applied for a
short time in the form of an embargo upon foreign trade, was
again put in practice; but the enforcement of it was so disastrous to our commerce that it raised immediately an outcry of alarm and rebuke. This outcry was loudest and most
vehement in New England, which already carried on an extensive commerce with foreign ports. The discussion of the
subject aroused, in addition to the usual passions of party, the
fiercest resentments of selfishness. Indeed, in a little while
the controversy was not so much the discussion of a question
of economic and political principle as an outbreak of private
and party animosities. The zealots on both sides looked upon
each other, not as men differing in opinion, and having a right
to differ, but as criminals and scamps. Family ties and ancient friendships were often broken by political dissensions.
In the eyes of a Federalist nearly every Democrat was a fellow of low habits and brutal manners, and in the eyes of a
Democrat nearly every Federalist was an upstart and the
sworn ally of monarchists and tyrants. Unhappily, this will-
ful misunderstanding was not confined to the ignorant classes
of society. "My father," writes Miss C. M. Sedgwick, in a
private diary, "one of the kindest of men, and most observant
of the rights of all beneath him, habitually spoke of the people
as Jacobins, sansculottes, and miscreants. I remember well,"
she adds, "looking upon a Democrat as the enemy of his
country, and at the party as sure, if it prevailed, to work our

destruction." These hostile convictions and prejudices were
fostered by the newspapers of the day, which put no qualification or stint upon their utterances. They were so furious in
their zeal, so unrelenting in their hatred, so coarse and brutal
in their modes of speech, that young Buckminster, writing to
his father from Paris in 1806, deprecates their excessive violence and bitterness as a serious damage to the reputation of
the Republic. "I only wish," he said, "I could let my friends
in political life in America know how painful, how mortifying,
how disgusting, how low, how infamous appear the animosities and calumnies with which our American papers are filled.
I am called every day to blush for the state of society among
us, and attempt but in vain to say something in our defence.
There is nothing I have more at heart than to impress upon
the minds of my countrymen the grievous injury which we
suffer in Europe from the complexion of our newspapers and
the brutality of our party spirit—the infamy of our political
disputes." *

Dr. Bryant was an earnest Federalist, and as a legislator,
who counseled with the leading men of his party at Boston,
more earnest than others less exposed to the heats of the con-
clave. He not only read the journals of his party, but he
allowed his family to read them, and his sons caught the prevailing rage. One day having accidentally discovered in the
handwriting of Cullen, the following apostrophe to Jefferson,
the leader of the Democrats, he was naturally very much delighted with it, and thought it an effective political weapon, if
not very fine poetry.

> " And thou, the scorn of every patriot name,
> Thy country's ruin and thy council's shame!
> Poor servile thing! derision of the brave!
> Who erst from Tarleton fled to Carter's cave;
> Thou, who, when menac'd by perfidious Gaul,
> Didst prostrate to her whisker'd minion fall;

* " Memoirs of Rev. J. S. Buckminster," by Eliza Buckminster Lee. Boston:
Ticknor, Reed & Fields, 1857.

And when our cash her empty bags supply'd,
Didst meanly strive the foul disgrace to hide;
Go, wretch, resign the presidential chair,
Disclose thy secret measures, foul or fair.
Go, search with curious eye for hornèd frogs,
Mid the wild wastes of Louisianian bogs;
Or, where Ohio rolls his turbid stream,
Dig for huge bones, thy glory and thy theme.
Go, scan, Philosophist, thy Sally's charms,
And sink supinely in her sable arms;
But quit to abler hands the helm of state."

The doctor encouraged the boy to prosecute his invective, which he did to the extent of five hundred lines and more, all pretty much in the same strain. These the father carried to Boston with him, where he had them printed in a pamphlet under the title of "The Embargo, or Sketches of the Times; a Satire, by a youth of thirteen; Boston; Printed for the Purchasers, 1808." Flattering the prejudices of the dominant faction, this philippic attracted a good deal of attention and was speedily sold. The "Monthly Anthology"—the great critical authority of the period—spoke in complimentary terms of the effort, saying:

"If this poem be really written by a youth of thirteen, it must be acknowledged an extraordinary performance. We have never met with a boy of that age who had attained to such a command of language and to so much poetic phraseology. Though the poem is unequal, and there are some flat and prosaic passages, yet there is no small portion of fire and some excellent lines."

It then quotes the following passage:

"Look where we will, and in whatever land,
Europe's rich soil, or Afric's barren sand,
Where the wild savage hunts his wilder prey,
Or art and science pour their brightest day.
The monster, *Vice*, appears before our eyes,
In naked impudence, or gay disguise.

" But quit the meaner game, indignant Muse,
  And to thy country turn thy nobler views;
  Ill-fated clime! condemned to feel th' extremes
  Of a weak ruler's philosophic dreams;
  Driven headlong on to ruin's fateful brink,
  When will thy country feel—when will she think!

" Satiric Muse, shall injured Commerce weep
  Her ravished rights, and will thy thunders sleep;
  Dart thy keen glances, knit thy threat'ning brows,
  Call fire from heaven to blast thy country's foes.
  Oh! let a youth thine inspiration learn—
  Oh! give him ' words that breathe and thoughts that burn! '

" Curse of our nation, source of countless woes,
  From whose dark womb unreckoned misery flows;
  Th' Embargo rages, like a sweeping wind,
  Fear lowers before, and famine stalks behind."

The Reviewer "regrets that the young poet has dared to aim the satiric shaft against our excellent President, but as the lines are a good specimen of the author's powers, we cannot resist the temptation of quoting them, conscious that the first magistrate of this country, secure in the impenetrable armor of moral rectitude, ' smiles at the drawn dagger and defies its point.'" Here follow the lines on Jefferson, already cited in a former page; but a more vigorous passage might perhaps have been found in this description of the factious demagogue:

" E'en while I sing, see Faction urge her claim,
  Mislead with falsehood, and with zeal inflame;
  Lift her black banner, spread her empire wide,
  And stalk triumphant with a Fury's stride.
  She blows her brazen trump, and at the sound
  A motley throng, obedient, flock around;
  A mist of changing hue o'er all she flings,
  And darkness perches on her dragon wings!

" As Johnson deep, as Addison refin'd,
And skill'd to pour conviction o'er the mind,
Oh might some patriot rise ! the gloom dispel,
Chase Error's mist, and break her magic spell !

" But vain the wish, for hark ! the murmuring meed
Of hoarse applause from yonder shed proceed ;
Enter and view the thronging concourse there,
Intent, with gaping mouth and stupid stare ;
While, in the midst, their supple leader stands,
Harangues aloud, and flourishes his hands ;
To adulation tunes his servile throat,
And sues, successful, for each blockhead's vote."

The prompt sale of the satire, coupled with the implied
challenge of the criticism, induced the father the next year to
bring out a second edition, in which the title ran thus : " The
Embargo, or Sketches of the Times ; a Satire ; Second Edition, corrected and enlarged ; together with the Spanish Revolution, and other Poems. By William Cullen Bryant. Boston. Printed for the author, by E. G. House, No. 35 Court
Street ; 1809." * Prefixed to the verses was this " advertise-
ment " :

" A doubt having been intimated in the " Monthly Anthology " of
June last whether a youth of thirteen years could have been the author
of this poem—in justice to his merits the friends of the writer feel
obliged to certify the fact from their personal knowledge of himself
and his family, as well as of his literary improvement and extraordinary talents. They would premise that they do not come uncalled
before the public to bear this testimony. They would prefer that
he should be judged by his works, without favor or affection. As the
doubt has been suggested, they deem it merely an act of justice to
remove it—after which they leave him a candidate for favor in common with other literary adventurers. They, therefore, assure the
public that Mr. Bryant, the author, is a native of Cummington, in

* A copy of this is to be seen in the New York Historical Library—the only one
I have been able to find.

the county of Hampshire, and in the month of November last arrived at the age of fourteen years. These facts can be authenticated by many of the inhabitants of that place, as well as by several of his friends who give this notice ; and, if it be deemed worthy of further inquiry, the printer is enabled to disclose their names and places of residence. February, 1809."

As the writer had now put his name in full to the title-page, he thought it advisable to prefix also a Preface, in the approved style of authorship. He said :

" PREFACE.

" The first sketch of the following poem appeared when the *terra-pin policy* of our administration, in imposing the embargo, exhibited undeniable evidence of its hostility to commerce, and proof positive that its political character was deeply tinctured with an unwarrantable partiality for France.

" Since that time our political prospects are daily growing more and more alarming—the thunders of approaching ruin sound louder and louder—and *faction* and *falsehood* exert themselves with increasing efforts to accelerate the downfall of our country.

" Should the candid reader find anything in the course of the work sufficiently interesting to arrest his attention, it is presumed he will not grudge the trouble of laboring through a few ' inequalities,' a few ' flat and prosaic passages.' *

" The poem is intended merely as a sketch of the times. The nice distinctions, the adequate proportions, the *light* and *shade* which give life and beauty to the picture, require some maturer and more skillful hand.

" The writer is far from thinking that all his errors are expunged, or all his faults corrected. Indeed, were that the case, he is suspicious that the ' composition ' would cease to be his own.

" *Fair* criticism he does not deprecate. He will consider the ingenuous and good-natured critic as a kind of schoolmaster, and will endeavor to profit by his lessons.

" CUMMINGTON, *October* 25, 1808. '

* A slight fling at his critic of the " Anthology."

Of the new poems in this second edition, the longest was called "The Spanish Revolution," a hundred and thirty-five lines, in the heroic measure also, celebrating the efforts of the Spanish patriots to resist the incursions of Napoleon. A few couplets describing a battle scene, which the boy, no doubt, thought extremely fine, must satisfy the reader's curiosity.

> "And now the peasantry, awaked to rage,
> With Gallic armies 'mid the streets engage;
> How dire the din! what horrible alarms,
> Of shrieks and shouts, and ever-clanging arms!
> Keen sabres glare, deep-throated cannons roar,
> And whizzing balls, in leaden volleys pour;
> Whilst clouds of dust amid the blue immense,
> Hang o'er the scene, in ominous suspense;
> Confusion o'er the deathful fray presides,
> Insatiate Death the storm of ruin guides;
> And wild-eyed Horror screaming o'er the fight,
> Invokes the curtains of chaotic night."

It is followed by an ode to the Connecticut River, in ten stanzas, dated May, 1808; by the "Reward of Literary Merit," dated 1807; eleven enigmas, of the same date; "The Contented Ploughman," a song, dated in June, 1808; "Drought," July, 1807; and a translation of Horace, 22d Carmen, Book I, rather gracefully and faithfully done. All these are in quatrains.

In his maturer years Mr. Bryant was naturally ashamed of his early political poems, both as poems and as expressions of opinion. I once asked him if he had a copy of the "Embargo." "No," he answered testily; "why should I keep such stuff as that?" More lately, when I told him that I had succeeded in borrowing a copy from a friend, his reply was: "Well, you have taken a great deal of trouble for a very foolish thing."

The pious grandfather, Deacon Snell, set the boy at much better work than writing satires on men and things that he knew nothing about, when he paid him for paraphrasing the Hebrew Scriptures. What he made of the first chapter of

the story of Job we have seen in the note on a previous page.*
A version of that noble ejaculation, the Hundred and Fourth
Psalm, is also spoken of there, but it has not been recovered.
In place of it, however, I find a version of David's lament over
Saul and Jonathan,† written about the same time, or shortly
afterward, which, as it is the first specimen of the poet's blank
verse—a measure that he subsequently carried to such per-
fection—I shall be pardoned, I hope, for reproducing it in a
note. ‡

---

* Page 22.

† II Samuel, i, 19.

‡ " The beautiful of Israel's land lie slain
On the high places.   How the mighty ones
Are fallen !   Tell it not in Gath, nor sound
The tidings in the streets of Ascalon,
Lest there the daughters of the Philistines
Rejoice, lest there the heathen maidens sing
The song of triumph.   Oh ye mountain slopes—
Ye Heights of Gilboa, let there be no rain
Nor dew upon you ; let no offerings smoke
Upon your fields, for there the strong man's shield,
The shield of Saul, was vilely cast away,
As though he ne'er had been anointed king.
From bloody fray, from conflict to the death,
With men of might the bow of Jonathan
Turned never back, nor did the sword of Saul
Return without the spoils of victory.
Joined in their loves and pleasant in their lives
Were Saul and Jonathan ; nor in their deaths
Divided ; swifter were they in pursuit
Than eagles, and of more than lion strength.
Weep, Israel's daughters ! over Saul, who robed
Your limbs in scarlet, adding ornaments
That ye delight in, ornaments of gold.
How are the mighty fallen in the heat
Of battle !   Oh, my brother Jonathan,
Slain on the heights !   My heart is wrung for thee ;
My brother, very pleasant hast thou been
To me ; thy love for me was wonderful,
Passing the love of women.   How are fallen
The mighty, and their weapons lie in dust !"

The poetry of the Old Testament is of such incomparable grandeur and beauty that the imagination of a child can not be more powerfully expanded than by rendering it into his own words. But the father, influenced by the literary spirit of his age, was more inclined to the classic models, and, when the boy, in November, 1808, went to Brookfield to begin his preparations for college, it was earnestly enjoined upon him to convert into English verse the passages of the Æneid and other books that he might take up. The father's letter to this effect we have not, but here is the boy's reply:

"BROOKFIELD, April 4, 1809.

"RESPECTED FATHER: You will doubtless find in the enclosed lines much that needs emendation and much that characterizes the crude efforts of puerility. They have received some correction from my hands, but you are sensible that the partiality of an author for his own compositions, and an immature judgment, may have prevented me from perceiving the most of its defects, however prominent. I will endeavor, to the utmost of my ability, to follow the excellent instructions which you gave me in your last. I have now proceeded in my studies as far as the Seventh Book of the Æneid.

"The Federal party here is now strengthened by the addition of a considerable number. The family are still favored with their usual degree of health. But I must conclude.

"Your dutiful son,

"W. C. B."

The poems enclosed were two (not one, as it is said in the Autobiography), and they hardly seem to deserve the severity of criticism applied to them by both father and son. They are too long for admission here, but an extract from one of them will not, perhaps, be out of place as a note.* It is the description of a storm, Book I, l. 19.

* " Eolus spake, and with a godlike might
Impelled his spear against the mountain's height.
Straight the freed winds forsake their rocky cell,
And o'er the earth in furious whirlwinds swell.

The second version, the account of Polyphemus, Æneid, Book III, line 618th, was more spirited, but is not of a nature to be quoted.

How thoroughly the lad entered into his classical studies appears from a poetical epistle addressed to his elder brother Austin, a little while after the foregoing letter was sent to his

---

The Southwest laden with its tempests dire.
Fierce Eurus and the raging South conspire ;
Disclose the ocean's depths with dreadful roar,
And roll vast surges thundering to the shore.
The cordage breaks, the seamen raise their cries,
Clouds veil the smiling day, and cheerful skies ;
Blue lightnings glare, redoubled thunder rolls,
And frowning darkness shrouds the dreary poles !
While instant ruin threatening every eye,
Hangs on the waves, or lowers from the sky !
Relaxed with shuddering fear, Æneas stands ;
And groaning, raises to the heavens his hands.
' Thrice happy ye who died in war,' he cries.
' In stately Troy, before your parents' eyes ;
Why fell I not, Tydides, by thine hand,
On Trojan plains, thou bravest of thy band ?
Then might I lie by mighty Hector's side,
Or where Sarpedon, great in battle, died ;
Where, with impetuous torrent, Simois rolls,
The arms and bodies of heroic souls.'

" A mighty wave descending from on high,
Death on its brow—before the hero's eye,
Fell on the ships which bore the Lycian crew,
And headlong from his seat the pilot threw.
Thrice the swift vortex whirled the vessel round,
And straight ingulphed it in the deep profound !
Then o'er the waves, in thick confusion spread,
Rose arms and planks and bodies of the dead.

" Now Ilioneus' sturdy barque gave way,
Achates' vessel owned the tempest's sway ;
Then round young Abas' ship its terrors roar,
And that whose bosom old Alethes bore.
Their joints were wrenched, and all, with gaping sides,
Receive, in drenching streams, the hostile tides."

father. The original contained some one hundred and eighty lines, but only a few of these are preserved :

> " Once more the Bard, with eager eye, reviews
> The flowery paths of fancy, and the Muse
> Once more essays to trill forgotten strains,
> The loved amusement of his native plains.
> Late you beheld me treading labor's round,
> To guide slow oxen o'er the furrowed ground ; *
> The sturdy hoe or slender rake to ply,
> 'Midst dust and sweat, beneath a summer sky.
> But now I pore o'er Virgil's glowing lines,
> Where, famed in war, the great Æneas shines;
> Where novel scenes around me seem to stand,
> Lo ! grim Alecto whirls the flaming brand.
> Dire jarring tumult, death and battle rage,
> Fierce armies close, and daring chiefs engage;
> Mars thunders furious from his flying car,
> And hoarse-toned clarions stir the raging war.
> Nor with less splendor does his master-hand
> Paint the blue skies, the ocean, and the land ;
> Majestic mountains rear their awful head,
> Fair plains extend, and bloomy vales are spread.
> The rugged cliff in threatening grandeur towers,
> And joy sports smiling in Arcadian bowers ;
> In silent calm the expanded ocean sleeps,
> Or boisterous whirlwinds toss the rising deeps;
> Triumphant vessels o'er his rolling tide,
> With painted prows and gaudy streamers, glide."

Meanwhile, the " Bard" was not so entirely absorbed in the fortunes of Æneas and his companions as to forget those of his own country. His indignant remonstrances had not succeeded in getting President Jefferson to resign his place and resume his scientific studies ; but the dire embargo was in

---

* This recalls the words of Burns's first dedication : " The poetic genius of my country found me—at the plough."

due course of time repealed.   Nevertheless, the clouds of danger that gathered about the nation were not thereby dissipated.   Napoleon Bonaparte had come to supply the place of Jefferson as the ogre of New England apprehensions.   All Europe, excepting England, now lay at the feet of that sanguinary and selfish despot; Italy was a dependency of France; Germany was overrun; and Spain and Portugal were possessed by his victorious troops.   In the despondency which these rapid successes impressed upon the general mind, it seemed as if the career of the conqueror would prove to be irresistible, and that, having subdued the Old World, his sombre helm might project its shadows over the New.   As we now see it, after the event, knowing how his difficulties multiplied with his triumphs, there was no real danger of such a catastrophe.   But the imaginations of his contemporaries were inflamed, and our youthful poet shared in the general fears.   He was not, however, mastered by them; and during a school vacation, in January, 1810, like David of old, he flung his stone of defiance at the Goliath.   Summoning to his assistance a mysterious and inexplicable personage, who had long haunted the American Parnassus, as "the Genius of Columbia," he dared "the son of glory" to an encounter with the "sons of freedom," and he put the despot to a speedy and ignominious flight before their invincible valor.*

I have cited these juvenile efforts purely as biographic material, and not as evidence of any peculiar poetic powers.

---

* This outbreak of patriotic valor may amuse the reader, and I append it:

THE GENIUS OF COLUMBIA.

Far in the regions of the west,
  On throne of adamant upraised,
Bright on whose polished sides impressed,
  The Sun's meridian splendors blazed,

Columbia's Genius sat and eyed
  The eastern despot's dire career;
And thus with independent pride,
  She spoke and bade the nations hear.

They show better than almost any other records the influences under which the lad was educated; but they do not as poetry bear witness to the real bent of his genius, or even foreshadow the characteristics of his later writings—that minute and loving observation of nature which became with him almost a religion—or that profound meditative interpretation of the great movements of the universe which amounted to a

> " Go, favored son of glory, go!
>   Thy dark aspiring aims pursue!
> The blast of domination blow,
>   Earth's wide extended regions through!
>
> " Though Austria, twice subjected, own
>   The thunders of thy conquering hand,
> And Tyranny erect his throne,
>   In hapless Sweden's fallen land!
>
> "Yet know, a nation lives, whose soul
>   Regards thee with disdainful eye;
> Undaunted scorns thy proud control,
>   And dares thy swarming hordes defy;
>
> " Unshaken as their native rocks,
>   Its hardy sons heroic rise;
> Prepared to meet thy fiercest shocks,
>   Protected by the favoring skies.
>
> " Their fertile plains and woody hills,
>   Are fanned by Freedom's purest gales!
> And her celestial presence fills
>   The deepening glens and spacious vales."
>
> She speaks; through all her listening bands
>   A loud applauding murmur flies;
> Fresh valor nerves their willing hands,
>   And lights with joy their glowing eyes!
>
> Then should Napoleon's haughty pride
>   Wake on our shores the fierce affray;
> Grim Terror lowering at his side,
>   Attendant on his furious way!
>
> With quick repulse, his baffled band
>   Would seek the friendly shore in vain,
> Bright Justice lift her red right hand,
>   And crush them on the fatal plain.
>
>   W. C. B.

CUMMINGTON, *January* 8, 1810.

kind of philosophy. There is nowhere in them any of the
inspiration or local coloring of the beautiful scenes in which
he lived. They do not breathe the odor of the soil, nor vi-
brate with the pulses of the mountain winds; even the day-
dreams and musings of childhood are not there; only factitious passions, excited by his political surroundings, and
wholly unsuited to his tender years. In manner, too, they
were imitative. "Such rhymes of boys," said Mr. G. W. Curtis
truly, "are but songs of the mocking-bird";* but it could not
easily have been otherwise. At the time the lad began to
write, the mode of versification, appropriated by Dryden and
Pope from Gallic originals, was universally and almost des-
potically in the ascendant. "The little Queen Anne's Man"
had not been, as Mr. Stoddard asserts, "long since dethroned
in England;"† he was still reigning in full power. The ten-
syllabled couplet, with its balanced antitheses and monotonous jingle, was the inevitable vehicle of all poetic expression; and the matter to be expressed was prescribed almost
as imperatively as the manner of the expression.‡ It is true
that Cowper, Thompson, Gray, Burns, and the Percy ballads, had introduced more simple and natural methods of
writing in metre; but these were not yet acknowledged by
the teachers or widely admired by the public.‖ As to our
American versifiers, they were the bond-slaves of the "system," as Mrs. Browning calls it, and rejoiced in their bondage, or rather were wholly unconscious of it. Every youth
who felt a desire to rhyme was condemned to follow strictly
in their footsteps. It would have been hardly less than a
miracle for a boy of the backwoods, whatever his native in-
stincts, to break away from the traditionary fetters and set
up a style of his own. In the experienced literary circles of

* "Commemorative Address," Dec. 30, 1878, p. 16. Scribner & Sons, New York.
† R. H. Stoddard. "Memorial Pamphlet," p. 38. New York, 1879.
‡ It is worthy of remark that, once emancipated from this measure, Mr. Bryant
never recurred to it for any purpose whatever.
‖ See Wordsworth's Prefaces—"Lyrical Ballads."

the mother country, where thought was certainly free to move in any direction, Wordsworth and his colleagues of the Lakes were nearly forty years in working out that return to the nobler old English models which is now deemed to have been a sort of regeneration of English verse.

It is, moreover, to be remembered that genuine original poetry is seldom, if ever, the product of immature intellect. As Davenant quaintly says, in his preface to Gondebart,* "these engenderings of unripe age become abortive or deformed." They are not the digestions of the author's own mind, but the suggestions of his books. Memory is, in truth, for such the mother of the Muses. When a youth of quick sensibilities reads a fine passage he admires it hugely, and because he admires it he fancies that he can do something like it; but what he does is a reproduction, and not a creation. For this reason it is that so few juvenile poems ever possess any enduring vitality. One looks in vain through the history of the world's literature for an exception. Even those dragnets, the Anthologies, which carry along a great deal of rubbish with a few pearls, cease very soon to contain them. If they survive at all, they survive, not on account of their intrinsic merit, but as exciting surprise that writers so young should, on the whole, have done so well, or because the authors of them have subsequently attained notoriety or fame. Certainly, Tasso's Lines to his Mother, written when he was nine years old, Cowley's Tale of Pyramus and Thisbe,† written when he was ten, and Pope's "Ode to Solitude," written in his twelfth year, are extremely interesting poems, but they are interesting because they were Tasso's, Cowley's, and Pope's. If these names had never been heard of again, the verses would have been forgotten. A certain lyrical faculty is possible to the very young—as we see in the case of the Davidson and Goodall children, not to mention others—but the true power

---

* Cited by Southey. "Poetical Works," vol. i. Preface to Minor Poems.

† Mr. Bryant himself thought Cowley's early pieces "the finest ever written at his age in the English language." "N. A. Review," No. 256, p. 369.

of poetry is, as Matthew Arnold somewhere says, the power to awaken in us a clear, full, fresh, intimate sense of the essential harmony of the objects about us, so bewildering and chaotic in their first impressions; and this power comes only out of the deeper experiences of life.

Nevertheless, these youthful verses possess, apart from the question of their poetic merit, a great deal of literary interest. Mr. Bryant is one of the few instances in which precocity was followed by a ripe maturity; and it is always pleasing to consider the first efforts of men of genius who have afterward made a name—to compare their rude, clumsy beginnings with the results of more cultured skill; and to remark the native as well as the traditional crudities and falsenesses out of which they have been compelled to work their way. From his tenth to his sixteenth year, this boy, shut up among the hills, away from the social influences that kindle ambition, had composed some thirty or forty different pieces of verse that are still extant, besides many others that are lost—making in all some thousands of lines—satires, elegies, odes, songs, and translations; work which certainly shows a decided literary faculty. All of it bears marks of negative good augury in the absence of all morbidness or affectation, proving it no mere febrile or hot-house growth, as all of it bears marks of positive good augury in a certain clearness, vigor, and dexterity of execution. He always seems to know what he would be at, and how to do it; and, though his matter and manner were both furnished him from without, it is easy to see, in his struggles to express himself in rhyme, the workings of that spirit which induced the little child to deviate in his prayers from those he heard around him, and to ask, on his own account, that he might "some time write verses that should endure." In considering the whole case, I do not recall from the history of literature any more remarkable example of early, continuous, and prolonged intellectual exertion than is to be found in the career of our poet.

CHAPTER FIFTH.

A. D. 1810, 1811.

IT was fortunate for the subject of this memoir that, when his father began to educate him, the love of the classics—an inheritance from England, widely cherished during our colonial period—was by no means extinct. Every person who expected to figure as a man of polite learning, or enter upon any of the liberal professions, knew that a knowledge of Greek and Latin literature was an indispensable preliminary. Every New England family, that could in any way compass the expense, was possessed of the ambition to send at least one of its members to college. In the Bryant family, the lot fell upon the second son—the eldest, Austin, having been provided for by his grandfather as a farmer, and the others being yet too young to be taken into account. Cullen, therefore, after having been instructed at home in the rudiments of Latin and French, was transferred, as the autobiography relates, to the care of his uncle at Brookfield, Parson Thomas Snell, who joined to his pastoral labors the preparation of a few lads for the higher seminaries. Cullen remained at Brookfield seven months, from November 8, 1808, to July 9, 1809, and was then removed (August 28th) to the house of the Rev. Moses Hallock, of Plainfield, who was somewhat noted, in his restricted sphere, as a successful teacher of youth. There he continued more than a year, when he was taken by his father to Williamstown to be examined for the Sophomore class, which he entered October 8, 1810.

Williamstown, though situated in one of the noblest mountain precincts of Massachusetts, was, at that time, a small straggling village of a few houses, with muddy and undrained streets, and without trees, presenting little of that loveliness of aspect which now renders it one of the most charming and picturesque of summer retreats. The college, scarcely older than Mr. Bryant himself, was no more than a grammar school, considering the range of its studies and the small number of its teachers. Dr. Bryant chose it for his son, partly because of its proximity to his place of residence, and partly because of the narrowness of his means. His tastes and associations would have inclined him to Cambridge, which enjoyed a wider repute, and was now under religious influences with which he sympathized, if he could have afforded to incur the additional expenses.

The brief references to his college career contained in Mr. Bryant's autobiography are supplemented by a few particulars in a letter to the Rev. Calvin Durfee, the historian of the college, written at Roslyn, Long Island, July 19, 1859.

"I entered Williams College," he says, "in the autumn of the year 1810, almost half a century since—having prepared myself in such a manner that I was admitted into the Sophomore class. At that time Dr. Fitch was president of the college, and instructor of the Senior class. I have a vivid recollection of his personal appearance—a square-built man, of a dark complexion, and black, arched eyebrows. To me his manner was kind and courteous, and I remember it with pleasure. He often preached to us on Sundays, but his style of sermonizing was not such as to compel the attention. We listened with more interest to Professor Chester Dewey, then in his early manhood, the teacher of the Junior class, who was the most popular of those who were called the Faculty of the college. Two young men, recent graduates of the college, acted as tutors, superintended the recitations of the two lower classes, and made their periodical visits to the college rooms, to see that everything was in order. These four were at that time the only instructors in Williams College.

"Before my admission, it had been the practice for the members of the Sophomore class, in the first term of their year, to seize upon the persons of some of the Freshmen, bring them before an assembly of the Sophomores, and compel them to go through a series of burlesque ceremonies, and receive certain mock injunctions with regard to their future behavior. This was called gamutizing the Freshmen. It was a brutal and rather riotous proceeding, which I can, at this time, hardly suppose that those who had the government of the college could have tolerated; yet the tradition ran that, if it was not connived at, no pains were taken to suppress it. There were strong manifestations of a disposition to enforce the custom after I became a member of the Sophomore class, but the Freshmen showed so resolute a determination to resist it that the design was dropped; and this, if I am rightly informed, was the last of the practice.

"The college buildings consisted of two large plain brick structures, called the East and the West College, and the college grounds, an open green, were between the two and surrounding them both. From one college to the other you passed by a straight avenue of Lombardy poplars, which formed the sole embellishment of the grounds. There was a smaller building or two of wood, forming the only dependencies of the main edifices, and every two or three years the students made a bonfire of one of these. I remember being startled one night by the alarm of fire, and, going out, found one of these buildings in a blaze and the students dancing and shouting round it.

"Concerning my fellow-students, I have little of importance to communicate. My stay in college was hardly long enough to form those close and life-long intimacies of which college life is generally the parent. Orton and Jenkins—I am not sure of their Christian names, and have not the catalogue of graduates at hand—were among our best scholars, and Northrop and C. F. Sedgwick among our best elocutionists. When either of these two spoke, every ear was open. I recollect, too, the eloquent Larned and the amiable Morris.

"The library of the college was then small, but was pretty well supplied with the classics. The library of the two literary societies into which the students were divided was a little collection, scarcely, I think, exceeding a thousand in number. I availed myself of it to read several books which I had not seen elsewhere.

"Where the number of teachers was so small, it could hardly be expected that the course of studies should be very extensive or complete. The standard of scholarship in Williams College at that time was so far below what it now is, that I think many graduates of those days would be no more than prepared for admission as Freshmen now. There were some, however, who found too much exacted from their diligence, and left my class on that account. I heard that one or two of them had been afterward admitted to Union College. There were others who were not satisfied with the degree of scholarship attained at Williams College, and desired to belong to some institution where the sphere of instruction was more extended. One of these was my room-mate, John Avery, of Conway, in Massachusetts, a most worthy man, and a good scholar, who afterward became a minister of the Episcopal Church, and settled in Maryland. At the end of his Sophomore year he obtained a dismission, and was matriculated at Yale College, New Haven. I also, perhaps influenced somewhat by his example, sought and obtained, near the end of my Sophomore year, an honorable dismission from Williams' College. With the same intention, I passed some time afterward in preparing myself for admission at Yale, but the pecuniary circumstances of my father prevented me from carrying my design into effect."

Mr. Charles F. Sedgwick, one of the class-mates mentioned, still survives, in the eighty-fourth year of his age, an honored citizen of Sharon, Connecticut; and in reply to a letter addressed to him by the biographer, asking his reminiscences of the youthful poet, was kind enough to return the following answer:

"SHARON, Conn., Sept. 22, 1879.

"DEAR SIR: I have your favor of the 8th inst., and will give such a reply as I am able to your inquiries regarding the college life of your honored father-in-law. His stay in college was so short that he had no time to develop those minute characteristics about which you inquire, and which a more extended term would have exhibited, but the general tenor of his college life is well preserved in my memory.

"He came with the reputation of having written some two or three minor poems, bearing upon the political questions then agitating the public mind, and which dealt out very pungent ridicule upon the Democratic policy of those days. I do not remember that I heard those poems alluded to by him, or in his presence, during his stay in college.

" He was well advanced in his sixteenth year, tall and slender in his physical structure, and having a prolific growth of dark-brown hair. I do not remember that I ever knew of any person in whom the progress of years made so great a change in personal appearance as in him.

" During his stay in college he associated with the more orderly and studious scholars, and was very modest and unobtrusive, though pleasantly familiar with his personal friends. His scholarship was respectable, and his lessons were well mastered. In the performance of the task, imposed upon each student, of reading a composition before the class in the presence of the tutor, he prepared a short poem, which received the commendation of the tutor, the Rev. Orange Lyman, afterward Presbyterian pastor at Vernon, Oneida County, N. Y. He also translated one of the odes of Anacreon, which he showed to a few friends. He gave me the perusal of it, but, as I have not the book, I cannot point out which ode it was. Except these two specimens, I remember nothing in his show of scholarship or in the incidents of his college life which foretold the brilliancy of his subsequent career. After Thanatopsis had made him famous, a tradition obtained some credit that it was conceived and written in some obscure locality among the mountains of Williamstown. I never gave the story credit, and at my last meeting with him in 1876, he stated that it was written at his home in Cummington.*

" I have only to add that Mr. Bryant was much respected by all his acquaintances in college, mild and gentlemanly in his intercourse with his fellow-students, and that his class-mates regretted his leaving them after so short a connection with the college. The corporation of Williams afterward restored his name to the college catalogue by conferring upon him the usual college degrees, and the college is proud to number him among its alumni.

" Very respectfully yours,
"CHARLES F. SEDGWICK."

The poem recited before the class was probably the " Version of a Fragment of Simonides," which has since been

---

* The tradition was nevertheless a natural one, as it was written about a month after his last visit to the college to attend the Commencement of his class, from which he had previously taken a dismission.

included in the collected works of Mr. Bryant.   There is an
"Indian War Song" of the same year, in which he pours
forth the sanguinary and vengeful feelings of a supposed Indian chief, with all the energy of a Greek chorus, and which,
though not distinguished by any unusual poetic excellence,
has yet a certain historical interest as the precursor of his
several poems relating to the aboriginal element of our poetic
traditions.   In this line of thought Freneau had preceded
him, but Freneau had never been able to manage the materials
with the same mastery of their more noble and pathetic associations.*

He was less successful in another attempt to declaim before
the class, in which he had selected a passage from "Knickerbocker's History of New York"—a work then recently published, and which he had been reading with great admiration
in his leisure hours—but the humor of which so convulsed him
with laughter when he attempted to recite it, that he was compelled to resume his seat, under the frowns of the tutor, but
amid an outburst of merriment from his companions.

The John Avery spoken of in the autobiography died at
an early age; but a letter which he wrote, while he was the
room-mate of Bryant, to Mr. Solomon Metcalf Allen, a son of
Dr. Thomas Allen, the first minister at Pittsfield, gives us another glimpse of the poet in those early days.†

---

* The reader will derive from this, the first of the eight stanzas of which the
" War Song " is composed, a pretty good conception of its tone and manner :

> " Ghosts of my wounded brethren rest,
>   Shades of the warrior-dead !
> Nor weave, in shadowy garment drest,
>   The death-dance round my bed ;
> For, by the homes in which we dwelt,
> And by the altar where we knelt,
>   And by our dying battle-songs,
> And by the trophies of your pride,
> And by the wounds of which ye died,
>   I swear to avenge your wrongs."

† I am indebted for this letter to Mrs. Erastus Hopkins, of Northampton, Mass.

"Bryant, I think I told you, means to leave Williams College. He will be no small loss to the class and to college.

"Many, especially in the Senior classes, have been unwilling to allow him the credit of writing the 'Embargo,' &c., but I am confident, if he lives and has the smiles of Providence, his writings will give sufficient evidence of his capability of writing them.

"The following is a specimen of his college poetry, which has not had the advantage of his father's criticism.

"It is a translation of Anacreon's ode to the 'Spring' contained in Græca Minora:

> "Lo! fragrant Spring returns again
> With all the Graces in her train!
> See, charmed to life the budding rose,
> Its meek and purple eyes unclose;
> Mark how the ocean's dimpling breast,
> Slow swelling sinks in tranquil rest!
> O'er the green billow heaving wide,
> The sportive sea-fowls gently glide;
> The crane returned from tropic shores
> Bends his long neck and proudly soars.
> Clear smiles the sun with constant ray
> And melts the shadowy mists away.
> The works of busy man appear
> Fair smiling with the smiling year;
> With future plenty teems the earth
> And gives the swelling olive birth.
> Haste, quick the genial goblet bring
> Crowned with the earliest flowers of Spring,
> While ruddy fruits depending bloom,
> Where late the blossom breathed perfume,
> Along the bending bough are seen
> Or peep beneath the foliage green.*

---

* In a private paper of Mr. Bryant, dated May, 1862, is another version of the "Spring," which must have been, I think, an attempt to recall that of his college days, which Avery preserved.

> "See what a shower the Graces fling,
> Of roses round the path of Spring.

"This will not suffer by comparison with Moore's translation of the same.

"JOHN AVERY, JR."

Mr. Bryant speaks of his residence at Williamstown as having been on the whole agreeable to him, but a poem which he delivered before one of the literary societies of the college conveys a somewhat different impression. It is a pretty severe satire upon the town, the college, and its authorities. He does not forget to celebrate the natural beauty of the place:

> "Hemmed in with hills, whose heads aspire
> Abrupt and rude, and hung with woods,"

but he deprecates the climate, which infects it at one season with "a lengthened blaze of drought," and, at another, drenches it with "the tempest's copious floods":

> "A frozen desert now it lies,
> And now a sea of mud,"

from which mud, he continues, the most deleterious exhalations arise:

> "And hover o'er the unconscious vale,
> And sleep upon the mountain side."

And then he asks:

> "Why should I sing those reverend domes,
>   Where Science rests in grave repose?
> Ah me! their terrors and their glooms
>   Only the wretched inmate knows.

> See how the billow on the breast
> Of ocean sinks to glassy rest.
> And here the wild duck swims, and there
> The crane goes journeying through the air.
> The great sun pours a constant ray,
> The shadowy clouds are chased away,
> And all that toiling man has done
> Looks bright beneath the glorious sun,
> Young berries stud the olive bough,
> The wine-cup wears a garland now,
> The fruit-buds into blossoms start
> And push the leafy shoots apart."

Where through the horror-breathing hall
The pale-faced, moping students crawl
   Like spectral monuments of woe ;
Or, drooping, seek the unwholesome cell,
Where shade and dust and cobwebs dwell,
   Dark, dirty, dank, and low."*

The spirit of invective, which dictated the " Embargo," was not entirely dead within the young man ; but in this case, I am inclined to believe, his objurgations were more playful than serious. · Mr. Bryant, in after life, always regretted, as he says in the autobiography, that he was not allowed to pursue his studies at Williamstown to the end of the course. He remained there only seven months, leaving in May, 1811, and, although he attended the Commencement exercises, September 3d of ·the same year, it was simply as a spectator. His scholastic life closed with this brief term, and was never resumed.

His return home, though a source of disappointment to himself, was an occasion of joy to the family. On the verge of manhood—handsome, exuberant in spirits, having new experiences to relate, and new compositions of his own to repeat, the younger brothers and sisters hailed his reappearance among them with delight. It was the signal for a renewal of their obstreperous games and their joyful wanderings in the woods. Older than most of the others, Cullen was regarded as a leader, both of their sports and their studies ; and his geniality and sweetness of disposition made him a most acceptable leader. He was at times quick-tempered, as it is called, but his little outbreaks of passion soon passed away, and were succeeded by the most affectionate demonstrations of kindliness and sympathy. His sisters, toward whom he was always extremely gentle and courteous, returned his love with more than sisterly devotion, while his brothers evidently regarded him as in some sort a superior being. " My earliest

---

* This poem, which has several stanzas, Mr. Arthur Bryant retained in his memory, from having heard his brother repeat it after returning home.

recollections of my brother," said Mr. Arthur Bryant, at a literary celebration in Chicago, in 1864, "are connected with his vacations, when I used to stare at him with astonishment and admiration, while he declaimed, with loud voice and extravagant gesticulation, sometimes his own verses, such as the "Indian War Song," and the translation of a chorus in "Œdipus Tyrannus," and sometimes those of other poets.

The boys, in fact, as they roamed about the hills, recited to one another. First, you might hear Cullen shouting out Strophe I of the Œdipus, as he had rendered it in English:

> "Where is the wretch condemned to death
>   From Delphi's rock sublime?
> Who bears upon his hands of blood
>   The inexplicable crime?
> Oh! swifter than the wingèd pace
>   Of stormy-footed steed,
> Fly, murderer! fly the wrath that waits
>   The unutterable deed!
> For lo! he follows on thy path
>   Who fell before thee late,
> With gleaming arms and glowing flame,
>   And fierce, avenging hate."

Then Arthur, or another, would take up Antistrophe I:

> "I heard the God of prophecies
>   From high Parnassus speak,
> Where lurks the guilty fugitive
>   Apollo bids us seek?
> 'Mong rocks and caves and shadowy woods,
>   And wild, untrodden ways,
> As some lone ox that leaves the herd,
>   The trembling outlaw strays;
> Yet vainly from impending doom
>   The assassin strives to haste,
> It lives and keeps eternal watch
>   Amid the pathless waste."

And so on through the whole chorus.

"I used," Mr. Arthur Bryant continues, "to commit his verses to memory, and attempt to imitate his elocution. I remember, too, that our grandfather, when his friends came to visit him, was wont to summon my brother to read the manuscript of his poems, and of once hiring him to write an elegy on the death of the Gerrymander.* I still retain in memory fragments and entire poems written about this period, many of which were never printed."

At the same celebration at Chicago, a brother still younger, Mr. John H. Bryant, said: "In my early childhood I looked up to him with a feeling of wonder and awe; and from that day my love and veneration for him have never faltered, but have grown deeper and stronger to this very hour. When I was yet a child, I well remember that his return home was always an occasion of joy to the whole family, in which I warmly participated, although not old enough to fully appreciate the cause of the delight. He was lively and playful, tossed me about, and frolicked with me in a way that made me look upon him as my best friend. He seemed to handle me so easily that I came to have great respect for his prowess and strength, and I used to brag to other boys about my stout brother; but I afterward learned that his strength was not remarkable, but that he had great skill and celerity in the use of it."

The autobiography says that our student, while at college, paid some attention to Latin prosody, besides engaging in a

---

* The Gerrymander was a monstrous figure which the Federal newspapers constructed out of the outlines made on the map of Massachusetts, by a peculiar arrangement of electoral districts, which Mr. Elbridge Gerry was said to have contrived in order to secure a legislature which would elect him to the United States Senate. Mr. Gerry was a man of great ability and distinction—member of the Provincial Congress, one of the Continental Congress in which Hancock and Adams served, a signer of the Declaration of Independence, a Judge of the Court of Admiralty, a Governor of Massachusetts in 1810, and Envoy to France, and Vice-President in Madison's time; but the effect of this caricature was to destroy him politically for the nonce; and up to the present time the word Gerrymander is used as a slang phrase descriptive of the fraudulent manipulation of electoral districts.

good deal of miscellaneous reading, but it does not refer to what cannot but be regarded as the greatest benefit he derived from his studies there—his introduction to the Greek poets. It was more than an introduction in his case; it was the awakening of his mind to the peculiar spirit and art of those writers. At least, one is compelled to infer as much from the fact that, from this time, for two or three years onward, his only translations, excepting a few from Horace—whose education at Athens had made him more or less Grecian—were confined to the Greeks. Among these translations, in addition to four of Lucian's "Dialogues of the Dead," rendered in prose, were several odes of Anacreon, the lines of Mimnermus of Colophon on the "Beauty and Joy of Youth," one of Bion's idyls, and choruses from Sophocles. It is true that seven months are but a short period wherein to acquire a knowledge of the rich world haunted by the Grecian muses (or of any other knowledge, in fact), but it is long enough to awaken the curiosity of a fresh and sympathetic young mind, endowed with poetic sensibilities, and yearning with poetic ambitions. He could hardly have acquired that familiarity with them, which faithful translation implies, without acquiring also some perception of their spirit and tone. The peculiarities of Greek literature lie deep, no doubt, and yet they are so pervasive that they lie on the surface no less; and any quick and thoughtful student, intent upon the object, may get at them in a little while. The simplicity of diction, as we call that exquisite choice of words which has no word too much nor any word out of place; the harmonious rhythms, beating like the pulses of a healthful body, and uniting the tenderest grace with robust and masculine strength; the vivid imaginativeness, that finds for the most subtle and visionary gleams of thought a perfect concrete form; and the austerity of judgment, that binds the most impetuous flights of imagination with chains of beauty, and subdues the ecstasies of passion to a god-like repose—these are qualities that may be seen at a glance, although they furnish food for the studies of a lifetime.

Mr. Bryant was at that period of life when the intellect is most restless, inquisitive, and daring, and it was quite impossible for him to have studied such models as he did and remain contented with the poetic judgments that he had been taught to form. At any rate, he was full of these new acquisitions when he returned home, and, although he gave some little time to the study of the natural sciences, particularly of chemistry and botany, his real interest lay with the poets. His old idols, the wits that shone and sparkled in the age of Anne, lost their lustre amid the splendors cast by the Grecian luminaries. He had loved them as a child for their pictures, their sentiment, and their wit, to say nothing of their musical jingle, but he was now, as a youth, beginning to study them in the light of a higher art. He soon saw that they were only men of the town, of the coffee-house and the drawing-room, who walked in slippers, and loved to dress in silk attire, and not men of the woods and fields, who walked upon the ground and saw nature with their own eyes. Cowper, Thompson, Burns, and Southey were discovered to be much better guides than his former models, and to them henceforth he devoted his attention.

These studies, however, did not seduce him from his rambles, during one of which his thoughts took a shape that proved to be of the greatest consequence to his poetic growth. He had been engaged, as he says,* in comparing Blair's poem of "The Grave" with another of the same cast by Bishop Porteus; and his mind was also considerably occupied with a recent volume of Kirke White's verses—those "Melodies of Death," to use a phrase from the ode to the Rosemary. It was in the autumn; the blue of the summer sky had faded into gray, and the brown earth was heaped with sere and withered emblems of the departed glory of the year. As he trod upon the hollow-sounding ground, in the loneliness of the woods, and among the prostrate trunks of trees, that

* "Autobiography," p. 37.

for generations had been mouldering into dust, he thought
how the vast solitudes about him were filled with the same
sad tokens of decay.   He asked himself, as the thought expanded in his mind, What, indeed, is the whole earth but a
great sepulchre of once living things; and its skies and stars,
but the witnesses and decorations of a tomb?   All that ever
trod its surface, even they who preceded the kings and patri-
archs of the ancient world, the teeming populations of buried
cities that tradition itself has forgotten, are mingled with its
soil; all who tread it now in the flush of beauty, hope, and joy,
will soon lie down with them, and all who are yet to tread it
in ages still unknown, "matron and maid, and the sweet babe
and the gray-headed man," will join the innumerable hosts that
have gone the dusky way.

While his mind was yet tossing with the thought, he hurried home, and endeavored to paint it to the eye, and render
it in music to the ear.   He began abruptly, in the middle of a
line:

> "Yet a few days, and thee
> The all-beholding sun shall see no more
> In all his course;"

and, working through the various suggestions of his theme, he
ended no less abruptly:

> "Thousands more
> Will share thy destiny; the tittering world
> Dance to the grave.   The busy brood of care
> Plods on, and each one chooses as before
> His favorite phantom; yet all these shall leave
> Their mirth and their employments, and shall come
> And make their bed with thee."*

This poem, for which he coined a name from the Greek,
"Thanatopsis," was, says the poet Stoddard, "the greatest

* This is the form of the poem as it was first published. See "Poetical Works,"
vol. i, notes.

poem ever written by so young a man." Certainly, it is
marked by a grandeur and profundity of thought, a breadth
of treatment, and an imaginative reach that surprises us in
one of his age—only seventeen; but what renders it more remarkable is the suddenness with which it breaks away from
everything he had hitherto attempted. There is nothing at
all in his antecedent efforts or aspirations to account for it
fully; nor in the models he studied. A germ of the leading
thought—a rude, uncouth germ—is to be found in Blair, who
asks:

> "What is this world?
> What but a spacious burial-field unwalled,
> Strewed with death's spoils, the spoils of animals
> Savage and tame, and full of dead men's bones.
> The very turf on which we tread once lived,
> And we that live must lend our carcasses
> To cover our own offspring; in their turns
> They too must cover theirs."

The versification may, perhaps, bear traces of Cowper and
Southey, although it is more terse, compact, energetic, and
harmonious than that of either of them; its pauses, cadences,
rhythms are different, and it has a movement of its own, a
deep organ-like roll, which corresponds to the sombre nature
of the theme. A lingering memory of the sublime lamenta-
tions of Job, an impression from the Greeks of that ineffable
sadness which moans through even their lightest music, and
his recent readings, may all have conspired to influence its
tone; but the real inspiration of it came from the infinite solitudes of our forests, stretching interminably inland over the
silent work of death ever going on within their depths, which
has been going on since the far beginning of time, and will be
going on till time shall be no more.

And as it came out of the heart of our primeval woods,
so it first gave articulate voice to the genius of the New
World, which is yet, as the geologists tell us, older than

the Old.   For the first time on this continent a poem was written destined to general admiration and enduring fame. It in fact began our poetic history, and, whatever great things have since been done or will yet be done, to "Thanatopsis" belongs the glory of the morning star, which glitters on the front of day, and only fades in the superior light it has itself announced.

Contrary to his custom, the youthful poet did not take this poem to his father for criticism, nor even read it to his brothers for their approval, but he carefully hid it away in a pigeon-hole of his father's desk, on which it had been written. Whether he considered it too incomplete to be shown, or was doubtful of the reception that might be vouchsafed the sentiment of it, which contemplated death, not as the penalty of one man's disobedience, but as a universal and even gracious fact in the economy of nature,* is not known. The probability is that it was merely allowed to slumber until it could be amended. The theme had so filled his imagination by its magnitude and suggestiveness, that any attempt to give it form, and particu- larly the attempt of a tyro, must have seemed to him pre-

---

* Two critics have said that "Thanatopsis" is a pagan poem, because there is no mention of the Deity in it, nor recognition of the Christian doctrine of resur- rection and immortality.   Certainly, in its original form there is no intimation of a belief in the continuous consciousness of the individual, showing the young poet's sympathy with the doubts and perplexities of the early part of the present century. But was such an intimation required by his theme?   Is the artist, who describes a great natural fact, obliged to include the supernatural?   Nature knows absolutely nothing of a hereafter ; and, if the poet had introduced the topic more positively, he would have departed from his main purpose.   His mind was directed to a single ob- ject—the universality of Death in the natural order, and the sentiments inspired by that fact; he therefore named his poem "Thanatopsis, or a View of Death"; and to invoke another order of thought would have been to break the unity of his contem- plations.   Apart, however, from the merely æsthetic question—what the critics allege as a defect of the poem is really one of its great claims to originality.   It takes the idea of Death out of its theological aspects and sophistications, and the perversions of conscience with which they are connected, and restores it to its proper place in the vast scheme of things.   This, in itself, was a mark of genius in a youth of his time and education.

sumptuous and inadequate to the last degree, and he reserved it for a time when maturer skill should qualify him to render his work a worthier expression of his thought. Imperfect as it was, however, the effort served to awaken him to a clearer consciousness of his powers, and of the direction in which they might be best applied.

CHAPTER SIXTH.

POEMS ON LOVE AND DEATH.

A. D. 1811–1814.

THE profession for which Cullen was originally intended was that of medicine, in accordance with an almost immemorial custom of his family. The father, grandfather, and great-grandfather had practised the gentle art of healing, and the father, in naming him after one of the most illustrious physicians of Scotland—William Cullen—wished to indicate his preferences as to the destination of his son. But the hardships encountered in his own course and the smallness of his material gains had somewhat modified his desires. Perhaps the boy's promise of intellectual powers turned his attention to other fields, in which he supposed they might be more brilliantly displayed. A merely literary career was, of course, not to be thought of, in the condition of our literature at that day. A few men, in past times, had endeavored to live by their wits, like Robert Treat Paine and Philip Freneau, but their examples were not encouraging, for Paine died a sot, and Freneau became a mere dependent upon official patronage.

The law, with its prospects of political preferment, presented greater attractions to youthful ability than any other walk, and, as Cullen had already shown in his satires some aptness for public discussions, it was decided that he should become a lawyer. His shy and delicate nature was not precisely fitted to the turmoils of politics or the rude conflicts of the bar; but the pursuit was an intellectual one, not wholly inconsistent with the indulgence of his poetic bents, and so he submitted

willingly to the choice of his parents. In December, 1811, he was put in charge of Mr. Howe, of Worthington, to be initiated into the mysteries of Blackstone, Stephens, and Coke. Mr. Howe was at this time a widower, but in the course of the next year was married again, to a Miss Robbins, of Boston, who, in some reminiscences written for the late William S. Thayer, Consul-General of the United States for Egypt, recalls the youthful poet.* "The first time I saw Mr. Bryant," she says, "was in the autumn of 1813; he was then a student in my husband's office, and about nineteen years of age. He was quiet, reserved, and diffident, so that I formed but little acquaintance with him; but I learned from my husband that he was a diligent student, not only of his profession, but of all the good books he had time for, including the classics and botany. He was a practical botanist, going to the woods and fields for his specimens. My husband feared that Bryant would be backward about speaking, and, I think, wrote to him afterward to accustom himself to the practice. I doubt if he ever satisfied himself in that branch of his profession." One reason why Mrs. Howe formed but little acquaintance with her husband's pupil was, that he was afraid of her, as it appears by a letter he wrote to one of his sisters. He had never seen a grand lady in his life, and he shrank from the encounter of one reputed to be so cultivated and so eloquent in conversation. He was not, however, as diligent a student as she represents. Too conscientious to neglect his studies altogether, he yet allowed himself to be drawn in other directions. A month after reaching Worthington he congratulated himself in a little poem † on his escape from the farm, because

---

* Communicated by Miss Sarah Thayer, of Northampton, a sister of Mr. W. S. Thayer.

† "AD MUSAM.

"So long neglectful of thy dues,
    And absent from thy shrine so long,
Say, wilt thou deign, Immortal Muse,
    Again to inspire thy votary's song?

now he might devote himself to the Muse without stint.   Accordingly, he turned his attention to spondees and dactyls quite
as much as to feoffments and fees-tail.   Mr. Howe was a skilful teacher, and lent him what assistance he could, carrying his
professional zeal so far, indeed, that one day, when he found
his pupil reading a book of verses, he seriously warned him
against such a sad waste of his time.   The book happened to
be Wordsworth's "Lyrical Ballads," which the young man
had picked up at home and taken with him; and the warning
was doubtless well deserved.   Mr. Richard H. Dana, writing
afterward, says, "I never shall forget with what feeling my
friend Bryant, some years ago, described to me the effect produced upon him by his meeting for the first time with Wordsworth's ballads.   He said that, upon opening the book, a
thousand springs seemed to gush up at once in his heart,
and the face of Nature, of a sudden, to change into a strange
freshness and life.   He had felt the sympathetic touch from
an according mind, and you see how instantly his powers
and affections shot over the earth and through his kind."
Mr. Dana's own partiality for Wordsworth may have colored his language a little; but there is no doubt that Mr.
Bryant regarded the volume as a precious discovery.   It
introduced him, as Mr. Dana says, to a kindred mind—to one
endowed, like himself, with pure and simple tastes, and exquisitely alive to all the sweet and gentle influences of external nature.   How hard it must have been to be debarred the
study of a work which disclosed to him such sources of new
delight!

> The time has been when fresh as air
>   I loved at morn the hills to climb,
> With dew-drenched feet and bosom bare,
>   And ponder on the artless rhyme;
> And through the long laborious day
>   (For mine has been the peasant's toil),
> I hummed the meditated lay,
>   While the slow oxen turned the soil."

WORTHINGTON, *January*, 1812.

But there were other reasons why he was not entirely satisfied with his studies of law. He wanted to get to college
again. His friend, John Avery, was at Yale, luxuriating among
its literary and scientific treasures, while he was confined to
the little village of Worthington, which he described in a letter to Avery as " consisting of a blacksmith-shop and a cow-
stable, at either of which places he might be found, while the
only entertainment it afforded was bound up in the pages of
'Knickerbocker.'" Avery's replies must have fostered his discontent, for he tells the "dear old chum" that, "with his acquisitions, he would be readily admitted to the Junior class."
Then he expatiated on the pleasures of reading Xenophon,
Thucydides, and Herodotus, with the hope of getting into
Longinus and Plato soon; what an unsurpassed cabinet of
minerals there was! how brilliant the lectures of Silliman on
chemistry and natural philosophy! how, at the debates, Dr.
Dwight himself presided, whose "decisions were most eloquent and instructive," he not being "afraid to give his opinions on the great principles of government!" But, concludes
Avery, after he had cast those tempting baits before the lone
student of the hills: "I approve of your philosophy, in general, that it is more noble to rule the passions than to penetrate the depths of mathematical science, or shine in the departments of literature." It was a good philosophy, indeed,
for one pining after opportunities of study that he knew
would never come.

Nor was the condition of public affairs, in which, like
.a good citizen, he always took some interest, such as to
give him much satisfaction. The federal party had lost
ground throughout the Union. Madison, the friend and
disciple of the hated Jefferson, was about to be chosen his
successor in the Presidency. A large majority of Republicans ruled in both houses of Congress; but, no longer restrained by the prudent counsels of Jefferson, they had become, under the fiery impulses of young Clay and young
Calhoun, a war party, bent upon embroiling the country in

hostilities with England. War was in fact declared a few months after the removal to Worthington (June, 1812), when the hot political contests that grew out of it, the threats of invasion from Canada, the raisings of troops, the varying reports of successes and defeats, the brilliant exploits of our navy on the lakes and on the ocean, and the disgraceful burning of Washington by the British—kept the public mind in such a ferment that, if Mr. Bryant shared in it, very little real hard study was to be done even in the backwoods.

There is, however, no evidence in any of his papers that he was unusually affected by the general agitation; on the contrary, it is remarkable that during these years, from the spring of 1812 to the autumn of 1814, when the domestic news, like that from abroad of Napoleon's gigantic expedition to Russia, with its terrible reverses, was so stirring, his Muse, though newly awakened by Wordsworth, was almost silent. Accustomed to put his feelings on all subjects into verse, there is not a word that relates to these great public occurrences excepting a Fourth of July ode, written at the request of the Washington Benevolent Society of Boston, made through his father.*

---

* This was a sort of Tyrtean blast, as the following specimen of it will show .

"Should Justice call to battle
   The applauding shout we'd raise ;
A million swords would leave their sheath,
   A million bayonets blaze.
The stern resolve, the courage high,
   The mind untam'd by ill,
The fires that warmed our leader's breast
   His followers' bosoms fill.
Our Fathers bore the shock of war,
   Their sons can bear it still.

" The same ennobling spirit
   That kindles valor's flame,
That nerves us to a war of right,
   Forbids a war of *shame ;*

The real reason of his silence at this period was, as I suppose, a contest going on in the youth's own mind, which had for him, as it will have for the reader, more interest than any public events. Carefully preserved among his papers —and he was for the most part inattentive in keeping what concerned himself only—are several fragments of poems expressive of the joys, the doubts, and the disappointments of love. These, when I opened them, seemed to me mere literary exercises, but on closer inspection they disclosed a seriousness of feeling and certain reactive effects upon his mind that led me to suspect that possibly a real experience lay behind them. I was confirmed in this suspicion by the reminiscences of Mr. Arthur Bryant, who says that, while his brother was a student of law in Worthington, a distinguished friend of their father came from Rhode Island on a visit to Cummington, bringing with him a beautiful and accomplished daughter, who fascinated the poet, so that for some time afterward they maintained an earnest correspondence. Of the incidents of the brief attachment, however, nothing more is known; but, if we are permitted to form conjectures from the poems themselves, it would appear that,

> For not in Conquest's impious train
>   Shall Freedom's children stand ;
> Nor shall, in guilty fray, be raised
>   The high-souled warrior's hand ;
> Nor shall the patriot draw his sword
>   At Gallia's proud command.

> " No ! by our Father's ashes,
>   And by their sacred cause,
> The Gaul shall never call us slaves,
>   Shall never give us laws ;
> Even let *him* from a swarming fleet
>   Debark his veteran host,
> A living wall of patriot hearts
>   Shall fence the frowning coast—
> A bolder race than generous *Spain,*
>   A better cause we boast."

while it was at first hearty and sincere, the course of it did not run smoothly, and the end proved very painful for some reason or other.

As these poems are fragmentary and unfinished, they are not quoted as poems, but to show how far they shadow forth a little romantic story. The earliest of them, mere random lines, is a vague intimation of worship at a distance, and endeavors to describe how a youthful poet, dreaming of his love, might see in the dawn that reddens the snowy hills, the blushes of life on the cheeks of the fair maid of his adoration. In the dusky air, he sees the soft dun shadow of her hair; in the beautiful stars above the summits, her lustrous eyes; and in the streams of the valleys, the currents of his own heart, that look up and exclaim,

> "How bright, but oh ! how far ! "

The second poem refers, but still remotely, to a mysterious charm, of which he has suddenly become aware:

> " Let no rude sound be uttered nigh,
>   Be heard no step profane,
> While tempered to the heaven-taught lyre
>   I pour the sacred strain.
>
> " There is a charm of heavenly birth,
>   A charm of mystick name,
> Of power the virgin's laughing eye
>   To light with lovelier flame,
>
> " That bids the rose-enamelled cheek
>   A riper blush assume,
> To beauty gives a fairer grace,
>   To youth a deeper bloom.
>
> " It dwells not in the teeming mine,
>   The diamond's caverned home,
> Nor where along their coral bed
>   The sea's green waters foam.

" Nor Africk sends this wondrous gift,
    Nor India's purple shores,
  Nor regions where the power of frost
    Has heaped his nitrick stores.

" But in the modest virgin's face
    Is all its influence seen,
  It loves the eye of timid look,
    The soft retiring mien," etc., etc.

WORTHINGTON, *August*, 1812.

He was enabled to speak more boldly in a version of the
words of old Paulus Silentiarius:

" The peerless rose no added charm receives
  From wreaths of flowers around its virgin leaves,
  Nor thou, sweet maid, from robes of costly care,
  Nor gems that sparkle in thy glossy hair;
  White is the pearl, more white thy bosom's snow,
  Among thy locks the gold forgets to glow,
  In vain the gem that India's shore supplies,
  The gleaming jacinth, emulates thine eyes,
  But thy moist lip and airy grace of frame
  By art unaided wake the unbidden flame,
  For these I pine—till to my ardent gaze
  Thy tell-tale eye the dawn of love betrays."

But, the poet stops to ask, shall he yield himself to this
pleasing but delusive passion—he that had formed for himself,
whose friends had formed for him, such ambitious hopes of
success, in a far different way.

" Yes, I have listened all too long,
  Deluder! to thy syren song.
  Ah, love! when first its musick led
  My cheated steps thy paths to tread,
  I never dreamed those airs divine,
  And those fair quiet walks were thine.

" And I would once have scoffed in scorn
　　At him who dared pronounce me born
　　To bend at beauty's shrine enchained,
　　And do the homage I disdained;
　　I little thought the hour to see,
　　When a blue eye could madden me.

" I seek the scenes that once I sought
　　To bring high dreams and holy thought,
　　That gave my early numbers birth,
　　The unpeopled majesty of earth—
　　One image still too loved to fade,
　　Is with me in the lonely shade.

" Yet, sometimes there dejected strays
　　The genius of my better days;
　　And I am troubled when I trace
　　The darkened grandeur of his face,
　　While thus he breathes his warnings high,
　　Betwixt rebuke and prophecy.

" ' When riper years this dream dispel,
　　Thy heart shall rue its folly well;
　　And thou with bitter tears shall gaze
　　On the blank train of wasted days;
　　And curse the withering spell at length,
　　That broke thy spirit's early strength.

" ' There were, in early life, of thee
　　Who augured high and happily ;
　　Who loved and watched the opening shoot,
　　And propped the stem and looked for fruit;
　　And they shall see its blossoms die,
　　Withered before a woman's eye.' "

Then he answers himself, half in jest and half in earnest, by
paraphrasing several odes of the old Grecian master, Anacreon
(the 14th, the 30th, and 36th), which relate how, resolving to
set the little god at defiance, the dimpled archer took his bow
and golden case of arrows, and dared him to the field. En-

cased in mail, like that which Pelides wore in battle, he stood manfully up to the enemy—but alas! and alas! he was pierced through and through for his rashness. Why attempt to defend the outposts, when the citadel was already entered? Overcome, and a captive, like that same little god, when bound by the rosy chains woven by the daughters of Beauty, he wished for no release ; it was so delightful a slavery. No, indeed, henceforth

> " To love, to love, shall be my law,"

and he desires through all the vicissitudes of time, even when age should bring gray locks and the decrepit frame, to bow still at the shrine of his queen.

Next follows a time of separation—the youth must go away to his studies, and the fair one, with her company, to her own people—indicated in two references. The first is this :

> " The home thy presence made so dear,
>   I leave—the parting hour is past;
>   Yet thy sweet image haunts me here
>   In tears as when I saw thee last.
>
> " It meets me where the woods are deep,
>   It comes when twilight tints depart,
>   It bends above me while I sleep,
>   With pensive looks that pierce my heart."

The other runs thus :

> " When on Fernandez' isle, whose cliffs upbear
>   Sweet dells that blossom in the unbreath'd air,
>   Stood the self-banished Scot, and saw the sail
>   That brought him, bound away before the gale,
>   And voices which he never more might hear,
>   Laughter and shout and song came to his ear
>   With faint and fainter sound, as o'er the main
>   The glad crew hastened to their homes again,
>   Then turned and cast his melancholy eye
>   On the lone scene where he must live and die,

And heard the eternal moaning of the tide
That cut him off from men—his spirit died
Within him, and the bitter tears came fast."

Left alone on the hills, as Selkirk was on his island, there was yet the resource of correspondence, and it was during this absence that the letters probably passed which Mr. Arthur Bryant recalls; but with the return of spring, a year later, borrowing from Virgil, who himself borrowed from Theocritus, he calls upon Galatea to come back from the sea-shore to the hills:

"Come, Galatea! hath the unlovely main
A charm thy gentle gazes to detain?
Spring dwells in beauty here; her thousand flowers
The glad earth here about the river pours;
Here o'er the grotto's mouth the poplars play;
Here the knit vines exclude the prying day.
Come, Galatea! bless this calm retreat;
Come, leave the maniack seas their bounds to beat."
WORTHINGTON, 1814.

Galatea must have come back, for we are informed:

"The gales of June were breathing by,
    The twilight's last faint rays were gleaming,
And midway in the moonless sky
    The star of Jove was brightly beaming.

"Where by the stream the birchen boughs
    Dark o'er the level marge were playing,
The maiden of my secret vows
    I met, alone, and idly straying.

"And since that hour—for then my love
    Consenting heard my passion pleaded—
Full well she knows the star of Jove,
    And loves the stream with beeches shaded."
WORTHINGTON, 1814.

A little later the outlooks are still favorable:

"Dear are these heights, though bleak their sides they raise,
 For here, as forth in lonely walk we fare;
Her cheek to mine soft Evelina lays,
 And breathes those gentle vows that none may share.
 Mine is her earliest flame—her virgin care—
The look of love her speaking eye that fills—
 To the known shade, when Eve's consenting star
Sees his soft image in the trembling rills,
 My lovely Oread comes—my charmer of the hills."

CUMMINGTON, 1814.

With Bion, he tells his solemn joy to the skies:

"Hail, holy star of love, thou fairest gem
 Of all that twinkle in the veil of night!
As the broad moon to thee, so thou to them
 Superior in beauty beamest bright.
 Lend me, while she delays, thy tender light.
Thou for whom Sol, to yield his turn to thine
 Stooped to the glowing West his hastened flight;
On deeds of guilt I call thee not to shine,
 Nor thefts, but those of love—and mutual love is mine."

WORTHINGTON, 1814.

But again doubts and misgivings intrude in the midst of it all; and something apparently has gone wrong:

"Ah, who would tempt the hopeless spell,
 Whose magic binds the slaves of Love?
The heart his power has touched can tell
 How false to peace his flatteries prove.

"Each silent sign by passion taught
 To tell the wish that thrills the breast,
The gaze with speechless meaning fraught,
 The glowing lip in secret pressed.

"The stolen hour by moonlight past,
 When hands are met and sighs are deep;
Are wanderings all, for which at last
 The heart must bleed, the eye must weep."

These doubts and misgivings are but the prelude to some
terrible rupture, when the delicious charm is suddenly broken,
and the wounded lover tramples his affection under the heels
of his pride.   He cries out in his pain and anger :

> " I knew thee fair—I deemed thee free
>   From fraud and guile and faithless art,
>   Yet had I seen as now I see,
>   Thine image ne'er had stained my heart.
>
> " Trust not too far thy beauty's charms ;
>   Though fair the hand that wove my chain,
>   I will not stoop, with fettered arms,
>   To do the homage I disdain.
>
> " Yes, Love has lost his power to wound,
>   I gave the treacherous homicide,
>   With bow unstrung and pinions bound,
>   A captive to the hands of Pride."

There the love seems to end; but contemporary in date
with these poems, or following closely upon them, is another
series of poems of a wholly different cast, which we cannot say
were in any way connected with the former, but which show, at
least, that the serene philosophy expressed in " Thanatopsis,"
a few years before, had been ruffled by certain storms of passion that opened quite another view of the dark abysses of
Death.   As if weary of life, and longing for its extinction, the
poet hears the voices of the grim tenants of the grave calling
upon him to take up his rest with them.   It is, as he names it,

> " A chorus of Ghosts ";

and it runs in this wise : *

---

* This piece was published ten years later, with the signature X.—not the usual B.
—in the New York " Review," with the seventh stanza, since supplied by Mr. Arthur
Bryant, omitted.   It conflicts somewhat with my interpretation of these poems, as
this one is dated February, 1814, which was before he had any reason to complain ;
but the date may have been put on years afterward, when his memory was not clear.

" Come to thy couch of iron rest !
　　Come share our silent bed !
　There's room within the grave-yard's bounds
　　To lay thy weary head.

" Come, thou shalt have a home like ours,
　　A low and narrow cell,
　With a gray stone to mark the spot;
　　For thee the turf shall swell.

" Cold are its walls—but not for thee—
　　And dark, but thou shalt sleep;
　Unfelt, the enclosing clods above
　　Their endless guard shall keep.

" Yes, o'er thee where thy lyre was strung,
　　Thine earliest haunts to hail,
　Shall the tall crow-foot's yellow gems
　　Bend in the mountain gale.

" There, as he seeks his tardy kine,
　　When flames the evening sky,
　With thoughtful look, the cottage boy
　　Shall pass thy dwelling by.

" Why shudder at that rest so still—
　　That night of solid gloom ?
　If refuge thou would'st seek from woe,
　　'Tis in the dreamless tomb.

" There is no tie that binds to life,
　　No charm that wins thy stay;
　To-morrow none will recollect
　　That thou didst live to-day.

" Come, we will close thy glazing eye,
　　Compose thy dying head;
　And gently from its house of clay
　　Thy struggling spirit lead."

WORTHINGTON, *February*, 1814.

But who are these ghosts that invite his company and promise him so much ? Do they know aught of the fate of a " dear

one" that, as we now learn, has gone to them? He will seek an interview with the awful monarch of the shades himself, and challenge him to disclose the secrets of his prison-house. At midnight he makes his appeal:

> " The night has reached its solemn noon,
>   And blotting half the sky;
> The clouds before the westering moon
>   In broad black masses lie.
> No voice is heard—no living sound,
>   Nor even the zephyr's breath;
> And I, where sheds the grove profound
> A night of deeper horror round,
>   High converse hold with Death.
>
> " He comes—but not the spectre grim
>   By fabling dreamers planned,
> With wickered ribs and fleshless limb,
>   And scythe and ebbing sand.
> But dim as through the polar shade,
>   When sails the gathering storm.
> A shadowy presence vast and dread,
> In terrors wrapt, which ne'er arrayed
>   Distinguishable form.
>
> " ' By all the dying feel and fear,
>   By every fiery throe,
> By all that tells thy triumphs here
>   And all we dread below;
> By those dim realms—those portals pale
>   Whose keys 'tis thine to keep,
> I charge thee, tell the thrilling tale!
> I charge thee, draw aside the veil
>   That hides the dear one's sleep!' "
>
> WORTHINGTON, 1814.

Death answers the invocation, not in person, but by sending the longed-for object herself to repeat the persuasions of the more general chorus:

"It was my love—that form I knew—
  The same that glazed unmoving eye;
And that pure cheek of bloodless hue,
  As when she slept with those that die.

"Why leave thy quiet cell for me—
  Have not my tears been duly shed?
Have I not taught the willow-tree
  To weep with me above thy head?

"And culled the earliest blooms of May—
  The latest sweets that Autumn knows,
To strew thy grave—and brush'd away
  From the cold turf the winter snows?

"I deemed that thou my dreams would'st bless.
  A seraph flush'd with heavenly bloom,
And gild with gleams of happiness
  My few brief years of care and gloom.

"But oh, that eye is ghastly bright,
  It glares with death, as mine will soon;
And that blanched brow is cold and white
  As the pale mist beneath the moon.

"Oh, wave not that dim hand again,
  Oh, point not to thy lowly cell;
For visions flash across my brain,
  And thoughts too horrible to tell.

"I may not follow thee, my love,
  Nor now thy dreamless slumber share;
The cold clods press thy limbs above,
  And darkness and the worm are there.

"Yet a few hours, and Nature's hand
  Itself shall sorrow's balm apply;
And I shall bless   kind command
  That cools this brow and seals this eye."

November, 1814.

This morbid condition of mind, whatever the origin of it, whether the result of personal experience or a mere dramatic attempt to bring out a peculiar situation, was not of long continuance. It passed off without harm, as such attacks commonly do. Allston says somewhere that young painters are apt to have a mania at one time or another for painting bandits—and it is not impossible that young poets have a similar desire to meddle with the dark secrets of the charnel-house.

CHAPTER SEVENTH.

THE LAW STUDENT.

A. D. 1814, 1815.

IN June, 1814, the student changed his residence from Worthington to Bridgewater, where he was soon engaged in the studies of his profession, and absorbed once more in public affairs. His grandfather, Dr. Philip Bryant, lived in Bridgewater, and for that reason, doubtless, he was transferred to that place. His own wish was to complete his course in Boston, and he makes frequent mention of it in letters to his father, for the sake of the advantages, he says, and not in a spirit of discontent. But the uniform reply of the father is, that he cannot afford the expense. "You have cost me already four hundred dollars at Mr. Howe's, and I have other children equally entitled to my care. Besides, my health is imperfect; I have suffered much from the fatigues of the last season, and, as I may not long be with you, I must do what I can for you all while I am still here."

Bridgewater was a larger town than any he had yet lived in—that is to say, it comprised more houses and people—and the conditions of intellectual and social life were more ample; but the best of the New England villages, in those days, contained few persons likely to appreciate a young man of genius and of delicate tastes, already enriched by a considerable knowledge of ancient literature, and cherishing visions of poetic fame. One of his fellow-students speaks of the place as "utterly destitute of good society," which he considers a benefit to one engaged in the dry study of the law. "A Bridgewater winter," he adds, "is more intolerable than a Bridgewater summer—the wind perpetually shifting from out to in—now rain, next snow —now a frozen collection of rough points for one to hobble over, then a swimming ocean of mud for one to wade through." But Mr. Bryant enjoyed his residence there, and always referred to it, in later years, as very pleasant. His teacher, Mr. William Baylies, was both a well-instructed jurist and a gentleman of cultivation and noble personal traits, whose friends were in the habit of comparing him, in appearance and character, with the model of the times, General Washington. Dignity of manner, a strong sense of justice, urbanity, elevated maxims of conduct, and disinterestedness, furnished the grounds of this comparison.* Under his influence, or it may have been to escape his former unhappy state of feeling, Mr. Bryant now devoted himself closely to study. In some lines, addressed "to a friend on his marriage," † he said :

> "O'er Coke's black-letter page,
> Trimming the lamp at eve, 'tis mine to pore,
> Well pleased to see the venerable sage
> Unlock his treasured wealth of legal lore ;
> And I that loved to trace the woods before,
> And climb the hills a playmate of the breeze,
> Have vowed to tune the rural lay no more,
> Have bid my useless classics sleep at ease,
> And left the race of bards to scribble, starve, and freeze."

---

* In an obituary notice of him, after his death in 1865, when he had reached his eighty-ninth year, Mr. Bryant said that "he was a man of imposing presence, kindly manners, and a close observer of character. His memory was stored with anecdotes of remarkable persons, the relation of which at times made him very entertaining. His tastes and habits of life were exceedingly simple, though his fortune was liberal, and his disposition of his income generous. He had a supreme contempt for the tricks of his profession, and for all indirect practices, and few lawyers ever exercised their profession so exempt from complaint and criticism." Mr. Bryant also wrote, at the request of relatives, a beautiful inscription for his monument.

† Published, three years later, in the "North American" for March, 1818.

A month after getting to Bridgewater his poetical faculties were put in request for a Fourth of July ode, which hardly broke in upon his routine, although it revived some of the old spirit of the politician. It was rather rhymed declamation than poetry, in which he took occasion to deplore the folly and ravages of the war and to rejoice in the downfall of Napoleon, whom the allies had shut up in Elba. He lauded the valor and persistency of England, and upbraided his own countrymen for having taken no part in the great work of independence achieved on the continent of Europe.* His assiduity of study is evidenced by the elaborate digests and notes that are found among his papers. They are arranged with extreme

---

* A few stanzas from this ode will show the spirit of it :

" Our skies have glowed with burning towns,
　　Our snows have blushed with gore,
　And fresh is many a nameless grave
　　By Erie's weeping shore.
　In sadness let the anthem flow—
　　But tell the men of strife,
　On their own heads shall rest the guilt
　　Of all this waste of life.

" Well have ye fought, ye friends of man,
　　Well was your valor shown ;
　The grateful nations breathe from war—
　　The tyrant lies o'erthrown.
　Well might ye tempt the dangerous fray,
　　Well dare the desperate deed :
　Ye knew how just your cause—ye knew
　　The voice that bade ye bleed.

" To thee the mighty plan we owe
　　That bade the world be free ;
　The thanks of nations, Queen of Isles !
　　Are poured to heaven and thee,
　Yes !—hadst not thou, with fearless arm,
　　Stayed the descending scourge ;
　These strains, that chant a nation's birth,
　　Had haply hymned its dirge."

care under appropriate divisions and headings, and with ample references to the authorities in old English treatises and the more modern American statutes and decisions. Together, they would form no incomplete manual of the rudimentary principles of the science, as it existed at that day. What is also remarkable in them is the neatness of the chirography. The young man had not yet formed his hand, such as it was afterward, rather copying his father in this as he did in his verses, but it is clear and full of character. One sees in it decision and vivacity, but only the germs of that flowing grace that marked it at a later period.

It is creditable to Mr. Bryant, young as he was, that his teacher at once took him into his confidence, and, during his absences as a legislator,* entrusted him with the control of nearly all his business. Letters passed between them constantly; on the one side giving reports of the state and progress of cases and soliciting instruction—on the other imparting that instruction, and with it the latest news of public affairs. As we were at war with a great naval power, it was an important time in the history of parties and of the nation. Public opinion of the propriety of the war and the modes in which it should be carried on was very much divided. The scenes of battle on the ocean or on the frontier were scarcely more fiery than those of Congress and the popular assemblies.

Mr. Bryant, it seems, had no difficulty in the preliminary tests of his profession. Addressing his father, August 16, 1814, he says:

"DEAR SIR: I went to Plymouth last week, where I stayed four days, and might, perhaps, have been obliged to stay a week had it not been for good luck in finding a Bridgewater man there with a vacant seat in his chaise. I there received a certificate in the handwriting of A. Holmes, Esquire, and sprinkled with his snuff instead

---

* Mr. Baylies had been a member of Congress for the years 1809, 1812, and 1814; and was re-elected in 1815, afterward in 1816–'17, and again in 1833–'34–'35.

of sand, for which I paid six dollars, according to the tenor and substance following:

" These certify that William C. Bryant, a student at law in brother
Baylies's office, has been examined by us, and we do agree that he be
recommended to be admitted an attorney at August Term, 1815, he
continuing his studies regularly all that time.

Br. Joshua Thomas,   }   *Committee of the Bar for*
Impress. Abm. Holmes. }   *Examining Candidates.*

August 9, 1814.

" By the bye, I ought to have mentioned, and perhaps I did mention in my last, that there is a bar rule providing that all students at
law who have not had the happiness and honor of an academic degree should be examined by a committee of three, any two of whom
will do, to decide how long such person shall study. Now, you will
see, the time fixed to admit me to the bar is before I emerge from my
minority. Whether this will be any objection or not I cannot tell—I
have not been able to find any law which makes it so, and the exam-
iners inquired my age at the time; but, if there should be any impropriety in being admitted next August, nothing is more easy, you
know, than to postpone it till November.

" When I was at Plymouth I went on to the Gurnet. There are
rather more than sixty men at the place, all stowed into about a
dozen or fifteen small tents. Their accommodations are not very
comfortable. There are seven guns in the fort—two twelves, two
twenty-fours, and three eighteen pounders.

" Yours affectionately,

" W. C. B."

To an old office companion at Mr. Howe's, Elisha Hub-
bard, who had removed to Northampton, he writes two weeks
later as follows:

" I have waited for you to write to me long enough to weary the
patience of the man of Uz, and I assure you I should really have been
angry at your conduct, had I not suspected that the fascinations of
some fair Northampton belle might have caused you to forget the existence of your old friends. If you will honestly own this to be the
fact, I will lay aside my resentment, for you know I am partial to
those errors which owe their origin to the tender passion. My situa-

tion here is perfectly agreeable: books enough; a convenient office, and for their owner, a good lawyer and an amiable man. The testimony which all classes bear to the uprightness of Mr. Baylies's character is truly wonderful. Everybody, even those who entertain the greatest dislike to lawyers in general, concur in ascribing to him the merit of honesty. You, who know how much calumny is heaped upon the members of our profession, even the most uncorrupt, can estimate the strict and scrupulous integrity necessary to acquire this reputation. Mr. Baylies is a man of no ostentation; he has that about him which was formerly diffidence, but is now refined and softened into modesty. As for old Worthington, not the wealth of the Indies could tempt me back to my former situation. I am here very much in my old way, very lazy, but something different in being very contented.

"W. C. B."

A few weeks later again, Sept. 19th, writing to another of his Worthington fellow-students, Mr. George Downes, he touches certain topics in a way which shows not only how far he had escaped from his late morbid communings with death, but that his studies did not withhold him from the usual pleasures of young men:

"I am certainly as well contented with this place as I could be with any, and I would not exchange it for Worthington if the wealth of the Indies were thrown into that side of the balance; yet I must acknowledge that, when I think of Ward's store, and Mills's tavern, and Taylor's grogshop, and Sears's, and Daniels's, and Briggs's, &c., &c., &c., such cool, comfortable lounging-places, it makes me rather melancholy, for there is not a tavern in this parish. A store with a hall, however, close to my door, supplies the place of one. We had a ball there last Friday, and it rained furiously. We had been putting it off for about a week, from day to day, on account of the wet weather, and at last, despairing of ever having a clear sky, we got together in a most tremendous thunder-storm, and a very good scrape we had of it. The next morning we set out, six couples of us, to go to a great pond in Middleborough, about thirteen miles from this place, on a sailing party, which we had likewise been procrastinating a number of days on account of the weather. When we began our

journey there was every sign of rain; the clouds were thick and
dark, and there was a devil of a mist; but the sun came out about
ten o'clock, and we had one of the most delightful days I ever saw.
Mine host and hostess were very accommodating; they gave us some
fine grapes and peaches, a good dinner, and tolerable wine. We had
a charming sail on the lake, and our ladies were wonderfully sociable
and alert, considering they were up till three o'clock the night before. At about eight in the evening we got back safe to the west parish of Bridgewater. . . . Yesterday we received orders from the
Major General of this division to detach eight hundred and ninety
men from this brigade to march to the defence of Plymouth. This
takes all the militia from this quarter. They marched this morning.
The streets were full of them a little while ago, but now the place is
as solitary and silent as a desert."

September 26th, he gave Mr. Baylies a more particular account of the military movements, and of the popular disposition in regard to them.

"DEAR SIR: We are in rather an unpleasant pickle in this part
of the country, General Goodwin having read General Cochran's letter, in which he communicated to Mr. Monroe his intention of de-
stroying all the towns on the sea-coast, posted off to Governor Strong,
and, after giving him some idea of the dangers which threatened the
goodly and important town of Plymouth, got permission to call out as
many men from his division to the defence of the peace as he thought
proper. A detachment was accordingly made of eight hundred men
from this brigade. We received the orders last Sunday week, and the
next Tuesday our people marched. Thirty are called from Captain
Lathrop's company, besides two sergeants, two corporals, two drum-
mers, and St. Leonard—thirty-seven from Captain Edson's—besides a
like number of sergeants, etc., and a captain and ensign. This draft
takes all the militia from this parish without being full—the companies being very small—some having got certificates and some being
sick and excused by the captain. Our streets are now very solitary—
the place is a perfect desert; you would hardly recognize the country
around your office if you were to see it; Briggs and Ben Howard and
Charles and Allen are gone—Eaton only is left to sell 'a little some-

thing to drink.' It is understood to be the intention of said Goodwin
to keep these men at Plymouth till winter as a scarecrow to the British fleet. The people here grumble heartily at the affair, and seem
angry that the General should think the safety of his pitiful village of
more consequence than their corn and potatoes. Those, however,
who stay at home are the most discontented. The soldiers are said
to enjoy themselves wonderfully, and some of them swear that they
would not come back if they could have an opportunity. They have
been attentively supplied with every comfort and convenience which
their situation could admit of; they are established at the rope-walks,
We are very anxious here to hear from Congress; our paper of to-day.
in which we expected the President's message, failed. I believe everybody knows what kind of talk to expect from the mouth of his Imbecility,* if he may be so titled; but the eyes of an attentive nation are
fixed upon their Legislature to see what steps they will take upon this
momentous occasion. How does the Southern autumn agree with your
constitution? I hope it has not given you the fever and ague which we
who dwell on the salubrious sands of the old colony dread so much."

In all his correspondence with Mr. Baylies, the young man
betrays an insatiable curiosity in regard to the progress of
events. Newspapers were not so many in those days, nor did
news fly as quickly as now, and country constituents depended
very much upon the letters of their representatives for knowledge of what was going on. "Who is this Dallas," Mr. Bryant asks, "that has been recently appointed Secretary of the
Treasury? is he a native of this country—is he competent?
What are the commissioners doing at Ghent? Do you mean
to impose any more taxes? If you do, I can tell you, the
people will revolt. There is no mistaking their spirit; you
know what it is; the same that animated 'the children of the
Hills,' at Cummington, who, when twenty-six men were called
for, stepped forward to a man!" "What are the views of the
Administration," he asks in October, "and the prospects of the
nation? Is all probability of peace cut off? Is the war to be

* His Imbecility was James Madison.

interminable? I earnestly wish that you would tell me something about these things, not only for my sake, but that of others, and you would save me much of such dialogue as the following: 'Any letters from Mr. Baylies to-day?'—'Yes.' 'Well, what does he write?'—'That it is very hot weather at Washington.' You may tell the Administration that, if the system of taxation proposed by the Committee of Ways and Means goes into effect, the people of the old colony will not like them any better for it. If Mr. Madison wants to make us sick of his war, let him lay upon our shoulders those 'burdens' which are so cheerfully and proudly borne; let him increase those 'taxes' which are paid with so much 'promptness and alacrity.' I cannot tell how mature the public feelings are —but the subject of a separation of the States is more boldly and frequently discussed, and the measures of our State Legislature are received among our party, as far as I can judge, with universal approbation, while the Democrats regard them with considerable alarm. Many are very boisterous about it, but perhaps they may become calm by the time the taxes are to be paid."

Mr. Baylies always replies with alacrity and patience, and encloses copies of "his Imbecility's" messages. In one instance he wrote three close pages in explanation of the proceedings at Ghent, and of his opinions as to the proper terms of peace. He seemed to regard his young student as a representative of the general community, and furnished him with full and explicit accounts of whatever was done or said at the seat of government.

Only five days later than the date of the last letter (October 10th) Mr. Bryant is completely possessed by the military fever, and writes his father a long and earnest letter, showing why he ought to go into the army, "for the defence of the State," be it remembered, not for the service of the United States. There is an intestine foe, he alleges, more dangerous than Great Britain, and it may be necessary soon to set up an independent empire.

"DEAR FATHER : Mr. Richards being about to return from a visit to his brother here, I have taken this opportunity to write by him. The militia, which were ordered to Plymouth and New Bedford upon permission obtained by General Goodwin, after he had made a terrifying representation to the Governor of the dangers which threatened the former of these places, are now about to return. The affair was laid before the Legislature, who considered it inexpedient that the greater portion of the laboring part of the community should be taken from their farms to be stationed in a petty village, which perhaps the British would never take any notice of. Two hundred are, however, to be left at New Bedford. Our people here grumbled very considerably at being thus destitute of hands to get in their corn and potatoes, but it was observed, however, that those who remained at home were the most discontented. The soldiers enjoyed themselves roundly, and were attentively supplied with every comfort and convenience which their situation could admit of. I escaped the draft, as, through the forbearance of the captain, I had not been once called upon to do military duty. I was, however, almost ashamed to stay at home when everybody besides was gone, but was not a little comforted by the reflection—in which, I believe, most people concurred with me—that the place was in no danger, that the detachment was entirely unnecessary, and, therefore, I might as well stay as go.

"Politics begin to effervesce a little here. People are afraid of paper money—afraid of exorbitant taxation, etc., etc. Democracy is, however, as obstinate, and inclined to justify its leaders, as ever. I presume that you in Hampshire begin to grow pretty warm by this time. The fact is, there is more party feeling, more of party union, in your part of the country than here. You are more of a newspaper reading people, and let the 'Hampshire Gazette' only give the word, which, by the by, it copies from some leading Federal paper, and every Federalist in the country has his cue, everybody knows what to think. Here the case is different; one takes the 'Centinel,' one the 'Messenger,' and one the 'Boston Gazette,' while by far the greater part take no paper at all. The consequence is that one is very warm, another very moderate, and another is in doubt how to be. I go upon the supposition that this parish affords a fair specimen of the habits and feelings of the people in this part of the State. .

"I have a question for you : Whether it would be proper for me to have anything to do with the army which is to be raised by voluntary enlistment for the defence of the State. Attached as you are to your native soil, to its rights and safety, you could not, surely, be unwilling that your son should proffer his best exertions, and even his life, to preserve them from violation. The force now to be organized may not be altogether employed against a foreign enemy; it may become necessary to wield it against an intestine foe in the defence of dearer rights than those which are endangered in a contest with Great Britain. If we create a standing army of our own—if we take into our own hands the public revenue (for these things are contemplated in the answer to the Governor's message)—we so far throw off our allegiance to the general government, we disclaim its control and revert to an independent empire. The posture, therefore, which is now taken by the State Legislature, if followed up by correspondent measures, is not without hazard. If we proceed in the manner in which we have begun, and escape a civil war, it will probably be because the Administration is awed by our strength from attempting our subjection. By increasing that strength, therefore, we shall lessen the probability of bloodshed. Every individual who helps forward the work of collecting this army takes the most effectual means in his power to bring the present state of things to a happy conclusion. A general spirit of devotion to the cause of the States, and of attachment to the measures into which we have been driven by the weakness and wickedness of our rulers, ought to pervade all ranks of men; no one should be induced to shrink from the contest on account of petty personal sacrifices. That even these would not be made, in case I should enter into the service, I am inclined to think, from the following reasons: 1st. If I enter upon my profession next year, I shall come into the world raw and rustic to a degree uncommon even in most persons of my age and situation—in all the greenness of a secluded education, without that respect which greater maturity of years and more acquaintance with the world would give me. 2d. As I understand the matter, the objection which is made to my spending five years in the study of the law is not upon the ground that I shall not come soon enough into business, but that the expenses attending my education would be greater than you could meet without injuring the interest of the family. In this reason I have always concurred, and this it is that has led me to endeavor to shorten the term of my studies as much as possible. If I should enter into the service of the State, I should procure the means of present support, and, perhaps with prudence, might enable myself to complete my studies without further assistance. I should then come into the world, as I said, with my excessive bashfulness and rusticity rubbed off by a military life, which polishes and improves the manners more than any other method in the world. It is not probable that the struggle in which we are to be engaged will be a long one. The war with Britain certainly will not. The people cannot exist under it, and if the government will not make peace, Massachusetts must. Whether there may be an intestine contest or not admits of doubt; and if there should be, the entire hopelessness of the Southern States succeeding against us will probably terminate it after the first paroxysm of anger and malignity is over. If these ideas should meet your approbation, you will make some interest for me at headquarters. The army, you will perceive, is to be officered by the Governor."

The same month, day not given, after detailing the state of several cases at law, he tells Mr. Baylies:

"You inquire what our people think of the new system of taxation. I believe that I mentioned something upon the subject in my last, and I can now still more confidently say that, if the taxes proposed are made, they will be, in my opinion, the cause of violent and unstifled discontent. Perhaps we *shall not* agree to pay them. This will, however, depend upon the determinations of our State Legislature, of which you have all the means of forming an opinion which we have here. I regret that I cannot give you a more particular account of the state of public feeling in these parts, but, as far as I am acquainted with it, there seems to be a deep presentiment of an approaching dissolution of the Union."

Again, not long after, he says:

"We hear that you legislators have got through with the conscription bill, and it is presented to the President to receive his sanction. God forgive the poor perjured wretch if he dares sign it. If the people of New England acquiesce in this law, I will forswear federalism forever."

We see in these letters, which, I have no doubt, represent the spirit of the times much better than more important public documents, what striking mutations party opinions may undergo in a very little while. From the origin of the government, the Republicans had professed themselves the opponents of Nationalism or Centralism, and the particular defenders of the rights, or, as it was called, the Sovereignty of the States. On the other hand, the Federalists, as their name imports, were sticklers for central supremacy and local subordination. Nearly all the earlier controversies of politics turned upon this point of the precise limitations to be affixed, respectively, to the general and the particular governments. But the attitude of parties was now changed, if not completely reversed. The Republicans, who were in possession of power, did not scruple in stretching the exercise of it to the utmost bounds, while the Federalists began to construe the organic law with literal strictness, questioning every aggression, and calling upon the States to interpose a check to the strides of Federal authority. The Legislatures of Massachusetts and other Eastern States not only denounced the war as "unpolitic, impracticable, and unjust," and demanded peace on almost any terms, but they concerted measures for the protection of their own citizens from "the violence and tyranny of the United States." They proposed an amendment to the Federal Constitution even, in the interests of the local jurisdictions. Governor Strong, of Massachusetts, supported by the courts, and by the executives of other States, refused to place the State militia under the command of officers of the Federal army. In several of the States, indeed, delegates were appointed to assemble in convention at Hartford,* to consider existing grievances and devise remedies. This body, in its public acts and enunciations, was restrained and prudent, taking great care not to advise a rupture with the Union as yet; but the constituents it represented were more outspoken.

* The convention met in Hartford on the 15th of December, 1814.

Unfortunately for his military and political projects, Mr. Bryant was taken ill in November, and compelled to return to Cummington. What his disease was is not told; but probably some incipient form of the pulmonary malady that threatened him more seriously a few years later.* His recovery he communicates to Mr. Baylies in a note, dated December, which has, perhaps, a trifle of literary interest:

"DEAR SIR: I have got back to Bridgewater safe and sound, and in much better trim than when I went from it. All the people in this quarter are well and kicking, except old Mrs. ——, who was in the ground before I returned. But here is no snow. All the indication of winter is very cold weather. But from Boston to Albany there is excellent sleighing, and on the hills of Hampshire the best I ever knew. I paid a visit to my old instructor, Mr. Howe. I found him among his sheep, *en deshabille.*† Business, he tells me, is languishing.

---

* It was about the time of this illness that Mr. Bryant seems to have received more natural views of the great enemy, Death, than those expressed on a former page, if we may judge by this little poem:

> "Oh, thou whom the world dreadeth! Art thou nigh
> To thy pale kingdom, Death! to summon me?
> While life's scarce tasted cup yet charms my eye,
> And yet my youthful blood is dancing free,
> And fair in prospect smiles futurity.
> Go, to the crazed with care thy quiet bring;
> Go to the galley-slave who pines for thee,
> Go to the wretch whom throes of torture wring,
> And they will bless thy hand, that plucks the fiery sting.
>
> "I from thine icy touch with horror shrink,
> That leads me to the place where all must lie;
> And bitter is my misery to think
> That, in the spring-time of my being, I
> Must leave this pleasant land, and this fair sky;
> All that has charmed me from my feeble birth;
> The friends I love, and every gentle tie;
> All that disposed to thought, or waked to mirth;
> And lay me darkly down, and mix with the dull earth."

BRIDGEWATER, *July*, 1815.

† Mr. Howe had caught the mania that prevailed for raising merino sheep, and devoted a good deal of time to the enterprise; not, however, with success.

"I met at Mr. Howe's with 'Lara,' a tale, which is advertised on the cover of the 'Analectic Magazine' as being written by Lord Byron. It seems intended as a sequel to the 'Corsair.' It possesses some merit, but I think it cannot be written by Lord Byron. The flow of this poet's versification is admirably copied, but it seems to me to want his energy of expression, his exuberance of thought, the peculiar vein of melancholy which imparts its tinge to everything he writes; in short, all the stronger features of his genius. Conrad, whose character you used to admire, and who makes his appearance in this tale as a Spanish peer, under the name of 'Lara,' is degenerated into a lurking assassin, a midnight murderer. But perhaps you have seen the poem. For my part, I never heard of it till I met with it at Mr. Howe's. May it not be the effort of some American genius?"

The student had scarcely got to work again when his brother informed him of the illness of their father, in a letter, which shows also how the whole family were saturated with Federalism and revolt. Austin Bryant writes from Cummington, January 25, 1815:

"DEAR BROTHER: Our father has been very ill for a month past; he was taken with a fever which has probably settled itself upon the liver. . . . I have heard nothing of your commission. People here tell me that you ought to have applied to some military character for a recommendation. Probably this might have more weight with the Governor. But be this as it may, I think you ought to have one, considering the eagerness with which you have sought for it. . . . What think you of the proceedings of the convention?* Our Federalists were much disappointed, saying that they dared not adopt any energetic measures, but would go on in the old way of supplication till the chains that were preparing to bind them to the earth were riveted. But I trust in God these things will never be. There is a redeeming spirit in New England which will resist every encroachment upon its liberties and stamp the oppressor under its feet. . . :"

Cullen's reply, February 5, 1815, is worthy of note, not only as an exhibition of the popular feeling, but as an early

* The Hartford Convention.

specimen of his ability and judgment in handling public questions.

"DEAR BROTHER: Yours of the 25th ult. I received yesterday. I am much afflicted at the news of my father's sickness. I trust you are doing everything in your power to make his situation as comfortable as possible. . . .

"The Governor's message at the beginning of the present session of our Legislature will be a sufficient answer to those people who ascribe the failure of my application for a commission to the want of a recommendation from some military character. You inform me that your federalists are much disappointed at the proceedings of our convention. This is not much to be wondered at, considering the general character and feelings of the citizens of Hampshire. They are impatient of oppression, and prepared to resist the least encroachment upon their rights. But what do they want done? Shall we attempt by force what we may perhaps obtain peaceably? The plan proposed by the convention, if it should meet with success, certainly appears competent to secure the interest of the Eastern States at the same time that it preserves the Union. If it should fail, it will not be our fault nor that of our convention. In that event we might resort to the first principles of things—the rights of mankind—the original, uncombined element of liberty—but, in the mean time, it appears to my judgment proper to make use of all the means for our relief which the constitution allows. For this purpose our delegates were chosen —this was the tenor of their instructions; all that the constitution would permit they have done, and they could not have done more without transgressing the commands of the people in whose service they were employed. They have publicly proclaimed the terms on which depends the continuance of the Union; they have solemnly demanded of the national government that the rights taken from them should be restored, and barriers erected against future abuses of authority. Now, if these things could be effected by a peaceable compromise, would it not be better than to resort to sudden violence? We should then be in possession of all the advantages which could be derived from a separation, without hazarding any of its dangers. Even if it were certain that this plan will fail, yet perhaps it would be necessary that we should adopt it to hold up as our justification to the world as we go along—to show that we act, not from factious motives or from a temporary burst of popular turbulence—to unite the wishes of all honest men in favor of our cause, and take from the mouths of our enemies all occasion of contumely. And this effect is, in a great measure, produced. Our southern friends (and Mr. Baylies gives me a very good opportunity of inspecting the southern papers) can scarcely find terms to express their approbation of the proceedings of our convention, while the ingenuity of Democracy is vainly exercised to find some plausible occasion to revile them. I conceive that the plan of conduct which they have recommended will make more proselytes and acquire more respect to the Federal party than anything that has been done for these ten years. It will strongly impress our adversaries with the idea of that dignified and temperate firmness which steadily advances to its object; and it is not altogether impossible that it may alarm them into compliance. If not, next June will be the season for further deliberations. It will be time enough to tell the world that the original compact between the States is dissolved. But, in my opinion, you people of Hampshire expected too much; you thought that the Eastern States were in a moment, and by a single effort, to be restored to peace, liberty, and independence. How, you did not know, but the convention were to devise the means. But the delegates were no necromancers; they were mere men like ourselves. They could not draw rain from the clouds nor call ghosts from the ground; evils of the magnitude which we suffer were not easily removed, nor were they to be approached by rash hands. They have conducted themselves like men aware of the high responsibility which rested upon them. Such are my ideas upon the subject, though I confess they are changed from what they were when I first saw the report of our delegates. I am, however, far from censuring or even wishing to diminish the high spirits and quick sensibility to oppression that prevails in your county. It is necessary to counterbalance the sluggishness of our towns on the shore.

"The reasons in favor of the conduct of our convention may, therefore, be reduced to the following: 1. Because their instructions limited their deliberations to constitutional measures. 2. Even if their authority had been unlimited, yet it were better to exhaust the catalogue of peaceable and constitutional expedients before we proceed to violence, especially as the plan now recommended has never been tried; and it is calculated to bring the parties to a certain and speedy issue upon the great points of dispute. 3. Because the plan now recommended bids fair to be a popular one, and to overcome by its moderation that strenuous opposition to our wishes which a more violent one would be likely to encounter. 4. Because it is necessary to make one lasting and distinct expression of the general will of the Eastern States, to give them an opportunity of granting our demands in preference to risking a separation before we appeal to those immutable principles of right and liberty given by God with his own divine image to man.   Yours affectionately,

                                          " CULLEN."

The application for a military appointment did not fail altogether; for, the next July (25, 1816), a commission as adjutant in the Massachusetts militia was sent to Mr. Bryant; but, after holding it for less than a year, he returned it to the hands of the adjutant-general (February 8, 1817). Before he received this right to buckle on his sword, the negotiations for peace, which had been going on at Ghent, were satisfactorily terminated. While the ink was still wet upon the paper addressed to his brother by our young and somewhat belligerent publicist, the result was announced to Congress, and proclaimed throughout the country (February 17, 1815). It was hailed with rejoicing everywhere; the Federalists flung up their caps because the fighting was over, though they still grumbled that not a single object for which the war was undertaken had been obtained, and the Republicans because the victory of Jackson at New Orleans, January 8th, enabled them to keep their reverses out of sight and to retire amid a blaze of glory.

In a letter, dated March 19, 1815, to Judge Howe, Mr. Bryant refers to the subject :

"I reciprocate most cordially your congratulations on the return of peace. This event, so much desired and so little expected, seems to have excited in every part of the Union a delirium of transport which has not even yet subsided. Yet, whatever may be our feelings on this occasion, I trust that we shall not *feel* much gratitude to the man who has so long and so successfully been employed in wasting the strength and debasing the character of the nation, merely because he has not suffered its very life-blood to flow from the arteries of the Union; still less, when it is recollected that he was compelled to this present treaty only by the necessity of affairs. . . .

"But God forbid that the Federalists should relax their exertions to drag back into that obscurity from which they ought never to have emerged the men who have brought upon the country so much distress and disgrace. I much fear, however, that this accommodation will incline the Federal party to indolence, and that, in the convalescent prosperity of the country, they will forget the mighty influence which has brought us so near to our ruin; and now, wearied with its only efforts, perhaps, pauses for some more favorable opportunity to destroy us.

"If the peace has blown my military projects to the moon, it perhaps may be a question whether it has not a little shattered your Merino speculations. I say a question, because I do not think it yet ascertained whether we might compete successfully with other nations in the exportation of wool; but our prospects in the law are, I think, rather brightened." *

* He expressed the same views of the war in an ode written for the Howard Society of Boston, of which I will cite a specimen:

"Ah, taught by many a woe and fear,
    We welcome thy returning wing;
And Earth, O Peace! is glad to hear
    Thy name among her echoes ring.
And Winter looks a lovelier Spring,
And hoarsely though his tempest roars,
    The gale that drives our sleet shall bring
The world's large commerce to our shores.

"My country, pierced with many a wound!
    Thy pulse with slow recovery beats.
War flies our shores, but all around
    The eye his bloody footprint meets,
    As when the dewy morning greets,
Serene in smiles and rosy light,
    Some prostrate city through whose streets
The earthquake past at dead of night."

The rejoicings over the return of peace were somewhat dashed, among those to whom the name of Napoleon was still a terror, by the news of his escape from Elba. Mr. Bryant, writing to his father, May 24th, says:

"I presume that you in Cummington, as well as we in Bridge-water, were a little surprised that Bonaparte should so suddenly resume the sceptre of France. The exile of Elba has outwitted all Europe. We, I think, may dread, in common with other nations, the consequences of this event. They, by due concert and proper measures, may, perhaps, ensure their own safety, even if they should not have the power or inclination to pull him again from the throne; we have no security against his artifices and emissaries but in the virtue of the people, which, I fear, is not wonderfully great."

Nevertheless, his apprehensions were not so great as to prevent him from applying himself for the rest of the summer to diligent preparations for his examination in August, to which he looked forward with anxiety. Writing to his friend Downes, in June, he says:

"The nearer I approach to the conclusion of my studies the more I am convinced of the necessity of industry. You, my friend, were born under a more fortunate star than I. You have everything in your favor in entering upon the practice of law, accommodating your conversation to every sort of people, and rendering yourself agreeable to all. The maturity of your manners will add much to the respect you will receive upon entering into life, and the natural placidity of your temper will enable you to contemn the little rubs which will, of course, attend the young practitioner. But I lay claim to nothing of all these, and the day when I shall set up my gingerbread-board is to me a day of fearful expectation. The nearer I approach to it the more I dread it."

Downes tells him in return that he must not give way to despondency, and thereby do injustice both to his application and to his talents. "If I were conscious," he says, "of possessing those qualities in the same degree, I would whistle all fears of the future down the wind." His distrust did not arise from any want of knowledge of the law—on which both Mr. Howe and Mr. Baylies took occasion to compliment him—but from conscious defects as a speaker. In July, Mr. Howe wrote him a long letter on the subject, instructing him how the art of speaking is to be acquired and improved, but predicting for him "the very highest rank in the fraternity of which he is soon to become a member." To this the student replies, August 8th, with not a little grace of allusion, as well as good sense :

"My Dear Sir : Your remarks upon public speaking I read with the more interest as they come from one who has practiced that art with such distinguished success. Yet I must acknowledge that their effect upon me was considerably lessened by the reflection that mere industry could never have supplied that eloquence. You must be content, sir, not to claim the whole merit of producing it to yourself. You must ascribe much of it to the bounty of Nature, assisted, I have no doubt, by art, but still entitled to the credit of furnishing the raw material which was afterward to be worked up into such polish and eloquence. I never could believe that the maxim, *orator fit*, holds good in its full extent. It may be true that any man of common sense and common utterance may, by practice and diligent endeavor, be brought to talk decently well upon some occasions, but what we currently term *eloquence*, according to my weak judgment, depends as much upon the original constitution of the mind as any other faculty whatever. This, heowver, is not the place for a disquisition of this kind.

"Next week, by the leave of Providence and the Plymouth bar, I become a limb of the law. You inquire in what part of the world I intend to take up my abode. I have formed a thousand projects; I have even dreamed of the West Indies. After all, it may be left to mere chance to determine. I hope soon to see you, and have the benefit of your advice upon this subject. My best remembrances to all who have not forgotten me. Believe me, sir, with the highest esteem and respect, Yours, etc.,

"W. C. Bryant."

On the 15th of August he left Bridgewater, with his credentials as an attorney of the Common Pleas in his pocket.

CHAPTER EIGHTH.

THE YOUNG LAWYER.

A. D. 1816–1819.

IT is worthy of note that the same year in which Mr. Bryant attained his majority and was admitted to the bar he adopted the poetic form he worked in for the rest of his life. During the perturbations of what may be called the Love and Death assault, the noble inspirations that breathe through "Thanatopsis" had been for a time forgotten. In the distractions of the interval, indeed, he seems to have feared that the Muses had deserted him altogether, and he implores their return.* As soon as he reaches home he begins to woo them back. The artificial style in which he was trained is definitively abandoned; his boyish heroics, those Tyrtæan drum-beats, are thrown aside; his amatory sobs and sighs are suppressed; his morbid colloquies with Death are outgrown; and, with his Greek studies in memory, and the influences of the new British school of Southey, Coleridge, and Wordsworth growing in force, he devotes himself to a minute study of nature. All his papers of this period bear witness to constant and ever-renewed attempts, in different forms, to paint her varying aspects. Fragments and sketches mostly, they resemble those rough outlines which artists are in the habit of making in preparation for larger canvases. He hums to himself of flowers, groves, streams, trees, and especially of winds which

---

* See "I cannot Forget with what Fervid Devotion," in its original form. Poetical Works, vol. i, notes.

abounded in the region where he lived.* Among other things, he began an Indian story, after the manner of Scott's highland poems, but, judging by the little of it that was executed, the descriptive quite overmastered the narrative parts. There was a great deal more of the old Pontoosuc forest in it

---

* Here are a few specimens out of many :

" The cloudless heavens are cold and bright,
The shrieking blast is in the sky,
And all the long autumnal night
Whirl the dry leaves in eddies by."

" The sun is risen, but wan and chill
Wades through a broken cloud ;
And in the woods that clothe the hill
November winds are loud."

" Hark ! how with frantic wing the blast
Buffets the forest bare,
Though long ago its branches cast
The last dry leaflet there."

" Where Westfield holds his gleaming course
Tall hills and narrow meadows washing,
And all at once with gentle force
Against a million pebbles dashing."

" The new-risen sun's mild rays adorn
The clouds beneath him rolled ;
And the first scarlet tints of morn
Have brightened into gold.
With many a note the wild is cheered ;
With many a rustling foot resounds ;
The squirrel's merry chirp is heard,
From knoll to knoll the rabbit bounds ;
The woodpecker amidst the shade
Is heard his drumming bill to ply ;
On whirring wings along the glade
Sweeps the brown partridge by."

" Now, e'er she bids our fields adieu,
With fragrant fingers June delights,
Profuse with flowers of sunny hue,
To clothe our plains and grassy heights.

than of the Indian; Nature, indeed, was winning him completely to herself, and one of the first fruits of her caresses
was the "Yellow Violet," written just before leaving Bridgewater, while on a visit to Cummington.* Another piece,
originally printed in the "North American" (1817) as "A
Fragment," now known as "An Inscription for the Entrance
to a Wood," is due to the same feeling. Composed in a noble
old forest that fronted his father's dwelling-house, it is an exquisite picture of the calm contentment he found in the woods.
Every object—the green leaves, the thick roof, the mossy
rocks, the cleft-born wind-flowers, the dancing insects, the
squirrel with raised paws, the ponderous trunks, black roots,

> Through banks of gold the stream is rolled,
> That half its gleaming waters hide,
> In gold the mountain rears its pride,
> In gold the sloping vales subside,
> The meadows wave in gold.
>
> "On either side, along the road,
> Glitters a yellow margin gay,
> But where the heifer crops her food
> Less glowing tints the tract betray,
> And far around as eye can see
> One blossomed waste is all the scene,
> Save verdant cornfields stretched between,
> Or groves or orchards rising green
> In summer majesty." (a)

* It was not published till some years later.

(a) Of this yellow flower, Mr. J. H. Bryant, in a letter to me, gives these particulars: "There is a very singular fact connected with the flowering plant which
produced the scene described in the stanza. This was the *Ranunculus acris;*
common name, Crowfoot, or Buttercup. It first made its appearance along the
road-sides of the hill-towns (as they are called) of Western Massachusetts early in
this century. The farmers, looking upon it as a pestilent weed, attempted for a while
to eradicate it by digging it up. But, in spite of them, it increased with astonishing
rapidity, and in a few years took possession of the soil of all that region. It occupied
the road-sides, the pastures and meadows, and every place except the woodland and
the small patches of ground planted with corn or other grain. It was a large,
branching, and profusely flowering plant, and gave that part of the country, when in
full flower, the appearance described in the poem. What is singular is, that, after
occupying the soil for some ten or twelve years, it began to disappear, and in ten or
twelve years more it was nearly extinct. Now it is rarely seen. It was a glorious,
entrancing sight, when, as far as the eye could see, the whole country was clothed in
bright yellow, the surface rolling and tossing in the June breezes."

and sunken brooks—is painted with the minutest fidelity, and yet with an almost impassioned sympathy.

Doubtless he would gladly have lingered in those shades; but the work of life was before him; his bread was to be won, and he knew not as yet where it was to be won. Boston, the great city of business and literature, was the goal of his own wishes; but how was he, an utterly unknown young man, to subsist in Boston, while the needed clients were finding out his talents and getting ready to entrust their interests to his skill? His father was in a condition to help him to valuable acquaintances, but he was not in a condition to provide him with means. The good friends, Howe and Baylies, too, were able to recommend him professionally at Northampton, or New Bedford, or Troy, all of which had been in contemplation; but the same difficulties existed in each as in Boston. How was he to live until success should come? There was, in fact, no alternative for him but to begin in some small country village, where, if the prospects of practice were not very alluring, the costs of subsistence at least might be managed. On the opposite hill-side from Cummington, about seven miles distant, and to be seen from his father's residence, was a hamlet called Plainfield, whither he resolved to go to try his fortune. He had been there at school, and the family once sojourned there for a little while, so that he would not be an entire stranger among its people. On the 15th of December he went over to the place to make the necessary inquiries. He says in a letter that he felt as he walked up the hills very forlorn and desolate indeed, not knowing what was to become of him in the big world, which grew bigger as he ascended, and yet darker with the coming on of night. The sun had already set, leaving behind it one of those brilliant seas of chrysolite and opal which often flood the New England skies; and, while he was looking upon the rosy splendor with rapt admiration, a solitary bird made wing along the illuminated horizon. He watched the lone wanderer until it was lost in the distance, asking himself whither it had come and to what far home it was flying.

When he went to the house where he was to stop for the night, his mind was still full of what he had seen and felt, and he wrote those lines, as imperishable as our language, "The Waterfowl." The solemn tone in which they conclude, and which by some critics has been thought too moralizing,

> "He who from zone to zone
>   Guides through the boundless sky thy certain flight,
> In the long way that I must tread alone,
>   Will lead my steps aright,"

was as much a part of the scene as the flight of the bird itself, which spoke not alone to his eye but to his soul. To have omitted that grand expression of faith and hope in a divine guidance would have been to violate the entire truth of the vision.*

What promise there was for a lawyer in a mountain hamlet like Plainfield, containing at the most a dozen houses, and those of farmers chiefly, it is difficult to see; yet that Mr. Bryant obtained some business is shown by a letter of Mr. Howe to Judge Eli P. Ashmun, of Northampton, asking him to correct a mistake that his young friend had fallen into as to a continuance in a case, and adding: "You have heard me

---

* The date of this poem, December, 1815, is to be remarked; for our accomplished and genial countryman, Dr. Oliver Wendell Holmes, in a lecture on Shelley, delivered in Boston in 1853, after quoting that fine passage from "Alastor,"

> "A swan was there;
> It rose as he approached, and, with strong wings
> Scaling the upward sky, bent its bright course
> High over the immeasurable main,"

added that: "The germs of two familiar and beautiful poems, written on this side of the water, might here be found." One of these poems, though it was not mentioned by name, was understood to be "The Waterfowl," but "The Waterfowl" is of earlier date. The preface to the first edition of "Alastor" is dated December 14, 1815; and the title-page is dated 1816, so that the volume could not have reached this country until some months afterward. Whether it found its way at all to so obscure a village as Plainfield is doubtful. As, however, "The Waterfowl" was not published till 1818, Dr. Holmes's mistake was natural enough, and when his attention was called to it, he corrected it with his usual grace and kindliness.

speak of him often as a man of great worth and intelligence."
At any rate, he remained in Plainfield only eight months,
when he received an invitation to a partnership with a young
lawyer named George H. Ives, of Great Barrington. Ives, in
his communication, says that he had been able to make from a
thousand to twelve hundred dollars a year by his practice, and
that with good office help the sum might easily be increased.
The offer was accepted with alacrity, and on the 3d of October, as he writes in his reminiscences of Miss Catharine M.
Sedgwick, Mr. Bryant made the journey from Cummington,
most likely on foot:

" The woods were in all the glory of autumn, and I well remember, as I passed through Stockbridge, how much I was struck by the
beauty of the smooth, green meadows on the banks of that lovely
river, which winds near the Sedgwick family mansion, the Housatonic,
and whose gently-flowing waters seemed tinged with the gold and
crimson of the trees that overhung them. I admired no less the contrast between this soft scene and the steep, craggy hills that overlooked
it, clothed with their many-colored forests. I had never before seen
the southern part of Berkshire, and congratulated myself on being a
resident of so picturesque a region."

Of these changes of domicile, writing to an old office-mate
in Bridgewater, soon after his arrival in Great Barrington, he
says:

" After leaving Bridgewater, and lounging away three months at
my father's, I went to practice in Plainfield, a town adjoining Cummington. I remained there eight months, but, not being satisfied with
my situation and prospects in that place, I left it for Great Barrington,
a pleasant little village in Berkshire County, on the banks of the
Housatonic, where I am now doing business with a young man of the
name of Ives. This town was originally settled by the Dutch about
the year 1730, and their descendants compose about one tenth of the
present inhabitants.* Its politics are highly Federal. I live about

* Many years later, in an article contributed to the " Landscape Book " (G. P.
Putnam, New York, 1868), he indulged in some curious speculations as to the Dutch

five miles from the line of the State of New York, and ten from that of Connecticut. In Plainfield I found the people rather bigoted in their notions, and almost wholly governed by the influence of a few individuals, who looked upon my coming among them with a good deal of jealousy. Yet I could have made a living out of them in spite of their teeth, had I chosen to stay; but Plainfield was an obscure place, and I had little prospect of ever greatly enlarging the sphere of my business. . . . I came into this place about the 1st of last October; since I have been here I have been wasted to a shadow by a complaint of the lungs,· but am now recovered."

The "complaint of the lungs" this letter refers to was a pulmonary weakness which had already assailed his father and a younger sister. The more serious effects of it, which befell them a few years later, he supposed he averted in his own case by avoiding the use of tea, coffee, and spices of every kind, by eating sparingly of meat, and by taking systematic exercise, in the open air when he could, and when he could not, in his rooms.

In spite of his ill health, Mr. Bryant set to work at his profession with earnestness, resolved to make himself master of

---

origin of the town which are worth quoting: "I have often reflected," he says, "upon what would have been the consequences if the power of England had met the fate that befell the power of Holland, and if that republic had flourished while England fell into decay. The Dutch emigration, of course, would have filled the valley of the Housatonic. Bilderdyk would have been at this moment the favorite poet of the people on that river; the romances of Loosje's would have taken the place of those of Walter Scott; the more devout would have read the sermons of Van der Palm, and the lovers of mirth would have laughed at the jokes of Weiland. So far as concerns the fine arts, the dwellings would have been more picturesque, comfortable Dutch homes, with low rooms and spacious *stoops*, embowered in trees, instead of the green, naked, and tasteless habitations of the Yankees. The painters who sought their subjects among the inhabitants of the valley would have painted interiors after the manner of Teniers, or elaborate and highly finished landscapes, in which fidelity to Nature was more regarded than selection of objects, after the manner of Cuyp." It is to be remarked, as an evidence of Mr. Bryant's retentiveness of memory, that this same paper contains two fresh and vivid descriptions of atmospheric phenomena, thunder-storms followed by strange plays of light, that he had seen forty years before.

it, and to achieve reputation and wealth. Of course, at the outset his practice was trivial—the collection of debts and the trial of small causes in the justice's court; but he was very diligent, and it grew as rapidly as the narrow stage on which he worked permitted. The old debate, which has kept itself alive among lawyers since the days of Cicero, as to the compatibility of literary studies with professional success, was constantly arising in his mind, and he seems to have concluded, at first, that he must abandon poetry altogether, even as a pastime, if he wished to keep up with his colleagues and rivals. But it was not without a struggle. Writing to his recent teacher, Mr. Baylies, he says:

"My dear Sir: I have at length summoned up industry enough to answer yours of the 7th of February last [1817]. I am obliged to you for the kind inquiries you make concerning my situation. You ask whether I am pleased with my profession. Alas! sir, the Muse was my first love, and the remains of that passion, which is not *rooted out* nor chilled into extinction, will always, I fear, cause me to look coldly on the severe beauties of Themis. Yet I tame myself to its labors as well as I can, and have endeavored to discharge with punctuality and attention such of the duties of my profession as I am capable of performing. When I wrote you last I had a partner in business. He has relinquished it to me. I bought him out a few days ago for a mere trifle. The business of the office has hitherto been worth about ten or twelve hundred dollars a year. It will probably be less hereafter, yet I cannot think it will decrease very materially, as I am very well patronized, and have been considered with more kindness than I could have expected. There is another office in town, kept by General Whiting, one of the senators from this district, who has a partner, Mr. Hyde. In 'arguing' cases I have not been very frequently employed. I never spouted in a court-house. While in Hampshire County, I did something in that way, and began to make long speeches at references' and in justices' courts, but since I came here my partner, who was respectable as an advocate, and had the advantage of longer experience, took that trouble off my hands. Since our separation, however, I am trying my hand at it again. . . . Upon the whole, I have every cause to be satisfied with my situation. Place a man where you will, it is an easy thing for him to dream out a more eligible mode of life than the one which falls to his lot. While I have too much of the *mauvaise honte* to seek opportunities of this nature, I have whipped myself up to a desperate determination not to avoid them."

Mr. Baylies encouraged him thus:

"I am pleased that your situation is so promising, and hope that your most sanguine expectations will be realized. It is not surprising that you should meet with difficulty in breaking off all connection with the Muse, as your love has ever met with so favorable a return. I do not, however, condemn your resolution. Poetry is a commodity, I know, not suited to the American market. It will neither help a man to wealth nor office. You recollect, no doubt, the lines of Swift, more applicable to this country than to his:

> "'Not Beggar's brat on bulk begot;
> Not Bastard of a Peddler-Scot,
> Are so disqualified by fate;
> To use in Church or Law or State
> As he whom Phœbus in his ire
> Has blasted with poetic fire.'"

So, a little later in the year, he writes a former fellow-student still hopefully:

"It may be said, with more truth of our profession than of any other, that industry is the road to success—and you, I hope, will be more diligent in the pursuit of knowledge than I was, or even seemed to be; for, while I appeared to study, I was half the time only dreaming with my eyes open. As essential to these habits of diligence, you are doubtless as well aware as I am that one should make himself satisfied with the profession he has chosen. Our profession may be a hard taskmaster, but its rewards are proportioned to its labors, which is as much as any way of life has to say for itself."

But, while he was striving to keep his business well in hand, and for that purpose to detach his mind completely from literature, the Fates were arranging it otherwise. Some time in June his father wrote to him from Boston that Mr. Willard

Phillips (an old Hampshire friend) "desired him to contribute something to his new review." " Prose or poetry will be
equally acceptable. I wish," the prudent doctor adds, " if you
have leisure, you would comply, as it might be the means
of introducing you to notice in the capital. Those who contribute are generally known to the *literati* in and about Boston." The younger Bryant was not tempted or was too busy
to reply, and so the ambitious father undertook to push the
matter in his own way. While his son was yet at Bridgewater, he had discovered the manuscripts of " Thanatopsis,"
the " Fragment," and a few other poems carefully hidden away
in a desk. A tradition in the family runs that, when he read
the first of these, he carried it to a lady in the neighborhood,
with tears streaming down his cheeks, and exclaimed : " Oh!
read that; it is Cullen's." Mrs. Howe, in her reminiscences,
relates that, " during Cullen's residence in Bridgewater, Dr.
Bryant brought us two manuscript poems—' Thanatopsis ' and
' The Waterfowl.' * We were greatly delighted with them, and
so was the father, who enjoyed our commendations of them
very much." He was so much delighted with them that he
resolved to carry them to Boston, to subject them to the judgment of his friend Phillips, whose new literary enterprise,
called " The North American Review," though but recently
established, had already acquired some name. It was the bantling of a club of young men, mostly lawyers of a scribbling
turn, who, in the winter of 1814–'15, proposed " to foster American genius, and, by independent criticism, instruct and guide
the public taste." Their first project had been a bimonthly
publication, but, on the return of Mr. William Tudor † from
Europe, full of the notion of a quarterly, the two plans were
combined in " The North American Review." The first number appeared in May, 1815. Mr. Tudor acted as editor till

---

* This is a lapse of memory. " The Waterfowl " was not then written, as we have
seen. It was the Inscription.

† Author of the Life of James Otis.

1817, when it passed entirely into the hands of a club, of which
the chief members were Richard H. Dana, Edward T. Channing, and Willard Phillips. President Kirkland and several
of the professors of Harvard College promoted its establishment. Dana, the son of Chief Justice Dana, was an ardent
lover of poetry, as well as a fine critic; Channing, a brother
of the more famous William Ellery Channing, was a cultivated
scholar, who two years afterward became Boylston Professor
of Rhetoric at Cambridge; and Phillips was a tutor in the
college, but later in life a judge of probate and a distinguished
writer of law books. They were all deeply imbued with the
spirit of that naturalistic revolution which was taking place in
the literature of England, and which they hoped to infuse into
American literature. Dr. Bryant carried his wares to Phillips, because Phillips some years before (1804) had been a
country neighbor. As "Thanatopsis," in the first draft, was
full of erasures and interlineations, he had transcribed it; but
the other pieces were in their original state. Mr. Phillips
was not at home when he called, and so he left his package,
with his name. When it was put into the editor's hands, he
read the poems with an absorbed interest, saw at once their
superiority to what he had been in the habit of receiving, and
he hastened with them to his fellows in Cambridge, to take
their opinions. They listened attentively to his reading of
them, when Dana, at the close, remarked, with a quiet smile:
"Ah! Phillips, you have been imposed upon; no one on this
side of the Atlantic is capable of writing such verses." It is
easy to imagine the surprise with which these editors—whose
best contributions before had been indifferent translations from
Martial or Boileau, or original pieces merely imitative of
some reigning English favorite—listened to the sombre but
majestic roll, as of the sea, in "Thanatopsis," or to the low,
soft music, as of the wind through innumerable leaves, in the
"Fragment." Dana, indeed, having just written a review of
Mr. Allston's "Sylphs of the Season," in which he spoke of it
as "a cause of grief and mortification" that it was the only ex-

ception in a wide waste of feebleness and nullity,* we can not wonder at his exclamation.   But Phillips rejoined, with some spirit, that he had not been imposed upon.   "I know," he said, "the gentleman who wrote the best of them, at least, very well; an old acquaintance of mine—Dr. Bryant—at this moment sitting in the State-House in Boston as Senator from Hampshire County."   "Then," responded Dana, "I must have a look at him," and, putting on his clogs and his cloak, he trudged over to Boston.   "Arrived at the senate," said Mr. Dana in a conversation afterward with the Rev. Robert C. Waterston, "I caused the doctor to be pointed out to me.   I looked at him with profound attention and interest; and, while I saw a man of striking presence, the stamp of genius seemed to me to be wanting.   It is a good head, I said to myself, but I do not see ' Thanatopsis' in it," and he went back a little disappointed. Mr. Waterston, in communicating the incident, thinks it "remarkable for a penetration and originality characteristic of Mr. Dana's sagacious judgment."

The two poems were published in September, but prefixed to " Thanatopsis" were four stanzas on the subject of Death † —which, though accidentally contained in the same bundle, had no connection with it, and were not intended for publication.   Much inferior in every way to the main poem, this unhappy juxtaposition may have prevented many readers from perusing it; at any rate it attracted no remark in the contemporary journals.   But in the immediate circle of the reviewers the excellence of both poems was acknowlegded and extolled, and the father and son were at once solicited to become regular contributors.   Mr. Phillips, addressing the son, in December, says: "I recollect the epitome of your present self, and with pleasure renew the acquaintance through your father. Your ' Fragment' was exceedingly liked here.   Among others,

* This review appeared in the same number of " The North American Review " in which " Thanatopsis " and the " Fragment " were printed—September, 1817.

† Written at the time of his dejection, described in chapter vi, *ante* p. 109.   See them in Poetical Works, vol. i, notes.

Mr. Channing, the clergyman (William Ellery Channing),
spoke very highly of it, and all the best judges say that it and
your father's ' Thanatopsis ' are the very best poetry that has
been published in this country." Whether this was the first
intimation the younger Bryant received of the uses that had
been made of his poems we cannot now tell; probably the
" Review " had preceded this letter, for in October I find that
he was instrumental in getting up a club to subscribe for it;
and, in forwarding the subscription, says: " I have one of the
numbers in my possession," which it is to be presumed was
that containing his own handiwork. On January 9, 1818, writing to his father, he observes, incidentally :

" We have subscribed for ' The North American Review ' here. I
wrote Mr. Phillips for it, and he answered me. He gave you the
credit, if it can be called by that name, of writing the ' Thanatopsis.'
I have sent you a correct copy of my version of ' The Fragment of
Simonides,' and another little poem which I wrote while at Bridgewater,* which you may get inserted if you please in that work. I
would contribute something in prose if I knew on what subject to
write." †

In February the father answered, from Boston : " I handed
the poems you sent me to Mr. Phillips, who has since informed
me that they were approved and admired. With respect to
" Thanatopsis," I know not what led Phillips to imagine I

---

* " To a Friend on his Marriage," not printed till March, 1818, in the same number with the " Version of Simonides," and " The Waterfowl."

† Mr. Bryant's interest in the " Review " increased from this time, and writing
to Phillips, April 13th, he says : " If your work sustains its present character, it will
soon acquire a reputation not easily to be shaken. A good Review has been a de-
sideratum in our literature. The public taste requires to be guided and reformed.
Our countrymen are assisted in forming their opinions concerning the numerous
modern publications imported into this country from Great Britain by the judgment
of the critics of that island. But, with respect to our native works, we have hitherto
had no such guide on which we could safely rely. Your work with its present promise, I think, will supply what we so much want, and constitute a kind of literary censorship, which, assigning to merit its just applause, and exposing unsupported pretensions, shall give a proper direction to our national tastes."

wrote it, unless it was because it was transcribed by me ; I left it at his house when he was absent, and did not see him afterward. I have, however, set him right on that subject, and told him what you said about writing for the ' Review.' " But if Phillips was set right others were not, for Edward Channing, nearly a year later, still refers to the poem as Dr. Bryant's, and Mr. Dana was under the same impression in 1821, when Mr. Bryant first went to Boston.

These small literary successes seem to have renewed Mr. Bryant's desire to remove from the narrow and sterile field in which he was to the livelier atmosphere of Boston. His father remarks, in reply to an intimation of the kind, that, " with regard to removing to Boston, there are some objections, one of which is that the county of Suffolk is crowded with lawyers. Still I think an industrious young man of talents and enterprise would in a few years force his way into notice among them. But will it not be better for you to continue where you are a few years, and lay a solid foundation, while you have your time to yourself without interruption? I, however, do not wish to influence your determination in respect to the disposition of your own affairs. Every young man who intends to make his way in the world and figure among his contemporaries must rely at last upon his own talent and exertions."

Mr. Phillips was too vigilant an editor to be put off with mere promises of contributions, and already had written to the younger Bryant, urging him to do something in prose, suggesting that a recent collection of American poetry by one Solyman Brown would furnish a good subject. The young lawyer, though somewhat inclined to undertake it, did not suppose himself in possession of the requisite materials. He applied to his father, February 20th, in regard to it, thus :

"DEAR FATHER: If I can procure the book he speaks of, I will undertake the subject mentioned by Mr. Phillips. To collect much further information than I at present possess, my situation here does not afford me many facilities. This place is like most other villages in this country—there are not many who suffer an excessive passion for books to interfere with other employments or amusements, and they encumber their houses with no overgrown collections. This scarcity of books, indeed, occasions me much inconvenience after having been accustomed all my life to have access to very respectable libraries. Most of the American poets of much note, I believe, I have read: Dwight, Barlow, Trumbull, Humphreys, Honeywood, Clifton, Paine. The works of Hopkins I have never met with. I have seen Philip Freneau's writings, and some things by Francis Hopkinson. There was a Dr. Ladd, if I am not mistaken in the name, of Rhode Island, who, it seems, was much celebrated in his time for his poetical talent, of whom I have seen hardly anything, and another, Dr. Church, a Tory at the beginning of the Revolution, who was compelled to leave the country, and some of whose satirical verses which I have heard recited possess considerable merit as specimens of forcible and glowing invective. I have read most of Mrs. Morton's poems, and turned over a volume of stale and senseless rhymes by Mrs. Warren. Before the time of these writers, some of whom are still alive, and the rest belong to the generation which has just passed away, I imagine that we could hardly be said to have any poetry of our own, and indeed it seems to me that American poetry, such as it is, may justly enough be said to have had its rise with that knot of Connecticut poets, Trumbull and others, most of whose works appeared about the time of the Revolution. Any facts which may occur to you on the subject, of which I might, perhaps, be unaware or ignorant, I should be obliged to you to suggest to me. I may visit Cummington before next June. I remember the 'American Review and Monthly Magazine,' published some eighteen or twenty years ago—a book which you have—contained considerable information on this subject, and some biographies.

"The Address you mention it is out of my power to send to you, as it was printed in the Berkshire 'Star,' and I have not the paper in which it appeared. It was hasty and imperfect, and I was reluctant to suffer it to be published, and should not have consented but for the solicitations of Mr. Wheeler, our parson. The good man was so importunate and so confident that it would be good on account of the quarter from which it came, it not being very common for young lawyers in this part of the country to harangue upon such subjects, that I could not well refuse him, but stipulated that the production should appear without my name.   It was, however, by some mistake, printed as the work of William C. Bryant, to which was carefully subjoined *attorney-at-law*."

The Address referred to in the last paragraph was one he had been requested to prepare for the Bible Society of Great Barrington, before which it was delivered on the 29th of January, and the next week published in the local paper of Stockbridge.   His general theme was " The Bible," of which he said : " Its sacredness awes me, and I approach it with the same sort of reverential feeling that an ancient Hebrew might be supposed to feel who was about to touch the ark of God with unhallowed hands."   His special topic, however, was the political and social influences of the Scriptures, and he tried to show, by glancing at the moral condition of the nations, that wherever they were allowed a free circulation among the people the great interests of human civilization were rapidly advanced.   In style it was exceedingly simple and concise, but, as a whole, showed a ready familiarity with the state of society in different parts of the globe.   This address made him more widely known to the people of Berkshire, and was of considerable advantage to him in his profession.   But his growing repute in law and literature seems not yet to have extinguished his military aspirations, for in a note to Baylies, dated April 14th, he says :

" The great folks at Washington, I see, make themselves pretty busy with the difficulties between this country and Spain.   If we should have a war with that country, and one could get a commission in the army, he might, perhaps, before it was ended, have an opportunity of garnishing his private history with a few South American adventures."

In the postscript he modestly asks :

" Do you read ' The North American Review ' ?   In the number for September (I believe), 1817, perhaps in the preceding number, there are some lines entitled 'Thanatopsis' and 'A Fragment,' by an old friend of yours, and in the number for March, 1818, three more 'Pair of varses' from the same hand."

At this time Mr. Bryant was called by his business to the city òf New York; it was his first visit to any considerable town, and it would be agreeable to know the impressions it made upon his mind; but the following brief letter to his father, dated June 20, 1818, is the only reference to the subject that remains:

"DEAR FATHER: Yours of the 11th instant I received on the 13th by my uncle, whom I had little time to see, as I was then just setting off to attend a court in Sheffield. I am obliged to you for the concern you express respecting my health. It has been considerably improved by my journey to New York. I was absent a fortnight; we were three days coming up the river, beating up one day and night against a furious head-wind, during most of which time I was obliged to lie flat on my back in my berth to prevent sea-sickness, of which I felt some qualms. While in New York I kept running about continually, and this constant exercise, together with being rocked and tumbled about in the vessel, operated on me as a restorative, and since my return my pain in the side and night-sweats have left me. I believe my affairs will not permit my visiting Cummington at present. My several absences of late render it proper that I should now give a little attention to my office, and, as I have taken off the tether from Major Ives and let him loose into the field of practice again, it has become necessary that I should use some diligence to prevent any part of that share of practice which I have obtained from falling into his hands. Perhaps, however, I may see Cummington some time in the course of the summer or autumn. I have written a review of Mr. Brown's book, and forwarded it to the publishers of 'The North American Review.' Luckily, I found the volume in this neighborhood, and escaped throwing away my money on it. It is poor stuff."

The review, called "An Essay on American Poetry," was printed in July. It was the author's first elaborate effort in prose, and while the style is on the whole graceful and finished, the judgments, though still somewhat influenced by prevailing opinions, are sensible and independent. In a very quiet manner the author dismisses the poetical pretensions of the rhymers who were then in vogue. He does not depreciate their products unjustly, or indulge in the slightest bitterness of criticism; on the contrary, his appreciations are more liberal than any we should now express, saying the best things he could of each writer; but, nevertheless, like a judge giving final sentence, he banishes the entire set to the limbo of oblivion. It is the coming poet, in fact, unconsciously disposing of his predecessors, and clearing away the rubbish to make room for others better qualified to do honor to the nascent genius of their country. Its principal effect is to show us the limitations in which our poetic literature was compelled to begin under the influences of an older literature in the same language, and from which it was almost impossible for tyros and stammerers to escape. Mr. Bryant's one demand is for a spirit of greater independence, for less imitation of form, for a more hearty reliance upon native instinct and inspiration; in a word, for greater freedom, greater simplicity, and greater truth.

What effect this quiet dethroning of much-worshipped little idols produced on the popular mind we are not informed; but Mr. Channing and his colleagues highly approved its tone, and said so to the author, who answered, September 18th, as follows:

"I am much gratified with the favorable reception that my contribution to 'The North American Review' has met with from the proprietors of that work, as well as with the obliging manner in which it has been communicated to me, and feel myself happy if I may be esteemed to have done anything to raise the literature of my country. In the mean time I may occasionally attempt something for your journal, and lend such assistance as might be expected from one situated as I am, *Musis procul, et Permesside lympha*, distant from books and literary opportunities, and occupied with a profession which ought to engage most of my attention. I have tried to write an essay for your next number, but could not satisfy myself.*   There is hardly any spot in the department of essays unoccupied.   With respect to writing another review, I will be contented with such a work as you may think proper to mention—provided you do not set me too diffi-cult a task.   I enclose you a small poem which I found by me, and which you may give a place in your journal, if you think it will do."

The poem enclosed was " The Yellow Violet," written some years before.   It was not published in the " Review," however, owing to the discontinuance of the department of " original poetry."   Mr. Channing, advising him of the change, takes occasion to commend his verses very highly, and to suggest that he ought to collect his fugitive pieces into a volume.   Mr. Bryant's reply (March 25, 1819) shows the moderate estimate that he put upon his poetical labors :

" Your favor of the 8th inst. has been received.   To commenda-tion so flattering as you are pleased to bestow on me, coming from such a quarter, I hardly know what to say.   Had you seen more of those attempts of mine, concerning which you express yourself so fa-vorably, your opinion would, perhaps, have been different.   The lines I sent you, you are at liberty to dispose of as you think proper ; but do not, by any means, take any trouble to make a place for them in your journal, and, above all, do not let them appear if they are not worthy of it. . . . If I can procure the ' Backwoodsman ' (a poem by J. K. Paulding) at any of the neighboring book-stores, I will review it for your June number.   If I do not get it, I will send some article for the miscellaneous department. . . . I may, perhaps, some time or other, venture a little collection of poetry in print, for I do not write much —and, should it be favorably received, it may give me courage to do something more.   In the mean time, I cannot be too grateful for the

---

* The essay on " The Happy Temperament," published in No. 9, p. 206, of the " Review," in which he tries to show that, while cheerful dispositions are to be cul-tivated, a true sensibility to the evils and sorrows of life is not only the cause of philanthropic exertion, but the source of peculiar satisfactions, which give balance and dignity to the character.   Similar thoughts are expressed by Coleridge in a son-net to Bowles.   The essay is worth reading as a clew to his own prevailing serious-ness.

distant voice of kindness that cheers me in the pursuit of those studies which I have nobody here to share with me."

Paulding's book he was unable to get, and so he did not review it, but he sent instead an essay on the use of " Trisyllabic Feet in Iambic Verse," which discloses how close and critical a student he was of the mere technique of his art. It was written, I suspect, some time before (probably in 1815), when he was breaking away from the school of Pope and adopting the broader methods of the later English school. He contends in it that the introduction of an occasional anapest in iambic measures, though seemingly irregular, really adds to the vivacity, if not the beauty, of the lines. He cites the older English authors—Shakespeare, the dramatists, and Milton—in proof of his position, alleging, moreover, that among the more modern writers the most successful are those who are freest from the trammels of the Queen Anne period.*

Meanwhile Mr. Bryant lost none of his interest as a good citizen in the local affairs of the town in which he lived. On the 9th of March, 1819, he was elected one of its tithing men, whose duties consisted in keeping order in the churches, and enforcing the observance of the Sabbath. I may add that soon afterward he was chosen town clerk by a vote of 82 out of 102. His principal function in this capacity was to keep account of the town's doings, such as the appointment of selectmen, surveyors of the highway, fence viewers, field drivers, and hog reeves. One may still see his records at Great Barrington, where they form an object of considerable curiosity to summer visitors. Written in a neat and flexible hand, it is remarked that almost the only blot is where he registers his own marriage, and the only interlineation where in giving the birth of his first child he had left out the name of the mother. These archives are a curious evidence of the extremely simple and primitive way in which New England towns were former-

---

* Wordsworth is not referred to throughout, which is one reason I have for thinking it was written some time before it was printed.

ly governed.   Each one was a little Democratic Republic, the people of which came together annually on the call of the selectmen, through the constable, to choose the several officers required to execute the laws, to fix the rates of local taxation, and then to adjourn for the rest of the year.   His salary as clerk was five dollars *per annum*, at which rate he held the place for the period of five years—all the time that he remained in the village.   A more important dignity, conferred upon him by the Governor of the Commonwealth, was that of Justice of the Peace, empowered to hear and try small causes as an inferior local court.   In this character, it appears, he performed the marriage ceremony twice, for contracting parties who objected to the service of the usual clergyman because they differed from him in religious opinion.   An old gentleman still living makes it a boast that he was "jined to his first old woman by Squire Bryant."

CHAPTER NINTH.

THE FIRST COLLECTION OF POEMS.

A. D. 1820, 1821.

WE have seen Dr. Bryant, the poet's father, complaining, in a letter on a former page, of over-exertion and impaired health. A hereditary weakness of the lungs, made worse by exposure to the bleak atmosphere of the hills, had long given his family cause for anxiety. His own skill, aided by that of Dr. Thatcher and other distinguished physicians of Boston, whom he knew, enabled him to alleviate the more painful symptoms. It was, however, only for a time. A visit made to the sea-shore in 1819, in which Cullen was his companion, brought no relief. On his return he was confined to his house, and in the spring of 1820 to his bed. Had he been able to command means and leisure for a sojourn in a more congenial climate, he might perhaps have been saved; but a life of almost incessant jogging, by night and day, in all weathers, over mountain roads that seemed rather the channels of torrents than ways of travel, had exhausted his vitality. He lingered until the 20th of March, when he died, a comparatively young man still, being only in the fifty-third year of his age. Even at this distance of time, one cannot but feel a profound regret that he who had so carefully tended the early development of his boy, and taken so natural a pride in the beginnings of his success, should not have lived to witness the full bloom of his genius and fame.

The event William, as he was now called, communicated to an aunt in these words:

<blockquote>
"CUMMINGTON, March 22, 1820.
</blockquote>

"DEAR AUNT CHARITY: I sit down to give you the melancholy news of the death of my father. He expired on Sunday, the 20th of this month, between the hours of seven and eight in the evening. It was not his fate to wait the gradual extinction of life which is the usual termination of the disorder under which he labored, and which would probably have carried him off soon. . . . I never saw anybody die before, but, judging as well as I am able, I thought his exit on the whole more easy than usual. . . . Let us hope that after all his sufferings our dear departed friend has gone to a happier world. A man so honest and upright in his conduct, so gentle in his temper, so forgiving of injuries, so full of offices of humanity—to which he sacrificed his health and perhaps his life—must be of those whom God rewards with felicity. Indeed, if it is not so, I think there is little hope for any one of the human race.

<blockquote>
"I am, dear aunt,
"Your affectionate nephew,
"WM. C. BRYANT."
</blockquote>

It was a blow that fell with great severity upon all the children, whom it deprived of their main protector and support, but upon none of them with a more crushing force than upon Cullen, who had been so intimately associated with his father from a tender age. The memory of this loss clung to him for many years. Some time before, he had written a "Hymn to Death"—not in the old querulous vein, but celebrating his triumphs over the lusty Leviathans who trample and consume the poor and weak ones of the earth—which he now recalled, in order to change its tone of praise into one of lamentation. For

<blockquote>
"He is in his grave who taught my youth
The art of verse, and in the bud of life
Offer'd me to the Muses—"
</blockquote>

And, again, eight years later, when speaking in "The Past" of

> "—earlier friends, the good, the kind,
> The venerable form, the exalted mind,"

he was thinking of

> " Him by whose kind, paternal side I sprung."

Faithful to his vow of not allowing his poetic impulses to interfere with his professional pursuits, Mr. Bryant does not appear to have written anything in verse save the fragment called " The Burial Place," begun and broken off in 1819, since he entered upon his practice in 1816. What few pieces he sent to " The North American Review " were taken from his scrap-book. But now, in 1820, his poetic susceptibilities were assailed from several sides at once. Soon after his father's death, while he was yet full of the sentiment it inspired, an appeal was made to him by the Unitarians, in aid of a collection of Hymns they projected. Mr. Henry D. Sewall, the editor, applied to Miss Catharine M. Sedgwick, of Stockbridge, to use her efforts in his behalf, and the result she communicates to her brother Robert, of New York, in a letter dated May 17, 1820:

"' I wish,' she says, 'you would give my best regards to Mr. Sewall, and tell him that I have had great success in my agency. I sent for Mr. Bryant last week, and he called to see me on his return from court. I told him Mr. Sewall had commissioned me to request some contributions from him to a collection of Hymns, and he said, without any hesitation, that he was obliged to Mr. Sewall, and would with great pleasure comply with his request. He has a charming countenance, and modest but not bashful manners. I made him promise to come and see us shortly. He seemed gratified; and, if Mr. Sewall has reason to be obliged to me (which I certainly think he has), I am doubly obliged by an opportunity of securing the acquaintance of so interesting a man.' "*

---

* Forty-four years after this Mr. Bryant printed, without publishing, a small volume of his Hymns, and sent a copy to Miss Sedgwick, who, in her reply, says : " My dear Mr. Bryant : But for your prohibition, I should at once, on the receipt of my precious little ' Hymns ' have sent to you my earnest thanks, and told you how vividly

This was the first time Miss Sedgwick had seen the poet; and Mr. Bryant, who never ceased to honor all the family for their virtues, and to be grateful to them for their attentions to him when he was quite unknown to the rest of the world, recalls his introduction to her in the reminiscences he wrote for her " Memoirs ":

" ' At that time,' he says, referring to his first arrival at Great Barrington, 'I had no acquaintance with the Sedgwick family; but the youngest of them, Charles Sedgwick, a man of most genial and engaging manners and agreeable conversation, as well as of great benevolence and worth, was a member of the Berkshire bar, and by him, a year or two afterward, I was introduced to the others, who, from the first, seemed to take pleasure in being kind to me. I remember very well the appearance of Miss Sedgwick at that period of her life. She was well formed, slightly inclining to plumpness, with regular features, eyes beaming with benevolence, a pleasing smile, a soft voice, and gentle and captivating manners. The portrait of her by Ingham, painted about that time, or a little later, although not regarded, I think, by the family as a perfect likeness, yet brings to my mind her image as I saw her then, with that mingled expression of thoughtfulness and benignity with which her features were informed.' "

At the instance of this amiable and accomplished family the young lawyer was called to pass through an ordeal by which every promising young professional man was formerly tried in this country—the delivery of a Fourth of July oration. It was spoken at Stockbridge, and with some success. Mr. William Pitt Palmer, many years afterward, in 1858, wrote of it, thus: "It was the first time," he says, "I ever saw the poet. He spoke from the pulpit of the Old Church; his delivery was modest and graceful. I got a position in the gallery near the speaker, and have not yet forgotten how fine, large, and promi-

they recall the day when the young poet, one of the first objects of my hero-worship, offered me in my dear home the six hymns ; and but for boring you, I would have described the color and form of his cloak, and the fire and expression of his countenance, but—"

nent his forehead appeared to me under the brown locks that
curled around it. He was already looked upon as a person of
unusual literary attainments—one of the first botanists of Berkshire, one of the best classical scholars in all Massachusetts,
and a poet *facile princeps* on this side of the Atlantic." This
address, though replete with patriotic sentiment, would not, I
fear, pass muster among the models of fervid anniversary eloquence. Distinguished by its purity of style and solid gravity
of thought, it must have fallen coldly upon the ears of the audience if they were at all accustomed to the turgidness and
inflation characteristic of such occasions. In one respect it is
still interesting to us, and that is, its indignant protest against
the " Missouri Compromise," a measure of contemporary Federal legislation, described as "extending the dangerous and
detestable practice of enslaving men into territory yet unpol-
luted with the curse." It was the earliest utterance of his
convictions not only in regard to the character of slavery, but
in regard to those party bargains euphuized as compromises,
which transact with evil, and debauch and degrade the public
conscience. Yet the raw simplicity of the country poet and
lawyer is seen in the expression of his belief that the people of
Missouri would have too much good sense and kindness of
heart to accept the pernicious privilege granted them by the
nation.

Mr. Dana's project of a periodical, to be called " The Idle
Man," and to consist of "poetry, essays, criticisms, and historical and biographical sketches," enlisted Mr. Bryant's
warmest interest from the beginning. As early as May, 1821,
Mr. Channing asked his assistance for it, suggesting that "a
literary frolic now and then is the best restorative for a conscientious, but overworked and jaded, attorney." In reply,
Mr. Bryant put " The Yellow Violet " at Mr. Dana's disposal,
and enclosed another piece, " Green River," which he had
picked out of his waste-basket, adding that his attorney-
ship "was not so absorbing that he might not turn off some
trifles occasionally," while "a connection with 'The Idle

Man' would be of more honor to him than he could be of
service to it."

When the first number of "The Idle Man" appeared,* he
wrote Dana that he was delighted with it, and "should think
better of the world if it liked it, too. It is an attempt to bring
us back to the purer and better feelings of our nature. When
I saw one of the articles," he goes on to say, "headed 'Mr.
Kean'" (an acute and powerful criticism of Kean's acting), "I
wished you had chosen a subject more likely to be popular;
but, before I had finished reading it, you had interested
me in it so much that I would not have exchanged it for
any other.† It is not possible for me in this retirement to
judge of the progress your work is making in the literary
world, but all whom I have seen that have read it speak
favorably of it. You must suffer the world to get in love
with it gradually, if you mean that they shall remain attached
to it long. I feel a strong confidence that it will succeed."
This confidence grew as the successive numbers appeared.
Mr. Bryant not only contributed some of his best poems
to it, such as "Green River," "A Winter Piece," "The
West Wind," "The Burial Place," "A Walk at Sunset," but
he commended it warmly in the newspapers and to private
friends.

If Mr. Bryant's self-imposed poetic abstinence was interrupted by the demand of his denomination for hymns, and
by his interest in Dana's enterprise, it was completely routed
by an enemy from another quarter—a pair of bright eyes.
Not long after his settlement in Great Barrington, at one
of the village "sociables" he met a Miss Fanny Fairchild,
who seems to have impressed him deeply from the first moment. She was the daughter of well-to-do and respectable
country people, who had cultivated a farm on the Seekonk,

* "The Idle Man." New York: John Wiley, 1821.
† The papers of "The Idle Man" have since been printed in Mr. Dana's collected works.

a tributary of Green River, but who were now dead, having been carried off almost together by a fever.* Their demise broke up the household, and Fanny became alternately an inmate of the homes of her married sisters, where her cheerful and social temper and unwearying industry made her an ever-welcome guest. She was in the nineteenth year of her age, "a very pretty blonde, small in person, with light-brown hair, gray eyes, a graceful shape, a dainty foot, transparent and delicate hands, and a wonderfully frank and sweet expression of face." The poet was drawn to her by the triple attractions of her orphanage, her good sense, and her loveliness; but the depth of his attachment was not revealed to him until the object of it was called to accompany a sister on her removal to East Bloomfield, in the Genesee Valley of New York. It was then an extreme limit of western emigration, and as, in default of canals, railways, and steamboats, her journey thither was made in high covered wagons, over bad corduroy roads, through an almost unbroken wilderness, and often exposed to the molestations of wild Indians or wilder white borderers, it was, of course, slow and tedious. The prolonged absence it required awoke her timid admirer to a painful sense of his loneliness. He began to pity himself very much in rhyme, and to pour out little ditties of complaint, yet full of tender recollections and yearnings. These are too unpremeditated and personal to be reproduced; but I may say that they differ much from the strains of a greener age— are calmer, less fluctuating, more assured in tone, and well represented by "Oh, Fairest of the Rural Maids!" which is the only one of them the author has cared to print.†

* The name of the mother's family was Pope, and it was connected in some way with Alexander Pope, the poet.

† Poetical Works, vol. i, p. 39. Of the others, the following may be given as a specimen :

> " Though summer sun and freshening shower
> Have decked my love's deserted bower,
> Though bees about the threshold come
> Among the scented blooms to hum,

On the return of Miss Fairchild from the West, the young couple engaged themselves to be married; and how earnestly and seriously they entered into the new relation is shown by a prayer, which they seem to have uttered together as a sort of betrothal vow to God. It was found among Mr. Bryant's papers, never having been read, probably, by any eyes but theirs until after his death.

"May Almighty God mercifully take care of our happiness here and hereafter. May we ever continue constant to each other, and mindful of our mutual promises of attachment and truth. In due time, if it be the will of Providence, may we become more nearly connected with each other, and together may we lead a long, happy, and innocent life, without any diminution of affection till we die. May there never be any jealousy, distrust, coldness, or dissatisfaction between us—nor occasion for any—nothing but kindness, forbearance, mutual confidence, and attention to each other's happiness. And that we may be less unworthy of so great a blessing, may we be assisted to cultivate all the benign and charitable affections and offices not only toward each other, but toward our neighbors, the human race, and all the creatures of God. And in all things wherein we have done ill, may we properly repent our error, and may God forgive us and dispose us to do better. When at last we are called to render back the life we have received, may our deaths be peaceful,

---

Though there the bindweed climbs and weaves
Her spotted veil of flowers and leaves;
Though sweet the spot, I cannot bear
To gaze a single instant there.

" Ah, there no longer deigns to dwell
The peerless One, I love so well,
And vainly may I linger near
The musick of her step to hear,
And catch from spheres of azure light
The glance my heart has proved too bright.
Fair is the spot—I own it fair,
But cannot look an instant there.

" Great Barrington, 1819."

and may God take us to his bosom. All which may he grant for the sake of the Messiah.

"GREAT BARRINGTON, 1820."

If ever solemn supplication to heaven was answered on earth, this one assuredly was, by a long life of reciprocal love, esteem, confidence, and helpfulness.

On the 11th of June, 1821, they were married at the house of the bride's sister, Mrs. Henderson,* and a few days later the groom communicated to his mother the facts and embarrassments of the occasion in this whimsical way: †

"DEAR MOTHER: I hasten to send you the melancholy intelligence of what has lately happened to me.

"Early on the evening of the eleventh day of the present month I was at a neighboring house in this village. Several people of both sexes were assembled in one of the apartments, and three or four others, with myself, were in another. At last came in a little elderly gentleman, pale, thin, with a solemn countenance, pleuritic voice, hooked nose, and hollow eyes. It was not long before we were summoned to attend in the apartment where he and the rest of the company were gathered. We went in and took our seats; the little elderly gentleman with the hooked nose prayed, and we all stood up. When he had finished, most of us sat down. The gentleman with the hooked nose then muttered certain cabalistical expressions which I was too much frightened to remember, but I recollect that at the conclusion I was given to understand that I was married to a young lady of the name of Frances Fairchild, whom I perceived standing by my side, and I

---

* The house is still standing in Great Barrington, an object of some interest to strangers. Fifty-five years after the event recorded in the text, Mr. Bryant and one of his daughters visited the place. He walked about it for some time, saying nothing; but, as he was about to turn away, he exclaimed: "There is not a spire of grass her foot has not touched," and his eyes filled with tears. His wife had then been dead nearly ten years.

† It was Mr. Bryant's duty, as town clerk, to publish the bans of marriage in the church, which was generally done by reading them aloud; but in his own case he pinned the required notice on the door of the vestibule and kept carefully out of sight.

hope in the course of a few months to have the pleasure of introducing to you as your daughter-in-law, which is a matter of some interest to the poor girl, who has neither father nor mother in the world.

"I have not 'played the fool and married an Ethiop for the jewel
in her ear.'* I looked only for goodness of heart, an ingenuous and
affectionate disposition, a good understanding, etc., and the character
of my wife is too frank and single-hearted to suffer me to fear that I
may be disappointed. I do myself wrong; I did not look for these
nor any other qualities, but they trapped me before I was aware, and
now I am married in spite of myself.

"Thus the current of destiny carries us all along. None but a
madman would swim against the stream, and none but a fool would
exert himself to swim with it. The best way is to float quietly with
the tide. So much for philosophy—now to business.

"Your affectionate son,　　WILLIAM."

When this singular epistle, in which his pride seems to be
awkwardly seeking excuses for a humiliating surrender, reached
the good mother, she is said to have exclaimed: "He make a
fool of himself! He never has done so yet, and couldn't if he
tried."

A few months after his marriage, Mr. Bryant was surprised
by a communication from the Secretary of the Phi Beta Kappa
Society of Harvard College, Mr. W. J. Spooner, requesting
him, "by a unanimous vote of the fraternity," to deliver the
usual poetical address at the next Commencement. At first
he shrank from the task, but at length consented to undertake it, although with many misgivings and doubts. In his
answer to Mr. Spooner, April 26th, he said:

"SIR: The honor thus conferred upon me is as unlooked for as it
is flattering; I did not even know that I was a member of your society till I was informed of it by your letter. I have concluded to accept the appointment, and discharge myself of it as well as I can.

"I have never attended an anniversary of the Phi Beta Kappa So-

* An expression used in a previous letter of his sister.

ciety, and must profess myself entirely unacquainted with the order of proceedings on that occasion. Of the general character of the performances I know only so much as might be gathered from reading a few of them which have occasionally fallen in my way. As you have kindly offered to give me any information I may desire on these subjects, I shall be obliged to you if you will mark out for me such a brief general outline as may prevent me from doing anything *outré* or getting foul of an interdicted subject."

Mr. Spooner responded in several pages, instructing him as to the sort of address expected of him, the probable composition of the audience, the time, place, and manner of delivery, and hinting also at the success or non-success of former poets. Mr. Willard Phillips wrote him a long epistle of admonition, particularly urging him to pay attention to his elocution. In Mr. Phillips's opinion nearly everything depended upon that ; and he thought that an indifferent poem, if it could be spoken in a fine manner, would achieve an undoubted success.

During the summer the leisure left him by his professional work was devoted to the preparation of this poem, which he found more of a labor than he had anticipated. "The composition of my address," he wrote to a friend, "owing partly to my having written but little, and partly to the difficulty of the stanza I have selected (the Spenserian), has come near to making me sick." Nevertheless, it was finished, and in August he went to Boston to fulfil his engagement. It was his first visit, of which we have any account, to a much-longed-for city, and it would be pleasing to learn his impressions of it and its people. But the following letter, addressed to his wife, August 25th, is the only one preserved out of his correspondence of the time, and I give it at length as characteristic :

"MY DEAR FRANCES: You observed in what an elegant style I went from Great Barrington to Sheffield. Seated on a rough board laid on the top of a crazy wagon, whose loose sides kept swinging from right to left, with a colored fellow at my right hand and a dirty old rascal before me who kept spitting all the way. I was jolted over a road that filled my mouth and ears and clothes with dust, and which the mulatto observed was 'very much like de desert of Arabey.' About half past eleven in the evening we arrived at Hartford. At half past six the next morning I was on my way to Boston, and about twelve o'clock at night I saw the rows of lamps along the great western avenue, and beyond them those of the Cambridge and Charleston bridges. We entered Boston over this great western avenue, which is not yet finished. I am now at Mrs. Vose's. Yesterday, in the afternoon, Mr. Phillips called on me in a chaise and carried me to Waltham. We passed by the seat of Mr. Otis, a fine, large building on a smooth, round eminence a little distance from the road, with a wood on the west. The approach to it was through a gravelled road of about an eighth of a mile in length, with a thick, dark row of trees and shrubbery on either side. He took me to the seat of Mr. Lyman, a Boston merchant, who has acquired great wealth in the India trade—the father of that Mr. Lyman who wrote the book about Italy. It is a perfect paradise; Phillips tells me that there is not a country-seat in the United States on which so much expense has been laid out. The owner is continually engaged in making improvements and alterations, the annual cost of which is not less than twenty thousand dollars. The house is a handsome building, shaded with exotic trees—the mountain-ash of Europe, with its large, numerous cymes of red berries; the English beech, with its smooth, lead-colored stem and purple foliage. Here I saw the Chinese sumach—a sort of apple-tree—which Phillips called the crab-apple, a pretty tree loaded with fruit of a delicate light yellowish-red color, about twice the size of a thornberry, and various other shrubs whose names I did not learn. In front of the house to the south was an artificial piece of water winding about and widening into a lake with a little island of pines in it, an elegant bridge crossing it, and swans swimming on the surface. A hard-rolled walk by the side of a brick wall about ten feet in height, and covered with peach and apricot espaliers which seemed to grow to it, like the creeping sumach to the bark of an elm, led us to a grove of young forest-trees on the top of an eminence in the midst of which was a Chinese temple. North of the house was a park with a few American deer in it, and a large herd of spotted deer—a beautiful animal imported from

Bengal. We visited the green-house. Here were pine-apples growing. The rafters were covered with the grape-vine of Europe, whose
clusters were nearly ripe. Here was the American aloe, whose ensi-
form leaves are as thick and as large as I am, a species of datura
with large, white flowers the size of a half-pint tumbler, and a thousand other curious matters. More than a hundred acres lie about
this seat without any enclosure, most of which is fine, smooth turf,
with occasional corn-fields. We took tea at Mr. Lyman's with several agreeable ladies. They said there was some elegant poetry in
the last 'Idle Man.'* Phillips has seen my thing,† and tells me it
will go well.

> "Your affectionate husband,
> "W. C. Bryant."

Mr. Bryant, during this visit, not only formed the acquaintance of the Danas, Channings, and others connected with
"The North American Review," for which he had written,
and with several of whom he corresponded, but he must have
been introduced to the professors of the college and to many
distinguished visitors. Allston was there, fresh from his intimacy with Coleridge; Sully, of Philadelphia, was there, engaged temporarily in his art, and hosts of others—statesmen
and lawyers of eminence—the Adamses, Quincys, Pickering,
Story, Mason, and Webster; but of these he says not a word.
That he enjoyed his intercourse with persons at once conspicuous and congenial we know from his later reminiscences;
but the letter to his wife makes no mention of them, though
it evinces a lively interest in the horticulture of the environs
of Boston. The beautiful results of art in the adornment of
the earth's surface were new to him, hitherto familiar only
with the wild beauties of the hills, and he made the most of
his opportunities.

His poem called "The Ages," a rapid survey of the general progress of mankind in virtue and knowledge, was, on

---

* This refers to his own pieces.
† I. e., his poem.

the whole, a marked success. The newspapers of the day make little reference to it, as it was not their habit then to speak of such things; * but there are several persons still living who remember it very well. Mr. Emerson was one of the class of that year, and I endeavored to get him to revive his impressions of the occasion, but, unfortunately, he was not in a state of health to enable him to comply with my request.†
Mr. John C. Gray, however, the orator of the day, although now in the eighty-eighth year of his age, has a distinct recollection of all that occurred. "Mr. Bryant and I were together," he writes, "in the same pulpit, in the old Congregational Church, where the services were held. Mr. Bryant was extremely modest and unassuming in his deportment. As I had closed my part of the duty, and was near him, I could listen attentively and hear every word. I said to myself at the time, 'If Everett had read this poem, what a sensation it would have produced!' It was read quietly, and perhaps with some monotony of manner, so that unless one gave a close attention, it did not produce its full effect. As a general thing, works of this kind, grave and thoughtful in substance, are not appreciated at the moment; but persons of discernment, who followed the thought without requiring an effective or powerful manner, or a clear and strong delivery, felt that Mr. Bryant's poem was an uncommon production. It placed him, as I thought, at the very head of American poets —and there has been, as I still think, his rightful place ever since. The audience was a distinguished one—a formidable one for a young man to front—John Quincy Adams, Timothy Pickering, John Lowell, Drs. Channing and Kirkland, Ever-

---

* The Boston "Daily Advertiser" of August 31st has simply the following notice :
"PHI BETA KAPPA.—The anniversary of this society was celebrated yesterday. The public oration was delivered by John C. Gray, Esq., and the poem by William C. Bryant, Esq. These interesting performances commanded the deep attention, and received the high approbation, of a very numerous and select audience."

† Mr. Emerson, I think, must have made the acquaintance of the poet, as I find little notes of introduction, etc., from him to Mr. B., written not long afterward.

ett, Dana, Shaw, and a multitude of others that are not often gathered in these days." Another contemporary, the venerable and accomplished Miss Eliza Susan Quincy, daughter and sister of a Josiah Quincy, recalls Mr. Bryant's appearance and address in a letter in which she says:

"There was a crowded audience in the ancient church. Mr. Bryant's appearance was pleasing, refined, and intellectual; his manner was calm and dignified; and he spoke with ease and clearness of enunciation. There was no attempt at oratorical display; but, considering the grave and elevated tone of the poem, it excited more repeated tributes of applause than could have been anticipated, and the last stanza rendered these testimonies of approbation vehement. A few days afterward Mr. Isaac P. Davis, a man noted for his very general acquaintance in society, during a visit to Quincy, informed me that Mr. Bryant's poem was generally considered the finest that had ever been spoken before the Phi Beta Society."

It was, in fact, considered so good by his immediate friends —the Danas, Channings, Allston, etc.—that they would not hear of his quitting Boston until he had consented to the publication of it, and of what else he had done in a poetical way. He immediately proceeded to put his few pieces together, and the proofs reached Great Barrington a few days after his return —the new volume itself in a few weeks. It can hardly, however, be called a volume; it was a small pamphlet of only forty-four pages, containing eight poems in all—"The Ages," "To a Waterfowl," "The Fragment from Simonides," "The Inscription for the Entrance to a Wood," "The Yellow Violet," "The Song," "Green River," and "Thanatopsis"—but such poems as had never before appeared in American literature. Brief as they were, and few as they were, they were yet of a kind to make a reputation; and, if the author had never written another line, his name would have been remembered with delight and honor for many years to come. Dana, in forwarding the poems, scolded him roundly for certain changes, not now to be guessed, that he had made in his text.

"I send you a copy of your poems," he said, under date of Cambridge, September 8, 1821, "as a glass for you to look into and see how handsome you are in print. 'We three'—Mr. Channing, my brother, and I—have taken a liberty with you, at which, I trust, you will not be offended. If you should be, our support under your indignation would be, that we suffer in a good cause. We have published 'The Yellow Violet' as you first wrote it, as also the line, 'Shall come and make their bed with thee'; and 'The Barcan Desert pierce.' What could have induced you to change 'the sweet babe' for that line and a half? As to 'the pale realms of shade,' a little after, it is utterly abominable. Nothing in the Elysian fields worse than it. As you first wrote it, nothing could have been more simple and solemn, and the objection made to the 'to earth' seemed to me at the time a hypercriticism. At any rate, I shall be glad to know what the caravan and 'shade' all mean now. Could I but have found your rough draft, we should have had your 'sweet babe' and the old caravan brought back to their proper places without a moment's hesitation. I believe that a poet should not be allowed to alter in cold blood; he grows finical. 'Make their bed with thee' is scriptural and holy; the alteration was neither good nor bad. Opposed as Mr. C. and I were to the change of 'The Yellow Violet,' we read original and alteration to my brother twice over, and he said that it would be a sin in us to allow the change, as it was in our power to prevent it, and that the town atmosphere must have got into your upper regions when you made that and the other changes. He was very sorry he did not see you before you left, and would have been at home had he known you were to leave before one o'clock. In good earnest, my dear sir, I am fearful that your feelings may be wounded by what we have done, and I wished my hands washed of the affair more than once. Yet I acted from the most thorough conviction that your poems would be injured by what you intended doing. And when you come, by and by, to read over those alterations which we could not put out, you will regret that it was out of our power. Forgive me the liberty I took part in, and I will forgive you your sad alterations, and we will shake hands."

Mr. Bryant, so far from being offended by the restorations, was thankful for them, and in his reply to Dana says:

"Yours of the 8th I received day before yesterday, and to-day the copy of my poems. I am infinitely obliged to you for the trouble you have taken with them, and submit as quietly as you could wish to your restoration of the altered passages. As to 'the pale realms of shade,' I have not a word to say in its defence. I dislike it as much as you can, and I had a secret misgiving of heart when I wrote it. I am now engaged with all my might in reviewing your book, 'The Idle Man,' and will send on the .fruit of my labors soon. . . . I am glad you do not mean to be discouraged by any symptoms of coldness with which the public have received it at New York. If it goes off well in Boston, and at the South, there is no fear that it will not soon do well enough in New York. The fires kindled at both ends of the pile will meet at last and be hottest in the middle. . . .

"In the mean time, I send you something of my own for your next number. It is a poem which I found unfinished among my papers on my return from Boston, and added the latter half of it on purpose for your work. You see my head runs upon the Indians. The very mention of them once used to make me sick, perhaps because those who undertook to make a poetical use of them made a terrible butchery of the subject. I think, however, at present, a great deal might be done with them. You may give what name you please to my poem." *

Mr. Willard Phillips endeavored to help his young friend along by printing in the October number of "The North American" an elaborate criticism of the poems. As this was the earliest printed notice they received, I quote a part of it.

"Of what school is this writer? The 'Lake,' the 'Pope,' or the 'Cockney'; or some other? Does he imitate Byron, or Scott, or Campbell? These are the standing interrogatories in all tribunals having the jurisdiction of poetry, and it behooves us to see that they are administered. He is, then, of the school of Nature, and of Cowper, if we may answer for him; of the school which aims to express fine thoughts, in true and obvious English, without attempting or fearing to write like any one in particular, and without being distinguished for using or avoiding any set of words or

---

* Mr. Dana called it "A Walk at Sunset." See Poetical Works, vol. i, p. 43.

phrases. It does not, therefore, bring any system into jeopardy to admire him, and his readers may yield themselves to their spontaneous impressions without an apprehension of deserting their party.

"There is running through the whole of this little collection a strain of pure and high sentiment, that expands and lifts up the soul, and brings it nearer to the source of moral beauty. This is not indefinitely and obscurely shadowed, but it animates bright images and clear thoughts. There is everywhere a simple and delicate portraiture of the subtle and ever-vanishing beauties of Nature, which she seems willing to conceal as her choicest things, and which none but minds the most susceptible can seize, and no other than a writer of great genius can body forth in words. There is in this poetry something more than mere painting. It does not merely offer in rich colors what the eye may see or the heart feels, or what may fill the imagination with a religious grandeur. It does not merely rise to sublime heights of thought, with the forms and allusions that obey none but master spirits. Besides these, there are wrought into the composition a luminous philosophy and deep reflection, that make the subjects as sensible to the understanding as they are splendid to the imagination. There are no slender lines and unmeaning epithets, or words loosely used to fill out the measure. The whole is of rich materials, skilfully compacted. A throng of ideas crowds every part, and the reader's mind is continually and intensely occupied with 'the thick-coming fancies.'"

Many persons, even his father's friend, Mrs. Lyman, thought this praise exaggerated and undeserved. Not so, Mr. Gulian C. Verplanck, author of " The Bucktail Bards" (1819), a political satire, and of several discourses that had already made him widely known, who wrote to Mr. Bryant, October 4th, in this way:

"SIR : I received a few days ago a copy of your poems from your friend, Mr. R. Dana. You will see how highly I think of their merits by the brief criticism in the paper which you will receive with this.* The 'American' is a paper of extensive circulation, and of

* The New York " American," October 4, 1821.

considerable importance in our State politics ; it is edited by a cousin of mine, who now and then indulges me with the use of his editorial columns for other purposes. An 'Anniversary Discourse,' which I published some time ago, having, by better luck than commonly falls to the lot of such publications, just reached a second edition, I have taken that opportunity to make some corrections and add a few notes and illustrations. I beg your acceptance of a copy.

" I am, with respect, yours, etc.,

"G. C. VERPLANCK.'

To this the poet answered from Great Barrington, October 10, 1821 :

" GULIAN C. VERPLANCK, Esq. :

" SIR : Yours of the 4th inst., together with the New York 'American' of the same date, and a copy of your 'Anniversary Discourse,' have just reached me.

" I had before seen the greater part of your Discourse in the shape of extracts in various publications, but I am happy in an opportunity to read, in its original connection, the whole of a work the free and liberal spirit of which, to say nothing of its other merits, too generally acknowledged to need any testimony of mine, had already so much interested me.

" Whether you think highly of my poems or otherwise, I hope, at least, that you think more of them than I was able to find in the paper you sent me. On unfolding it, I found the two inside pages entirely blank, through some blunder, I suppose, of the press. I conclude, however, from the intimation in your letter, that the notice was a favorable one, and I am grateful for the assistance afforded me at a time when it may do me much service.

" I am, sir, with much respect, yours, etc.,

"W. C. BRYANT."

At length a more perfect copy of the paper arrived, and Mr. Bryant was gratified to see his merits recognized by one who held an acknowledged position in literature outside of Boston. Verplanck discerned at once the quality of the verses before him, and he spoke in the warmest terms of " their exquisite taste, their keen relish for the beauties of nature, their magnificent imagery, and their pure and majestic morality."

His little venture attracted some attention, even in England, where a collection of " Specimens of American Poetry " (Allman, London, 1822), made by Mr. Roscoe, brought it to the notice of the reviewers. A writer in " Blackwood " (June, 1822) graciously said : " Bryant is no mean poet ; and, if he is a young man, we should not be surprised at his assuming, one day or another, a high rank among English poets." In justification of this prophecy the critic adduced " Thanatopsis " and " The Waterfowl," which showed " really superior powers." This recognition, however, did not prevent " Blackwood," two years later, from taking all its praises back, in an article which denied " the existence of anything like American literature or American authors." " All their writers are but feeble dilutions of English originals. Some of the pieces of Bryant having found their way by piecemeal into England, and having met with a little newspaper praise, which was repeated with great emphasis in America, he is set up by his associates as a poet of extraordinary promise ; but Mr. Bryant is no more than a sensible young man of a thrifty disposition, who knows how to manage a few plain ideas in a handsome way. ' The Waterfowl,' though beautiful, has no more poerty in it than the Sermon on the Mount (!), and his blank verse is a mere imitation of Milman," which was a curious sort of imitation, seeing that his blank verse anticipated Milman's by some years.* The " Retrospective Review " took the same tone, and, after admitting that " Mr. Bryant stood at the head of the American Parnassus," found that " he copied Lord Byron in his Spenserian stanzas, and in his blank verse reminds us at once both of Cowper and Wordsworth."

Strictures like these, however much they may have been deserved in times past, were getting to be no longer pertinent. A new life, full of the richest promise, was already begun in

* " Blackwood," September, 1824.

this country. The year embraced in this chapter, which saw
the publication of Mr. Bryant's little volume, belonged to a
significant and notable time in our literary annals. It was
then that Cooper published his " Spy "; Washington Irving
his " Sketch Book " and " Bracebridge Hall "; Halleck his
" Fanny "; Sands and Eastburn their " Yamoyden "; Dana
his " Idle Man "; Hillhouse his " Percy's Masque "; Percival
his " Prometheus "; Miss Sedgwick her " New England Tale ";
Channing his earliest essays in the " Christian Disciple ";
Daniel Webster his " Plymouth Oration "; and Edward Livingston his " Penal Codes." " Many voices have followed
these," as Bayard Taylor said in his address at Halleck's
grave; " but we must never forget the forerunners, who were
even in advance of their welcome, and created their own
audiences."

CHAPTER TENTH.

THE LAW ABANDONED.

A. D. 1822–1824.

IT was at this time, I am disposed to believe, that Mr. Bryant's political opinions underwent certain modifications which
it is important to notice. He was still a Federalist, attended
the meetings of his party, served on committees, and, when necessary, discussed the character and claims of candidates for
office in the newspapers.* But a great change had been going

* If one may judge from the following *jeu d'esprit*, however, found among his
papers, he was more disposed to make fun of the politicians in general than to take
part in their contests :

> " All things must have an end—empires and thrones—
>   Speeches and messages—though ne'er so long—
> There is an end to smiles, an end to groans,
>   To C——'s sermons and to B——'s song.
> All things must have an end—that high behest
>   Has brought the Sixteenth Congress to its close, (*a*)
> And packed its members off to East and West,
>   To Florida in flowers and Maine in snows.
>
> " Some carry home the unspoken speech again,
>   Some mourn a luckless bill tó its long sleep
> Untimely sent, as dies upon the plain
>   The tender poppy trod by huddling sheep.
> Some glory to have proved their length of wind,
>   Some that a starveling measure struggled through,
> One sighing statesman leaves his heart behind,
>   Another, some cool hundreds lost at loo !

(*a*) The Sixteenth Congress closed March 3, 1821.

on in both the tone and direction of political controversy since the days of his young enthusiasm for State rights and rebellion. After the peace of 1815 the old parties were more or less fused or extinguished, and a period of quietude followed, which, during the administration of Monroe, who was elected to the presidency in 1821 by an almost unanimous vote, was called "the era of good feeling." New questions of difference, however, arose out of the altered circumstances of the nation. A considerable manufacturing interest had grown up in the Northern States during the war with England, which at the close of it desired to be continued. The conditions of peace revived and stimulated more active interchanges in domestic commerce, and schemes for the promotion of it came into the ascendant. The Eastern States demanded tariffs to shelter them from foreign competition, and enlarged harbors for their shipping; the Western States wanted highways and canals to put them in easier communication with the East; and the South was not backward in clamoring for such internal improvements as might facilitate the access of their crops to the

> "Homeward to Boston Webster hies to breathe,
> Jove-like, the incense that in every nook
> Smokes up to his Olympus from beneath—
> With clerkly Everett, who his trade mistook—(a)
> Shrewd Woodbury hastens to his own hearth-fire,
> And Gorham grave and Dwight of manners bland,
> And knowing Anderson and McIntyre,
> And Burges with old Lemprière in his hand.(b)

> "And Carolina welcomes Drayton home,
> Hayne, and McDuffie of the fearless voice ;
> And in the news that White and Polk are come,
> The gorgeous vales of Tennessee rejoice.
> But there the wild-cat in the depth of woods
> Trembles to feel the south wind's softer breath,
> For well she knows that with the opening buds
> Crockett returns, whose very stare is death." (c)

(a) Mr. Everett had been a clergyman, and became a politician.
(b) Tristam Burges, of Rhode Island, noted for his classical quotations.
(c) Davie Crockett, famous for his eccentricities and his rifle.

seaboard cities and to a great and growing inland population. How these various enterprises should be fostered and sustained became a principal object of legislative solicitude.

Mr. Bryant, during this lenten time, while new issues were getting into shape, devoted his leisure to studying the political history of his country. This led him to reconsider the grounds of his traditionary opinions, and to scrutinize more closely than he had done before the principles and tendencies of various past and dominant parties. His attention was particularly directed to the doctrines of political economy, which, though still wearing a gloss of newness on this side of the Atlantic, were in much favor with inquiring and independent minds in Europe. His friends the Sedgwicks, like himself of Federal affinities, were yet disposed, by their reading and reflections, to a generous hospitality toward conclusions which the treatises of Smith, Say, Thornton, and Ricardo, but especially the great debates in the British Parliament in the time of Huskisson (1820), rendered more and more popular in Europe. Theodore Sedgwick, indeed, the foremost of the family, and a man of eminent character and parts, had long been a decided advocate of freedom of exchange.* Either following

---

* Mr. Theodore Sedgwick, the second son of Judge Theodore Sedgwick, who died in 1813, was greatly admired by Mr. Bryant, and doubtless exercised considerable influence over his opinions and conduct. In a memoir of this distinguished friend, written for "Griswold's Biographic Annual" in 1839, he describes him as one "whose character deserves to be held up to the imitation of all men engaged in political life, or in public controversies of any kind. He was a man of many virtues, but he enjoyed one distinction of difficult attainment, that of being a politician without party vices. In the question respecting the powers of government and the proper objects and limits of human laws, he took part with great zeal, deeming them highly important to the welfare of mankind ; yet he bore himself in these disputes with such manifest sincerity, disinterestedness, and philanthropy, and with such generosity toward his adversaries, as to make them regret that he was not on their side. Nothing could excel his dislike of the ignoble ferocity into which party men allow themselves to fall, save his abhorrence of the unmanly practices to which they sometimes resort. It is with a feeling of deep reverence that I essay to speak of such a man." Further on, speaking of Mr. Sedgwick's work, entitled "Public and Private Economy," he says : "It is full of wise and just views, and informed by a warm and

his lead or impelled by his own researches, Mr. Bryant took the same view. What he learned from these sources was, that the great economic movements of society, or the complex actions by which human wants are supplied, are as uniform and regular as any other aggregate of causes and effects, or that, if they vary, it is within calculable limits: in other words, that social phenomena are subject to laws with which it is injurious to interfere in any artificial manner. But, having arrived at this fundamental principle, he saw that it carried with it, to a certain extent, the readjustment of other more general political notions. He observed that in the proceedings of Congress, where economic subjects were perpetually coming up in one shape or another, the leading statesmen were apt to take position in regard to them according to their proclivities of constitutional doctrine. Those who inclined to a protective system were also inclined, or bound by the necessities of the case, to broad constructions of the powers of the national Government, while those who were emancipated from old economic errors were as earnestly disposed to a rigid exegesis. It was pretty evident, therefore, that, while he was nominally ranked as a Federalist, his place, when parties should divide and organize on economic grounds, would be inevitably on the side of the Republicans.

Mr. Dana, in his correspondence with Mr. Bryant, urges him not to trouble himself about such questions, but to undertake a poem of greater length than any he had yet written. "We talk of you a great deal down at my brother's," he said, "and want you to write a poem as much longer than

genuine philanthropy. Its principal design was to promote the object that lay nearest the heart of the author, that of narrowing more and more the limits of poverty, ignorance, and vice among his countrymen, of inspiring them with the love of personal independence, giving them habits of reflection, teaching them reverence for one another's rights, and thus bringing about that equality of condition which is the most favorable to the morals and happiness of society, and to the harmonious working of our institutions." I cannot but here remark that, secluded as the whole of Mr. Bryant's early life was, he was rarely favored by the enjoyment of intercourse with such men as Judge Howe, Mr. Baylies, and the several Sedgwicks.

'The Ages' as may please you. Fix upon a subject, and turn over the plan in your mind; get as full of the matter as you have leisure to be, and write as you find time." Again, in November, he renews the advice: " Have you turned the matter over and gathered in your thoughts?. There are men of talents enough to carry on the common world, but men of genius are not so plenty that any can afford to be idle, neither can any man tell how great the effect of a work of genius is in the course of time. Set about it in good earnest." Mr. Bryant did not set about it, nor take any notice of the suggestion. With all the fire of youth in him, he yet despaired of an achievement which he seemed to agree with a later opinion of Poe in thinking impossible for any man—a long poem which should also be a good poem.*

A subject of much public excitement at the time was the revolt of the Greeks from the tyrannic and cruel rule of the Turks. I can well remember, though a mere child then, the depth and intensity of feeling with which the whole community, even the children, followed the incidents of the heroic struggle of the children of Leonidas against the Moslem. How we pitied and extolled the Greeks, and how we execrated the Turks! The same enthusiasm which carried Byron from the delights of Genoa and Venice to his deathbed at Missilonghi, animated a large number of our young men, who, like Dr. Samuel G. Howe, were disposed to go in person to the assistance of the oppressed. Mr. Bryant's zeal never attained to such a degree of warmth, but exhaled in poetic expressions and a popular address on the Greek Revo-

---

* Mr. Bigelow, in his memorial address to the Century Club, says : " Like Horace, like Burns, like Beranger, but unlike most other poets of celebrity, Bryant never wrote any long poems. I once ásked him why. He replied : 'There is no such thing as a long poem.' His theory was that a long poem was as impossible as a long ecstasy ; that what is called a long poem, like ' Paradise Lost' and the ' Divine Comedy,' is a mere succession of poems strung together upon a thread of verse, the thread of verse serving sometimes to popularize them by adapting them to a wider range of literary taste or a more sluggish intellectual digestion."

lution. These were, however, of service in keeping sympathy alive by a generous intellectual appreciation. His address, delivered at Great Barrington in December, 1823, is marked by impressive thought and a fine manly fervor, rather characteristic of the scholar than of the statesman. His love for the Greek language seems to have diffused itself over the whole race by which it was spoken. " Nothing ignoble or worthless," he assumed, " can spring from so generous a stock. It was in Greece that civilization had its origin, and the grand impulse which she communicated to the human mind will never cease to the end of time. It was there that poetry, sculpture, all the great arts of life, were invented or perfected, and first delivered down to succeeding generations. Greece was the real cradle of liberty in which the earliest republics were rocked. We are the pupils of her great men, in all the principles of science, of morals, and of good government; her genius, in short, in every department of intellectual creation, has instructed, overcome, and awed the world; she preserved learning and religion when all the rest of Europe was a prey to barbaric invasion, and the world owes her a debt of gratitude which it would be pusillanimous to forget, or to fail to return in heaping measures of assistance and benefaction." Turning, then, to the present condition of Greece, he painted in pathetic colors her martyrdoms and sufferings, and urged the people, almost in agonizing tones, to rush to her rescue and relief.

Mr. Bryant did not take his friend's advice in regard to a long poem ; but what he did set about, strange to say, was a farce intended for the stage. It is uncertain whether he had ever seen a play ; and his genius, though not devoid of a sense of humor, was hardly of a comic cast. Yet he determined to try it in that vein. A duel having been recently achieved by two Southern Hotspurs, under preliminaries and conditions more wiredrawn than even Touchstone's catalogue of the degrees of courtly punctilio, he thought it presented an admirable opportunity for bringing the practice of duelling itself, still popular in nearly all parts of the country, into deserved ridicule. He therefore tried to expose it to irresistible laughter. Of this piece, called "The Heroes," one must say, as Brummel said of his cravats, "These are our failures." The situations were perhaps funny enough; the dialogue was brisk with repartee, and the characters not unamusing in their mock-heroic eloquence and attitudes. But, as a whole, it was illy adapted to representation. His good friend, Charles Sedgwick, to whom the play was communicated, like Lord Burleigh, shook his dubious locks. He thought the satire effective, but doubted whether the jokes and squibs would be appreciated, owing to lapse of time. Nevertheless, he was willing to submit the matter to his brother Henry, who, because he lived in New York, was supposed to be a better judge, and it was sent to him for decision. The arbitrator gave no encouragement whatever to the aspiring dramatist.* But the incident, small in itself, had important effects. Mr. Henry Sedgwick saw enough in the sketch to make him think that, if Mr. Bryant would remove to the city, he might, perhaps, run a successful career as a writer for magazines. Accordingly, in returning the farce, he urged a consideration of the subject with some degree of earnestness. "The time," he wrote, "is peculiarly propitious; the Athenæum, just instituted" (a library and reading-room since merged, I think, in the Society Library), "is exciting a sort of literary rage, and it is proposed to set up a journal in connection with it. Besides, 'The Atlantic Magazine,' which has pined till recently, is beginning to revive in the hands of Henry J. Anderson, who has a taste or whim for editorship, and he unquestionably needs assistance. Bliss & White, his publishers, are liberal gentlemen; they pay him

---

* "I send you a letter from New York about the farce," wrote Charles Sedgwick. "Happily for me, you are too well acquainted with the opinions of the Sedgwick tribe to take in dudgeon Mr. Harry's free sayings about it. To tell you the truth, I was rather amused by his surprise at seeing a farce written by you, and by his comparisons on the subject, and, as I could send you his letter easier than tell what he said, I do so."

$500 a year, and authorize an expenditure of $500 more. Any deficiencies of salary, moreover," Mr. Sedgwick adds, "may be eked out by teaching foreigners, of whom there are many in New York, eager to learn our language and literature. In short, it would be strange if you could not succeed where anybody and everything succeeds." The prospects thus presented, it must be confessed, were not brilliant or alluring, but Mr. Sedgwick's zeal was sufficiently persuasive to induce Mr. Bryant to make a flying visit to the metropolis on a prospecting tour, as the miners would say. Writing to his wife of his arrival, under date of New York, April 24, 1824, he says nothing of his objects, yet glances at a few noteworthy persons:

"MY DEAR FRANCES: I have, on the whole, made up my mind not to come home this week. The weather has been so bad that I have seen little of the city as yet, and, as there is no knowing when I shall be here again, I think I had better take time to look about me before I leave the place. . . . I dined yesterday at Mr. Robert Sedgwick's in a company of authors—Mr. Cooper, the novelist; Mr. Halleck, author of 'Fanny'; Mr. Sands, author of 'Yamoyden'; Mr. Johnson, the reporter (of the Court of Appeals), and some other literary gentlemen. Mr. Cooper engrossed the whole conversation, and seems a little giddy with the great success his works have met with. *Hier, au soir nous allames, Mons. Ives et moi, chez une famille Française, ou nous jouames au whist et parlames Française tout le temps.** . . . I got in on Sunday morning at five o'clock, and heard two sermons from Parson Ware, and very good ones too. Tuesday we had Sparks, editor of the 'North American Review,' to dine with us—a man of very agreeable manners; he was on his way to Boston from Baltimore. Please to tell Dr. Leavenworth, if I do not get home before Monday, to make my apology to the world, and get somebody to take down the votes for me† and make the proper memorandums. Good-

---

* These scraps of French hide no secrets, and are retained only to show a habit, which Mr. Bryant long followed, of writing a part of his familiar notes to his family in the language which they happened to be learning at the time.

† I. e., as town clerk.

by—*Baisez la petite Fanchette pour moi*—and give my regards to the family.   Your affectionate husband,

"WM. C. BRYANT."

It was to this visit, doubtless, Miss C. M. Sedgwick refers in a letter from New York to her brother Charles at Lenox : *

"We have had a great deal of pleasure," she says, "from a glimpse of Bryant. I never saw him so happy, nor half so agreeable. I think he is very much animated with his prospects. Heaven grant that they may be more than realized. I sometimes feel some misgivings about it; but I think it is impossible that, in the increasing demand for native literature, a man of his resources, who has justly the *first* reputation, should not be able to command a competency. He has good sense, too, good judgment, and moderation, and never was a man blessed in a warmer friend than he has in Harry; and besides Harry there are many persons here who enter warmly into his cause. He seems so modest that every one is eager to prove to him the merit of which he is unconscious. I wish you had seen him last evening. Mrs. Nicholas was here, and half a dozen gentlemen. She was ambitious to recite before Bryant. She was very becomingly dressed for the grand ball to which she was going, and, wrought up to the highest pitch of excitement, she recited her favorite pieces better than I have ever heard her, and concluded the whole, without request or any note of preparation, with 'The Waterfowl' and 'Thanatopsis.' Bryant's face 'brightened all over,' was one gleam of light, and, I am certain, at the moment he felt the ecstasy of a poet."

Without abandoning his profession, on his return from this visit he devoted himself to literary work with more earnestness than he had ever before displayed. The "North American," having rejected a critique of his on the "Idle Man," was closed to him ; † but a new field had been opened by the timely

---

* This letter is dated in February, 1822 ("Life and Letters of C. M. Sedgwick," by Mary E. Dewey) ; but I can find no evidence of Mr. Bryant's having been in New York during that year.

† Mr. Phillips having invited him to write a review of the book, he complied. But in the interval, and before his article arrived, the editorship of the Review was

establishment ·in Boston of the "United States Literary Gazette," a periodical conducted by a young lawyer of a literary turn, since known as the venerable Judge Theophilus Parsons, who earnestly solicited his aid.* He began to write for
him in the latter part of 1823, and continued to write through
the year 1824, until some time in 1825. It proved the time of
his most prolific poetic effort. Between twenty and thirty
poems were then produced, the names of which alone suggest
the rare value of his collaboration. They were "The Massacre
at Scio," "Rizpah," "The Rivulet," "March," "The Old Man's
Funeral," "Sonnet to ——," "An Indian Story," "Summer
Wind," "An Indian at the Burial-Place of his Fathers," the
song called "The Lover's Lessons," "Monument Mountain,"
the "Hymn of the Waldenses," "After a Tempest," "Autumn Woods," "Mutation," "November," "Song of the Greek
Amazon," "To a Cloud," "The Murdered Traveller," "Hymn
to the North Star," "The Lapse of Time," "The Song of the
Stars," and the "Forest Hymn." Never before had so many
bits of verse of equal excellence been contributed to the same
periodical within the same limits of time. They show that
the writer's monotonous drudgery, "scrawling strange words
with a barbarous pen," had not dimmed his eyes to the delicate beauties of Nature, nor abated the force of his imagination. In the "March," "The Rivulet," "Monument Mountain," "Autumn Woods," "After a Tempest," and the "Forest
Hymn," we have some of the finest work of his life, equal to
the best in the little volume of 1821, and hardly surpassed in

changed. It passed into the hands of Mr. Alexander and Edward Everett, gentlemen
of fine scholarship and taste, but who, adhering still to the classic English models of
the Queen Anne period, were not admirers of either the opinions or style of Mr.
Dana. Mr. Dana's habitual study of the older English writers, and his warm admiration of Wordsworth and Coleridge, in spite of the arbitrary dicta of Jeffrey in the
"Edinburgh," put him somewhat in advance of his contemporaries. His peculiarities of thought and expression seemed strange and unnatural, if not affected,
then, although we should now regard them not only as perfectly natural, but as really
beautiful.

    * Mr. Parsons died in 1882, after this was written.

later years. His principal theme is Nature, which he treats
as one whose mission it was to show an uncongenial world
what beauty lay concealed in our vast, uncouth, almost savage
wilds of woods and fields. But his enthusiasm for the Greeks
finds elegiac or lyrical vent now and then; and the region in
which he lived, once the home of a powerful tribe of Indians,
whose solitary descendants wandered back at times, from their
new settlements toward the setting sun, to gaze upon the
graves of their race, suggested pathetic stories out of their
traditions.* Among these pieces there is one which has a deep
and tender personal meaning. It is the "Sonnet to ——," his
sister, a dearly loved companion of earlier days, who was then
in the last stages of the disease of which the father had died a
few years before. She was a person of rare endowments and
sweetness of disposition, and well might he pray that

> " —death should come
> Gently to one of gentle mould like thee,
> As light winds wandering through groves of bloom
> Detach the delicate blossoms from the tree."

She died in the twenty-second year of her age, and thereafter the old familiar places wore a gloom for him, which, perhaps, inclined him more willingly to the change of residence
Mr. Sedgwick had suggested. The memory of this cherished
companion of his childhood he carried with him for years, as
may be seen in the allusive lines of "The Past," and of "The
Death of the Flowers."

The reader will be both amused and surprised to learn that,
when Mr. Bryant was asked to name the compensation he expected for these writings, he fixed upon two dollars for each
piece, and seemed, says Judge Parsons, writing to me, abun-
dantly satisfied with the terms. The publishers, however
(Messrs. Cummings, Hillard & Co.), appreciating the worth of

---

* The people of Stockbridge have erected a monument to the memory of the
Stockbridge tribe of Indians, who were the friends of their fathers.

their contributor, offered him two hundred dollars a year for an average of one hundred lines a month—about sixteen and a half cents a line—expressing, at the same time, "their profound regret that they were unable to offer a compensation more adequate." Even this was more than he got by his book; for it appears, from accounts rendered him by Mr. Phillips two years later, that since 1821 some seven hundred and fifty copies had been printed, of which only two hundred and seventy were sold, so that the profits of the author in five years, all expenses told, amounted to just fifteen dollars, *minus* eight cents—less than two dollars for each of the pieces contained in the volume.*

But if the pecuniary harvest was small, that of fame was more considerable. The poetry of the "Gazette" attracted a great deal of attention, so much so, indeed, that a volume entitled "Miscellaneous Poems"† was made of it, and the "North American" thought the publication of it a signal event in our literary history.‡ It is, perhaps, worthy of note that Mr. Bryant himself formed a high opinion of the poetry of the "Gazette" other than his own; for, noticing it afterward in the "New York Review,"§ he said: "We do not know, of all the numerous English periodical works, any one that has furnished within the same time as much really beautiful poetry. We might cite, in proof of this, the 'April Day,' the 'Hymn of the Moravian Nuns,' and the 'Sunrise on the Hills,' by H. W. L. (we know not who he is), or more particularly those exquisite *morceaux*, 'True Greatness,' 'The Soul of Song,' 'The Grave of the Patriots,' and 'The Desolate City,' by P., whom it would be affectation not to recognize as Dr. Percival." The H. W.

---

* A gentleman met Mr. Bryant in a New York book-store a few years ago, and said : " I have just bought the earliest edition of your poems, and gave twenty dollars for it." " More, by a long shot," replied Mr. Bryant, "than I received for writing the whole work."

† Boston : Cummings, Hillard & Co., and Harrison Gray, 1826.

‡ "North American Review," vol. xxii, p. 43, 1826.

§ Vol. i, p. 289.

L., whom he did not know, then an undergraduate of Bowdoin College, has since come to be pretty well known as Mr. Henry W. Longfellow.

Mr. Dana was so ardent a friend that he lost no opportunity in urging Mr. Bryant to protracted effort. Writing from Cambridge, July 4, 1824, he says:

". . . . So much by way of preface. And now to my object— which is, to learn from you what you have done, *without the bar*, besides the little you have written for Parsons. I shall expect from you a full and honest account of yourself. Your 'Rivulet' was delicate and tender and beautiful; but it sometimes ran so near 'Green River' that they mingled their murmurings. I suppose 'Green River' was not at all in your mind, and that you have not been aware of this? I doubt whether it is well for the mind to work much in this way—to write from some occasional thought, or chance object. However beautiful what it produces may be, it is not called upon for the exercise of all its strength; it acts in detachments. But, if it is about undertaking a great work, there is a plan to be sketched out on a large scale. The powers are *all* astir gathering from abroad, out of all quarters. Then there is such a movement within—such a thronging of events and images, and such a press of thoughts and feelings—that, if a man had time to look into himself, he would be as much in wonder at the change there as at the sight of a suddenly peopled desert. A man does not feel himself completely till he grapples with something that will *hold him a tug.* . . .

"Two gentlemen, lately from England, report that Cooper is in high snuff there. They say he ranks at least with Irving, and that no works meet with a quicker sale. I was sorry on Phillips's account to see such a review of 'The Pilot.' It can do no harm to Cooper; he is to the windward of the American reviewers, at least. It seemed to me altogether unworthy of Phillips in point of ability. I am afraid he meant to steer a middle course between Cooper's petty enemies and those who have the good sense and the fairness to relish him and speak well of him. I had no thought of running on to this length. Channing, Allston, and my brother desire to be remembered to you, and hope to hear of you shortly through me."

Mr. Bryant answers, July 8th:

". . . You inquire whether I have written anything except what I have furnished to Parsons. Nothing at all. I made an engagement with him with a view, in the first place, to earn something in addition to the *emoluments* of my profession, which, as you may suppose, are not very ample, and, in the second place, to *keep my hand in*, for I was very near discontinuing entirely the writing of verses. As for setting myself about the great work you mention, I know you make the suggestion in great personal kindness toward myself, and I cannot sufficiently express my sense of that unwearied good-will which has more than once called my attention to this subject. But I feel reluctant to undertake such a thing for several reasons. In the first place, a project of that sort on my hands would be apt to make me abstracted, impatient of business, and forgetful of my professional engagements, and my literary experience has taught me that it is to my profession alone that I can look for the steady means of supplying the wants of the day. In the second place, I am lazy. In the third place, I am deterred by the difficulty of finding a proper subject. I began last winter to write a narrative poem, which I meant should be a little longer than any I had already composed ; but finding that would turn out at last a poor story about a Spectre Ship, and that the tradition on which I had founded it had already been made use of by Irving, I gave it up. I fancy that it is of some importance to the success of a work that the subject should be happily chosen. The only poems that have any currency at present are of a narrative kind—light stories, in which love is a principal ingredient. Nobody writes epic, and nobody reads didactic poems, and as for dramatic poems, they are out of the question. In this uncertainty, what is to be done? It is a great misfortune to write what everybody calls frivolous, and a still greater to write what nobody can read.

"I am glad to hear that Miss Sedgwick's new novel, ' Redwood,'* finds so much favor with your friends, and I think that when you have read it you will call it a good book. What you tell me of the success of our countryman, Cooper, in England, is an omen of good things. I hope it is the breaking of a bright day for American literature, the

---

* It was dedicated to Mr. Bryant.

glory and gladness of which shall call you again from your retirement."

Again, on the 16th of November, 1824, Mr. Dana recurs to
the subject:

"Cooper holds you in great admiration. G. C. Verplanck talked
about you, too. So far as I could discover in a two days' visit in the
city, you are mighty popular. They all say what I have said to you—
till I begin to think myself impertinent—that you must write a longer
poem than you have yet written. . . . A poem of fair length, with selections from what you furnished Parsons (which he can't refuse you,
as you work dog cheap), together with the contents of your little volume, and the addition of two or three small pieces never before published, will make the world look upon you as a man of quite a comely
size and port when you issue forth again. I should think you would
find very little difficulty in making yourself, abroad as well as at home,
a man of consequence, as you seemed from your letter to me to be
doubting what steed to mount. This much I will say: Mount what
one you may, you will put such spirit into him that you will soon say,
in the words of him who will never speak more, 'The horse doth feel
his rider.' When you have got well agoing, joy me with the news
thereof."

In another letter Dana takes occasion to inform him that
he is getting a name in England. In "Blackwood's Magazine"
for June, he says, referring to a criticism already cited, "is a
notice (slim enough, to be sure) of Roscoe's 'Selections of
American Poetry'; and they seem to be fully aware that you
are another sort of a man from those bound up with you.
They say that if you are a young man you will undoubtedly
take your rank with their leading poets. This is a good deal
for Blackwood to say of any American." Phillips was of opinion, also, that this faint notice of him abroad had produced
great effect on the currents of domestic opinion. "Many of
your countrymen," he remarks, "deemed you inferior to Percival; my poor praise in the 'North American' they thought
an extravagant eulogium; but, now that you have been repro-

duced by Roscoe in England, the question is settled, and they
have become your most decided admirers." *

The narrative poem of the "Spectre Ship," mentioned in
the letter of July 8th, is still partly extant in manuscript. It is
a story founded upon the tradition told by Cotton Mather, in
his "Magnalia Christi," of a vessel which, in the time of the
Pilgrims, sailed from New Haven, having a large body of returning emigrants on board, but which was never heard of
again.† The interest of it was made to hang, as far as I can
gather from the indications of the fragments, on the adventures of a young lover who leaves his orphan sweetheart behind him to suffer the various calamities of Indian captivity on
shore, while he suffers from the no less barbarous treacheries
of the sea, until they are at length restored to each other's
arms by some of those miraculous agencies known to novelists
and poets. In what way he was going to weave the supersti-
tious element into his story does not appear. Nevertheless, the
scheme gave ample scope for descriptions of forest and sea, in
calm and storm, and was suggestive of incidents as romantic
as any of those that Scott has immortalized. Mr. Bryant, however, did not carry his execution of it beyond a few hundred
lines, of which it may be repeated what has been already said
of his projected Indian tale, that the descriptive parts overbal-
ance the narrative. He could tell a simple story well, as he
has since proved by "Sella" and "The Little People of the
Snow," but whether he was equal to the dramatic exigencies
of a sustained and complicated plot admits of some doubt.
His genius was meditative, not epical; and while we possess
such poems as "The Fountain," "The Rain-Dream," "Among

---

* Narrowness or provincialism of judgment was then one of the most formidable
obstacles in the way of our native writers, and I am not sure that we are yet wholly
free from the impediment.

† Mr. Longfellow has some verses on the same subject, beginning :
"In Mather's 'Magnalia Christi'
Of the old colonial time,
You will find in prose the legend
Which is here set down in rhyme."

the Trees," "The Night Journey of a River," and others of
the kind, we may easily forgive him his want of ambition or
ability to reach success in other walks of his art.

Many letters of this time show Mr. Bryant's incessant activity in services to other writers. Charles Sedgwick thanks
him gratefully for his review of Miss Sedgwick's "Redwood,"
which, as it was inscribed to him, he only undertook at the urgent request of Mr. Jared Sparks, now become the editor of
the "North American."* Mr. Thomas J. Upham, since distinguished as a metaphysician, but then aspiring to be a poet,
submitted his first effusions to Mr. Bryant's correcting hand.
He revised in manuscript, also, the poems of Henry Pickering,
author of "The Ruins of Paestum," and afterward made them
the subject of a careful notice in the "North American."†
James T. Hillhouse, a writer who had before come into note
at home and abroad, thought it advisable to send the manuscript of "Percy's Masque" to him to be looked over. "Being resolved," Mr. Hillhouse wrote, "to venture once more
into the perilous field of dramatic poetry, I am anxious that
my weapons of warfare should be inspected and approved by
skilful eyes." Mr. Bryant read the poem with care, and commended it to public favor in an elaborate review.‡ Besides
these, many minor writers, ambitious to avail themselves of
his taste and judgment, enclosed their manuscripts to him, soliciting his opinion, and sometimes hinting that they would not
be offended if he should rewrite the weaker parts. He was patient and good natured with all, and often at pains to return
elaborate corrections and advices.

In these labors he was actuated by an urgent desire to help
the cause of American letters. "We should ill fulfil," he said,
"the task we have undertaken (as reviewers) if we did not occasionally pause, amid our severer labors, to notice the early
blossoms which the spring-time of our literature is calling up
along our path." "It is a matter of no small gratification," he

---

* "North American Review," No. 11, p. 384.   † No. 19, p. 42.   ‡ No. 20, p. 245.

goes on to say, "in watching the progress of American poetry, to see it assuming something of an original and national character—to see the embalmed body that lately was worshipped as a nymph, symmetrical, indeed, but cold, lifeless, and without human emotion, laid quietly in the grave, and a new-born being arise, full of youth and life, though sometimes awkwardly putting forth her strength, and sometimes affected in her attempts at gracefulness, and decking herself, in infantile fondness, with a profusion of ornaments and flowers."

As the books he criticised have largely passed away, so his criticisms of them have lost their interest for us now, yet they furnish, incidentally, hints of the writer's opinions on some topics connected with his art that may be pondered with profit. Thus, in the notice of "The Ruins of Pæstum," we discover what he regarded as the besetting fault of the writers of that day—haste; haste in composition, and haste in rushing before the public. "No kind of composition," he remarks, "requires a more perfect abstraction of mind than poetry, or a more intense and vigorous exertion of the faculties, and he who covets its rewards cannot dispense with its discipline. Improvisators have never produced a lasting work. When Parnassus is to be scaled, he only reaches the summit who boldly climbs its heights through brambles and briers, and fearless of precipices, and not he who sidles safely and slowly along circuitous paths, taking his ease when he will." Again, he remarks that to fly into print before one has given the last touches to his work, and made it as good as he is able, "offends decorum as much as a gentleman would who should walk into an assembly with a long beard, an unbrushed coat, and a dirty pair of boots." Similarly, in the review of "Redwood," we find a suggestive discussion of the adaptation of American life to the purposes of the novelist; and in that of "Hadad," * a little later, some wise thoughts on the propriety of using scenes and characters from Scripture as themes for dramatic treat-

---

* "New York Review," vol. i, p. 1.

ment, illustrating his conclusions by references to Milton, Cowley, Byron, Moore, Montgomery, Cumberland, Dwight, and
Hannah More.

It is to be inferred, from the persistency as well as variety
of his literary work at this time, that Mr. Bryant was verging
more and more toward a definite committal of himself to literature as a vocation. He did not neglect his practice of law;
on the contrary, his exertions were greater, and his reputation
as a lawyer was growing. He was called to argue cases at
Northampton, at New Haven, and before the Supreme Court
at Boston.* None the less, "Green River" shows that his
heart was not in it; he wanted to get away from the "sons
of strife, subtle and loud"; and the letters that passed between himself and several intimate friends now turn mainly
upon his wish to quit it all forever. Mr. Phillips rebukes
him frankly for his desire to abandon a career in which success is so entirely assured. Mr. Charles Sedgwick is more
guarded, but proposes that he should go to New York to
see what can be done there. In a letter of November 4, 1824,
he says:

"MY DEAR SIR: I have thought a great deal of your project since
court. The law is a hag, I know, wearing the wrinkled visage of antiquity, toward which you can feel no complacency. Though it
comes to us fraught with the pretended wisdom of ages, it wears an
ugly drapery of forms, and the principles of virtue and the simple
perceptions of truth are so involved in clouds of mystical learning
and nonsense that the finest mind must needs grope in obscurity and
be clogged with difficulties. Besides, there are tricks in practice
which perpetually provoke disgust. The end, indeed, may be good,
and success certain, and eminence, too, but the process is perplexing,
and the way not pleasant. I can not bear, however, to have you quit
the profession, for many weighty personal reasons; and I feel a great
interest that you should prove that your genius which delights the

---

* A late Senator of the United States from Connecticut, Mr. Truman Smith,
writes me that he was associated with Mr. Bryant in the conduct of an important trial
at New Haven, in which he evinced the very highest learning, acumen, and assiduity.

world can surmount the barriers of the least inviting and most laborious profession. Still I do not know how you ought to decide. If I
had your mind and a very prevailing desire for literary occupations, I
should run the hazard of indulging it. If you do this, I hope, before
you form any definite plan, you will go to New York and see what
you can find there worthy of your notice. I do not know how useful
my brothers may render themselves in this way, but of one thing I
can assure you: neither of them will be wanting in that zeal which
characterizes a friend. Whenever and whatever you decide, may
God bless you.   Yours, affectionately,
                                                    "C. S."

Whether he went to New York in compliance with this advice is not told; but Phillips's continued expostulations make
it clear that his purpose is at last fixed. He will turn his back
upon Themis, and be henceforth constant to the Muses. In
speaking of the reasons of this change later in life, Mr. Bryant
averred that he could never make up his mind to undertake a
cause, of the rigid and entire justice of which he was not fully
persuaded; and that, with such feelings, the law afforded him
little prospect of emolument. He further alleged that the decisions of the courts were not in accordance with equity, citing
in proof one of the last cases in which he was employed. It
seems that a person named Tobey had said of another person
named Bloss that he had burned down his own house to secure the insurance money. Tobey, on being prosecuted for
slander, Mr. Bryant acting as attorney for the prosecution,
was mulcted some five hundred dollars; but on an appeal from
the lower courts to the Supreme Court, it was decided, for
mainly technical reasons, that, as a man has a right to do as
he pleases with his own, the accusation was not slanderous.*
"Thus, by a piece of pure chicane—in a case the merits of

---

* The case is reported in 2d Pickering, Massachusetts Reports, p. 320. Chief
Justice Parson's decision is thus summarized: "Simply to burn one's store is not unlawful, and the words, '*He burnt his store*,' or '*there is no doubt in my mind that he
burned his own store, he would not have got his goods insured if he had not meant to
burn it*,' or a general allegation that the defendant charged the plaintiff with having

which were with my client, and which were perfectly understood by the parties, the court, the jury, and everybody who
heard the trial, or heard of it—my client was turned out of
court, after the jury had awarded him damages—and so deprived of what they intended he should receive." Disgusted,
therefore, alike by his non-success and the reason of it, he
flung up his briefs and turned his looks elsewhere.* His long-
ings, as we have seen, had been for Boston, the undoubted literary centre of the time, where Allston, Pierpont, Sprague, and
others were diffusing a mild poetic radiance over the better
achievements of learning and eloquence.   But the pivot was
now shifting.   New York—already illustrated by Irving and
Cooper—harbored some sparkling wits in the persons of Halleck, Drake, Verplanck, and Sands.   Yet it was a desperate
venture to undertake to live by literature in its existing state.
Irving and Cooper were our only successful professional authors, and both of them possessed some little hereditary fortune.   Verplanck and Sands were lawyers, and Halleck was
in a mercantile business.   What promise was there for a writer
of poetry—and that poetry of a refined, not popular, cast—in a
great commercial town?

There are still living a few persons who remember Mr.
Bryant in the Great Barrington days, † and I have obtained
from them, by letter or personal communication, some reminiscences of the impression he made upon his village contemporaries.   Mr. Leavenworth, who would otherwise have been

wilfully and maliciously burnt his own store, will not sustain an action for slander
without a colloquium or averment setting forth such circumstances as would render
such burning unlawful, and that the words were spoken of such circumstances; and
the want of such colloquium will not be cured by an innuendo."

* See, " I broke the Spell that held me long."—Poetical Works, vol. i, p. 99.

† These are Mr. E. W. Leavenworth, former member of Congress from the Syra-
cuse district, in whose father's house Mr. Bryant boarded, and who studied law for
a short time in his office; Mrs. George Pynchon, *née* Rossiter, who saw him in society; Colonel Ralph Taylor, for a while his room-mate; Mr. Isaac Seeley, his successor as town clerk; Mr. George Hains, whom, as justice of the peace, he married
to Miss Hannah Avery; and Mr. Edward P. Woodward and wife.

our best witness, was too young to remember much of him; but he distinctly recalls his solitary, brooding habits, and his dislike of his occupation; his love of the thickets along Green River and the Housatonic; and his reticent, almost austere manner with strangers, contrasted with his cheerful, entertaining, joyous way among his friends. Mrs. Pynchon relates that he was simple and scrupulously neat in his dress, wearing commonly blue cloth made in city fashion, which to rustic taste seemed a little dandified. Occasionally he attended evening parties, and took part in games and frolics, but was never demonstrative, and much less hilarious. The young women liked his bright eyes and clustering light-brown hair, and "set their caps for him"; but he once gave them great offence by saying that "farmers' daughters always walked as if they were carrying swill-pails"—for which ungracious speech, however, he made amends by marrying a farmer's daughter in the end. He drank wine now and then, but was rigidly temperate in both eating and drinking, making his diet chiefly of fruits and vegetables, and his beverages of milk and water. "A more perfect gentleman," said one good lady, "never existed; and yet he had a strange fondness for talking with queer and common people—farmers, woodmen, and stage-drivers. He would crack his jokes with them at any time, and yet seemed to avoid more respectable people." Colonel Taylor says he liked to wander most of anything, and when he met an acquaintance his first salutation was, "Come, what say you for a stroll"—which stroll, once begun, was apt to last for the greater part of the day. "He was a passionate botanist," adds the same authority; "knew the name of every tree, flower, and spire of grass; and was curious also about the antiquities of every place, and yet when you told him anything he seemed to know it all before. He relished a jest heartily—even broad jokes—got off some of his own, and his laugh, when he did laugh, began with a queer chuckle, spread gradually over the whole face, and finally shook him all over like an ague." "He was commonly gentle, courteous, and polite; but he allowed of no fa-

milarities; and impertinence or vulgarism he rebuked on the
spot, no matter who the offender.   Once, when some young
men, a little 'sot' with liquor, were teasing another somewhat
more intoxicated than themselves, he reproached them for
their inebriety and cruelty, predicting that they would all
come to a bad end; and every one of them did die a drunkard."
In court he often lost his self-control when provoked by adversaries; and on one occasion a neighbor met him bouncing
out of the door, almost white with rage, and exclaiming: "If
old Whiting says that again, I will thrash him within an inch
of his life."   "The fun of this was," says Colonel Taylor, "that
while Mr. Bryant was spare, almost diminutive in size, the
other fellow, General Whiting, was quite a giant.   Little as he
was, however, he was fearless, and would have undertaken,
and done it, too, if he liked."   "He was punctual in going to
church, owning half a pew in the Congregational Church, but
he was terribly prone to pick the sermons all to pieces."

As a poet he was scarcely known to his neighbors until he
had gone up to Cambridge to deliver his Phi Beta Kappa address.   Even then he was not without rivals for village fame.
One of these, David Hitchcock, a cobbler, whose "Shade of
Plato" and "Social Monitor" may yet be seen in type,* used
to pay, it is said, for his corn and potatoes with his doggerel.
Another, Emanuel Hodget, like Homer, sang his verses through
the streets.   Meeting Mr. Bryant one day, he accosted him
thus: "Well, Squire Bryant, they say you are a poet like me;
is that so?   I've never heerd any of your varses; would you
like one of mine?   Here goes:

> 'Squire Bryant is a man so bold
> He scorns to be controlled;
> And keeps his books under his arm,
> For fear they may be sold.' "

Mr. Bryant used to repeat this effusion with great glee;
but many of his listeners could not understand why he laughed

* They were printed in thin volumes at Stockbridge, in 1812.

at it so much. One among them, at least, was an exception, a French officer of Napoleon's army, and a friend of Lafayette, named Bouton, who gave him lessons in French and fencing, and became a most sincere and admiring friend. They corresponded in French when Bouton removed to another village, and in one of the latter's letters is this remonstrance: " Ah, my good friend, why dost thou despair because the fickle jade Fortune is not kind to thee? Thou shouldst snap thy fingers at her as I do. Hast thou not an amiable wife, a lovely child, and talents to win thee a name? Yes, Europe may fondle England's spoiled child of genius (Byron), but posterity will prize thee more than him "—a sagacious forecast, not flattery, if I may judge from the prevailing tone of the old soldier's epistles. Byron was then uppermost in everybody's mind, and it is told of Mr. Bryant that once as he approached a group of village youths one of them exclaimed: " See Bryant; because he is a poet he wears his shirt-collar turned over in imitation of Byron!" " Silence, sir!" was the poet's only response; " poor Byron is now no more," and his eyes moistened as he spoke. Judging by his sentiments in after years, he no doubt disliked the loose, cynical, and sophisticated man; but, like every one who lived from 1816 to 1824, he could not but feel the power and the passion of the bard, and his heart might well have softened at the thought of a career so young, so brilliant, so wasted, for which the redeeming future was now suddenly closed forever.*

---

* Mr. Bigelow, in his memorial address to the Century Club, said : " I don't remember to have heard him ever cite a line or an opinion of Byron, who was never one of his favorites. Some twenty-five or thirty years ago a person claiming to be a son of the poet appeared in New York with some poems and letters which he said had been written and given him by Byron, and for which he sought to find a market among our publishers. I spoke of the matter one day to Bryant, and his reply surprised me more than it would have done after my opinions of Byron were more settled. Looking up with an expression which implied more than he uttered, he said : ' I think we have poems enough of Byron already.' " No less, in the anthology which he supervised, there are more quotations from Byron than from any other contemporary poet.

CHAPTER ELEVENTH.

"A LITERARY ADVENTURER."

A. D. 1825, 1826.

MR. BRYANT visited New York in both January and February, 1825, a "literary adventurer," as he describes himself.* His route was by stage to Hartford, where he expected to take a steamer, but, as no steamer was ready to sail, he continued by stage, and reached the city after a journey of three days and a night. In his first letter to his wife, announcing his arrival, he says: "I have no leisure to report progress as to my projects; but I will do the best I can while I am here, and decide as soon as possible whether to remain or not. Sedgwick is constantly occupied with my affairs."

New York, at the time of these visits, was a considerable city, but hardly yet the metropolis. Boston surpassed it in literary repute, and Philadelphia vied with it in commercial activity. The completion of the Erie Canal, however, celebrated but a year before by grand illuminations and parades, having opened trade to the boundless prairies of the West, was giving it a start to supremacy. As yet its population did not exceed a hundred and fifty thousand souls. A line drawn from Catharine Street, on the East River, along Canal Street to the Hudson River, would have formed the northern boundary of the thickly settled parts. Broadway, the principal thoroughfare, was built up as far as Canal Street; beyond that to Prince Street only a few straggling houses were to be seen,

* Address on G. C. Verplanck,

and then came orchards and fields. I can myself remember to have played as a boy on a stone bridge that crossed a stream in Canal Street coming from the Kolch, a considerable pond near the site of the present Tombs, and to have hesitated in going beyond it, in dread of imaginary savages, or of the press gangs that stole little boys and carried them to sea. Lispenard's meadows, near by, had just been filled up and graded for building lots. Greenwich village, a few miles out, was a summer resort and place of refuge when the yellow fever raged, as it often did in the overcrowded districts. A favorite suburban walk was along the bank of the North River, as far as the State prison, at the foot of Amos Street, overlooking the harbor with its stately ships and its steam-boats, still somewhat of a novelty. Dr. Hosach's Botanic Garden, covering some twenty acres of ground (near Forty-seventh Street), and filled with rare plants, native and exotic, was generally an attractive place.

Within the city the streets were narrow, and about as dirty as they have ever since remained, but they were then frequented by loose pigs, were badly lighted by rusty oil lamps, and poorly watched by constables in huge capes and leather caps. Some few were exceptionally fringed with trees—elms, plane, and catalpas—and the park, finely shaded, was the play-ground for children in the day-time, and a social gathering-place for their elders in the evening. The richer and more fashionable denizens lived around the Battery, and Maiden Lane was the center of the more splendid shops and stores.*

More compact than now, the inhabitants were generally more intimately acquainted with one another. Everybody knew everybody, and everybody took part in what was going on. The resources of enjoyment—theatres, operas, concerts, balls, and excursions—were limited, but they were open to all.

---

* For many of these facts about the city I am indebted to a paper prepared for me by my friend Chief Justice Daly, who speaks from his own personal recollections. It is not the place, or I should avail myself more largely of his interesting communication.

Family visiting was common, so that it was easy to get into
"society"; and the taverns were not so much frequented by
wayfarers as by residents, to whom they answered the purpose
of clubs and restaurants.   Each one of them, in fact, had its
special circle of gossips and clever men.   All the celebrities of
the professions, the stage, or of literature were there to be met
with; and, seated at little tables on the well-sanded floor, with
pipes in their mouths, and jugs of punch at their elbows, they
discussed politics, books, play-actors, and the events of social
life.   In one of these clubs, founded by Cooper, called the
Bread and Cheese Club, which met in Washington Hotel, on
the site of Stewart's late wholesale store, Mr. Bryant encountered many of the distinguished men of the day—James
Kent, Thomas Addis Emmet, Edward D. Griffin, among the
lawyers; President Duer, and Professors Renwick, McVickar,
Anthon, and Moore, of Columbia College; the poets Percival,
Hillhouse, Halleck, and Sands; and the artists Vanderlyn,
Morse, Jarvis, and Dunlap.

He was, however, chiefly indebted to the brothers Sedgwick—Henry and Robert, both men of high standing at the
bar—for his social opportunities.   "Their houses," he says,*
" were the resort of the best company in New York—cultivated
men and women, literati, artists, and occasionally foreigners of
distinction.   Here I often found Verplanck, who had shortly
before published his work on the 'Evidences of the Christian
Religion,' and was then occupied in getting through the press
his able 'Essay on the Doctrine of Contracts.'   Here I met
the novelist J. Fenimore Cooper, who, however, soon after
had a difference with Robert Sedgwick, which put an end to
his intimacy with the family.   At these houses I met Robert C.
Sands, the wit and poet, whose 'Yamoyden,' written by him
in conjunction with James Wallis Eastburn, had just before
appeared; and Hillhouse, author of 'Percy's Masque,' and the
finer drama of 'Hadad,' which he was then writing.   Halleck,

* " Memoirs of Miss C. M. Sedgwick."

then in the height of his poetical reputation, was among the
visitors, and Anthony Bleeker, who read everything that came
out, and sometimes wrote for the magazines, an amusing companion, always ready with his puns, of whom Miss Eliza Fenno,
before her marriage to Verplanck, in 1811, wrote that she had
gone into the country to take refuge from Anthony Bleeker's
puns. Here were frequently seen Morse, then an artist, unconscious of the renown which was yet to crown him as the author
of the most wonderful invention of the age; and Cole, the
landscape painter, in the early promise of his genius. Here,
too, the clear, magnetic voice of Mrs. Nicholas was sometimes heard reciting Halleck's ' Marco Bozzaris,' or one of
Lockhart's ballads from the Spanish, to a spell-bound and
breathless audience."

"Henry D. Sedgwick was a philanthropist and reformer,
without the faults which too often make that class of persons
disagreeable. He was foremost in all worthy enterprises, but
did not fatigue people with them. He took a deep interest in
the project of reducing our statutes to a regular and intelligible code, and wrote an able pamphlet in its favor. I remember
vividly the personal interest he took in one of the authors of
that code—Benjamin F. Butler, then of Albany, and afterward,
under the administration of Jackson, Attorney-General of the
United States—how much he was impressed with the purity
of his character and the singleness of his mind, and how much
we all admired him, on a visit which he made to New York,
then a young man, with finely-chiseled features, made a little
pale· by study, and animated by an expression both of the
greatest intelligence and ingenuousness. Mr. Sedgwick was
warmly in favor of that change which has since been made in
our laws—giving the wife the absolute disposal of her own
property—the advantages of which he was fond of illustrating
by the marital law of Louisiana. He was a zealous friend of
universal freedom, and allowed no escaped slave from the
South to be sent back if he could prevent it. I remember going with him on board a vessel just arrived from a Southern

port, lying at a wharf in New York, in which it was said that
a colored man was detained in order to be sent back into slavery. We found no indications of the presence of any such
person, but, if we had, he would have been immediately liber-
ated by a writ of habeas corpus."

Three days after his arrival in New York, February 21st,
Mr. Bryant writes to his wife:

"My dear Frances: It will not be possible for me to set out
from here till Thursday next, which will bring me to Hudson on Friday afternoon. . . . My friends here are making some interest to obtain the approbation and patronage of the Athenæum for a literary
paper to be established under my direction, and I think there is a
pretty good prospect that they will succeed. The Athenæum at present is all the rage, and I think there is great probability *q'un journal
etabli sous ses auspices aurait une circulation fort étendue.** At all events,
I shall make the experiment. *Mons. Hillhoues, Dr. Wainwright,
prêtre de l'eglise Anglicane, Mons. Verplanck et beaucoup d'autres savans
de New York se sont intéressés pour moi dans ce projet, et j'ai a ce que je
pense, sujet d'espere que mon attentat n'echouera pas.* † *Baissez la petite
Fanchette pour moi. Ayez, je vous prie, un soin particulier de votre santé
et croyez moi.*

"*Pour la vie,*
"*Avec la derniere passion,*
"*Votre ami, etc.,*
"Wm. C. Bryant."

The attempt did fail, for some reason or other. Mr. Bryant's reputation had preceded him, ‡ and helped him to ac-

---

* That a journal established under its auspices will have a wide circulation.

† Mr. Hillhouse, Dr. Wainwright, prelate of the English Church, Mr. Verplanck,
and many others are very much interested in my project, and I have reason to hope
that my attempt will not fail.

‡ No less, a venerable lady informs me that at a great *conversatione* in the house
of one of the leaders of society, at which she was present, a gentleman read the "Waterfowl" from a newspaper slip, and no one present could tell him the name of the
author. So, Mr. Coleman, the editor of the "Evening Post," a sort of literary Aris-
tarchus, reprinted "Thanatopsis," May 11, 1824, with these remarks: "Hearing a

quaintances, but it is possible that his religious opinions stood somewhat in his way. The Unitarian sect, to which he belonged, was small in numbers, and not in good odor with its orthodox rivals. Its first society had been formed in a parlor only a few years before, 1819, Mr. Edward Everett preaching the first sermon, and a year later, when Dr. Channing came on from Boston to address it, was refused admittance to any of the usual places of religious meeting. At length the College of Physicians and Surgeons opened a room to it, and thereby stirred up a hornet's nest.* But whatever the hindrances, after waiting several days, Mr. Bryant returned home greatly disappointed.

A month later he came back to the city to renew his attempt, and writing to his wife, March 23d, says:

"My dear Frances: I suppose you would like to know whether I broke my neck in going out to Hudson last Thursday. I can assure

literary friend, whose taste and judgment we respect, speak highly of the poetic talents of William Cullen Bryant, and of his effusions published in 1821, we procured the book, and now present the following beautiful poem, as fully justifying the eulogium."

* Dr. J. W. Francis was one of the physicians who were bold enough to let the room to Dr. Channing's friends, and in describing the commotion it caused, adds: "Some three days after that memorable Sunday I accidentally met the great theological thunderbolt of the times, Dr. John M. Mason, in the book-store of that intelligent publisher and learned bibliopole, James Eastburn. Mason soon approached me, and in earnestness exclaimed, 'You doctors have been engaged in a wrongful work ; you have permitted heresy to come in among us, and have countenanced its approach. You have furnished accommodations for the devil's disciples.' Not wholly unhinged, I replied: 'We saw no such great evil in an act of religious toleration ; nor do I think,' I added, 'that one individual member is responsible for the acts of an entire corporation.' 'You are all equally guilty,' cried the doctor, with enkindled warmth. 'Do you know what you have done ? You have advanced infidelity by complying with the request of these sceptics.' 'Sir,' said I, 'we hardly felt disposed to sift their articles of belief as a religious society.' 'There, sir, there is the difficulty,' exclaimed the doctor. 'Belief; they have no belief; they believe in nothing, having nothing to believe. They are a paradox ; you can not fathom them. How can you fathom a thing that has no bottom ?' I left the doctor dreadfully indignant, uttering something of the old slur on the sceptical tendencies of the faculty of physic."—"Old New York," p. 154.

you that it is as sound at this moment as your own, notwithstanding your prediction. However, I met with what was almost an equivalent. I got wet by riding half a mile in that tremendous thunder-shower, and afterward drove to Hudson, a distance of ten miles, in a damp great coat and pantaloons. I waked the next morning giddy and almost blind with a cold. I thought to go to New York in the steamboat on Friday, but none went down that day. Then I engaged a passage in a sloop, and had my baggage carried on board of her, and after waiting there from three o'clock till six in the afternoon, during which time I was chiefly employed in pulling at a rope to help get her away from the dock, against a strong northwest wind, the vessel ran upon the bottom of an old wharf in the river and stuck. I went back to my quarters in the city. The next day (Saturday) the Olive Branch came along about noon; I got on board of her, and Sunday morning at five o'clock found myself in this city.

"Here I am trying to starve myself well, going hungry amid a profusion of good cheer, and refusing to drink good wine amid an ocean of it. But all will not do; I am continually in the steamboat. Sitting or standing, I feel the roll and swell of the water under me; the streets and floors of houses swing from side to side as if they were floating in a sea. However, I am not much alarmed as long as my lungs are free from the distemper, which they seem to be hitherto. My negotiations with the 'Atlantic Magazine' are going on, but I do not know exactly what will come of them. . . . Mr. Hillhouse's 'Hadad' is out. He has presented me with a copy, which I shall bring up with me. . . . Monday evening I was at one of the *soirées* of Dr. Hosack. There was a crowd of literary men—citizens and strangers —in fine apartments splendidly furnished, hung with pictures, etc. I saw Captain Franklin among others, who is just arrived from Europe, and is going on another Polar Expedition, by land.* Two other gentlemen of the expedition were with him. He does not look like a man who has suffered the hardships of which his narrative gives an account. He is square built, rather short, inclining to corpulency, with the complexion of a shoemaker. Kiss Fanchette for me.

"Your affectionate husband,

"W. C. BRYANT."

* This was Sir John Franklin on his second voyage to the Arctic Seas.

The "Atlantic Magazine," here spoken of, a monthly periodical which had been established in 1824 under the charge of Mr. Robert C. Sands, was now in the hands of Mr. Henry J. Anderson, and leading a precarious life. It was proposed to amalgamate it with an earlier periodical, called the "Literary Review," and issue them under the name of the "New York Review and Athenæum Magazine," with Mr. Anderson and Mr. Bryant as editors, and "the co-operation of several gentlemen, amply qualified, to furnish the departments of Intelligence, Poetry, and Fiction." This arrangement was carried into effect, and the first number of the new review was announced to appear in June. Enclosing a prospectus to Mr. Dana, in April, Mr. Bryant wrote, not very hopefully: "I have given up my profession, which was a shabby one, and I am not altogether certain that I have got into a better. Bliss & White, however, the publishers of the 'New York Review,' employ me, which at present will be a livelihood, and a livelihood is all I got from the law." Dana, in response, promised him every sort of assistance, and, as an earnest of his purpose, enclosed a contribution which he called "The Dying Crow." Dana's letter, dated Cambridge, April 15th, discloses a bit of literary history, showing that, although the older man considerably, he was yet much the younger poet. He says:

"I send you my first attempt—perhaps my last—in blank verse. I may as well say in *verse*, for I never wrote thirty lines before in any measure. It may be too long; though, as it is a musing, meditative affair, I do not know that such an objection holds against it. At any rate, I would not go through the toil of compressing it. . . . Does the movement offend thee, thou veteran in verse? The truth is, though I have read a good deal of poetry, and been delighted with its music, I never thought or cared about its rules. So I came to my work raw and ignorant. Though I have said so much about my 'Crow,' you must not think that I expect you, as a matter of course, to show him to the public. . ."

"What a magnificent hymn you wrote for the last 'Literary Ga-zette'!"*

Before this letter was received, Mr. Bryant had gone to Great Barrington, to settle up the remnants of his business, and to provide a home for his little family during the summer. It was impossible for him, however, to take a final leave of the grand old woods, which for ten years had been the sanctuaries of his musings, and which perhaps he might never see again, at least on the familiar footing of the past, without offering to the Mightiest, amid their majestic solitudes, "his solemn thanks and supplications." As he walked the columned aisles beneath the verdant roof, hearing only the soft winds that ran along the summit of the trees in music, he sang in grave and measured language his "Forest Hymn," pouring out his soul in worship to that universal Spirit which others, less simple and austere, find only in houses made with hands.

On his return to the city he took lodgings with a French family, of which he gives this account (May 24th):

"My dear Frances: I am now boarding at M. Evrard's. The family speak only French, and what is better, very good French; and what is better yet, are very kind and amiable people. Mr. E. is a bigoted Catholic, and is taking great pains to convert me to the true and ancient faith. I have been so far wrought upon by his arguments that I went yesterday to vespers in St. Peter's Church; but my convictions were not sufficiently strong to induce me to kneel at the elevation of the host. As I have a great respect for family prayer among all denominations of Christians, I intend asking M. Evrard the favor of being permitted to attend his. On these occasions, it is said, he utters with inconceivable rapidity a long list of such petitions as the following:

'Sainte Marie, priez pour moi,
Chaste Vierge, priez pour moi,
Mére adorable, priez pour moi,
Mére de Dieu, priez pour moi.'

---

* The "Forest Hymn." Mr. Bryant was still a writer for the "Gazette," though Mr. Parsons had yielded the control to others.

" I have had one or two turns of being a little homesick since I have been here, but I think if you and Francis were with me I should pass my time quite as pleasantly, to say the least, as I did in Great Barrington. In the mean time I have become a great church-goer; I went three times yesterday, including the Roman Catholic service, which is more, I believe, than I have done before these ten years."

To Dana's letter, which arrived in his absence, he replied the next day, 25th:

" MY DEAR SIR : On coming to New York about a week since, I found two letters from you which seemed from their dates to have been waiting for me some time. In one of them I was very glad to find a contribution in verse for my magazine. I am surprised after reading it to hear you say that you never wrote thirty lines before in any measure. You have come into your poetical existence in full strength, like the first man. Not that I was surprised to find the conceptions beautiful—that I was prepared for, as a matter of course —but you write quite like a practiced poet. The printer has got it, and you shall see your first-born in print next week. It will be admired, without doubt. The only fault I find with it is, that you give rather too many magnificent titles to a bird the popular associations connected with which are not generally of the dignified kind you mention. I can speak also of his character from my own experience, having once kept a tame crow, and found him little better than a knave, a thief, and a coward. As for the trochees, etc., never fash your mind about them. They are well enough. I would not alter them if it could be done without injuring the beauty of the expression. I hope to receive more favors of the same kind from you. Choose a subject worthy of your genius, and you will do nobly. In the mean time, if you have any prose that you can spare, I should be very glad to publish it in my journal. . . . I suspect that in the course of the week we shall be sorely perplexed to get matter for the miscellaneous department. A talent for such articles is quite rare in this country, and particularly in this city. There are many who can give grave, sensible discussions on subjects of general utility, but few who can write an interesting or diverting article for a miscellany. . . .

" I do not know how long my connection with this work will continue.   My salary is $1,000; no great sum, to be sure, but it is twice what I got by my practice in the country.   Besides, my dislike for my profession was augmenting daily, and my residence in Great Barrington, in consequence of innumerable quarrels and factions which were springing up every day among an extremely excitable and not very enlightened population, had become quite disagreeable to me. It cost me more pain and perplexity than it was worth to live on friendly terms with my neighbors ; and, not having, as I flatter myself, any great taste for contention, I made up my mind to get out of it as soon as I could and come to this great city, where, if it was my lot to starve, I might starve peaceably and quietly.   The business of sitting in judgment on books as they come out is not the literary employment the most to my taste, nor that for which I am best fitted, but it affords me, for the present, a *certain* compensation, which is a matter of some consequence to a poor devil like myself."

Again in a few days (May 28th) Mr. Bryant recurs to the same subject :

"MY DEAR SIR : You will see in the copy of our magazine (for June) which I send you, that I have changed your crow to a raven. I do not know how you will like the metamorphosis, but it is a change only of the title of your poem, and I have not ventured to take any such liberty with the verses.   My reason for doing this was that the *title* was not a taking one; Anderson was of the same opinion, and urged me strongly to make the alteration ; and Mr. Halleck (author of 'Fanny,' etc.), to whom it was shown, while he admired the beauty of the poetry, thought the title unfortunate.   The raven is a North American bird, common in the interior of the United States, and naturalists say that his habits are similar to those of the crow.   I hope you will forgive the liberty I have taken, as it was only with a view to draw to your poem the attention it deserves.   You will appear in our magazine in company with Mr. Halleck.   The poem entitled 'Marco Bozzaris' was written by him, and I think is a very beautiful thing. Anderson was so delighted with it—he got it from the author after much solicitation—that he could not forbear adding the expression of his admiration at the end of the poem.   For my part, though I entirely agree with him in his opinion of the beauty of the poem, I have

my doubts whether it is not better to let the poetry of magazines commend itself to the reader by its own excellence. The lines which follow yours were written by your humble servant." *

To his wife he writes, June 3d :

"MY DEAR FRANCES: I send you by Mr. Charles Sedgwick, who
is about setting out for Lenox, the first number of the 'New York
Review,' which he has kindly undertaken to put into the post-office
there along with this letter. I think it is a pretty good number. I
speak with reference to the articles which I did not write myself. . . .
Our subscription list is going on pretty well; we have already about
five hundred in the city and one hundred in the country, besides the
Boston subscribers of which no return has yet been made. . . . This
week has been a chapter of terrible accidents in New York. Last
Friday a Swiss who had just arrived in this country was murdered
by two of his fellow-passengers. Yesterday morning at six o'clock
the boiler of one of the steamboats plying between this city and
Brunswick exploded at the wharf, as she was just setting out with one
hundred passengers on board, and four of the hands were scalded to
death and others badly injured; and this morning about two o'clock
a Mr. Lambert, returning from a party a little out of the city, with
some of his friends, was assaulted by a party of drunken apprentices,
and a fray ensued in which he was killed.†

"I like my boarding-house better and better. It is almost impossible to conceive of a man of more goodness of heart and rectitude
of principle than M. Evrard. He is very religious, very charitable,
and very honest—a proof of the utter folly and presumption of all
those who arrogate to their own sect the exclusive title of Christians.
Here is a bigoted Catholic—a man who believes that miracles are
wrought by good men at this late day; who kneels to the consecrated
wafer as to the body of God himself; and who invokes saints and
angels to pray for him—and yet his religion, mistaken as it is in these
points, is as full of piety toward God and kindness to his neighbor as
that of any man I ever knew, while it is much more amiable and
cheerful than that of many sects. On the whole, I think that a *good
Catholic* is quite as good as a *good Calvinist.*"

* "A Song of Pitcairn's Island."
† Rather startling incidents for an emigrant from a quiet country village.

The next week (June 12) he continued his reports:

"My dear Frances: I envy you very much the pure air, the breezes, the shade, and the coolness which you must enjoy in the country, while I am sweltering under a degree of heat which I never experienced in my whole lifetime for so long a period. For six days the thermometer has hardly been below 80°, day or night. I cannot write except in the morning, when the air is a little cooler; but in the middle of the day, when the thermometer is at 85° or 87° Fahr., it is almost impossible to call up resolution enough even to read. Yesterday, in the afternoon, I rode a few miles into the country; I found it worse, if possible, than the city. The roads were full of carts, barouches, chaises, hacks, and people on horseback passing each other; and a thick cloud of dust lay above the road as far as the eye could follow it. It was almost impossible to breathe the stifling element.

"Along with these inconveniences, however, there is one advantage which, to me, is of considerable importance. The nights are very dry. I do not perceive that the night air is at all more damp than that of the day. There is a window at the head of my bed, and I have slept with it wide open for six nights past without experiencing the least inconvenience—without perceiving anything like that current of moist air which in the country you always feel coming from an open window in the stillest nights. A cough which I have had hanging upon my lungs ever since last March has left me entirely. Upon the whole, I think that a change of climate is likely to prove rather beneficial to my health than otherwise. I lodge in Chambers Street, near the Unitarian Church, which, of course, I attend pretty regularly. M. Evrard, my host, has lived here twenty years, and during that time no epidemic fever has prevailed in this quarter. His house is at some distance from that part of the city in which the yellow fever made so many victims a few years since. The North River is at a short distance from us. I see it whenever I put my head out of the window; and whenever the wind is westerly it comes to us from over a body of water several miles in width. . . ."

His work on the "Review" was rather more laborious than he had anticipated. Mr. Anderson, his colleague, and Mr. Sands, who was now joined with them, were both active writers, but the laboring oar fell to his hands. He had complained of the drudgery of the law, and now found himself involved in drudgery of another kind quite as trying. To read and give an account of trashy novels and flimsy verses; to prune and patch the manuscripts of ambitious but inexperienced writers; to provide essays, tales, and poems of his own—were by no means agreeable tasks. Besides, the city was insufferably hot, dirty, and stuffy, and he missed his rambles in the woods. Still, he put as good a face upon it as he could, and says to Mrs. Bryant, the latter part of June:

"Notwithstanding the heat, the noise, and the unpleasant odors of the city, I think that if you and Frances were with me I should pass my time here much more pleasantly than at Great Barrington. I am obliged to be pretty industrious, it is true, but that is well enough. In the mean time, I am not plagued with the disagreeable, disgusting drudgery of the law; and, what is still better, am aloof from those miserable feuds and wranglings that make Great Barrington an unpleasant residence, even to him who tries every method in his power to avoid them."

He speaks encouragingly, but he was in reality despondent. The prospects of the "Review" were not bright; he was very much alone; and his heart was ever going back to his mountains. His mood is indicated in those sweet and pensive lines on "June"—gentle aspirations destined to become a prophecy—wherein he hopes his grave at least shall be made in the season of flowers and singing birds, and where,

> "—through the long, long summer hours
>   The golden light should lie,
> And thick young herbs and groups of flowers
>   Stand in their beauty by."

It was a great relief to him, in the latter part of June and July, to be able to make a flying visit to Cummington, and, standing on his native hills again, while the mountain wind, most spiritual thing of all the wide earth knows, lifted his

brown locks, to indulge in the grand reveries that appear in
" The Skies," and the " Lines on Revisiting the Country."

He was more contented with the city when his family
joined him in the autumn, for he was less solitary. His habits,
to say nothing of his reserve and diffidence, withheld him from
miscellaneous companionships. What leisure his labors on the
" Review " left him he devoted to perfecting his knowledge of
French and Provençal, and to the acquisition of the Italian,
Spanish, and Portuguese languages. He had his intimacies,
but they were few. Cooper and Verplanck were occasional
visitors ; Anderson attracted him by his profound and various
knowledge and courteous manners ; and Sands's acquisitions
and humor rendered his fellowship delightful. With William
Ware, the Unitarian clergyman, whose refinement and culture
were afterward so beautifully exhibited in "Zenobia," " Pro-
bus," and " Julian," he formed a lifelong friendship. And there
were others to whom he may be said to have attached himself
as a class—the artists. They were men for the most part like
himself—of great simplicity of character, fond of the beauties
of nature, and struggling, in the midst of poverty and untoward
circumstances, to win a place, however humble, for themselves
and their country in the higher walks of intellectual exertion.
In their company he was at home ; they made him a member
of their little societies and conclaves ; he took part in all their
efforts to bring the fine arts forward in the estimation of an
indifferent or ungenial public, and, by his persistent advocacy
of their claims at that early day, helped to gain for them the
high repute they now enjoy.

How patiently and faithfully he discharged his duties of
editor may be seen in this letter of September 1st to his friend
Dana :

" MY DEAR SIR : I intended answering your letter before this, but
I have been exceedingly lazy and somewhat hurried during the hot
weather that has continued almost ever since I received it. I have
found time, however, to look over the lines you sent me, and, as you
seemed to give me leave to make some alterations, I have in particular

taken the liberty, whenever I found you out of the pale which the law-givers of versification have put up to confine poets in, to catch you and bring you back, and put on your fetters again. There are two lines which I am confident you left on purpose to try me:

> 'O'er hills, through leafy woods, and leafless;
> To me, who love the stream to trace, etc.' *

I tried by reading these lines over and over to make them agree in time and measure; but, finding that impossible, I altered them, and in doing this was obliged to alter several of the neighboring lines. I must confess that you had one good reason—I have written *good reason*—but that is wrong—you had one apology for leaving the lines as they were—namely, the difficulty of making them otherwise.

"I have also ventured to make some changes where the sentences were continued from one couplet to the beginning of another, or where they began near the end of one couplet and were continued to the middle of the next—a practice sometimes exceedingly graceful in the heroic measure, but which, if frequently introduced in octo-syllabic verse, produces harshness. In other cases where I thought the idea not sufficiently brought out, I have taken the liberty to amplify it a little. But you will see all the mutilations I have made when you receive the journal, which I will send on the heels of this letter.

"One thing I have done: I have respected the thoughts in all the alterations I have made, and it is a great excellence of your verses that they are full of thought. You are, however, more at home in blank verse than rhyme—at least, you are so in the specimens you have sent me.

"I saw Cooper yesterday. He is printing a novel entitled 'The Last of the Mohicans.' The first volume is nearly finished. You tell me that I must review him next time myself. Ah, sir! he is too sensitive a creature for me to touch. He seems to think his own works his own property, instead of being the property of the public, to whom he has given them; and it is almost as difficult to praise or blame them in the right place as it was to praise or blame Goldsmith properly in the presence of Johnson."

* Fragment of an Epistle.

Again, he writes to Dana in January, 1826:

"I like your poem very much. I have not yet been able to discover the popular name of your bird,* but I wish you would take the
trouble to make a little change in the metrical construction of it, and
send me the alterations in your next. I refer to the following lines:

> "'With the motion and roar
> Of waves driving to shore.'

And also,

> "'To thy spirit no more
> Come with me, quit the shore
> For the joy and the light
> When the summer birds sing.'

These lines do not correspond in measure with the lines which occupy
the same place in the other stanzas. All other lines in the poem are
such as the ear will acknowledge for iambics, but these are in a kind
of tripping measure, which is not in harmony with the rest of the
poem, and is disagreeable from its unexpectedness. Besides, they do
not, as it seems to me, suit with the general solemn and plaintive effect
of the whole. Cannot you substitute iambics for these? The abbre-
viation *long* I should be glad to see altered, for it is certainly an inno-
vation; but if you insist upon it I shall retain it. †

"It is true, as you say, that there is a want of *literary entertainment*
in our journal. But as to the multitude of clever men here who might
furnish it, let me say that we have some clever men to be sure, but
they are naughtily given to instructing the world, to elucidating the
mysteries of political economy and the principles of jurisprudence,
etc.; they seem to think it a sort of disgrace to be entertaining.
Since the time of Salmagundi, the city has grown exceedingly grave
and addicted to solid speculations. Paulding sometimes writes for
our magazine, and we pick up the rest of it as well as we can."

---

* It is now entitled "The Little Beach Bird."
† These lines now stand:

> "With the motion and the roar
> Of waves that drive to shore."

And,

> "And on the meadow light
> When birds for gladness sing."

In the autumn of 1825 Mr. Bryant had been invited by the
Athenæum Society to deliver a series of lectures on " Poetry,"
and, having accepted the invitation, he prepared four lectures
for delivery in the April following.   The more prominent
residents of the city were making a systematic effort to raise
its intellectual tone and scope, and for that purpose organized
courses of lectures on many subjects.   Professor Charles Anthon was engaged to discourse on " Roman Writers," Professor Renwick on " Chemistry," Professor McVickar on " Taste
and Beauty," Mr. S. F. B. Morse on " Painting," Mr. William
Beach Lawrence on " Political Economy," and Dr. John
Frederick Schroeder on " Oriental Literature." *   Mr. Bryant
could not, of course, in the brief compass allowed him, pretend
to give anything like an exhaustive or complete view of the oldest and most prolific of the arts—the very literature of which
fills volumes, if not libraries.   As, moreover, his lectures were
intended to be merely a popular defence and recommendation
of Poetry as one of the grand means of human culture, and
not to be addressed to adepts or even students, they required
no elaborate discussions of its philosophy, conceived either in
the spirit of the English school of Addison, Kames, and Blair,
or of the more recent and deeper æsthetics of the Germans.
He could not so much as dwell upon its technical rules, or the
history of its development, or the characteristics of different
countries and ages, or even the merits and defects of the great
writers by whom it had been most signally illustrated, and he
therefore confined himself to a brief consideration of its nature,
its influences, and its relations to the general progress of mankind.   As these elementary views will probably be printed in
his collected works, I give no analysis of them.   Suffice it to

* Some of the lectures at the Athenæum were not without results. Among the
lecturers was Professor James Freeman Dana, of New Haven, whose subject was
" Electro-Magnetism," a science then in its infancy ; and among the hearers was S.
F. B. Morse, the artist, whose thoughts, already turned to the possibility of utilizing
the electric current, took a shape which a few years later issued in the Electro-Magnetic Telegraph.—" Life of Morse," p. 161. New York : D. Appleton & Co., 1874.

say that his several topics were handled with clearness, insight, and facility as well as amplitude of illustration. The discussions, though not profound as we should now esteem them, gave occasion for many happy and instructive remarks, and, as an expression of the views of a master on important phases of his own peculiar walk, they are suggestive and interesting.

While delivering these lectures, Mr. Bryant was also active in another and kindred movement. There had been for years in New York an institution called the American Academy of Art, of which Jonathan Trumbull was President, and Chancellor Livingston, De Witt Clinton, and other conspicuous citizens were members. It gave yearly exhibitions of pictures, mostly borrowed from private owners, and it professed to furnish instruction in an irregular way to students in the elements of drawing. The artists were dissatisfied with it as a representative of their body, not only because its means of education were inadequate, but because it was almost exclusively managed by laymen. To supply its deficiencies, they organized at first a simple Drawing Association (November 8, 1825), which met in the old Almshouse building, behind the City Hall. This soon expanded (January 18, 1826) into the more ambitious enterprise of a National Academy of the Arts of Design. Mr. S. F. B. Morse, one of the most active promoters of the scheme, was chosen the first President of it, and Messrs. Durand, Dunlap, Inman, Cummings, Ingham, Agate, and a few others composed the membership. It opened schools, gave exhibitions, and instituted a series of lectures on anatomy, perspective and cognate subjects, among which mythology and history, in their relation to the plastic arts, were included. In 1826 Mr. Bryant was appointed one of the professors of the new academy. When he began his labors does not appear on the records, but he read to the classes five lectures on "Mythology" in December, 1827, which were repeated in February, 1828; again in January, 1829, and finally in November, 1831. This continuance of them through five years would show how highly they were estimated, if we had not the grateful votes of the Academy testifying to their worth. Confining his treatment to the Greek and Roman mythology, and to the *Dii Majorum Gentium* in this, the lecturer gave the fullest historical details within his sphere of the origin and growth of the ancient faiths, accompanied by such allegorical interpretations as they had suggested to former writers or to his own fancy. He has succeeded wonderfully in compressing the wide, weltering, almost chaotic mass into a consistent and intelligible form, and imparting life, beauty, and meaning to the stories which have come down to us rather as crude, grotesque, and indecent fantasies than as "the fair humanities of old religion." *

Meantime the "Review" was getting on as it could—that is, not swimmingly. Compared with the ample dimensions and vivacious contents of our later periodicals, with "The Century" and "Harper's," it was but a meagre and dull affair.

---

* The distinction with which he opens the first lecture I think worth preserving: "The Painter and the Sculptor," he says, "are connected with the ancients, with their religion and with their notions of all that is noble and beautiful in humanity, by nearer ties than any other students of antiquity—nearer than even the Poet or the Philosopher. You live among the remains of the ancient world, and, with the creations of ancient genius before your eyes, you copy the noble features moulded by the old artists ; you imitate forms that were wondered at and worshipped in the age in which they were produced—attitudes and faces which even yet inspire the beholder with a sort of religious awe, seem to fill the air around them with the emanations of their own superhuman beauty. On the other hand, between the modern student and the fathers of ancient history a veil is interposed which is never wholly withdrawn—the veil of a dead language. He must labor long and severely before he can surmount this difficulty. He is detained in things which have no connection with the pure spirit of ancient literature—in grammatical rules, the meaning of words, and forms of construction. It is as if you had to acquire the sense of sight by a surgical operation before you could look upon the remains of ancient sculpture around you. After all his labor he must content himself with incomplete conceptions of the pathos, the force and harmony shrined in the majestic but disused dialects which he studies—dialects which to no man in modern times convey the ideas they express with that grace and energy which belongs to the language of his birth. If he recurs to translations, he is still more unfortunate, for these are but shadows of their glorious originals."

It wanted, I think, distinctiveness, perhaps aggressiveness of character. Many of the disquisitions were heavy, and the criticisms, though sensible, were not pungent.* It was, no doubt, as good as any of its contemporaries, even the " North American," on which it was modelled. In one respect, its poetry, it far surpassed them all. Of Mr Bryant's own works it contained: " The Song of Pitcairn's Island," " The Skies," " Lines on Revisiting the Country," " I Cannot Forget," " To a Mosquito," " Romero," " The Close of Autumn " (" Death of the Flowers "), " The New Moon," " A Meditation on Rhode Island Coal," " Hymn to Death," " An Indian Girl's Lament," and one or two others, not since acknowledged. Some of them, written in the country, are equal to his best; but others, particularly the humorous pieces—effects, no doubt, of Sands's lively fellowship—are not so much admired. Dana also contributed to it his best things: " The Dying Raven," " Fragments of an Epistle," " The Husband and Wife's Grave," and " The Little Beach Bird." It introduced to the public Halleck's " Marco Bozzaris," " Burns," " Wyoming," and " Connecticut," † which are his best; several of the earlier efforts of Longfellow, which, however, were not his best, and of N. P. Willis, who wrote under the name of Roy. Mr. George Bancroft, since eminent as an historian, aspired to poetry then, and

* They were not, however, without keen critical insight, as this notice of Disraeli's " Vivian Gray " may show. " This is a piquant and amusing novel, though its merits are not of a very high order. . . . The foundation of the story is extravagant. The powers, purposes, and influence of a mature man are attributed to a boy of twenty; and the work is rather a series of sketches than a regularly built story. The hero has no mistress but politics, and no adventures but political adventures. The other prominent characters are all fools or knaves, and all are more or less forced and unnatural. Their aggregate makes a strong picture, which dazzles, but does not satisfy. The style of writing is dashing and careless, occasionally rising into hasty extravagance, and at times sinking into mawkish sentimentality. The morality of the book is loose. It is, in fact, little more than a picture of the vices and follies of the great, with an active spirit in the midst of them, making their vices and follies the stepping-stones to his ambition."—December, 1827.

† The three last after it was changed to the " United States Review."

translated for it from Goethe and Schiller, and Mr. Caleb Cushing opened his varied career in it by gentle flirtations with the Italian Muses.

Two subjects were given prominence in the prose department which greatly needed codling at that time, the Fine Arts and the Italian opera, the former of which I suspect Mr. Bryant took care of, and the latter Mr. Anderson.* Mr. Bryant's principal prose articles were: "Hillhouse's Hadad," " Memoirs of Count Segur," "Provençal Poets," " Scott's Lives of the Novelists," "Moore's Sheridan," "Rammohun Roy's Precepts of Jesus," "Wayland's Discourses," " Webster's Address," "Recent Poetry," "Richard Henry Lee," "Percival's Poems," "A Pennsylvania Legend," "Sketches of Corsica," " Wheaton's Pinkney," etc. Of these articles the interest now has wholly passed away. They are for the most part well written, and some of them exhibit research. His portrait of Sheridan, after Moore, is full of character-painting; he breaks a lance with the potent Sir Walter even as to the comparative worth of the Romancers; shows himself in advance of his day in religious liberality when he speaks of Rammohun Roy; and the "Sketches of Corsica" enable him to trace the peculiar characteristics of Bonaparte, his wild passion for war, his rancorous revengefulness, his duplicity, his contempt for wo-

---

* A mercurial but accomplished Italian teacher, Lorenzo Da Ponte, a former friend of Mozart and of the eccentric Joseph II, of Austria (and whose adventures in Europe furnished the materials of a diverting autobiography), pervaded New York, and possessed it with some degree of his own enthusiasm for his native language and his national music. It was by his help that a company of singers, under the management of Signor Garcia, was persuaded to try its fortunes in the new world, and to transplant, if it could, a rare exotic to a somewhat reluctant soil. Mr. Anderson was intimately connected with Da Ponte (having afterward married his daughter), and through him Mr. Bryant, who cared nothing for music, though a great deal for the Italian language and literature, was brought in contact with this strange world. For a time he and his family occupied the same boarding-house with the Garcia's, where they learned to admire the wild fawn of the herd, the Signorita Felicite, then in the seventeenth year of her age, beautiful, capricious, charming, and affectionate, who afterward, by the grace, the versatility, the brilliancy, and the terrible grandeur of her operatic performances, acquired a world-wide fame as Mme. Malibran.

men, and his brigandage, to the barbarous ferocities of his
Corsican blood.

But the "Review," whatever its merits or defects, found
no public.   It was born at an unfavorable time—during one of
those periodical storms which, under the name of financial
crises, sweep over the world with destructive power—and the
little venture felt the effects of a gale in which, in the old world,
the more stupendous fabric reared by the genius of Scott
went down.   In March (1826) it was merged with the " New
York Literary Gazette " into the " New York Literary Gazette,
or American Athenæum "; and in July into " The United
States Gazette " of Boston, under the title of " The United
States Review and Literary Gazette "; big names all of them,
but scarcely more than names.   In the final arrangement Mr.
Bryant was allowed a quarter ownership and five hundred dollars a year salary, with a prospective increase contingent upon
the increase of subscribers, who never came.   A divided control, one editor (Mr. James G. Carter, afterward Charles Fol-
som) holding the reins at Boston, another, Mr. Bryant, at New
York, must have been a hindrance instead of a help.   The outlook for our " adventurer " grew more and more dark.   In spite
of his struggles, his projects had failed, or threatened failure ;
and the " Journey of Life " opened upon him in the sombre
hues of his little poem, where

> " The lights that tell of cheerful homes appear
> Far off; and die like hope amid the glooms."

Lest resources should be altogether wanting, he renewed his
license to practice law in the courts of New York (March,
1826), and was associated for a time with Mr. Henry Sedgwick in the prosecution of a claim for the recovery of a part
of the fund which had been raised in behalf of the Greeks, but
which had in some way been perverted.   But I do not find
that he appeared in any of the courts.   Just when his affairs
were at the worst he was requested to act temporarily as assistant editor of the New York " Evening Post."   I say tem-

porarily, because the place had been already offered to his friend Dana, who had not yet answered. Mr. Bryant, indeed, was deputed to consult him about it, and went to Boston for that purpose, but found him reluctant to leave his home at Cambridge, to say nothing of an offer made him by the Boston " Centinel," which, being only a weekly, would exact less labor. Writing to Verplanck from Cummington, August 26th, as to the results of his mission, he said : " Dana seems desirous to have the place in the office of the 'Evening Post' kept in reserve until he has heard what could be done nearer home." Nothing came of it ; but it is curious to think what that journal would have become in the hands of so decided a monarchist in politics and so high a churchman in religion. As late as October 2d, when Mr. Bryant wrote to his wife in the country, the matter was not yet determined. He says :

"I shall send you a number of the ' Evening Post,' either by Mr. Van Deusen or by the mail, containing an account of the ' Commencement of Columbia College,' and will also mark with a pencil such paragraphs as are written by me. I have got to be quite famous as the editor of a newspaper since you were here, and a few of my friends —Mr. Verplanck in particular—are anxious that I should continue in it. Some compliments have been made to me about its improvement in character. The establishment is an extremely lucrative one. It is owned by two individuals—Mr. Coleman and Mr. Burnham. The profits are estimated at about thirty thousand dollars a year—fifteen to each proprietor. This is better than poetry and magazines."

It certainly opened a prospect much more seductive than that which lay immediately before him.

CHAPTER TWELFTH.

THE SUBORDINATE EDITOR.

A. D. 1827, 1828.

THE " Evening Post," on which Mr. Bryant was now employed as a subordinate, was one of the oldest journals of the
city. Founded in the first year of the century by William
Coleman, under the auspices of Alexander Hamilton, Colonel
Varick, Archibald Gracie, Colonel Troupe, and other Federalists of note, it steadily maintained their political opinions up
to the close of the Second War. As the lines of party demar-
cation were then more or less obliterated, it became somewhat
independent ; and it continued so until the presidential contest
of 1824—a sort of personal scrub-race between four or five
opposing candidates—when it so far threw off its old bonds as
to support Crawford of the South against Adams of the East
and Clay and Jackson of the West.

Newspapers, however, were not then the voluble organs of
public sentiment they have since become. Advertising sheets
mainly, adding to their local chronicles and digests of foreign
intelligence, an occasional comment on public questions or
characters, they preferred for the most part to confine their
disquisitions to squabbles with one another.* The more solid

---

* Cheetam and Duane, for example, were editors of rival gazettes, to which the
" Evening Post " paid its compliments in this wise :

> " Lie on, Duane, lié on for pay ;
> And, Cheetam, lie thou too—
> More against truth you cannot say,
> Than truth can say 'gainst you."

matter came from without—from Lucius Crassus, or Publius,
or Viator, or a Constant Reader.   Even criticisms of literature
and the fine arts were apt to appear as communications.   Neither the news nor the discussions exhibited any great boldness
or hurry of enterprise.* / But Mr. Coleman, the editor of the
" Evening Post," having been a lawyer, was something of a
scholar, and gave to it a considerable literary repute.   It was
for this reason chosen in 1819 as a vehicle for the waggeries of
two young rhymers—Fitz-Greene Halleck and Joseph Rod-
man Drake—who under the name of Croaker & Co. obtained a
great deal of notoriety.   They satirized the men and things of
the day—Cobbit, Dr. Mitchell, the aldermen, and the theatres
—in a humorous manner, mingling occasionally graver strains
with their fun.† When jests less good-natured than theirs
found their way into print, the consequence was apt to be a
meeting at Hoboken early in the morning.   Coleman himself,
the law partner of Aaron Burr for a time, adopted his notions
of the duel.   His pen was now and then too sharp at the nib,
and compelled him to " make his proofs " according to French
phrase.   Once, at least, he was in hiding for some days for
having put an adversary under the sod.   But he was now getting old and self-indulgent, and glad to avail himself of a new
hand.

During Mr. Bryant's year of apprenticeship, as it may be
called (1826–'29), we are able to trace his handiwork in more
discriminating and elaborate notices of new books, in larger
extracts from foreign journals showing the progress of science, in constant presentations of the claims of artists and
their works to public regard, in more careful characterizations
of public men, and in almost daily suggestions of reform in
city affairs—a new water supply, a better organized police,
cleanlier streets, and a more elegant style of architecture in
shops and houses.   Mr. Bryant's fine taste was perpetually

---

* News arrived slowly : in five days from Albany, a week from Washington, and
one or two months from Europe.
† Drake's " American Flag " was among these.

urging him to these repeated appeals to improvement; and they are mentioned here because the services that journalists render the communities in which they live in this way, small in the detail but important in the results, are not generally appreciated. He was also outspoken in his opposition to the practice of duelling, which prevailed more or less all over the country, denouncing it with the utmost severity, and to the licensing of money lotteries, which filled the streets with shops for the sale of chances, and every fortnight attracted anxious and noisy multitudes into the Park to witness the turn of the fatal wheels.

In politics there was no evidence of his activity, except on the subject of free-trade. It has been frequently represented that he first induced the "Evening Post" to support that doctrine, but such is not the case. The journal was committed to it before his accession to the staff. In the city of New York, indeed, it was popular with the merchants and more eminent citizens. One finds on published lists of delegates to free-trade conventions, or attached to calls for free-trade meetings, such well-known names as those of Albert Gallatin, Peter Jay, James Kent, John Duer, Morgan Lewis, James G. King, Peter Remsen, Isaac Bronson, Reuben Withers, Jonathan Goodhue, Jacob Lorillard, Gardner Howland, Charles H. Russell, and others. A majority in both houses of Congress, however, voted for protection, and there was not a journal this side of the Potomac, except the "Evening Post," which endeavored to controvert its fallacies. In the northern parts of the Union, the seaboard towns particularly, a few friends of freedom were to be found, while the people of the interior of the Atlantic States and the entire population of the West seemed to acquiesce without scruple in the policy of legislative favoritism and discrimination. Mr. Bryant, who, as we have seen, had for some years been a student of political economy, was able, in this respect, to animate and strengthen the polemics of his journal.

Nevertheless, he was only as yet a subaltern, and engaged,

besides, in the management of his staggering monthly, now
"The United States Review." His contributions to it in
prose were many, but not significant for us; while his poetical pieces, "October," "The Damsel of Peru," "The African
Chief," "Spring in Town," "The Gladness of Nature," "The
Greek Partisan," "The Two Graves," and "The Conjunction
of Jupiter and Venus," though spirited enough in their way,
are hardly up to his old mark.* His residence in the city had
enlarged his knowledge of, and deepened his interest in, the
ways and doings of men, but it seemed to need the genial
breezes of the country to awaken his harp to its finest tones.
In the "Summer Ramble," which he contributed to the "Mirror," we hear again the soft voices of the grass, and the strains
of tiny music, that swell

> " From every moss-cup of the rock,
>   From every nameless blossom's bell."

Mr. Dana, some time in 1826, announced to Mr. Bryant
that he was about to do himself what he had often urged
upon him—that is, publish a poem of some length and in book
form. In pursuance of this purpose, the manuscript of "The
Buccaneer" was forwarded to Mr. Bryant early in 1827, with
a request that he should look over it, and suggest such revis-
ions as might seem to be advisable. He wrote of it (June 1,
1827) as follows:

". . . . The first moment I was able I finished the examination
of your work. I should, however, apologize. I have a good deal of
work to do. I drudge for the 'Evening Post' and labor for the
'Review,' and thus have a pretty busy life of it. I would give up
one of these if I could earn my bread by the other, but that I cannot
do. I have delayed attending to your manuscript from time to time,
just as I often delay writing poetry, until I should feel able to do it

* Some of these, he said to his brother once, were written when he was greatly
overworked, and he desired to leave them out of his edition of 1832, but his friends
—probably Anderson and Sands—would not hear of it.

better justice. I have delayed it too long, but it was not from mere laziness.

"You are mistaken in supposing the piece did not take well with me. I think very highly of it. It has passages of great power and great beauty, and the general effect, to my apprehension, is very fine. Did you tell me not to show it? I cannot find the letter which accompanied the manuscript, and I may have sinned, for I have shown it to Verplanck, who approved, and we have agreed that it should be printed. . . .

"It is difficult to judge in what manner the public will receive your work. I believe the reception will be respectful. I hope it will be cordial, but fashion has a great deal to do with these things; and, though there is a better taste for poetry in this country than there was ten years ago, there are yet a great many who count the syllables on their fingers—e. g., Mr. Walsh * and all that class of men. But we will try what we can do for it. I have not marked all the passages which I thought required amendment, because I was not certain where the fault lay. There is occasionally a startling abruptness in the style, and Matt is treated by the poet who relates the story with a sort of fierce familiarity which is sometimes carried too far. If I have thus, both here and in the notes I have made, dwelt upon the blemishes, it is not because they are more numerous than the beauties, but because I wish the work to be entirely free of them. They are blemishes of execution merely, and I, who have been an apprentice in the trade of verse from nine years old, can only wonder how, with so little practice, you have acquired so much dexterity. There are passages of strong pathos, and, indeed, the whole work is instinct with this quality; the descriptions are also striking, and as many powerful lines might be picked out of the poem as out of any other of the size that I know." †

---

* Robert Walsh, probably, the editor of a Philadelphia periodical.

† This amusing note from Halleck belongs to this time:

"DEAR BRYANT: Mr. Morris, the editor of the 'Mirror,' has asked me to say to you that his engraving of the seven, or nine—I forget which—'Illustrious Obscure' is completed. He has made me what I ought to have been, and very possibly shall be—a Methodist parson. As for the character in which you appear in the plate, he wishes you to call on him and judge for yourself. The barber-shop sort of im-

The book was published in the autumn, and, in order to help it along, Mr. Bryant, at the request of Mr. Sparks, the editor, wrote a review of it for the "North American.'* In a letter to Dana of February 16, 1828, he refers to the matter thus:

"MY DEAR SIR: I am glad you are so well pleased with my review of your poems. It is pretty well received, I believe, by the reading world, and thought a fair criticism. Mr. Walsh, to be sure, says that your poems are 'too broadly and strongly eulogized,' but Mr. Walsh's opinion on poetry is not worth anything, and, although it yet passes for more than it is worth, its real value is beginning to be better understood than formerly. Mr. Walsh is the greatest literary quack of our country, and deserves to be taken down a peg or two. It would do him good, for the creature really has some talent; and, if he would be content to drudge in a plain way, might be useful. I saw Mr. Greenough (the sculptor), and am obliged to you for introducing me to so agreeable a man, and one of such genuine tastes and right opinions.

"P. S.—I ought to answer your question about the New York 'Evening Post.' I am a small proprietor in the establishment, and am a gainer by the arrangement. It will afford me a comfortable livelihood after I have paid for the *eighth part*, which is the amount of my share. I do not like politics any better than you do; but they get only my mornings, and you know politics and a belly-full are better than poetry and starvation.

"I should also express my pleasure at learning of the success of your poems in Boston. To confess to you the truth, I had strong misgivings as to their reception—very strong; but I knew that there had been a change in the tastes of the people there, and that the popularity of Wordsworth's poems, whether real or fictitious, had prepared

mortality with which this engraving honors us is most particularly annoying, but how could we help ourselves? '*Il faut se soumettre*,' as they say in French, or, as that prince of corporals and philosophers, Nym, with his usual brief eloquence, expresses it, 'Things must be as they may.'   Y'rs truly,

"*Wednesday, 16th Jan'y, '28, 11 o'clock.*"   " HALLECK.

* "North American Review." Dana's Poems, No. 26, p. 239, 1827.

the way for you. As to the reception here, you know we are a prosaic, money-making community, and nothing takes unless it be a new
novel, or some work on a subject of immediate interest; but they have
been read with pleasure by the few who know how to value such
things. We did what we could in the papers both before and after
the work appeared.

"W. C. B."

Mr. Dana's warnings against politics—that " vile blackguard
squabble," as he calls it—were as yet hardly needed ; Mr. Bryant's interest in it was no doubt quickened by his new propri-
etorship in the " Evening Post," but he was not absorbed by it.
The " Review " having finally collapsed, his attention was given
to a new literary project originated by Sands. A fashion of
decorated annuals, caught by French and English publishers
from the " Annalen " of the Germans, was now reigning in the
United States, and the booksellers of the principal cities vied
with one another in the production of Tokens, Souvenirs,
Amaranths, and Amulets, of light miscellaneous contents, but
sumptuously printed and adorned. " Mr. Elam Bliss, a worthy
member of the trade," says Mr. Verplanck,* "mentioned a
thing of the kind to Mr. Sands, who, after consulting with Mr.
Verplanck and Mr. Bryant, hit upon the scheme of a yearly
publication which should combine the characteristics of an annual with those of a miscellany from the pens of two or three
authors writing in conjunction." By the kindness of several
artists, with whom the writers were on terms of intimacy,
some respectable embellishments were gotten together, and
the " Talisman " for 1828 was prepared in· the latter part of
1827.† It was put forth in the name of an imaginary editor,

---

* " Memoir of Robert C. Sands," prefixed to his works. Harper & Brothers, New
York, 1834.

† Out of this casual association of artists and literary men the Sketch Club arose.
Cooper's club, the Lunch, was no more, owing to his departure for Europe, and
the Sketch Club was meant to be a sort of substitute. Its meetings were continued
until it was merged in what is now " The Century Club," one of the largest and
most prosperous clubs of the city.

Mr. Francis Herbert, who professed to draw his materials, tales, essays, and verses out of a portfolio, which had been slowly gathered in the course of years of travel and research. He was, of course, one of those omniscient and ubiquitous individuals, easily found in such cases, who had visited every part of the earth, made himself familiar with the languages, the literature, and the manners of people of all ages and climes, and capable of writing, with equal ease, on every kind of topic, and in every variety of style. A petty volume with a few engravings in it was a small result for such grand pretensions, but it had no less a considerable literary success.

It would be difficult to conceive of editorship under pleasanter circumstances than those in which the " Talisman " was compiled. Mr. Sands resided at Hoboken, where his father's hospitable house was made the headquarters of the trio. It was in the midst of a pleasant hamlet of the most beautiful surroundings. The New Jersey shore of the Hudson River, from the peninsula of Paulus Hook (Jersey City) to beyond Weehawken on the north, presented a singularly picturesque outline of indented coves and wood-fringed promontories, stretching away over level meadow-lands to a bolder background of heights. Wandering through the tangled undergrowth of the woods to the little grassy plot where Hamilton fell in his duel with Burr, and so many other mortal quarrels were voided, or stretching themselves upon the sunny top of a cliff that commanded a magnificent view of river, bay, and city, now belonging to the King estate, the editors would concoct their projects for the annual. Sometimes the members of the Sketch Club would join them in these excursions, and take minutes of the views that were to be afterward engraved.*

---

* On one of these rambles they encountered a Frenchman, who gave himself out as having been an intimate of the household of the grand Napoleon. Unfortunately, he said, he had lost all his most valuable papers in the retreat from Moscow. It appeared, when he was more closely questioned, that these were receipts for the preparation of favorite dishes. At present he was in search of rattlesnakes, which, he averred, when properly cooked and sauced, were the most delicious of edibles.

On returning home they would reduce their wandering talks to manuscript, Sands, as the readiest penman, commonly acting as amanuensis, while the others walked the room or lolled upon chairs. How the house would ring, says Miss Sands, surviving sister of Robert, with eloquent declamations and roars of uproarious laughter! Often the passing stranger would stop, thinking rather of jolly fellows at a feast than of sober and sedate scholars in the throes of composition. Sands, in fact, had a propensity for innocent and playful mischief, and on these occasions would divert his companions with stories of his adventures among the primitive Dutch settlers of Communipaw, whose festivals and frolics he sometimes attended. Or else he was getting up one of his many literary practical jokes. "It was his sport," says Mr. Verplanck, "to excite public curiosity by giving extracts, highly spiced with fashionable allusions and satire, from the forthcoming novel—which novel was, and in truth is, yet to be written—or else to entice some unhappy wight into a literary or historical newspaper discussion, then to combat him anonymously, or, under the mask of a brother editor, to overwhelm him with history, facts, quotations, and authorities, all manufactured for the occasion." * This pedantic sort of fun was much in vogue at one time with the wits of "Blackwood" and other magazines, but has now fallen into disuse. Mr. Bryant seems rather to have liked it, and often took part with Sands in his mystifications. "Did you see a learned article," he wrote to Mr. Verplanck, at Washington, "in the 'Evening Post' the other day about Pope Alexander VI and Cæsar Borgia?

---

* "One of these pranks occurred in relation to the Grecian Crown of Victory, during the excitement in favor of Greek liberty, when, after several ingenious young men, fresh from their college studies, had exhausted all the learning they could procure, either from their own acquaintance with antiquity, or at second hand from Lemprière, Potter, Barthelemi, or the more erudite *Paschalis de Corona*, Sands ended the controversy by an essay filled with excellent learning, that rested mainly on a passage of Pausanias, quoted in the original Greek, but for which it is vain to look in any edition of that author."

Matt. Paterson undertook to be saucy in the 'Commercial' as to a Latin quotation in it, so we—i. e., Sands and myself—sent him on a fool's errand.   He has not been able as yet, I believe, to find the 'Virorum Illustrium Reliquæ,' though he says Da Pontè has a great many queer old Latin books, and he has an indistinct remembrance of a work that has *virorum clarorum* on the title-page!"   Again, he says: "You have doubtless seen the learned epistle of Mr. John Smith to the editors of the 'Evening Post?'   The poems were concocted, as well as the greater part of the translations, by Sands and myself; some by Anderson, Paine, and Da Pontè.   We look upon it here as a very learned *jeu d'esprit*."   The joke consisted in taking a familiar couplet and running it through all the languages, ancient and modern, inclusive of several Indian dialects.   These quips and quirks were sometimes flung into the camps of political adversaries, where they exploded like fire-crackers, and produced a great deal of spluttering and noise, but not much damage.   One of the more successful flings was levelled at Miss Fanny Wright (afterward Madame Darusmont), the forerunner of those ladies, now not so scarce, who lecture on Infidelity and Marriage, or what Miss Wright used to call Nolige (Knowledge).   Writing to Verplanck still, he says, slyly: "I suppose you saw an 'Ode to Miss Wright' in the 'Post' not long since?   It has passed for Halleck's among the knowing ones, and Carter was so cock-sure of it that he republished it in the 'Statesman,' and laid a wager with Colonel Stone that Halleck was the author.   Mr. Walsh must have fallen into the same mistake, for he republished it with praise." *

On one occasion Miss Sands remembers that Verplanck came rushing to the house, early in the afternoon, in a state of breathless excitement, exclaiming: "Oh, Sands, I've got such a poem!   Gray's 'Elegy' is nothing to it.   I picked it up at

* When Mr. Halleck was asked if he wrote the ode, he promptly answered, "No; and there is but one man in New York who could have written it, and that is Bryant."

the publishers, and all the way across the river it has been ringing in my brain.

> "'Far in thy realms withdrawn
> Old Empires sit in sullenness and gloom!'"

and he then repeated the whole of Mr. Bryant's poem "To
the Past." At the close the two editors congratulated each
other with the fervor of those who find a treasure.

Nor were the rambles of the editors confined to the woods;
as scholars, they had antiquarian tastes, and often explored together out-of-the-way places in the city itself, where odd characters were to be found, or which were distinguished by historical associations. They gazed, of course, upon the spot in
Wall Street where Washington had been inaugurated as the
first President of the United States, recalling the forms of
Hamilton, Madison, the elder Adams, Jay, Knox, Sherman,
Lee, Clinton, Ames, Ellsworth, Gouverneur Morris, and others
who stood around him as he took the oath administered by
Chancellor Livingston. They lingered about the fine old
house at the head of Pearl Street, where he afterward received
his friends. Sometimes they paced the shores of the North
River, just above the present Barclay Street ferry, where
Jonathan Edwards, temporary pastor of the Wall Street
Church, used to walk backward and forward while he medi-
tated the mysteries of eternal preordination and free-will, as
the eternal murmurs of the ocean fell upon his ears. At
other times they sought out the house in Stone Street where
the philanthropic Oglethorpe, the founder of Georgia, lodged
on his first visit to America; or that on the corner of Broadway looking on the Battery, which had been the headquarters of Wolfe, the conqueror of Canada, and afterward of
Howe, who fell at Ticonderoga; or the old two-story structure in Cedar Street, in which Jefferson conversed with Tal-
leyrand and Billaud de Varennes; and they tried to learn
the places that Volney and Cobbett, the Abbé Correa and
General Moreau, and Tom Moore and Jeffrey had frequented.

Of all these sites, no one was more attractive than the massive wooden building, with a lofty portico, supported by Ionic columns, on the hill at the corner of Varick and Charlton Streets, where Lord Amherst had lived, where President Adams entertained foreign ministers and the more conspicuous senators and congressmen, and Aaron Burr resided at the height of his career. All these places, celebrated by the editors in their " Reminiscences of New York," have since been swept away by the remorseless besom of metropolitan progress.

The " Talisman " was continued in the years 1829 and 1830 —making three volumes in all—when other occupations on the part of the writers—of Mr. Verplanck in Congress, of Mr. Bryant as editor of the " Evening Post," and of Mr. Sands as editor of the " Commercial Advertiser "—put an end to a work which had been a source of a vast deal of amusement to them, if not of much profit.* A few years later the principal contents were republished as " Miscellanies," and obtained a wider and more lucrative popularity.†

Mr. Dana's earnest remonstrances against " politics," which we have read, were prompted as much, doubtless, by anxiety as to the direction in which Mr. Bryant's preferences tended as by his general sense of the degraded methods of our political warfare. Regarding the Democratic polity with small

---

* Mr. Bryant's poetical contributions to the " Talisman" were : " A Scene on the Banks of the Hudson " ; " The Hurricane " ; " William Tell " ; " Innocent Child and Snow-white Flower " ; " The Close of Autumn " ; " To the Past " ; " The Hunter's Serenade " ; " The Greek Boy " ; " To the Evening Wind " ; " Love and Folly " ; "The Siesta " ; " Romero " ; " To the River Arve " ; " To the Painter Cole," and "Eva," including " The Alcayde of Molina " and " The Death of Aliatar." It is a proof how little the " New York Review " had been known that two or three of these were republished from it without seeming detection. His prose pieces were : " An adventure in the East Indies " ; " The Cascade of Melsingah " ; " Recollections of the South of Spain " ; " Moriscan Romances " ; " Story of the Island of Cuba " ; " The Indian Spring " ; " The Whirlwind " ; " Early Spanish Poetry " ; " Phanette des Gantelmes " ; " The Marriage Blunder " ; and parts of " The Devil's Pulpit," and of " Reminiscences of New York."

† " Miscellanies," by G. C. Verplanck, Robert C. Sands, and W. C. Bryant. New York: Elam Bliss, 1832.

admiration, he felt still less for the parties which struggled for ascendency under it. As for the more popular or radical of those parties, he did not hesitate to express the utmost aversion, and yet it was toward that party his friend Bryant was rapidly gravitating. In its enmity to the dogma of protection, the "Evening Post" had gradually fallen into an attitude of antagonism to the administration of John Quincy Adams. Perhaps a little leaven of old Federal prejudice, which deemed Adams guilty of party treachery when he disclosed the real *animus* of the New England leaders during the war, tinctured its dislike. At any rate, as early as June, 1827, it took the field in favor of the nomination of General Jackson. Its avowed reason was that Jackson had pronounced himself friendly to "a judicious tariff," which was interpreted to mean a mitigation of the existing customs duties; but another motive may have operated upon Mr. Bryant's mind. Like many other literary men of the time, Irving, Cooper, Bancroft, Verplanck at home, and, in later years, Landor abroad, he had formed a very high opinion of the personal character of the General. His known simplicity and frankness, his incorruptible honesty, his strong sense of justice, his popular sympathies, his fearless directness in moving to his ends, were qualities that captivated not the common people alone, but simple-hearted men everywhere who loved manliness and energy. Jackson was comparatively untried in civil affairs; scholastically ignorant; of irascible, if not unbridled passions, and impatient of restraint; but his integrity was spotless, and his will in the execution of his purposes inflexible. Moreover, there was a certain degree of heroism in his life of the frontier, and as a military chief among the everglades of Florida, which captivated the imagination.

At the outset, the partizanship of the "Evening Post," though it was decided, was not immoderate; but it was found, as the campaign advanced, that a personality like Jackson's admitted of no half-way attachments or dislikes. He was either, as his friends averred, "a noble old Roman," or, according to his enemies, a monster of violence greatly to be dreaded. Mr. Bryant was disposed to concur with the former, and, as the controversial heat increased, his admiration warmed. His regular adoption, however, among the Democratic train-bands was owing to an incident which, considering his habitual reticence and dignity, is somewhat amusing. Jackson's chief glory dated back to the 8th of January, 1815, when he won the victory of New Orleans, so that his partisans inscribed the anniversary of that day among the festal days of the calendar, always to be celebrated by dinners, songs, speeches, and fireworks. The poet, at the instigation of a friend, had written an ode for one of these occasions, which, containing a sonorous and rollicking refrain, gave great pleasure to the admirers of "Old Hickory," who took it up and made it popular. Mr. Verplanck, writing from Washington, January 9, 1828, describes its early fortunes thus, using names from the "Talisman":

"MY DEAR FRANCES: I am sorry to tell you that, although from 'The North American Review' we have learned the merits of your work, yet as Mr. Walsh thinks the praise given by the eastern critic too high, we are altogether at a loss to decide on your literary rank, not a single copy of your *coup d'essai* having reached us.

"Your political demonstrations have succeeded far better. I received from Mr. Hoyt a copy of your ode for the 8th of January, which was, I trust, sung with splendid effect, admirable music, and the finest voices, at the Masonic Hall.* If it was not—I told a lie to our Jackson friends.

"At the Jackson dinner yesterday, after an admirable speech from Livingston, full of interesting anecdotes of the 'Matins of St. Victoria '—for that he said is the Catholic name of the 8th—something was said about New York, to which the president (not Mr. Adams, but General Van Ness) requested me to reciprocate. I made a little speech—regretted that the letter of the venerable and patriotic chairman of our New York dinner conveying an official toast had by some

---

* Where the Democrats of New York kept their festival.

unaccountable accident miscarried. But, that we might as far as possible sympathize with my constituents, I told them that I would read a noble effusion of poetry, at that moment doubtless thrilling every bosom in the Masonic Hall. Perhaps my partiality for the author (who, etc., etc.) might deceive me, but it seemed to me to breathe the purest spirit of poetry—I was sure that it did that of the purest patriotism.

"I then read the ode with due emphasis, and a little theatrically. Vice-President Calhoun nodded approbation. Van Beuren (*sic*) was in ecstasies, so was the Speaker (Taylor), and Kremer shouted clamorous delight. After divers cheers I renewed: 'Mr. President, in the absence of any official instruction from my gestive constituents, permit me, instead of substituting a sentiment of my own, to offer you in their name as a toast the last stanza of the verses I have read: "Drink to those who won," etc.' *

"This was received with enthusiasm. The company (and at that period they were all in a mood to judge of poetry and sentiment, for they had merely got to a point of temperate excitement) shouted and clapped, the music brayed, the cannons fired, and Colonel Hayne swore that the Jackson cause had all the poetry as well as all the virtue of the land.

"Remember me to M. DeViellecour, Miss Huggins, and our other friends.   I am yours, very truly,

"G. C. VERPLANCK."

Mr. Bryant answered, February 16th, thus:

"MY DEAR SIR: I have not written, I believe, since Mr. Herbert got his letter containing an account of the reception of his ode at the dinner at Washington. He was wonderfully delighted with it, and so also were his friends. The artist who made Plutarch Peck's coat, with his usual interest in everything that relates to American letters, called to obtain a sight of it, and a copy was dispatched to M. Viellecour, who returned a note expressive of the gratification with which he had perused it. Mr. Herbert was observed to look wonderfully complacent for a day or two, but his face grew longer when Mr. Walsh

---

* This ode I once found in the "Evening Post," but have been unable to get at it again.

said that the ode had been praised too highly, and the critical Charles King declared it prosaic. However, a couple of articles which lately appeared in the 'Enquirer,' in which justice is done to both Mr. Walsh and his Jak Rugby, have restored their usual serenity to the features of our excellent friend.

"The tariff does not seem likely to be popular to the eastward. It was amusing to observe by the papers how it was received. The Jackson papers in that quarter seized upon it as a proof that the Jackson party was friendly to manufactures, or at least willing to give their friends fair play. The Adams papers preserved a dead silence for a while, and then the storm broke forth. The 'Boston Courier' attacks the whole bill tooth and nail, as you probably have seen by this time. The dissatisfaction with the tax on molasses seems to be pretty general; it reaches from Albany to Portland. An article from the 'National Journal,' in which it is said that the bill does not meet the views of the real friends of the American system, is copied into almost every administration paper that I take up; and they all take their cue from it. I think the New England members will be forced, as you predict, to vote against it.   W. C. B."

These letters are good specimens of those that passed between Mr. Verplanck and Mr. Bryant at this time, which are nearly all of them curious mixtures of allusions to the ideal characters of the "Talisman," or its progress, and of discussions of politics. Mr. Verplanck was preparing a new tariff bill, as Chairman of the Committee of Ways and Means, and Mr. Bryant gave him what help he could with the details. Sometimes Verplanck would impart to him the drift of opinion in Washington, with innuendos and speculations as to the movements of the great chiefs, which he would use in his newspaper, "in advance of the mails," and he in return would give the Congressman the gossip of the city, and what the newspapers or prominent authorities were saying about their literary bantling. On one occasion I find that Washington Irving, who was Secretary of Legation at London, ventured information (but not improperly) as to the negotiations about the West India Trade, which the editor turned to use, doubtless to the disgust of his contemporaries, whom he anticipated. But the interest in these desultory notes is now too remote to justify more than a few brief extracts.

"MAY 9, 1828: I publish to-day yours of the 5th, or at least a part of it, but so altered that the authorship need not be claimed by you unless you please. It has also been thought best to publish Mr. McDuffie's·letter. I made an apology for you on the day after the article appeared in the 'Commercial '; but the merchants said it was *sly,* and did not think it quite satisfactory. It, however, had the effect of disgusting them with Blunt, if they were not disgusted before. The letters published to-day, particularly Mr. McDuffie's, will set the matter right. . . .

" The demand for the 'Talisman' continues, and you must do your share for another year. Inman has a design illustrating Moore's poem of the Dismal Swamp, which I hear spoken highly of, and which he wishes engraved for the 'Talisman.' Will you pick up from the Virginians some particulars of the Dismal Swamp while you are at Washington, which some of us may weave into a narrative, or make a florid description out of."

"DECEMBER 29, 1828: The American Academy of Arts have filled their gallery with copies of Italian and Flemish paintings, which an Italian has brought over for originals. Some are good copies, say Morse and the other artists, but for the most part daubs. By the bye, do not let Colonel Trumbull paint the other four national pictures. They will be taken down again in twenty years; and the Colonel has got thirty-two thousand dollars already for his copies. Give one to Allston while he is not only alive but in the vigor of his genius. Give one to Morse, who is going abroad next spring to Rome, who will study it there, and give five years of his life to it. Give one to Sully, and, if the colonel cannot do without the remaining one, let him have it as a matter of grace."

"JANUARY 27, 1829: As to the degree of favor with which the 'Talisman' has been received, I can only say that the impartial opinions seem to place it even higher than last year. I suppose you have seen Buckingham's opinion of it, placing it, in point of literary merit, above all other works of the kind. The 'Middletown Gazette,' a paper in which I showed you a criticism on Charles King's style, expressed the same opinion, but committed a great blunder as to the authors, ascribing the book to Paulding, Halleck, and myself. The 'Norfolk Herald' paid a high compliment to Mason's engraving of the Dismal Swamp, which it said gave a pleasing view of the Great Feeder, with a lady crossing the lake by the fire-fly lamps in a canoe rowed by an Indian. As I told you beforehand, Coleman cannot abide the scenes at Washington—not liking the ridicule of fat women; and Lewis Tappan is outrageous against the 'Simple Tale,' which he looks upon as an impious sneer at the charitable and religious societies, of many of which he is a principal pillar."

"FEBRUARY 9, 1829: People have done talking about Miss Wright here, and now the common topic is General Jackson's health. As often as about once a week somebody sets afoot a report that he is dead. This morning there is a good deal of anxiety because he has not got to Washington yet, although he has been allowed eight whole days to travel thither from Pittsburgh. As we have all set our hearts on his being president, I solemnly believe that, if he were to take it into his head to die before he is declared to be elected, it would occasion tenfold more vexation and disappointment than if Mr. Adams had received a majority over him. We should all think it very unkind of him, after all the trouble we have been at on his account. Besides, you know that everybody is in an agony of curiosity to know who he will put into his Cabinet. If he should slip off to the other world without solving this riddle, we should never forgive him. Do you not intend to make some great speech this session that we can publish in the 'Post,' with REMARKS, 'earnestly inviting the attention of our readers'? Or will it be soon enough to take that trouble another session."

"FEBRUARY 27, 1829: Having a spare moment, I think I cannot employ it better than in taking you to task for letting General Jackson make so bad a Cabinet. Van Buren is very well, but how comes Ingham to be the Secretary of the Treasury? It does not signify to say that he is not exactly in favor of the tariff as it now stands; he is a tariff man, infected with the leaven of the American system. Then as for capacity, I should judge, from what I have seen of him in letters and speeches, that he is no great matter. We are very much inclined to grumble here at the appointment of Ingham. Eaton, I have no doubt, would have stood quite as high in the general estimation as to talent; I mean, if he had never written the 'Life of Jackson.' Branch is a man, too, of whom we know little in this quarter, and that little does not give us a high opinion of him. Berrian's appointment will be highly satisfactory. I allow, the Cabinet is as good as the last; the Treasury Department is a little better filled, but where are the great men whom the General was to assemble round him, the powerful minds that were to make up for his deficiencies? Where are the Tazewells, the Livingstons, the Woodburys, the McLanes, etc.?"

"NEW YORK, AUGUST 5, 1829: * You will see in to-day's 'Evening Post' an extract from a letter concerning a new picture by Washington Allston of a mother and child. I copied it from a letter which Verplanck has just received from Dana. Dana says that 'The Past' suited him exactly, and spoke of its 'naked strength,' in which he thought it exceeded anything I had written. He added that, if Bryant must write in a newspaper to get his bread, he prayed God he might get a bellyful. Dana speaks in the same letter of a poem he has been writing, and says he thinks he shall deliver it at Andover. What has he to do with Andover, I wonder? I hope he is not studying divinity, to make himself a Calvinistic parson. He is inclined to Calvinism, you know, but I hope he will not Andoverize himself.

"Yesterday was the Commencement of Columbia College. It rained violently, and, therefore, I neither attended the exercises nor went to the dinner. Theodore Sedgwick, the younger, had the valedictory, and acquitted himself with great credit. Mr. Verplanck spoke highly in praise of his performance. I like Leggett, so far, very much. He seems to be an honest man, of good principles, industrious, and a fluent though by no means a polished writer."

"DECEMBER, 1829: † We are greatly obliged to you for such oracular hints, for so they are received, as you have occasionally given us since you went on to the capital. They are copied everywhere, even

---

* To Mrs. Bryant.   † To Mr. Verplanck again.

in the 'American.' The President's message has been very favorably received here. Those who are concerned in the United States Bank did not like the part relating to that institution, but even on that subject there is not much excitement, notwithstanding the opposition journals have tried hard to kindle one. How came Eaton to suffer his report to appear so overcharged with verbal inaccuracies? Partly, I suppose, by having an ignorant copyist for the press, and partly by his own ambition to be fine; but in either case he is inexcusable. It has given the small critics of the opposition something to talk about.

"The 'Talisman' I have little to tell you about. If you see the 'Courier,' you must have seen Paulding's article about it, and Brooks's certificate to its merits. Bliss does not talk of making much money by the concern."

" DECEMBER 24, 1829: The other day Mr. Sands showed me the third volume of a work called 'Tales of an Indian Camp,' published in England by Colburn, and which Carey and Lea are to republish here. You may perhaps have seen some preliminary puff of the book, in which the author is said to be a Mr. Jones—J. A. Jones, I believe, the same who wrote the sonnet on Webster and then edited a Jackson paper in Philadelphia. And what do you think I found Mr. Jones had been doing in this third volume? Only transplanting my story of the 'Cascade of Melsingah' bodily into his work, leaving out my introduction and fitting it with a short one of his own, altering slightly the beginning and end of several of the paragraphs, and putting a new sentence at the close of the whole, but otherwise copying verbatim about twenty pages of Mr. Herbert's composition. It is the same old coat with a new cuff and collar. Not the slightest acknowledgment of the obligation is made in any part of the book. What adds to the man's impudence, he relates in the course of the work, with the utmost gravity, as Mr. Sands tells me, that in his childhood he was attended by an Indian servant, from whom he learned the superstitions and traditions he has made use of in compiling the book. This theft from me is not, however, the only one the work contains. The 'Notes to Yamoyden' are stolen in the same wholesale manner. It will be necessary that the critics should be prepared to vindicate Mr. Herbert's literary rights when the book comes out. For my own part, I intend to expose the robbery, and if the book comes in your way you will not forget what is due to our old friend. Sands has seen Carey. He seems to entertain the proposition favorably, and promised to write, with an offer of terms." *

These letters are important only as showing how the poet was getting more and more busy with politics and politicians —a connection which for the time paralyzed his poetic activity, so that for nearly three years after the close of the " Talisman " he wrote nothing in verse that he has since been willing to acknowledge.

* This relates to the republication of the " Talisman " as " Miscellanies."

CHAPTER THIRTEENTH.

A. D. 1829–1832.

By the death of Coleman, July, 1829, Mr. Bryant was left chief editor of the " Evening Post "—in the ownership of which also he acquired an additional interest by an arrangement with Mrs. Coleman. His life-work was now to be begun—not that which most subtly and widely influenced his countrymen, but that which absorbed the greater part of his attention, and most taxed his energies. He had abandoned his profession and come to the city to engage in a purely literary career, and here he was involved in journalism, of which so much is mere hackwork and routine. It is no winged Pegasus he mounts, to curvet and caracole in the air, amid the plaudits of onlookers, but a sorrier steed, as fiery, perhaps, as his fabled brother, whose path lies on the dusty highways of life, and among the clamors of noisy and ferocious combatants. Could he have anticipated at the time the whirlpool of agitation and toil into which it would plunge him for the greater part of his days?

His personal character—his stern self-respect, and pervading sense of responsibility in all that he did—lifted his employment at once into a region of elevation and dignity. Knowing the power of the press, if wielded in a worthy manner, knowing also its temptations to time serving and slackness of performance, he resolved that if in his hands it fell short of the noblest ideals, it should not be for the want of upright purposes and persistent endeavor.   Of the spirit in which he approached his task, I shall allow him to speak in a passage which furnishes a clew to his subsequent career, and which may not be wholly devoid of instruction to his fellow-journalists even at this later day : *

"The class of men," he said, "who figure in this country as the conductors of newspapers are not, for the most part, in high esteem with the community.   It is true, they are courted by some, and dreaded by others—courted by those who are fond of praise, and dreaded by those who are sensitive to animadversion; courted by those who would use their instruments for their own purposes, and dreaded by those whose plans may suffer from their opposition—but, after all, the general feeling with which they are regarded is by no means favorable.   Contempt is too harsh a name for it, perhaps, but it is far below respect.   Nor does this arise from the insincerity or frivolousness of their commendation or their dispraise in the thousand opinions they express in matters of art, science, and taste, concerning all of which they are expected to say something, and concerning many of which they cannot know much, as from the fact that professing, as they do, one of the noblest of sciences, that of politics—in other words, the science of legislation and government—they too often profess it in a narrow, ignorant, ignoble spirit.   Every journalist is a politician, of course; but in how many instances does he aspire to no higher office than that of an ingenious and dexterous partisan ?   He does not look at political doctrines and public measures in a large and comprehensive way, weighing impartially their ultimate good or evil, but addicts himself to considerations of temporary expediency.   He inquires not what is right, just, and true at all times, but what petty shift will serve his present purpose.   He makes politics an art rather than a science—a matter of finesse rather than of philosophy.   He inflames prejudices which he knows to be groundless because he thinks them convenient.   He detracts from the personal merits of men whom he knows to be most worthy.   He condemns in another party what he allows in his own.   In short, he considers his party as a set of men who are to be kept in office, if

---

* " Memoir of William Leggett," "Democratic Review," July, 1829.

they are already in, or placed in office, if they are not, at any hazard, instead of making it his duty to support certain doctrines and measures, and to recommend them to the people by reason and argument, and by showing their beneficial effects and the evils of opposite doctrines and different measures. . . . Yet the vocation of the newspaper editor is a useful and indispensable, and, if rightly exercised, a noble vocation. It possesses this essential element of dignity—that they who are engaged in it are occupied with questions of the highest importance to the happiness of mankind. We cannot see, for our part, why it should not attract men of the first talents and the most exalted virtues. Why should not the discussions of the daily press demand as strong reasoning powers, as large and comprehensive ideas, as profound an acquaintance with principles, eloquence as commanding, and a style of argument as manly and elevated, as the debates of the Senate?"

Running through this exposition of his professional creed are references to the philosophy or science of politics, which are not vague words with him. Already a firm believer in the doctrines of political economy, as they had taken shape in the English and Continental treatises, he had persuaded himself that society, in satisfying its natural wants, or in procuring, assimilating, and distributing the means of its nourishment, acted as a spontaneous organism. In this respect the social nature of man, like external nature, was subject to fixed and invariable laws, which scientific induction might discover and formulate, but which it was beyond the power of legislation to modify, except arbitrarily and to the detriment of human well-being. But if such is the case, if in this important order of its functions, society is capable of operating harmoniously without political interference, and impelled alone by permanent and indefeasible impulses, what is the use of government? In what sphere, to what extent, under what limitations, may the hand of authority interpose in the regulation of social movements? Mr. Bryant's answer was that commonly given by the disciples of *laissez faire*, but with a difference. Government, he said, is the organ and representative

of the whole community, not of a class, or of any fraction of
that community. Its primary duty, therefore, is to maintain
the conditions of universal liberty or the equilibrium and harmony of the social forces so that the energies of the individual
may the most freely act and expand, according to his own
judgment, his own capacities, his own views of the duties and
destinies of man here upon earth. It must not undertake directly any enterprises of its own—religious, intellectual, artis-
tic, or economical—but it must secure a perfectly safe and
open field to every kind of enterprise and to every one of its
members. In a word, its functions are juridical—to protect
and maintain rights—and not paternal or eleemosynary—to en-
courage, nurse, and coddle interests, save in so far as those
interests are general, or common to every member of the
body-politic. Liberty, justice, order, are its supreme, almost
exclusive ends, and not prosperity, which will come of itself
when those ends are attained. On this theory of the State,
Mr. Bryant contended, our institutions as a nation are dis-
tinctively built, and either we must give up our pretensions
to democracy or carry them out with a manly courage to
every logical and practicable result. Whether he was right
or wrong in his notions, it cannot be denied that his exalted
conception of the true nature of governmental agency gave a
rare dignity to his discussions, and won for him, in the end,
a public confidence that has seldom been surpassed in any
editorial career.

He was all the more convinced of the soundness of his political philosophy because it was at one with his moral in-
stincts. Holding that the proper aim of morality was not
a mere outward obedience to an established rule, but an inward recognition of the true manhood of man, or reverence
for that rationality, conscience, and freedom which are the
sole and characteristic attributes of human nature, the em-
phatic injunction of the Apostle, " Honor all men," consti-
tuted for him the practical side of ethics. It brought, as he
thought, his politics into a complete unity of principle with

his religion, "the perfect law of love" displayed in the life and teaching of Jesus Christ. He was, in a word, thoroughly, radically, intensely a Democrat, but of the positive rather than the negative school of democracy, which, insisting upon the rights of the individual, maintains also the duties of the individual to every one of his fellow-men.

Baldly stated as they are here, these opinions would seem to be the merest doctrinarianism; yet in theory, as in practice, Mr. Bryant was very far removed from the simple *doctrinaire*. His principles, I think, never came to him as a system. They were the results of his feelings rather than of his thoughts or of any deliberate process of reflection. His profound love and respect for his fellow-men; his unwillingness to ask for himself what he would not concede to another and to all others; his humility, his sense of justice, his yearning for progress in all the nobler arts of life; and his deep, religious reverence for a humanity which the Most High had not disdained to assume with a view to its ultimate glorification on earth as in heaven—these were the sources of his abstract political convictions. Nevertheless, in the discharge of his actual duties he was eminently practical. No one, indeed, not even the statesman in power, is more imperatively required to consider the real condition and feelings of society than the political editor who aspires to be a teacher and guide of men. All his problems come to him in the concrete, as something to be resolved there and then, and to be resolved in a way that will satisfy a large number of his contemporaries. If he should treat them in the abstract only, he would soon be without an audience. He may, like the statesman, secretly worship an ideal of policy, and be forever reaching toward the realization of it in his practical measures; but he must also, like the statesman, take into account the opinions and tendencies of his fellows, or the living spirit of his age and nation. Mr. Bryant was a careful observer of these circumstances; he read with attention the newspapers and magazines of all parties; he conversed freely with men of all conditions, and particularly with the plain people whom he encountered in his many rambles; and he cultivated the habit, in his discussions, of always arguing from the specific instances in hand. Thus, in his innumerable strictures upon our tariff legislation, he seldom recurs to general principles, but dwells upon the duty on iron, the duty on woollens, the duty on salt, etc., showing its immediate influence on society as it is, and in all its ramifications of interest. Of course, he carries with him, without expressing them, his fundamental convictions, as everybody must do who would not render his reasonings a jumble of transient expedients, but the special case is relied upon to enforce his conviction, rather than the conviction to enforce the special case. It was a part of his strategy, I may further observe, never to fly violently in the face of existing prejudices if it could be helped, but to dislodge them by attacks on the flank and rear. If, however, victory was not otherwise to be obtained, he had the courage to march boldly and openly to the point of attack, and to take the consequence of battle.

Unfortunately, he found himself, from the outset of his editorial career, in sharp conflict with a large and powerful force of public opinion. A mass of schemes growing out of the needs of our young and impatient material civilization confronted him, which not only proceeded upon theories of government the reverse of his own, but which threatened to swamp all rational notions of government in a deluge of selfish and avaricious clamors. These schemes were prosecuted by a great party, strong alike in numbers, intelligence, and wealth, and upheld by leaders distinguished for intellect and eloquence. One segment of this numerous body, comprising the bankers and merchants, endeavored to control, by means of allied incorporations, the issues of paper currencies, which exercised all the functions of money; another part, composed of the manufacturers, demanded bounties in the shape of prohibitory and discriminating taxes against foreign rivals; and a third raved for subsidies to enable them to construct local roads and canals, and to clear out unnavigable harbors and rivers in the name of internal improvements. They all agreed in one thing—in mercenary intentions against the common treasury. It required no extraordinary reach or astuteness of sagacity to see what a stupendous means of bribery their conjoint bids for favors were likely to become in our popular Congressional and Presidential elections; or how much they tended to an overwhelming concentration of power in the hands of successful party managers; or what an evil lesson they taught practically to the masses of people, whom they persuaded that national prosperity depends not upon individual energy and individual economy, but upon the fostering care and corrupting patronage of government. It was in this light, at least, that Mr. Bryant saw these projects, and he set himself against them with all his ardor and ability.

It was for some time doubtful during Jackson's candidacy whether, if elected, he would turn the Federal power in favor or against the enterprising classes, as they were called. Originally brought forward by Federalists, he was yet known to be not of their way of thinking. During a brief senatorial term he had rather given in to the prevailing views, and voted for tariffs and internal improvements. But after his nomination, and before his election, he looked decidedly in another direction. Educated in the tenets of the old Republicans, and professing an earnest sympathy with the masses rather than classes of the people, his known character and unknown views awakened a dread of him which lent a great deal of passion and bitterness to the contest. It raged in the end with a vehemence that had scarcely been equalled since the days of Jefferson. On reaching the chair of State, Jackson was not long in letting it be understood that the reins of government were in his hands. Professing to be guided by a spirit of the utmost impartiality and justice, he did not conceal his very decided party proclivities. "The blessings of government," he said, "like the dews of heaven, must fall upon all alike," which was not a consolatory remark for those who lived upon its special favors.

The administration of Jackson, beginning only three months before Mr. Bryant's editorship, was a stormy one throughout. His whispered suspicions of the National Bank, the charter of which was to expire in a few years; his vetoes of road and harbor bills on the ground of their want of national scope and bearing; the enmity of his friends, less ambiguous than his own, to the device of protection, which they seemed determined to defeat in detail, if not in gross; his plan for the removal of the Indian tribes beyond the limits of the States— furnished themes for excited debates on home affairs; while at a later day his vigorous prosecution of our claims against France, and his frank but determined dealing with Great Britain in questions of colonial trade, kept alive in many minds a hovering fear of foreign complications.

It is for history, not biography, to write an account of these disputes. Suffice it to say that in all of them the President had no more efficient supporter than the "Evening Post." It caught a good deal of its hero's courage and energy, and could be at times, in spite of its habitual decorum, exasperating and fiery. Once indeed — and only once in the whole course of his fifty years of editorial experience—Mr. Bryant so lost the control of himself that he inflicted personal chastisement upon an adversary who had given him the lie direct. It was the impulse of a moment, as the parties passed each other in the street, and regretted almost as soon as it was done. The next day Mr. Bryant recounted the incidents of the affair impartially, stating the gross provocation that he had received, but apologizing to the public for having so indiscreetly taken the law into his own hands. He could never afterward hear the matter alluded to without annoyance, and particularly when it was intimated to him that the person who had given the offence was not the one who had been subjected to its penalty. With the exception of this unfortunate occurrence, Mr. Bryant, though railed at with the vulgar and violent vituperations of our journals, confined his replies to words which were trenchant and severe enough, but never transcending the bounds of allowable party warfare. Nor was he often blinded by the smoke of battle to the shortcomings and misdeeds of his party associates. He castigated them, when he had occasion, with the same plainness of phrase that he used toward his adversaries, and not infrequently incurred their displeasure. We shall see, as the anti-slavery feeling took form and prominence, that his journal was not afraid of prodding even the " old lion " in his den.

In one respect, I feel bound to say, the " Evening Post " permitted its party attachments to close its eyes to a most deplorable phase of Jackson's administration. There were in it no rebukes—rather defences, or, if that word be too strong, pleas in abatement — of the practice of removing political opponents from office, which did not originate with Jackson, but was greatly extended by him, under the pernicious maxim that " to the victors belong the spoils of the enemy," and which has since grown into a prodigious and most menacing abuse. It is true that Mr. Coleman, who was an ardent admirer of Edmund Burke, had before committed the journal to the opinion that administrations should be kept entirely in the hands of their political friends. He justified himself by quotations of passages in Burke's " Thoughts on Present Discontents," * which argue that, while it is "the business of the speculative philosopher to mark the proper ends of government," it is the business of the politician, who is the philosopher in action, "to pursue every just method to put the men who hold his opinions in such a condition as may enable them to carry their common plans into execution with all the power and authority of the State." It was not seen, or if it was seen it was concealed, that Burke's words apply only to chiefs of departments, who control the policy of government, and not to subordinates, who are

* Burke's Poetical Works, vol. i, p. 530, *et al.* Boston edition.

mere ministerial agents, while he protests in so many words against the use of "proscription." Jackson himself, before his election, enunciated the true principle. "The chief magistrate," he said, "of a great and powerful nation should never indulge in party feelings. His conduct should be liberal and disinterested, always bearing in mind that he acts for the whole, and not a part, of the community." But the pressure of hungry supporters, acting upon his too ready and impassioned resentments, overcame the scruples of his better judgment, and the example of proscription which he set, only too faithfully followed by his successors of all parties, has converted our political contests into reckless scrambles for office, generated a class of professional politicians, who control the entire machinery of elections, and opened the way and given impulse to systems of bargaining and corruption which are the most imminent and fearful dangers of the republic. Mr. Bryant, in process of time, discovered the tendencies of this detestable bigotry,* and took a prominent part in the endeavor to arrest and correct its evils. Alas! how little has yet been accomplished toward a real amelioration!

Our editor's interests were not confined to the affairs of his own country. The decade, beginning in 1830, the reader will remember, was the heyday of what Carlyle used to ridicule so scornfully as "glorious enfranchisements" and "rose-water millenniums," when the minds of the race both in Europe and America were full of regenerating effervescences. It was the day of political revolution in France, Belgium, Poland, Italy, and South America, of Catholic and West India Emancipations, of reform bills in England, and of various smaller philanthropies, moral and social, everywhere—such as improved jurisprudence, wholesomer dietetics, disciplined prisons, so-

---

* "The practice of sweeping and indiscriminate dismissions from office for opinion's sake," he wrote, "corrupts our elections, embitters party quarrels, and makes many cowards and many hypocrites. Its effect is to put bad men in office, by rendering party zeal a principal qualification, and causing appointments to be made with too much haste to be made well."—"Evening Post," but not till November 28, 1842.

cietary experiments, and fervent religious revivals. Mr. Bryant did not escape the prevalent tendencies. He watched the larger struggles with earnest attention and outspoken sympathy; he signed and commended calls for meetings gotten up to express opinions, or to raise money, in behalf of the European revolutionists; and, rejoicing in their successes, he participated in feeling, if not always in person, in the processions and dinners that celebrated their supposed triumphs. Even for the less imposing revolts of the South Americans against the Spanish yoke, he uttered many a friendly word, defending the character and conduct of such chiefs as Bolivar, and earnestly urging the patriots to renewed exertions whenever they seemed about to fail. O'Connell in Ireland excited his warm admiration, and when the victory was achieved he joined heartily in the commemorating festivities. He must, I infer, have made himself somewhat prominent in these demonstrations; for in a letter from Garnier Pages,* dated Paris, June, 1830, he is addressed as one " whose occupations and labors, as well as personal character," would be of the greatest assistance to the liberal cause in Europe. " We have," continues M. Pages, "the most incomplete notion of the United States, which yet furnishes us the model that we wish to imitate. You have arrived at that happy state in which you have nothing to think of but the conservation of the political well-being you enjoy, while we in France must fight continually to acquire what you already possess. May I then ask of you, who are so competent to give them, the instructions that we so much need in our circumstances? " etc. I have no means of saying to what extent Mr. Bryant put himself in relation with the continental leaders, or that he did so at all.

His zeal in the smaller reformatory movements was less marked; for, while he approved the objects of many of them, such as the Prison Discipline and Anti-Capital-Punishment Societies, he kept somewhat aloof from reformers themselves,

* A member of the Provisional Government of 1848.

who were apt to be shallow yet overbearing men, of less agreeable companionship and chatter than the trees and birds he found in the woods. He once or twice presided at unimportant meetings, but I do not discover that he cared to speak. His adherence to the doctrines of Hahnemann in medical practice dated from a later period; and, although the preachers of "the vegetable gospel" claimed him as a convert, we have seen that his habits of living were a matter of necessity, imposed upon him long before by the state of his health.

In all his professional labors Mr. Bryant had a most able associate in William Leggett, whom he called to his assistance shortly after the death of Coleman. He was a native of the city, who for a few years had served as a midshipman in the navy, which he abandoned because of some real or fancied tyranny on the part of a superior officer. For a while, then, he wrote tales and verses that acquired him local repute enough to justify the issue of a weekly periodical called the "Critic," of several of the later numbers of which he composed the entire contents—reviews, essays, tales, biographical notices, and poems, besides putting it in type and delivering it to its subscribers. At the outset of his engagement, Mr. Leggett stipulated that he should not be asked to write on politics, "a subject he did not understand, and for which he had no taste," but in less than a year he overcame both his ignorance and aversion, and wrote fluently and copiously on questions of free-trade, currency, abolitionism, and constitutional law. It must be said, however, in excuse of this appearance of haste, that he was an unusually industrious student, quick of perception, ardent in the love of truth, supremely disinterested, and if too rapid in the formation of his judgments, and fearless in the expression of them, frank in the avowal of his errors, and always amenable to instruction. As he had been, like Mr. Bryant, a known writer of verses—in his case such as young sailors are apt to perpetrate during moonlight nights at sea— the wags of the opposition press lost no time in christening them "The Chaunting Cherubs of the 'Evening Post.'" More impetuous in temperament than his chief, he sometimes needed restraint, but for the most part his writing added to the vigor of the journal and helped to raise it to the leadership it soon attained.

Arduous and incessant work on his paper left Mr. Bryant no time for poetical labor. After the pieces prepared for the last number of the " Talisman"—early in 1829—he wrote no poetry for some years, as I have said—once, in 1832, after a visit to the Western prairies, but not again until his residence in Europe in 1835. Resolved, however, not to be lost to the literary world altogether, he prepared, in 1831, a volume of poems, comprising all that he had published since the little pamphlet of 1821 was printed. It contained about eighty additional pieces—not a luxuriant crop for ten years, considering quantity, but of rare worth and significance in respect to quality.* When it appeared, the reviews, with the single exception of a Philadelphia periodical, which thought but poorly of it, recognized its merits. Mr. William J. Snelling, in the " North American," pronounced it "the best volume of American poetry that had ever appeared." † Mr. Longfellow, in the same number, ‡ referred to his translations " as rivalling the originals in beauty." " He is," said Mr. H. W. Prescott, in the next number, § discoursing of American literature in general, " placed by general consent at the head of our poetic literature. His writings are distinguished by those graces which belong to naturally fine perceptions and a chastened taste. A deep moral purity, serious but not sad, tinctures most of his views of man and nature, and insensibly raises thought from the contemplation of their lower objects to that of the mind who formed them." Mr. Hugh Swinton Legaré had before confessed, in the " Southern Quarterly," ‖ that, proposing to sub-

* Poems. By William Cullen Bryant. New York : Elam Bliss, 1832.
† "North American," April, 1832.
‡ April, 1832.
§ July, 1832.
‖ "Southern Quarterly Review," February, 1832.

ject them to rigid criticism, he had turned down the pages he wished to remark upon, but found, before he got through, that he had turned down nearly every leaf in the volume for commendation. Other writers were no less generous; and it was this chorus of approval, doubtless, that induced him to test the hospitality of England toward a new American production. At the suggestion of Mr. Verplanck, he sent a copy of his book to Washington Irving, who, as our pioneer in prose, it was natural to suppose, would lend a helping hand to a pioneer in poetry. He was then residing abroad; and, though Mr. Bryant was unacquainted with him personally, he had every reason to rely upon his amiability and kindness. Some time before, Irving, writing to his friend Brevoort, from Madrid, in 1826, had said: " I have been charmed by what I have seen of the writings of Bryant and Halleck. Are you acquainted with them? I should like to know something about them personally; their vein of thinking is quite above that of ordinary men and ordinary poets; and they are masters of the magic of poetic language." * This expression had been communicated to Mr. Bryant, who would have scrupled else to ask the services of a stranger. He wrote to Mr. Irving, December 29, 1831, as follows:

"SIR: I have put to press in this city a duodecimo volume of two hundred and forty pages, comprising all my poems which I thought worth printing, most of which have already appeared. Several of them I believe you have seen, and of some, if I am rightly informed, you have been pleased to express a favorable opinion. Before publishing the thing here, I have sent a copy of it to Murray, the London bookseller, by whom I am anxious that it should be published in England. I have taken the liberty, which I hope you will pardon a countryman of yours, who relies on the known kindness of your disposition to plead his excuse, of referring him to you. As it is not altogether impossible that the work might be republished in England,

---

* " Life and Letters of Washington Irving," vol. iii, p. 241. New York : Putnam's Sons, 1880.

if I did not offer it myself, I could wish that it might be published by a respectable bookseller in a respectable manner.

"I have written to Mr. Verplanck, desiring him to give me a letter to you on the subject; but, as the packet which takes out my book will sail before I can receive an answer, I have presumed so far on your goodness as to make the application myself. May I ask of you the favor to write to Mr. Murray on the subject as soon as you receive this. In my letter to him I have said nothing of the terms, which, of course, will depend upon circumstances which I may not know, or of which I cannot judge. I should be glad to receive something for the work, but, if he does not think it worth the while to give anything, I had rather that he should take it for nothing than that it should not be published by a respectable bookseller.

"I must again beg you to excuse the freedom I have taken. I have no personal acquaintance in England whom I could ask to do what I have ventured to request of you; and I know of no person to whom I could prefer the request with greater certainty that it will be kindly entertained. I am, sir,

"With sentiments of the highest respect,

"Your obedient and humble servant,

"WILLIAM CULLEN BRYANT."

"P. S.—I have taken the liberty to accompany this letter with a copy of the work."

Mr. Verplanck wrote to Mr. Irving two days later, commending the project of his friend:

"WASHINGTON, *December* 31, 1831.

"DEAR IRVING: My friend Bryant, some of whose poetry I know you have read and admired, has been collecting, and is about to publish, a volume of his poems in New York. I need not praise them to you. A letter received from him this morning informs me that he has sent a copy of them to Murray, and has referred him to you as to the character of the work. I believe that I am answerable myself for this liberty, though he asks me 'to inform him (you) of the liberty he has taken.' His object is an honorable publication in Europe, though I take it for granted that profit would be acceptable, which I am happy to say is not necessary. You will receive a copy of the work, which I have not yet seen in the present shape; but his lines ' To the Past,' ' Lament of Romero,' ' Summer Wind,' and everything painting our scenery, I am sure can be eclipsed by nothing of our own day; the first, I have thought, by nothing in the language.

" I have the honor to be,

" Yours, very truly,

" G. C. VERPLANCK."

The fortunes of the book in England we shall learn in the next chapter.

CHAPTER FOURTEENTH.

SUCCESS OF THE POEMS.

A. D. 1832.

EARLY in the year 1832, one of the most active of his life, Mr. Bryant visited Washington, with a view, as I conjecture from hints in one of his letters to Mr. Verplanck, to establish a permanent correspondence for his paper. Up to that time "our regular correspondent" was hardly known, and editors depended for special news upon their relations with members of Congress. He may have desired also to make the acquaintance of the leading men of the day, but, knowing his later habit of avoiding personal contact with politicians, it is not very probable. His few familiar letters to his wife, giving an account of what he saw fifty years ago, may possess an interest for some of the thousands of travellers who are familiar with the capital in these days.

"JANUARY 23d : I wrote you yesterday, giving an account of my arrival here. Since that time I have called on Mr. Verplanck. He took me last evening to the house of Mr. Woodbury, Secretary of War, whom we found in the midst of his family and two or three friends—a fine-looking man, with a prepossessing face, and of agreeable conversation. After a stay of about three quarters of an hour we went to Mr. McLane's, Secretary of the Treasury, where we found more display. Mr. McLane is a quiet man, of small stature and unassuming manners. His wife, the mother of ten children, is a lady of great vivacity and a good deal of address, full of conversation, and talking to all the guests with great fluency. The eldest daughter is

a young lady, as I should judge, of sixteen. There were several ladies, half a dozen members of Congress, and Mr. Poinsett, late Minister to Mexico. Among the ladies was a daughter of the ex-Em-
peror Iturbide, looking much as you might suppose Mrs. Salazar * to
have done at the age of eighteen. A young lady of the name of
Christie played a psalm-tune or two on the piano, accompanying the
music with the words. One of the hymns sung was Watts's ' Sweet
fields beyond the swelling flood.'

" This morning I went to visit the Capitol. We first entered the
Representatives' Hall, a spacious building, but not well designed for
its purposes; speakers experience great difficulty in making themselves heard in it. Mr. Verplanck next took us to the library, an elegant room, and literally well stocked with books. We then went to
the gallery of the Senate Chamber, and waited for the Senators to
assemble. The Senate Chamber is not a large nor handsome apartment, compared with the Representatives' Hall. We saw Harry
Clay, who has what I should call a rather ugly face. He is a tall,
thin, narrow-shouldered, light-complexioned man, with a long nose,
a little turned up at the end, and his hair combed back from the
edge of his forehead. We saw, also, the Vice-President, Calhoun,
who, you know, is the presiding officer of the Senate. He is a man
of the middle size, or perhaps a little over, with a thick shock of hair,
dull complexion, and of an anxious expression of countenance. He
looks as if the fever of political ambition had dried up all the juici-
ness and freshness of his constitution. He despatched the business
of the body over which he presided with decision and rapidity. Afterward we went to the gallery of the other House, and saw Mr.
Adams, Mr. Everett, and others, and heard two or three short
speeches on trifling questions. Becoming tired of these, we climbed
to the top of the great dome of the Capitol. From this elevation we
descried the whole city, with all its avenues leading in various directions over a vast extent of surrounding country, through which flow
the waters of the Potomac. This afternoon we dined with Mr. Cambreling; Colonel Drayton and Mr. Powlett, two very agreeable men,
were of the party. We were going to see 'Old Hickory,' but it was

---

* A Spanish lady with whom Mr. Bryant's family boarded in New York for a
time.

too late before we were ready, as the old gentleman goes to bed at nine o'clock."

"JANUARY 25th : Yesterday I called, with Mr. Wetmore, on the Secretary of State, Mr. Livingston. To-day I dined with Mr. Verplanck. Several members of both Houses were present. To-night I am going to see the President, and afterward to Commodore Patterson's to a party."

'. JANUARY 29th : When I wrote you on Wednesday, I was about to call at the President's. We went with Mr. Cambreling in a carriage to the palace, on a bitter cold night, about seven o'clock in the evening. We were told by the servant that the President was engaged up-stairs, and could not be seen. C. proposed, however, that we should go in and see Major Lewis and Major Donaldson (private secretaries), which we did. Soon after, I observed that C. was out of the room, and in a few minutes he entered with the President—a tall, white-haired old gentleman, not very much like the common engravings of him. He received us very politely, and after about three quarters of an hour, in which he bore his part very agreeably in the conversation, we took our leave. Mr. Van Buren had been rejected that day by the Senate, and when that subject was alluded to the 'lion roared ' a little. We then went to Commodore Patterson's, where there was a party made up of various materials—the families of heads of departments, naval officers, members of Congress, foreign ministers and *attachés*, and others. Of the ladies, some were pretty, but the prettiest was a Mrs. Constant, from New York. On Thursday evening Mr. Verplanck took us to Governor Cass's. We saw him *en famille* with his two daughters; he is, as you may have heard, a widower—a grave-looking, rather dark-faced man of fifty years of age. On Friday evening we dined with Mr. Livingston, Secretary of State. The entertainment was, I think, altogether the most sumptuous and elegant I ever witnessed. There were no guests but Major Lewis, who lives with the President, Dr. Frienhau, and ourselves. We afterward went to a party at Mr. McLane's. It was much like a New York party, but more crowded. Three rooms were filled with company, and in two of them there was dancing. On Saturday we dined with Thomas L. Smith, formerly of New York, now Register of the Treasury. Major Barry, the Postmaster-General, was a guest —a man of slight make, and apparently the wreck of a man of talents.

"This morning we took a walk of a mile and a half to George-town, which is, in some sort, the parent of Washington. It is situ-ated close on the shores of the Potomac, and looks like an old town, compared with Washington. The country about it seems to be pleas-ant with hills, valleys, and woods. The shores of the Potomac above the town are beautiful and varied. We crossed the river on the ice to what was formerly a part of Virginia, but is now included in the District of Columbia, and found ourselves in a wood that clothed the slope of a hill. We returned in a driving snow-storm. . . . I have heard no elaborate speeches yet from the great men, but I have heard a specimen of the manner of most of them in their debates. I have heard Hayne, Webster, Clay, and others in the Senate, and Drayton, Adams, Cambreling, Archer, and Everett in the House. McDuffy I have not heard."

Soon after his return, Mr. Bryant was gratified by the re-ceipt of a letter from Washington Irving, giving an account of his discharge of the duty with which he had been intrusted. It was dated at Byron's former home, Newstead Abbey, Jan-uary 26th:

"DEAR SIR: I feel very much obliged to you for the volume you have had the kindness to send me, and am delighted to have in my possession a collection of your poems, which, separately, I have so highly admired. It will give me the greatest pleasure to be instru-mental in bringing before the British public a volume so honorable to our national literature. When I return to London, which will be in the course of a few days, I will ascertain whether any arrangement can be effected by which some pecuniary advantage can be secured to you. On this head I am not very sanguine. The book trade is at present in a miserably depressed state in England, and the publishers have become shy and parsimonious. Besides, they will not be dis-posed to offer you anything for a work in print for which they cannot secure a copyright. I am sorry you sent the work to Murray, who has disappointed me grievously in respect to other American works intrusted to him; and who has acted so unjustly in recent transactions with myself as to impede my own literary arrangements, and oblige me to look round for some other publisher.* I shall, however, write to him about your work, and if he does not immediately undertake it, will look elsewhere for a favorable channel of publication.

" Believe me, my dear sir,

" With the highest consideration,

" Very truly yours,

" WASHINGTON IRVING."

Murray's answer to Irving, dated Albemarle Street, February 2d, was curt and to the point:

" MY DEAR SIR: I received Mr. Bryant's poems yesterday, and I am very sorry to say it is quite out of Mr. Murray's power to do anything for him, or with them. I send the volume to you in compliance with your request. I am, dear sir,

" Yours, very truly,

" J. MURRAY, Jr."

Mr. Irving, nothing daunted, applied to other publishers, and at length succeeded in finding one in Mr. Andrews, who consented to undertake it on the condition that a line in the " Song of Marion's Men," which reads—

" The British foeman trembles,"

should be changed to

" The foeman trembles in his camp,"

to avoid wounding British susceptibilities. The book was published in March, 1832, with a dedication to Samuel Rogers, which spoke in the warmest terms of the poems contained in it.

" ' The descriptive writings of Mr. Bryant,' said Irving, ' are essentially American. They transport us into the depths of the primeval forest, to the shores of the lonely lake, the banks of the wild, nameless stream, or the brow of the rocky upland, rising like a promontory from amid a wide ocean of foliage, while they shed around us the glories

---

* A temporary misunderstanding, which was subsequently repaired.

of a climate fierce in its extremes, but splendid in all its vicissitudes. His close observation of the phenomena of nature and the graphic felicity of his details prevent his descriptions from ever becoming general and commonplace, while he has the gift of shedding over them a pensive grace that blends them all into harmony, and of clothing them with moral associations that make them speak to the heart. Neither, I am convinced, will it be the least of his merits, in your eyes, that his writings are imbued with the independent spirit and buoyant aspirations incident to a youthful, a free, and a rising country.'"

Mr. Rogers accepted the dedication in these friendly words:

"MY DEAR IRVING: I wish I could thank you as I ought, but that is impossible. If there are some feelings which make men eloquent, mine are not just now of that class. To have been mentioned by you with regard on any occasion, I should always have considered as a good fortune. What, then, must I have felt when I read what you have written. If I was a vain man before, I am now in danger of becoming a proud one; and yet I can truly say that never in my life was I made more conscious of my unworthiness than you have made me by your praise.

"Believe me to be

"Your very grateful and very sincere friend,

"SAMUEL ROGERS.

"*March* 6, 1832."

Mr. Irving announced the success of his negotiations, in a letter to Mr. Bryant from London, March 6th:

"MY DEAR SIR: I send you a copy of the second edition of your work, published this day. You will perceive that I have taken the liberty of putting my name as editor, and of dedicating the work to Mr. Rogers. Something was necessary to call attention at this moment of literary languor and political excitement to a volume of poetry by an author almost unknown to the British public.

"I have taken the further liberty of altering two or three words in the little poem of 'Marion's Men'—lest they might startle the pride of John Bull on your first introduction to him.

"Mr. Andrews, the bookseller, has promised to divide with you any profits that may arise on the publication, and I have the fullest reliance on his good faith. The present moment, however, is far from promising to literary gains, and I should not be surprised if the returns are but trifling.

"Believe me, my dear sir,

"Very respectfully and truly yours,

"WASHINGTON IRVING.

"WM. C. BRYANT, Esq."

That Mr. Bryant was pleased with what Irving had done for him, appears by this note to Verplanck of April 20th:

"MY DEAR SIR: Your letter seems to have been all powerful with Washington Irving. I sent him a copy of my poems, and another to Murray, referring him to Irving. On receiving the volume, Irving wrote me a letter, saying that he would do what he could for me, but he was sorry that I had given the work to Murray, who had occasioned him a great deal of trouble in the transactions he had with him respecting his own works. A few weeks after receiving the letter I received another, informing me that Murray declined doing anything with the work, and that it has been placed in the hands of J. Andrews, of New Bond Street, who was to divide with me any profit that might arise from its publication. Yesterday I received from Mr. Irving a copy of the London edition, with his name on the title-page as editor, and a dedication to Rogers prefixed to the poems, in which the kindest things are said of them. This was doing so much more than I had any reason to expect, that you may imagine the agreeable surprise it gave me.

"Why do you never write? The 'Evening Post' is in an eclipse since you have withdrawn the light of your countenance. The other papers are ahead of it in the revelation of State secrets and mysteries of policy.   Yours truly,

"WM. C. BRYANT."

As soon as a copy of the English republication was received in this country, Mr. Bryant took occasion to thank Mr. Irving for his services as follows:

"MY DEAR SIR: I have received a copy of the London edition of my poems forwarded by you. I find it difficult to express the sense I entertain of the obligation you have laid me under by doing so much more for me in this matter than I could have ventured, under any circumstances, to expect. Had your kindness been limited to procuring the publication of the work, I should still have esteemed the favor worthy of my particular acknowledgment; but by giving it the sanction of your name, and presenting it to the British public with a recommendation so powerful as yours, on both sides of the Atlantic, I feel that you have done me an honor in the eyes of my countrymen, and of the world.

"It is said that you intend shortly to visit this country. Your return to your native land will be welcomed with enthusiasm, and I shall be most happy to make my acknowledgments in person.

"I am, sir, very sincerely yours,

"WM. C. BRYANT."

Mr. Irving was crossing the ocean on his way home at the date of the foregoing letter, which was intended to reach him in Europe. As soon as Mr. Bryant heard of his return, he addressed him this second letter of acknowledgment, which was the first received, from Philadelphia, May 22d:

"MY DEAR SIR: I wrote you some time since to express my thanks for the kind interest you have taken in the publication of my book in England, but perceiving your name in the morning paper among those of the passengers of the last Havre packet, I conclude that my letter has not reached you. I take this opportunity, therefore, of doing what my absence from New York will not permit me to do at present in person—namely, to say how exceedingly I am obliged to you for having done so much more for my book than I was entitled, under any circumstances, to expect. I was not vain enough to think you would give it to the British public with the sanction of your name, or take upon yourself, in any degree, the responsibility of its merit. To your having done so I ascribe the favorable reception —for such it is, so far as I am able to judge—which it has met with in Great Britain, as well as much of the kindness with which it is regarded in this country.

"I am, sir, very gratefully and truly yours,

"WM. C. BRYANT."

A brief interchange of sentiment between Mr. Bryant and Mr. Dana, from which I make a few extracts, had taken place in the interval.

"NEW YORK, APRIL 9th: You were right in expecting a copy of my poems. I made out a list of persons to whom I intended to present copies, before the work was out, and I put down, first, the names of three old and good friends—yours and Channing's and Phillips's.

". . . The review in the 'American Quarterly'* was written, it is said, by Dr. McHenry, author of 'The Pleasures of Friendship, and other Poems'; but Walsh has said, in his paper, that it was written at his particular request, and adopted by him as soon as he saw the manuscript. It is supposed, also, that it received some touches and additions from his pen. Walsh has a feeling of ill nature toward me, and was doubtless glad of an occasion to gratify it, but I believe that, as you say, the article will do me no harm.

" You ask about the sale of the book. Mr. Bliss tells me it is very good *for poetry*. I printed a thousand copies, and more than half of them are disposed of. As to the price, it may be rather high at $1.2 5 but I found that, with what I should give away, and what the booksellers would take, little would be left for me if a rather high price was not put upon it, and so I told the publisher to fix it at a dollar and a quarter. If the whole impression sells, it will bring me $300, perhaps a little more. I hope you do not think that too much. I have sent the volume out to England, and Washington Irving has had the kindness to undertake to introduce it to the English public. . . . As for the *lucre* of the thing on either side of the waters, an experience of twenty-five years—for it is so long since I became an author— has convinced me that poetry is an unprofitable trade, and I am very glad that I have something more certain to depend upon for a living.

" I wish the critics of poetry in this country understood a little more of the laws of versification. The tune of

'Rŭm ti, rŭm ti, rŭm ti, etc.,'

is easily learned, but English verse not only admits but requires something more. He who has got no further than rŭm ti knows no

* A severe and almost abusive criticism.

more of versification than he who has merely learned the Greek alphabet knows of Greek. Yet people undertake to talk about the rules
of English prosody who are evidently utterly ignorant of the usage,
the established usage, of the great mass of English poets who deserve
the name. I have half a mind to write a book in order to set our
people right on this matter, but I fear nobody would read it."

"APRIL 10th: I have this moment received the 'American
Monthly.' If you see Mr. Channing, give him my best thanks for
what he has so well and kindly said of my writings.

"As to the *great poem* or the *long poem* of which you speak, I must
turn it over to you to be written. One who has achieved such a triumph as you have over ill-natured critics, winning a reputation in
spite of them, should not let his talent sleep the moment it is acknowledged.

"I am going to remove to Hoboken on the first of May, where I
will give you a chamber. But do not come till I get back from the
West, for to the West I am going in the course of about four weeks,
with no other purpose in the world than to look at it. I have a brother
settled in Illinois, so I shall go down the Ohio till it mingles with the
Mississippi, and up the Mississippi till it meets the Illinois, and up
the Illinois to within twenty miles of Jacksonville, where my brother
lives.

"I have written you an egotistical sort of letter, but you will excuse me in consequence of having lately published a book. My regards to all my friends in Cambridge.   W. C. B."

Mr. Dana's reply was from Cambridge, April 20th:

". . . I wish that your half a mind to write a book on English
versification might become an entire one. Nor am I quite so sure that
it would not be read. Let me see: there are all the manufacturers
of verses for monthly magazines, daily papers, and albums—no small
number. Then you have only to call it 'The Verse Class-Book; or,
Prosody made Easy,' and have it reviewed in 'The American Journal
of Education,' and recommended to all academies and boarding-
schools, and your fortune is made at once. But, seriously (if you,
with your half mind, were half serious), I should be glad to see such

a work as you would write, illustrating your principles with such selections as you would make from our master poets and from the
Greeks and Latins, where you wished to point differences or resem-
blances. We have no work deserving the name of a treatise on English prosody. Every departure from the ordinary rule is set down to
neglect, or ignorance, or laziness; for instance, the trisyllable—with
how much beauty you have used it (a little too frequently, perhaps,
for what is peculiar)! How exquisite it is in Shakespeare, and how
fine in Milton, I need not say. To me, *sometimes*, in an impassioned
line, when Milton makes a break, the trochee following the iambus
gives an abrupt, startling energy to the passage, which it would hardly
have had if he had adhered to the common rule. And I believe that,
in many cases, though he may not have so written it premeditatedly,
he retained it designedly.

"To think of the infinite variety of sound that one with a bold
mind and a harmonious ear may pour forth! It seems to me that
versification has never been treated upon philosophically enough,
merely as the utterance of thought and feeling, and taking the character and undergoing all the changes of these. Sensible remarks, and
plain moral reflections in verse, for instance, would naturally fall into
a Pope-like measure. Fiery, impassioned thought and feeling take
the abrupt and somewhat harsh one; feelings and thoughts more
lofty and imaginative would as naturally swell into a full and rich harmony. Pope's verse, for instance, was the result, I should say, not of
system, but of the general cast of his thoughts and feelings. He may
have made it into a system, but that was after-work. I am so sensible
of my own defects in versification that it is unpleasant to me to speak
of myself in relation to the subject, or I would say that I have thought
that, without the slightest premeditation, my own movement in verse
was, in its poor degree, frequently subject to all these changes from
within. I know it may be said that versification should run through
all the changes without losing either its melody or harmony; nor
have I the least wish to accommodate the laws of verse to my heinous
transgressions. I love the melody and harmony of others' tongues,
though I have none in my own. I am pleased with sounds I cannot
myself give forth. I began *too late*, and am too impatient, also, of the
labor, or rather am not enough skilled to preserve all the meaning and
strength, and give harmony too. Write such a work as I know you

can write, and I promise you I will be your diligent pupil. . . . I visited New Bedford and Newport. While in Newport I walked at the rate of eight and ten miles a day. The sea and I held stupendous dialogues! How spiritual the sea is!—how it seems to swallow one up in the Infinite! How bleak it is of a rainy day, and how awfully white the curl of its breakers in contrast! . . .

"Channing was pleased with your remembrance of him in yours to me, and sends his most sincere regards. I learn by to-day's paper that the English edition of your poems has made its appearance, with a dedication to Rogers, by Irving. Samuel Rogers! never mind, dear sir, it will help to favor. If the English will but give you fair play, how they will bow and scrape to you at home! and, then, how silly Walsh will look! Let him go; revenge is bad for both head and heart.   R. H. D."

The reception of his book in England was, on the whole, favorable—very much so, considering what the tone of British criticism had been up to this time;[*] but the praise or blame was alike superficial. The critics spoke of qualities that any reader might see at a glance, without discerning that peculiar genius which placed the writer among the great meditative poets of all time. The "Foreign Quarterly Review,"[†] which commended his descriptive fidelity, his quiet beauty of style and moral purity, yet complained "of a want of finish, such as we find in Gray, Goldsmith, Moore, and Campbell." "Although Mr. Bryant," the critic goes on to say, "occasionally recalls

---

[*] A few years before, the "Retrospective Review" (a) remarked : "In respect to the poetry of our friends, the Americans, little can be said at present. Their verses are too like ours to call for particular mention. Their principal writers of verse are Mr. Barlow, Mr. Paulding, Mr. Linn, Mr. Pierrepont, Maxwell Eastburn, Dabney, Mr. Allston, who has contrived to reconcile the two muses of poetry and painting, and, finally, the author of 'Fanny' and William Cullen Bryant. The author of 'Fanny' takes 'Beppo' for his model, and Mr. Bryant, who certainly stands first in the American Parnassus, copies the style of Lord Byron, in his Spenserian stanzas, and in his blank verse reminds us at once both of Wordsworth and Cowper."

[†] February, 1832.

(a) Vol. ix, p. 311, 1824.

Cowper, Wordsworth, and Rogers," he is "by no means a copyist," "writing in the same spirit, it is true, but without descending into imitation." "His sketches of Nature surpass those of Thompson, and 'The Ages,' written in the manner of 'Childe Harold,' though inferior to it in brilliancy and power, is superior to it in thought and sentiment." The loudest applause came from John Wilson, the Christopher North of "Blackwood," then a stalwart figure in the literary world, who, himself a poet and not unwilling to pick a brother to pieces, as his dissection of Tennyson shortly after shows, was warm, and even enthusiastic.* "The 'Song of Pitcairn's Island,'" he said, "is the kind of love poetry in which we delight"; the "Hunter's Serenade" he pronounced "a sweet, lovely lay"; and the "Marion's Men" "a spirit-stirring, beautiful ballad, instinct with the grace of Campbell and the vigor of Allan Cunningham." But the chief charm of the poet's genius he found to consist in "a tender pensiveness, a moral melancholy, breathing over all his contemplations, dreams, and reveries, even such as in the main are glad, and giving assurance of a pure spirit, benevolent to all living creatures, and habitually pious in the felt omnipresence of the Creator." The inspiration of many of his poems is traced to "a profound sense of the sanctity of the affections. That love which is the support and the solace of the heart in all the duties and distresses of this life is sometimes painted by Mr. Bryant in its purest form and brightest colors, as it beautifies and blesses the solitary wilderness. The delight that has filled his own being, from the faces of his own family, he transfuses into the hearts of the creatures of his imagination, as they wander through the woods, or sit singing in front of their forest bowers." Though he disagreed with Irving, thinking Bryant less "American" than Cooper, he quoted admiringly the poems descriptive of the landscape of the New World, and gave long

---

* "Blackwood's Magazine," April, 1832. Mr. Bryant, in his various visits to England, tried to see Wilson, but was not, I believe, on any occasion successful.

passages from others, which "could only have emanated from a genius of very high order."

The trip to Illinois, alluded to in a foregoing letter, was undertaken by Mr. Bryant in order that he might see his brothers, who were among the earliest settlers of that as yet unsettled State. After the death of their father, the children of the family were left pretty much to shift for themselves. Austin, the elder, took charge of the homestead, where the mother and daughters remained; Cyrus, after trying to be a merchant in South Carolina, taught the natural sciences at Mr. Bancroft's school in Northampton; Arthur was for a while at West Point, but abandoned it because of ill health, and went to the West as a farmer (1830); John followed him the next year, and sooner or later the whole family were gathered at Princeton, Illinois. They carried out the pioneer traditions of their grandparents and parents, and took up their abode in the wilderness, which they not only helped to tame, but where they were active in moulding its raw civilization into that of a highly advanced and powerful community. During these wanderings and trials William was in correspondence with one or the other of them, endeavoring to further their interests as he could, and not forgetting their mental improvement, as these extracts from letters to brother John, himself a poet of no mean pretensions, will show:

"NEW YORK, NOVEMBER 21, 1831: I am glad that you are so well pleased with the country, considering that you have become, as I suppose is the case, a landed proprietor; and I have no doubt, from your account, that, if you should choose to leave the place, you will be able to sell again at an advanced price.

"As for yourself, I hope you are not in too great a hurry to marry. When you do, I hope you will take the step with wisdom and reflection. Marry a person who has a good mother, who is of a good family that do not meddle with the concerns of their neighbors, and who, along with a proper degree of industry and economy, possesses a love of reading and a desire of knowledge. A mere pot-wrestler will not do for you. You have tastes for study and elegance, and must not link yourself to one who has no sympathies for you in your admiration for what is excellent in literature. A woman, too, whose religious notions are fanatical would be a plague to you. By the way, I suppose you have heard of the great religious excitement which prevailed last winter and spring in the western part of Massachusetts. Four-days' meetings, an expedient for the spread of fanaticism borrowed from the Methodists, were held everywhere, and when I visited Cummington, although the rage was somewhat cooled by the necessity the farmers found of attending to their business, prayer-meetings were held at four o'clock in the morning at the village, and meetings in the day-time twice a week. People would trot about after prayer-meetings for the sake of listening to unprofitable declamations about the meta-physics of the Calvinistic school, who would never stir a step to furnish their minds with any useful knowledge. . . .

"I have seen several poetical things by you, some of them very well, in the Jacksonville papers. I must repeat, however, the injunction to study *vigor* and *condensation* in your language and originality in your ideas. Your blank verse might also be improved by greater variety in the pauses. Affairs go on prosperously with me. The 'Evening Post' has increased in subscribers within the last year, and I am in hopes by making it better to obtain still more. I shall want them to pay the new debt I have contracted. I intend to visit Washington this winter to look at the old General and his Cabinet. It appears that the *unlucky*, I was going to say, but revoke the word—it appears that the late dissolution of his Cabinet has, instead of diminishing his popularity, made the old gentleman more popular than ever. At the next election he will 'walk over the course.'"

"NEW YORK, FEBRUARY 19, 1832: I have received several of your poetical compositions published in the 'Illinois Herald.' The lines on leaving the place of your nativity are very well. Those addressed to Kate are flowing and easy, but with some weak passages. The poem on winter also is unequal. The New Year's address was, I suppose, like most things of the kind, written in haste. Indeed, it is a pity to spend much time on what is so soon laid by and utterly forgotten, or what cannot possibly interest the reader afterward. As to the politics of the address, I think that, if they were not your own, I should not have put them in verse. I saw some lines by you to the skylark. Did you ever see such a bird? Let me counsel you to draw your images, in describing Nature, from what you observe around you, unless you are professedly composing a description of some foreign country, when, of course, you will learn what you can from books. The skylark is an English bird, and an American who has never visited Europe has no right to be in raptures about it. Of course, your present occupation necessarily engrosses the greater part of your time, and leaves you but little leisure for writing verses. What you write, however, you should not write lazily, but compose with excitement and finish with care, suffering nothing to go out of your hands until you are satisfied with it. I have visited Washington, where I passed ten days. I saw the President, who appears to be a sensible old gentleman, of agreeable manners, and the four Secretaries who compose a very able Cabinet—the most so that we have had since the days of Washington. Of fashionable society I saw something. The only peculiarity I observed about it was the early hours that are kept—the balls beginning at eight and breaking up at eleven, and the refreshments being all light, and no supper. I heard a few words from most of the distinguished men in Congress, but no speeches of length or importance. If I come, I cannot set out until the middle of May. I shall move the 1st of May, I think, to Hoboken, and the semi-annual dividend of the profits of the 'Evening Post' is made on the 15th of May. My stay in Illinois will be short. The family at Cummington talk of going to Illinois next fall if the farm can be sold. . . .

"I send you, by Mr. Coddington, a copy of my poems, and I have also given him one, according to your request. The book sells, I believe, tolerably well—that is, for poetry, which in this country is always of slim sale. I do not expect, however, to make much by it. If it brings me two hundred or two hundred and fifty dollars, I shall think myself doing pretty well. Poetry, at present, is a mere drug, both in this country and in England. Since Byron's poetry, I am told that nothing sells. I have, however, sent my book to England to try its luck, offering it for what I can get, and if I can get nothing, consenting that it shall be republished for nothing, provided it be done respectably."

The journey to Illinois was no easy one in those days, when the Indians were still abroad, and the modes of conveyance of the rudest kind. It took Mr. Bryant a fortnight to accomplish it, going across the Alleghanies by stage, down the Ohio River and up the Mississippi to St. Louis by steamboat, and then over the prairies by wagon or on horseback. One incident is curious enough to be recorded. While alone in these "gardens of the desert" he encountered a company of raw Illinois volunteers, who were going forward to take part in the Black Hawk Indian War. They were led by a tall, awkward, uncouth lad, whose appearance particularly attracted Mr. Bryant's attention, and whose conversation delighted him by its raciness and originality, garnished as it probably was by not a few rough frontier jokes. He learned, many years afterward, from a person who had been one of the troop, that this captain of theirs was named Abraham Lincoln.

Mr. Bryant found his brothers in possession of lordly estates in land, but at a hard grip with poverty. They were clearing the soil, planting trees, and raising rough log homes. He remained with them a week, making excursions into the neighboring wilds, and then returned, by way of Louisville, through Kentucky, Virginia, and Maryland, whence, hearing that cholera was in New York, he quickened his steps. He found his family already removed to a pretty cottage near the home of the Sands's, at Hoboken, and snugly domiciled just in time to escape the pestilence. It had broken out with great fury, and, being a new and almost unknown scourge, the terror created can scarcely be imagined at this day. I remember passing through New York at the time, on my way from Princeton College, which had been dismissed in apprehension of the disease, and it seemed to me like a town suffering siege. The streets were deserted, many shops and houses were closed, every face wore an expression of despondency and fear, and almost the only noises heard in the streets were the rattle of the death-carts as they carried off the dead. All that fearful summer our editor was compelled to remain at his post, endeavoring to calm the general panic and enliven the general

gloom by such cheerful and assuring accounts as the circum-
stance might warrant.

　　In the autumn Mr. Dana and Mr. Bryant exchanged words
that referred to these subjects.　Mr. Dana began October 3d,
from Newport, whither he had gone on account of ill-health:

　　"MY DEAR SIR: Your kind purpose in inviting me to pass part of
the warm weather with you at Hoboken, upon your return from the
West, was, like much else, brought to nothing by that power before
which great and small gave way—the cholera.　By this time I suppose
your city is as gay as ever, and in full dance over the graves of the
thousands who have gone down to death since that plague entered it.
As I never dance, I shall not visit you for that purpose now; and, for
the sake of moralizing, why, there is enough at home and in my own
bosom for that.　I do hope, however, that you and I shall meet by
another summer.　Why may we not meet on this fair island? unless
you fear that your poetic taunts may rise up against you.*

　　"My dear sir, what are you doing in the poetics?　Your name is
up, and you must not follow the adage and lie abed.　It is a little
amusing to see how, with all our patriotism, our men of real genius
must send abroad for their good names.　Look at the miserable notices of your poems at home, and then consider how you stand in
England.　I read a review of you in 'Blackwood.'　I was at points
with the reviewer in some things; but, upon the whole, thought there
was a good deal of fair commendation.　The long talk about the want
of description peculiar to our scenery and customs was owing in a
measure to Irving's sweeping remark.　In the few things in which it
has been your object to describe what is peculiar to our country, you
have done it; but these do not justify Irving's unqualified assertion.
Why must everything be daubed over with our treacle?　(I don't
mean *your maple sugar*.)　I perfectly nauseate it.　By-the-by, with all
my respect for Mr. Irving, I must be allowed to say that his dedication to Rogers showed much effort to little effect, and was withal very
un-English.　I will not say it was unworthy the dedica*tee*, but it was
unworthy both the dedica*ted* and the dedica*tor*.　When you write

　　* This alludes to Mr. Bryant's fling at the island in his "Meditation on Rhode
Island Coal."

(will you?), let me know in what English periodicals besides 'Blackwood' you have been noticed. I never read our reviews unless, for instance, you are concerned, and seldom see them."

Mr. Bryant's reply was from New York, October 8th, as follows:

"MY DEAR SIR: . . . You are right; we have had a fearful time in New York, the pestilence striking down its victims on the right hand and the left, often at noonday, but mostly in darkness, for of the thousands who had the disorder three quarters were attacked at the dead of night. I have been here from the 12th of July, when I returned from the westward, till the present time, coming every morning from Hoboken to attend to my daily occupation, every morning witnessing the same melancholy spectacle of deserted and silent streets and forsaken dwellings, and every day looking over and sending out to the world the list of the sick and dead. My own health and that of my wife and youngest child in the mean time have been bad, with a feeling in the stomach like that produced by taking lead or some other mineral poison. Since the second week in September the state of things has changed, and my own health was never better than it is at this moment.

"I am much obliged to you for conveying to me the proposal of the booksellers—I forget their names—to print a second edition of my book. There are, I believe, about a hundred copies of the first on hand, and I must see them fairly off before I print again. Bliss *sells* as slow as Old Rapid in the play *sleeps*. Any other bookseller would have got off the whole before this time; but he is a good creature, and I could not find it in my heart to refuse his instances to be permitted to publish the book. What you say of 'Blackwood's' animadversions about scenery, etc., is just. I am a little mortified that the transatlantic critics will not look at my 'Past,' which I think my best thing. You ask who has noticed me abroad. 'Blackwood' you have seen. My book was made the subject of a rather extravagant but brief notice in Campbell's 'Metropolitan.' They say it is also noticed at some length in the last number of 'The Foreign Quarterly Review,' which I have not seen. 'The Athenæum,' 'The Literary Gazette,' and some of the other weekly literary journals—no great authorities in matters of criticism—spoke of the work when it first appeared, and made large extracts. I read somewhere that it was reviewed in 'The Penny Magazine,' which, though less than a 'twopenny' affair (pronounced '*tuppeny*'), comes out under the auspices of the Society for the Diffusion of Knowledge, and has a circulation of, I believe, fifteen thousand copies.

"I have seen the great West, where I ate corn bread and hominy, slept in log houses, with twenty men, women, and children in the same room. . . . At Jacksonville, where my two brothers live, I got on a horse, and travelled about a hundred miles to the northward over the immense prairies, with scattered settlements, on the edges of the groves. These prairies, of a soft, fertile garden soil, and a smooth, undulating surface, on which you may put a horse to full speed, covered with high, thinly growing grass, full of weeds and gaudy flowers, and destitute of bushes or trees, perpetually brought to my mind the idea of their having been once cultivated. They looked to me like the fields of a race which had passed away, whose enclosures and habitations had decayed, but on whose vast and rich plains, smoothed and levelled by tillage, the forest had not yet encroached.* . . .

"P. S.—Dr. Anderson, who has just called, tells me that he has no doubt that the notice of my poems in 'The Foreign Quarterly' was written in this country. The critic's notion of prosody is the same as Dr. McHenry's, etc."

Before setting out for Illinois, Mr. Bryant was employed on a volume of Tales which he had projected, which was to be called "The Sextad," from the number of authors engaged in it, but, Verplanck having backed out, it took the name of "Tales of the Glauber Spa." It was published soon after his return.† His own share in it, besides the editorship, was confined to two stories—"Medfield" and "The Skeleton's Cave" —his friends, Miss Sedgwick, and Messrs. Sands, Leggett, and

---

* These thoughts were embodied in the poem on the " Prairies," which Mr. Bryant wrote while his mind was full of the subject, and contributed to the " Knickerbocker Magazine."

† "Tales of the Glauber Spa." By several American authors. 2 vols. New York: J. & J. Harper, 1832.

Paulding, contributing the rest. It was intended to be anonymous. "But the newspapers," said the "Evening Post," "those inveterate enemies to secrecy, have undertaken to point out the several partners in the joint stock. To Miss Sedgwick they ascribe one story, 'Le Bossu,' and, whether from deference to her as a lady, or whether from their candid opinion of her intrinsic merits as a writer, they have allotted to her the best tale in the collection. To Mr. Paulding they ascribe two stories, 'Childe Roeloff's Pilgrimage' and 'Selim'; to Mr. Sands two, 'Mr. Green' and 'Boyuca'; and the remaining three tales they apportion between ourselves" (Bryant and Leggett). It then proceeds:

> "Whether this ascription is correct or not so far as the others are concerned, is not for us to say; but, for ourselves, we may and do solemnly assert that we were never at Glauber Spa in our lives; that we never had anything to do with Sharon Clapp, or his son Eli, or his wife, or his daughters; that we never tasted of either 'oxhides' or 'gin' from the fountain at Sheep's Neck; and, finally, that we believe Mr. Clapp's story is a piece of sheer fiction, manufactured out of whole cloth, and with no other object than 'to do' those respectable gentlemen, Mr. John and Mr. James Harper, out of a portion of their well-gotten gains."

But it was not a propitious time for tale-writing. Day by day the politics of the nation was growing hotter. The question was no longer one of party supremacy, but of national existence. Legislation for special interests was bringing forth its fruits. The manufacturers, in their zeal to secure an exclusive home market for their products, had raised the rates of the tariff so high that it virtually destroyed the foreign market of the cotton planters, who, impetuous by nature, and domineering by position and habit, were not satisfied to oppose the evil under which they suffered by argument and appeals to the justice of the country, but threatened a resort to force. Entangled in the fine-spun theories of constitutional construction so acutely reasoned by Mr. Calhoun, they talked of nullifying the laws of Congress by State ordinances, which, with singular infatuation, they professed to consider a peaceable remedy. Mr. Bryant felt keenly the wrongs inflicted upon the South by the pernicious policy of protection, and had battled against it more earnestly and persistently than any other man at the North. His persuasions, indeed, had brought a considerable number of his Democratic allies to his views. But he would not allow his party connections to seduce him into any kind of approval of the remedial measures proposed by the nullifiers. Long before the interposition of Jackson he pronounced their plans impracticable and disorganizing, and he warned them against the incipient treason that lurked in their after-dinner toasts and speeches. While adhering to the doctrine of State Rights as an imperative maxim in matters of administration, he looked for remedies and modes of adjustment in cases of conflict between Federal and State authorities, to the determinate jurisdiction of the Supreme Court, where it could be applied, and where it could not be applied, to remonstrances to Congress, to appeals to the people in their elective capacity, to addresses to other States invoking justice, and to amendments of the Constitution in the manner prescribed. Should these constitutional and peaceful methods, however, prove inadequate, he was willing to resort, in the last extremity, to the natural right of resistance to oppression, but he called it revolution. Nullification and secession were, in his eyes, revolution in disguise, and they were not justified by the circumstances. He therefore earnestly supported Jackson's Union Proclamation of December 11th, extolling its teachings, and approving its menaces of legal prosecution, and, if need be, of war. Fortunately, war was evaded; the leaders in Congress came to their senses; the more odious features of the tariff were repealed by the compromise tariff of 1833, and a promise given of the final extinction of that kind of destructive legislation.*

---

* The " Evening Post " regarded the Compromise Tariff as a timid but certain abandonment of the protective policy, and rejoiced accordingly : " We should be un-just to the cause we have constantly and zealously maintained were we not to ex-

This year, 1832, fatal to so many human beings because of the pest, was particularly marked by the number of distinguished men who had died in the course of it—Goethe, Scott, Cuvier, Champollion, Bentham, Adam Clarke, Charles Carroll, and the young Napoleon. Mr. Sands had written a poem on the subject, called "The Dead of Thirty-Two," and three days after the publication of it (December 17th) he sat down to complete an article on "Esquimaux Literature" for the first number of the "Knickerbocker Magazine,* when, as his pencil had just traced the line,

"Oh, deem not my spirit among you abides,"

he was smitten by a paralysis of which he died. Below the line, in the original manuscript, several irregular pencil-marks were observed, extending nearly across the page, as if traced by a hand that moved in darkness, or no longer obeyed the impulses of the will. During the brief interval of lethargy that followed the attack, the only words he uttered were, "Oh, Bryant, Bryant!" † In the same number of the magazine that

press our deep and sincere gratification that the glorious principle of free-trade is proclaimed by a solemn legislative act of this country, and the restrictive system given over to a sure though lingering dissolution. . . . This journal has persevered in the cause through good report and ill report ; it has never intermitted, never slacked, never lowered its tone, from the fear of going too fast for the party to which it has been attached ; for which course we have received much abuse, . . . and been fiercely threatened with vengeance ; but we have gone on unmoved."—March 4, 1833. In these sanguine anticipations the writer was destined to great disappointment. Selfish interests are not so easily dislodged.

* Mr. Bryant's "Arctic Lover to his Mistress" was intended to form part of this article.

† "He was," said Mr. Bryant, " a man of extraordinary powers and attainments, joined to a disposition of equal humanity and goodness. His classical acquisitions were rare in an age not fruitful in ripe Latin and Greek scholars, and his acquaintance with the tragedians of Athens was scarcely less familiar than is that of the modern English scholar with the dramas of Shakespeare. In the literature of his own language his reading was unusually large and various, and to this he had added an intimate knowledge of that of several languages of Europe. He possessed an intellect of great activity, a quick and prolific fancy, and a vein of strong, racy, original humor."

contained the fragment of his latest production was a short memoir of his life by the friend whose name was the last upon his lips.* The same friend also set on foot the project of a volume of his collected writings, which he helped the editor, Mr. G. C. Verplanck, to compile. †

* " Knickerbocker Magazine."   No. 1.   New York : Peabody & Co., 1833.
† " The writings of Robert C. Sands."   In prose and verse.   With a Memoir of the Author.   Harper & Brothers, 1834.

CHAPTER FIFTEENTH.

THE BATTLE WITH THE BANK.

A. D. 1833, 1834.

THE battle of arms was averted ; but the battle of opinion went on, with scarcely less fury than before. Jackson, having routed the nullifiers, was determined to rout the speculators as well—traders on borrowed capital he called them. In his first message (1829) he had questioned the constitutionality and uses of the United States Bank—the charter of which would expire in 1836—and, though at first unseconded by his own party in Congress, he renewed his attacks until the final veto of the bill rechartering the institution in 1832. The questions raised were mainly economical, but they were soon complicated with mere party questions, and the contest was carried on with unexampled violence.

In its tug for life the bank encountered no more active and sleepless enemy than the " Evening Post," which not only approved the measures of the President and the reasons he gave for them, but took a broader ground of hostility to all special acts of incorporation, and to all attempts, by means of legislation, to remove any kind of business, banking in particular, from the general conditions applicable to every kind of business. Its opinions gave offence to the mercantile classes, which were largely the dependents or patrons of the bank. They had looked on with some impatience, if not formal dissent, when it argued against the dissipation of national funds in various local jobs of pretended improvement; but they left

that account to be settled by those who were directly concerned.   Many of them, too, formerly the advocates of a free
commercial system, were now inclined, by political affinities,
to take part with the manufacturers, whose schemes in their
own behalf were seriously menaced by the logic and ridicule
of the " Evening Post."   But, now that it assailed the bank,
it was making a thrust at their own vitals.   They believed, as
sincerely as they believed their Bibles or their ledgers, that
without that regulator, a safe, sound, uniform paper currency
was impossible.   No domestic exchanges, save at enormous
trouble and cost, could be effected without it; no easy collection and transfer of the public revenues made.   In a word,
nothing but confusion, disturbance, panic, and loss in the
whole vast field of commerce and industry if it should be destroyed..   Thinking thus, they could not maintain, by their advertisements and subscriptions, a journal that was blowing its
trumpet at the very head of the hostile forces.   Accordingly,
they withdrew in large numbers, which, however, had the
effect only of inflaming its zeal and fixing its determination.*

Out of this fiery furnace Mr. Bryant was glad to escape, in
the summer of 1833, by making a visit with his wife to Canada.   Just before his departure he was invited by a committee
of prominent citizens—Dr. Hosack, James G. King, Vice-
Chancellor McCoun, and others—to prepare an address on
the occasion of a benefit to be given to William Dunlap, the
historian of the stage, when Charles Kemble and his accomplished daughter Fanny, and a young actor named Edwin
Forrest, had volunteered to appear; but he either distrusted

---

* In the midst of his political distractions Mr. Bryant could yet find time to
amuse himself with such trivialities as the New Year's addresses of his carriers.   It
was a custom then of the lads who distributed newspapers to salute their " patrons "
on the first day of January—as poets laureate do their sovereigns—in doggerel lines,
which recounted the events of the year and predicted good times to come.   Whether
anybody read these effusions it is hard to say.   They are, for the most part, unread-
able now, though I presume that, if the recipients of them had known that the first
poet of the land was disguising himself as an humble newsboy, they would have given
more attention to his matutinal lays.

his powers to write for occasions * or was so eager to get off that he declined the honor.† He went by way of his favorite Berkshire Valley, in Massachusetts, through Vermont to St.

---

* How very much he was indisposed to write, or even to translate, for occasions, appears in this letter to Miss Sedgwick, dated New York, February 12, 1834:

"Dear Friend : I am sorry to decline any request in which you take an interest, particularly when it is urged with so much delicacy ; but I have two good reasons for not undertaking the translation of the ode on the supposed death of Pellico, of which you shall judge. In the first place, I have several things on my hands at present which occupy all my leisure. In the second place, I have looked over the ode, and doubt my ability to produce such a version as would satisfy my friends and myself with anything like a reasonable expenditure of trouble. You know that our English tongue is, of all languages, the most intractable for the purposes of poetic translation, both from the peculiarity of its idioms and the paucity of its rhymes. It is, therefore, a work of vast dexterity and patience—the *ne plus ultra*, I had almost said, of poetic *skill*, though not of poetic genius—to produce a translation in English which shall be a decidedly good poem in itself, animated with the fire and spirit of an original, and at the same time a faithful transfusion of the ideas of its prototype. In the things of the kind which I have executed, I have not kept close to the original, but I should not like to take liberties of the kind with the ode you send me, which is really beautiful and affecting, and deserves to have all its thoughts and images preserved unmarred and unchanged.

"I am, very sincerely, yours, etc.,

"W. C. Bryant."

† Not, however, without having made some attempts of that kind. Among his papers is a prologue, written for the opening of a theatre, not named. It seems to me quite as good as those of Johnson or Goldsmith ; but, unfortunately, the writer has taken his notions of theatres from books rather than from actual experience, for he supposes that Æschylus and Euripides have as full possession of the stage as Shakespeare, judging by these lines :

" Here shall by turns to wondering crowds be shown
    Each glorious triumph that the stage has known.
    Scenes that have made the tears of ages flow,
    And words that thrilled and melted long ago.
    Orestes, maddening with his fancied guilt,
    Shall talk with Furies o'er the blood he spilt ;
    And pale Medea, with a sterner air,
    Walk in her calm and terrible despair.
    And Cæsar, slain that Rome might yet be free,
    Submit, and die with Roman dignity.
    And poor Ophelia plait the idle wreath
    For her sick brow, and sing of love and death.

Johns, and thence to Montreal and Quebec, which are such miniatures of the Old World that he came back with a strong desire to visit Europe.

For a while Mr. Bryant was now busied with Mr. Dana's literary affairs, and subsequently with his own, to which these extracts from their letters refer:

"NEW YORK, JUNE 21, 1833: I have called on the only book-sellers here who would be likely to undertake the publication of your work. The Carvills declined on account of the 'times,' observing that they had already on hand some manuscripts which they had paid for a year or two since, and which they had delayed publishing on account of the state of their own affairs and of the book market. They, however, treated the application very respectfully, and did not decline until they had heard all I had to say, and considered the matter. On going to the Harpers, I found that your friend Mr. Wood had *prevented* me, as we used to say in the old English dialect, which Dr. Webster threatens to reform when he mends the common version of the Bible. Mr. Wood appears to have said everything that could be said on the subject, and to have left the brothers impressed with a high opinion of your talents, but they could not be persuaded that the book would be what they called a *selling book*, at least in such a degree as to induce them to offer anything for it.

"You do well in republishing your prose. It will be better received at the present than formerly. Your poetical reputation will cause it to be sought for and read, and the public can no longer be confined to the cold and artificial style of writing which was then held up as the standard.   W. C. B."

"NEW YORK, OCTOBER 2, 1833: I had received your volume of poems—for which I thank you very much—before writing the notice you speak of, in the 'Evening Post.' * It was a hasty article—hasty, I mean, for a subject to which I was so desirous to do justice—and I

And Lear, bareheaded in the storm that tears
The pelted woods and strews his aged hairs,
Find colder than the winds upon his breast
The love of those who feigned to love him best."
* They had been printed at Boston in the interval.

saw, on reading it over after it was printed, that I had not been very happy in speaking of the merits of the poem entitled 'Factitious Life.' I had neglected to say anything of the satire of the piece, which was happy and well directed.   I have seen the notice of your book in the 'Christian Register.'   It was not written by a person capable of judging of your writings, but I thought that the writer meant his article to be a friendly one.   By the way, I have to make amends for what I said about a critic of my poems in the 'Foreign Quarterly Review' before I had seen his article.   You may remember what I wrote to you on that subject.   Since that time I have seen the 'Review,' and have not the slightest doubt that the writer meant to be exceedingly kind, condescending, and patronizing, and all that; the misfortune was, that he did not know how to criticise poetry.   I have no right to complain, for he wrote in a friendly spirit, and praised me enough, I believe, though not in the right place.   What is the reason that none of the critics in England or America, except Channing, in noticing my things, have said a word about 'The Past'?

"After all, poetic wares are not for the market of the present day. Poetry may get printed in the newspapers, but no man makes money by it, for the simple reason that nobody cares a fig for it.   The taste for it is something old-fashioned; the march of the age is in another direction; mankind are occupied with politics, railroads, and steamboats.   Hundreds of persons will talk flippantly and volubly about poetry, and even write about it, who know no more of the matter, and have no more feeling of poetry, than the old stump I write this letter with.   I see you predict a change for the better in your new preface to the 'Idle Man.'   May it come, I say with all my heart, but I do not *see* the proof of it, or, rather, if I were called upon to point out any sign of its approach, I could mention no other than the change which criticism has undergone in speaking of your writings.   Beyond this I discern no favorable indication.   The edition of my poems published by Bliss is all sold but a handful of copies. . . . I think of publishing another edition soon, and will get you, when I am ready, to inquire what your booksellers will give for being allowed to publish a thousand copies."

"NEW YORK, OCTOBER 17, 1833: Will you see your booksellers, Russel, Odiorne & Co., and ask whether they will give me two hun-

dred and fifty dollars for one thousand copies of my book. Mr. Bliss
has offered me a check for two hundred dollars as soon as I put the
book into his hands. If your booksellers do not offer me more, I
shall let him have it. If they should not care to do anything about
it, will you inquire what my volume could be printed for at Cambridge, and let me know when you write.' I shall probably add to it
half a dozen pages, not more. My manuscript poem, of which you
speak, was not finished, and was not quite good enough to publish.
Will you resolve a critical doubt for me? John Wilson finds fault
with the passage in the 'Forest Hymn,'

> '—No silks
> Rustle, nor jewels shine, nor envious eyes
> Encounter—'

as out of place, and I am rather inclined to think him right."*

"NEW YORK, NOVEMBER 2, 1833: I have completed the bargain
with Mr. Odiorne, and have given him my book with such corrections
and additions as I have been able to make. I shall avail myself of
your kindness to look over the proofs. As most of the type-setting
is to be done from printed copy, I hope it will not give you much
trouble. Should anything occur to you respecting my book, whether
in the way of objection to any parts, or otherwise, you will do me a
favor to write to me about it. I need not say how much I am obliged
to you for making the bargain with the publishers for me. I have a
little piece by me in blank verse entitled 'The Prairies,' for which I
have directed room to be left. It is not yet quite finished; the conclusion gives me some perplexity. The winding up of these things
in a satisfactory manner is often, you know, a great difficulty. I have
sometimes kept a poem for weeks before I could do it in a manner
with which I was at all pleased. All this is in favor of your advice to
write a long poem. I will do it one of these days. I will write a
poem as long, and, I fear, as tedious, as heart could wish. I congratulate you on having become a centre-table poet. Your verses will be
repeated by youths and maidens, and you will be their poet through
life."

* The lines were omitted in later editions.

"New York, November 11, 1833: I am much obliged to you, certainly, for giving yourself so much pains about my verses. Since you think so ill of 'The Robber' as to place it below everything I have written, it shall not go into my book, and I formally authorize you to take the proper measures for excluding it.

"The phrase in 'The Past' (wisdom 'disappeared') I am not quite certain is a defect. I have sometimes thought it was a boldness. Disappeared is used nearly in the sense of *vanished, departed, passed away;* but with more propriety than *vanished,* since that relates to a sudden disappearance. At all events, I do not find it easy to alter the stanza without spoiling it.

"It was the 'Edinburgh Review' which remarked on the rhyme *boughs* and *bows* in the 'Evening Wind.' The grammar in the three last lines in that stanza is probably not clear, for the critic blundered in copying it, and made nonsense of the passage. Suppose the rhyme and construction be amended in this manner:

> 'Go, play beneath the linden that o'erbrows
> The darkling glen where dashing waters pass,
> And stir in all the fields the fragrant grass.'

And let the second line in the same stanza read thus:

> 'Curl the still fountain bright with stars, and rouse,' etc.

"As to the passage in the 'Forest Hymn,' remarked upon by Wilson, I see that, in attempting to mend it, I have marred the unity and effect of the passage. The truth is, that an alteration ought never to be made without the mind being filled with the subject. In mending a faulty passage in cold blood, we often do more mischief, by attending to particulars and neglecting the entire construction and sequence of ideas, than we do good. I think a better alteration than I made would be this:

> 'Communion with his Maker. These dim vaults,
> These winding aisles, of human pomp or pride
> Report not. No fantastic carvings show,' etc.

"As to the other passage in the same poem, about 'life,' and 'blooms and smiles,' I remember very well when I wrote the word 'blooms' that I had a vague idea of its impropriety, but I did not

know why until you showed me. I have rung half a dozen changes
on the faulty line. You shall choose:

> '—yea, seats himself
> Upon the tyrant's throne—the sepulchre—'
> ' As in defiance, on the sepulchre—'
> ' In loneliness upon the sepulchre—'

" The words 'that to the graves seem,' in the second line of ' The
Prairies,' strike me as feeble. I wish the commencement of that
poem to stand thus:

> ' These are the gardens of the desert, these
> The unshorn fields, boundless and beautiful,
> And fresh as the young earth ere man had sinned—*
> The prairies,' etc.

' To sup upon the dead ' I do not like. ' Bosom ' and ' blossom '
are in Wordsworth, whose rhymes are generally correct:

> ' Fill your lap and fill your bosom,
> Only spare the strawberry blossom.'

" But I will think of it. I have cleared away the rubbish, as far
as I am able, from the first part of the volume at least, and, since you
have kindly undertaken to read the proofs for me, I will give you the
trouble to see that the changes noted above are duly made."

Mr. Dana's answer was from Cambridge, December 7,
1833:

" The printing of your volume has gone on rather slowly. . . .
They will make a handsome volume of it, I think. You delivered up
' The Robber ' like a man. After writing you, I felt a little troubled
about it, lest I had taken too great a liberty. True, I would gladly
have received a like advice from you, whether I finally determined to
follow it or not; but, then, you are a master in these matters, and I
scarcely so much as a learner in them. Allston was up here to see
me after I received your letter, and I told him that you had directed

---

* This verse is not now in the poem, but in its place:
  " For which the speech of England has no name."

its omission. He said he was glad you had, and added: 'It is the only thing of Bryant's that has not pleased me.'"*

* This ballad was first printed in the "Mirror," where it was highly commended by Mr. N. P. Willis. As my readers would no doubt like to compare their own judgments with those of Dana, Allston, and Bryant, I shall enable them to do so by copying what they suppressed:

"THE ROBBER.

" Beside a lonely mountain-path,
  Within a mossy wood,
That crowned the wild, wind-beaten cliffs,
  A lurking robber stood.
His foreign garb, his gloomy eye,
  His cheek of swarthy stain,
Bespoke him one who might have been
  A pirate on the main,
Or bandit from the far-off hills
  Of Cuba, or of Spain.

" His ready pistol in his hand,
  A shadowing bough he raised;
Glared forth, as crouching tiger glares,
  And muttered as he gazed:
' Sure, he must sleep upon his steed!
  I deemed the laggard near.
I'll give him, for the gold he wears,
  A sounder slumber, here;
His charger, when I press his flank,
  Shall leap like mountain deer.'

" Long, long he watched, and listened long,
  There came no traveller by;
The ruffian growled a harsher curse,
  And gloomier grew his eye;
While o'er the sultry heaven began
  A leaden haze to spread,
And, past his noon, the summer sun
  A dimmer beam to shed;
And on that mountain summit fell
  A silence deep and dread.

" Then ceased the bristling pine to sigh,
  Still hung the birchen spray,
The air that wrapped those massy cliffs
  Was motionless as they.

" Your substitute for *boughs* and *bows* did not suit me much better than it did you; and I thought that, rather than injure the beautiful

Mute was the cricket in his cleft,
But mountain torrents round
Sent hollow murmurs from their glens
Like voices underground—
A change came o'er the robber's cheek,
He shuddered at the sound.

" 'Twas vain to ask what fearful thought
Convulsed his brow with pain.
' The dead talk not,' he said at length,
And turned to watch again.
Skyward he looked ; a lurid cloud
Hung low and blackening there,
And through its skirts the sunshine came,
A strange, malignant glare ;
His ample chest drew in with toil
The hot and stifling air.

" His ear has caught a distant sound,
But not the tramp of steed ;
A roar as of a torrent stream
Swol'n into sudden speed,
The gathered vapors in the west
Before the rushing blast,
Like living monsters of the air,
Black, serpent-like and vast,
Writhe, roll, and, sweeping o'er the sun,
A frightful shadow cast.

" Hark to that nearer, mightier crash !
As if a giant crowd,
Trampling the oaks with iron foot,
Had issued from the cloud !
While fragments of dissevered rock
Come thundering from on high,
And eastward from their eyrie cliffs
The shrieking eagles fly,
And, lo ! the expected traveller comes
Spurring his charger by.

" To that wild warning of the air
The assassin lends no heed.
He lifts the pistol to his eye,
He notes the horseman's speed.

original, it had better be left as it was, judging from your expressing yourself, rather doubtingly, that, as the public had already seen it, it might run once more. For another edition you may perhaps alter it to your mind, or conclude to let it stand. The word *o'erbrows*, in your alteration, sounded affectedly to me. I know well that it was with you—'a forced put' at a change. What you say about making alterations 'in cold blood' is true enough. If *you* feel it, who are so much master of the *art*, you may rely upon it, it has made my head and heart ache in trying to give harmony to my rough metre, or to change an expression to my mind.

"My objection to *disappeared*, in 'The Past,' was not what you suppose, and I like your remarks upon the distinctive meaning of it. My objection was, that, although merely an elliptical expression, it affected me like a participle *passive*, and this impression was probably deepened by the rhyming word. The alterations in the 'Forest Hymn' have been made according to your directions. In the second, as you left a choice, I took, without hesitation, the first proposed change:

'Yea, seats himself
Upon the tyrant's throne—the sepulchre.'

"The change in 'The Prairies' introduced as you directed. In 'The Lapse of Time,' fourth stanza, besides the rhyming words *glow* and *go*, you have 'Could I *forego* the hopes,' etc. I had no time to

Firm is his hand and sure his aim ;
But, ere the flash is given,
Its eddies, filled with woods uptorn,
And spray from torrents driven,
The whirlwind sweeps the crashing wood,
The giant firs are riven.

" Riven and rent from splintering cliffs,
That rise like down in air.
At once the forest's rocky floor
Lies to the tempest bare.
Rider and steed and robber whirled
O'er precipices vast,
'Mong trunks and boughs and shattered crags,
Mangled and crushed, are cast.
The catamount and eagle made
That morn a grim repast ! "—" New York Mirror," 1833.

write you about it, so you must *forego* a change this time, and let it *go*. In your new piece, 'The Arctic Lover,' you have, as a rhyming word, *bespread*. I don't believe that this is a word after your own heart, and guess it was used because you could not make out your line to your mind by the simple *spread* without more trouble than you were willing to give it at the time. Where used at all, I believe it is applied to smaller things, such as flowers and the like, but fur hides are rather too sizable articles. You can think of it against your next edition. I have played the critic enough for the present. You may think it would have been quite as well if I had begun my work early enough for you to have passed judgment upon my suggestions before printing."

" JANUARY 10, 1834 : Buckingham applied to me for a review of your book for his monthly. I declined on the score of health. It was indeed a reason, but not *the* reason. For us poets, as Judge Story would say, to be exhibiting ourselves before the public in the character of reviewers of one another, strikes me unpleasantly. A friendly paragraph or so in the newspapers, or an incidental well-speaking of one another, is right, and may do good, in so far as it will show a curious world that it is possible for two men to follow the same art, and not hate each other; anything beyond that might be taken according as it was. You may remember that I pointed out in your Agricultural Ode, p. 204,

> ' Till men of spoil disdained the toil.'

In ' Jupiter and Venus,'

> 'Kind influences. Lo! their orbs burn more bright.'

It troubled me to read it as measure. You may be amused at my objecting to a movement in your measure. But my *ear*, I hope, has always been more musical than my tongue; besides, your own excellence in these things gives a queerness to any defects in you. I may walk over Parnassus in a shag Petersham—people expect nothing better of me ; but it won't do for you, my dear sir—nothing short of superfine broadcloth must you be abroad in. You may have seen a review of me in the ' American Monthly' by Longfellow; it is respectable in point of talent, but what I liked it for was a certain air of

frankness and heartiness. As for my versification, I am as sensible of
my defects as he can be. Mr. Felton, Greek Professor at Cambridge,
has reviewed me in the ' Christian Examiner.' The article is a different one, and an abler, than I expected. He made me feel that he
had stretched his praise too far in parts, which gives me always a
feeling of pain which I can't describe. Still, he has been free in his
objections, which takes off from this feeling of excess. I feel grateful
to him, I am sure.

"Times are changed since your review of me was rejected by
certain gentlemen connected with the 'North American,' and I wish
the hearts of those individuals were changed toward me. The kind
feeling toward me which these late instances have shown have touched
me even to sadness; as *praise* I have hardly thought of it, it has gone
so straight to my heart."

"NEW YORK, APRIL 22, 1834:* It is some time since I went
through your book for the purpose of noting such passages as appeared to me capable of amendment—though, from my delaying to
write, you might think that I had neglected it. You shall have my
animadversions since you ask for them, though I do not place much
stress on them. The line, page 33,

> ' I feel its sunny peace come warm and mild
>   To my young heart,' etc.,

strikes me as faulty. The epithet *mild* I think tautologous as applied to peace. It is much like 'mild and gentle sympathy' in my
Thanatopsis. In 'Thoughts on the Soul' I am certain I found a
bad rhyme when I read the first edition. I have gone over it two
or three times in search of it, but can not find it. I have marked
the line,

> ' Life in itself, *it life* to all things gives,' p. 89,

as a harsh inversion. In the ' Husband and Wife's Grave,' the line,

> 'Of uncreated light have visited and lived,'

is an Alexandrine, which rarely has a good effect in heroic rhyme,
and is not used at all in blank verse, and, as I think, with good
reason.

* From Mr. Bryant to Mr. Dana.

"Page 118 :

> 'Dear Goddess, I *grow* old, I trow;
> My head is *growing* gray.'

"In this passage the word 'grow' is repeated without any beauty of effect.

"Page 134 :

> 'Nor live the shame of those *who bore their part*,' etc.

"Is not this passage obscure?

"Page 141 :

> '*Quere* as to the phrase *go* and care '

"Page 128 :

> 'But fluttered out its idle hour.'

"Can the word 'flutter' be applied to a flower in this manner?

"These are all the verbal faults which I have found in reading over your poems several times. I am sorry I have not a better list to present to you, for the sake of gaining credit for my diligence; but we must take things as they are. . . .

"I am sorry your health continues so bad. My own is much better than usual. I have gradually discontinued the uses of coffee and tea, and now I have given them up altogether. I have also, by degrees, accustomed myself to a diet principally vegetable, a bowl of milk and bread made in my house of unbolted wheat at breakfast, and another at noon, and nothing afterward. This is not my *uniform* diet, but nearly so. Its effect upon me is so kindly that, while it is in my power to continue it, I do not think I shall ever make any change. All indigestion, costiveness, slight obstructions of bile at one time, and the excessive production of it at another, disagreeable sensations in the head, nervous depression, etc., etc., are removed by it, while the capacity for intellectual exertion without fatigue is much increased; in short, I do not recollect that I have enjoyed better health or more serene spirits since my childhood than I have done for more than six months past. I mention these things that you may think of them—though I know it is said that 'what is one man's meat is another man's poison.'

"The line you remark upon as faulty,

> 'Kind influences—lo, their orbs burn more bright,'

is not to my ears unmanageable. I thought that I had a parallel for it in Milton, but I do not find it. Some critic in 'Buckingham's Magazine,' I believe, noticed the line as harsh, but I paid no attention to the criticism, being in the habit of disregarding all that is said about my versification.* But since it seems faulty to *you*, who are quite as great a heretic as I am in this matter, I will consider of it and perhaps amend it. It is only leaving out the *S*, you know. I thank you for the other passages you have marked, and will not fail to profit by your animadversions."

"MAY 9th: . . . Since I wrote the foregoing, I have packed up my goods, broken up housekeeping, and accompanied my wife and children to Berkshire, where I left them the latter part of last week, and now I am again without a home, ready to wander whithersoever my inclination may lead—provided I can *raise the wind*. But I must have a word with you concerning the question you put anent your versification. In this art I think you have a manly taste, and a vigorous, and ofttimes a happy, execution. In this it appears to me that you have the advantage of most of our writers in verse. The only fault that I find with you is, that you sometimes adopt a *bad order of the words* for the sake of the measure, or rather you let the bad order stand, for want of diligence to overcome the difficulty. Perhaps, however, you do right. I have sometimes been conscience-smitten at wasting so much time in making a crabbed thought submit to the dimensions of the metre, to frame a couplet or a stanza, so that the tune of it perfectly pleased my ear, at the same time that the expression, the thought, was the most perfect that I could command. I fear that the process has been attended with a loss of vigor and freshness in the composition. Your general system of versification pleases me—in that of Mr. Longfellow, I see nothing peculiar. So do not let them plague you about your versification."

Judging by the tone of these letters, one might suppose the writer of them in the midst of a quiet and contented literary leisure. But Mr. Bryant was really living in the very vortex of a popular tumult. The April in which some of them were

---

* Edgar A. Poe condemned it also in " Godey's Lady's Book."

written saw the outbreak of an election riot, which could only be quelled by calling out the troops; and three months later began those violent assaults upon the abolitionists, which ended in conflagrations and murders. In the latter of these, the "Evening Post" was constantly threatened by the mob.*

---

* The "Evening Post" of July 11th, referring to these events, says: "The fury of demons seems to have entered into the breasts of our misguided populace. Like those ferocious animals which, having once tasted blood, are seized with an insatiable thirst for gore, they have had an appetite awakened for outrage, which nothing but the most extensive and indiscriminate destruction seems capable of appeasing. The cabin of the poor negro and the temple dedicated to the service of the living God are alike the objects of their blind fury. What will be the next mark of their licentious wrath it is impossible to conjecture. If the unprincipled journal which has raised this storm is capable of directing it, we ourselves may expect to feel the vengeance of a mob, mad with passion, or drunk with the mere excitement of their audacious proceedings."

CHAPTER SIXTEENTH.

THE FIRST VISIT TO EUROPE.

A. D. 1834–1836.

THE fiercest of the abolition riots Mr. Bryant escaped by a voyage to Europe, which he says he had resolved upon provided his journal should not be knocked to pieces by the mob or merchants. He seems to have concluded that there was no danger on that score, and on the 24th of June set sail with his family in the good ship Poland, Captain Anthony, for Havre. For once, and the only time in his life, he applied for an office. He asked the Secretary of State, Mr. McLane, through Verplanck and Cambreling, congressmen from the city, to be appointed bearer of despatches, a place that carried no emoluments with it, but offered certain facilities of entrance on landing, etc. He was promised it, but it never came, and the State Department had some difficulty in explaining the why and wherefore to his friends. After a windy and cold, but not protracted, voyage, he reached France on the twentieth day. Among his fellow-passengers he mentions the notorious Madame Lalaurie, who, a little while before, was driven from New Orleans by a mob, because of her excessive cruelty to her slaves. "She was a portly, polite Frenchwoman," writes Mr. Bryant, "and her husband, who seemed a good sort of man, was devoted in his attentions to her, though she diverted herself from the time we sailed by gambling with a vulgar, disagreeable Frenchman." Her story had preceded her to France, and when she went to the theatre at Havre, her pres

ence becoming known, she was hissed by the audience, greatly
to the delight of some of her American fellow-passengers.
More agreeable companions were found in a young Swiss, the
Count de Portalis, and Mr. J. H. Latrobe,* his travelling tutor.
The journey from Havre to Rouen was made by the Seine—a
route not now frequented—and they reached Paris in the midst
of the festivals of July, which enabled them to see the great
city in all its splendor and gayety.

Mr. Bryant's original intention had been to spend his time
chiefly in Spain, by the language and literature of which he
was singularly fascinated; but that country was in the midst
of one of its chronic convulsions, and he turned his face toward
Italy. After tarrying several weeks in the French metropolis,
he went by way of Lyons, Marseilles, and the beautiful Cor-
niche road along the shores of the Mediterranean to Genoa.
He passed a month in Rome and one in Naples, two months in
Florence and four in Pisa, mingling much in the Italian society of all, and then came back by way of the Tyrol to Mu-
nich, where he remained three months, and to Heidelberg,
which kept him four months. As some account of these movements is to be found in the "Sketches of Travel," which will
form a part of his collected works, I shall here insert but
three extracts from his private correspondence. The first is
to the Rev. William Ware, giving his impressions of Italian
scenery:

"FLORENCE, OCTOBER 11, 1834: Talking of pictures reminds me of
Cole's fine little landscape taken from the bridge over the Arno, close
to the lodgings which I occupy. You may recollect seeing it in the
exhibition two years since. It presented a view of the river travelling
off toward the west, its banks shaded with trees, with the ridges of the
Apennines lying in the distance, and the sky above flushed with the
colors of sunset. The same fine hues I witness every evening, in the
very quarter and over the very hills where they were seen by the artist

---

* Mr. J. H. Latrobe, of Baltimore, with whom an acquaintance was formed,
which was continued in after years.

when he made them permanent. There has been a great deal of prattling about Italian skies—the skies and clouds of Italy do not present such a variety of beautiful appearances as those of the United States—but the *atmosphere* of Italy, at least about the time of sunset, is more uniformly fine than ours. The mountains then put on a beautiful aërial appearance, as if they belonged to another and fairer world —and a little after the sun has sunk behind them the air is flushed with a radiance that seems reflected upon the earth from every point of the sky. Most of the grand old palaces in Florence are built in a gloomy, severe style of architecture, of a dark-colored stone, massive and lofty; and everywhere the streets are much narrower than with us, so that the city has by no means the cheerful look of an American town; but at the hour of which I am speaking the bright warm light shed upon the earth fills the darkest lanes, streaming into the narrowest nook, brightens the sombre structures, and altogether transforms the aspect of the place. . . .

"Thus far I have been less struck with the beauty of Italian scenery than I expected. The forms of the mountains are more picturesque, their summits more peaked, and their outline more varied than those of the mountains of our own country ; and the buildings, of a massive and imposing architecture, or venerable from time, seated on the heights, add much to the general effect. But, if the hand of man has done something to embellish the scenery, it has done more to deform it. Not a tree is suffered to retain its natural shape, not a brook to flow in its natural channel; an exterminating war is carried on against the natural herbage of the soil; the country is without woods and green fields; and to him who views the vale of the Arno 'from the top of Fiesole' or any of the neighboring heights, grand as he will allow the circle of the mountains to be, and magnificent as the edifices with which it is embellished, it will appear a vast dusty gulf, planted with ugly rows of the low, pallid, and thin-leaved olive, and of the still more dwarfish and closely pruned maples on which the vines are trained. The simplicity of natural scenery, so far as can be done, is destroyed; there is no noble sweep of forest, no broad expanse of meadow or pasture-ground, no ancient and towering trees clustering with grateful shade round the country seats, no rows of natural shrubbery following the course of the rivers through the valleys. The streams are often but the mere gravelly beds of torrents, dry during the summer, and kept in straight channels by means of stone walls and embankments; the slopes are broken up and disfigured by terraces, and the trees kept down by constant pruning and lopping, until somewhat more than midway up the Apennines, when the limit of cultivation is reached, and thence to the summits is a barren steep of rock without soil or herbage. The grander features of the landscape, however, are beyond the power of man to injure: the towering mountain summits, the bare walls and peaks of rock piercing the sky, which, with the deep, irregular valleys, betoken, more than anything I have seen in America, an upheaving and engulfing of the original crust of this world. I ought in justice to say that I have been told that in May and June the country is far more beautiful than it has been at any time since I have seen it, and that it now appears under particular disadvantages in consequence of a long drought. . . ."

The next is addressed to Horatio Greenough, the sculptor, who was engaged on his statue of Washington, ordered by the Government, and who appears to have consulted Mr. Bryant as to certain intimations given him from home:

" PISA, FEBRUARY 27, 1835 : I am glad to hear that you are so far advanced with your statue. Never mind as to what Mr. Everett says about the necessity of sacrificing your taste to what he may suppose to be the taste of the public. As you are to execute the statue, do it according to your own notions of what is true and beautiful, and when Mr. Public wants a statue made after his own whims, let him make it himself. If you undertake it, give us a Greenough; the statue deserving it, the popularity will come sooner or later. Mr. Everett talks like a politician, but a politician of a bad school, nor has he gained much by following his own maxims. I hope to be permitted to see your model when I come to Florence."

The third, written the day after that to Mr. Ware, is the close of a note to Miss Sands, which sums up his general impressions, under an evident feeling of home-sickness:

" FLORENCE, OCTOBER 12, 1834: I am tempted to ask what I am doing so far from my native country. If one wants to see beautiful or majestic scenery, he needs not go out of the United States; if he is looking for striking and splendid phenomena of climate (I say nothing of uniformity of temperature, for there Europe has the advantage), he needs not leave the United States; if he delights in seeing the great mass intelligent, independent, and happy, he *must* not leave the United States; if he desires to cultivate or gratify his taste by visiting works of art, there are some means of doing so in all the great American cities, and they are all the time increasing. If he wishes to make the comparison between a people circumstanced as are those of a republic and the nations which live under the rickety governments of the Old World—*à la bonne heure*, as the French say—let him do it, and, after having made the comparison, if he is a just and philanthropic person, who looks to the good of the whole, and not to the gratification of his individual tastes, he will be willing to return and pass the rest of his life at home. If he dislikes being plagued with beggars, if he hates idleness and filth, if he does not like to feel himself in a vast prison wherever he travels in consequence of what is called the passport system, which subjects him to constant examinations and delays in going from one place to another, he must not go to France or Italy; and if he cannot bear being cheated and defrauded by rapacious hotel keepers, servants, and shopkeepers, who are desirous, as the phrase is here, to 'profit by circumstances,' he must not travel in Europe at all. Do not suppose, however, by this that I have finished my travels, and am coming back. I am only making a plain statement of inconveniences, to which I am willing to submit, temporarily at least, for the sake of gratifying my curiosity."

At Heidelberg his residence was rendered particularly pleasant by introductions to English, American, and German families; but it was interrupted by news of the dangerous illness of his colleague, Mr. Leggett. Resolving to return home at once, although it was in the depth of winter, he left his family in the care of friends until the spring should bring a safer time for travel. On the 25th of January he set out for Havre, in order to take the first packet for New York. It was not among the least of the regrets occasioned by this abrupt departure that it deprived him of the society of Mr. H. W. Longfellow, who had joined his circle a few days before.

Beyond a dinner or two, and some strolls in the pine forests, the poets found few opportunities for communion. Mr. Bryant had all the more occasion to feel how much enjoyment he had lost when his friend, a year or two later, imparted his European impressions to the public at large in the charming pages of "Hyperion."

On arriving in Havre, Mr. Bryant secured a passage by the packet ship Francis I, which was advertised to sail on the 2d of February, 1836, but, owing to head winds, did not leave port for a week. When the winds became more favorable she put to sea, but, as they suddenly chopped round again, blowing a gale, she was driven into Plymouth, where she remained for another week. Mr. Bryant, availing himself of the detention to land in England, was able to see a few commercial towns, but not the rural interior which he desired. At length they got off, but the weather turned up rough again, and he was kept ill almost from shore to shore, making a dreary and irksome passage of nearly fifty days on the water. He reached New York on the evening of the 26th of March, to find that his publisher, Mr. Burnham, had died in the interval, and that his colleague, Mr. Leggett, though a little better, was still very ill. A few days after landing, he was met by the following invitation to a public dinner:

"NEW YORK, *March* 31, 1836.

"To WILLIAM CULLEN BRYANT.

"DEAR SIR: Learning with pleasure your arrival in New York, and desiring to express our high sense of your literary merits and estimable character, we beg leave to congratulate you upon your safe return, and to request that you will name a time when you will meet your friends at dinner.

"Very respectfully and sincerely, your obedient servants,

"WASHINGTON IRVING,
"F. G. HALLECK,
"A. B. DURAND,
"G. C. VERPLANCK," etc.*

* The other names attached to the letter were William Dunlap, Samuel F. B. Morse, Thatcher G. Payne, Robert Sedgwick, W. T. McCoun, Henry James Ander-

To this offer Mr. Bryant modestly replied as follows:

" NEW YORK, *April* 2, 1836.

" GENTLEMEN : It is unnecessary for me to say how much the honor you have done me has increased the pleasure of my return to my native land, and how high a value I place on such a testimony of kindness from hands like yours. I cannot but feel, however, that although it might be worthily conferred upon one whose literary labors had contributed to raise the reputation of his country, yet that I, who have passed the period of my absence only in observation and study, have done nothing to merit such a distinction. This alone would be a sufficient motive with me, even were there no others which I might mention, to decline your flattering invitation.

" I am, gentlemen, with greatest consideration and regard,

" Your obedient servant,

" WM. C. BRYANT."

A few brief extracts from letters to his wife will now best show how he was occupied after his return:

" APRIL 14th : On arriving at New York I went to the American Hotel, where I was put into a little room containing two beds. I went to the other hotels and could find no better accommodations. Mr. Payne came to make me a thousand apologies for not answering my letter and to invite me to his house, saying that his wife had enjoined it upon him not to return without me. Mrs. Ware (her husband was then absent) insisted upon my staying with them till I could find lodgings. I told Payne I would go to his house, where I am still. Just as he had gone, Dr. Anderson came to ask me to occupy a chamber in his house.

" I think I told you in my last that I found New York much changed—the burning of one of the finest quarters of the city,* and

son, H. Inman, John W. Francis, Theodore S. Fay, George D. Strong, C. Fenno Hoffman, C. W. Lawrence, Prosper M. Wetmore, George P. Morris, Henry Ogden, Edward Sanford, Morgan L. Smith, J. C. Hart, and J. K. Paulding.

* On the night of the 16th of December, 1835, the coldest that had been known for fifty years, a fire broke out, which, after raging for three days, consumed more than six hundred houses ; among them the Merchants' Exchange—a fine marble structure—the old South Dutch Church, and nearly all the banks of Wall Street. The loss was estimated at nearly twenty millions of dollars.

the building of many elegant new houses, churches, and other public buildings,* have given it quite a new aspect. Astor's new hotel is an edifice of massive granite, and the new university, in the Byzantine style of architecture, is the finest public building in the city. Everything in New York is become exorbitantly dear—wages, rents, provisions—the latter have risen one half; but, now that the Hudson is open (it was closed till three days ago), it is thought they will decline somewhat in price. People of small fixed income complain that they cannot live as formerly, and some talk of going abroad to find a cheaper country."

"NEW YORK, APRIL 27th: Miss Martineau is yet in town, and is the great lioness of the day. Mr. Ware is a great admirer of hers. She goes on the 2d of May to Stockbridge, and from Stockbridge to Niagara, and from Niagara to Chicago; in June she will return again to New York, and in August sail for England. Miss Martineau is a person of lively, agreeable conversation, kind and candid, but rather easily imposed upon, and somewhat spoiled, perhaps, by the praises she has received, and the importance allowed to her writings. She came out with a Miss Jeffrey as her companion, who returned to England the first of this month. Miss Martineau's friends fear that she intends to anticipate Miss Martineau by publishing the journal of her travels. She has seen exactly what Miss Martineau has, and as she has two good ears, which Miss Martineau has not, she has heard a great deal more."

"MAY 6th: I am going this afternoon to Great Barrington, and this letter will be carried by the packet of the 8th. Since I wrote what you have read of Miss Martineau, I have been told by Miss Sedgwick that she has some queer notions about this country, and some strange stories about our people, and that *we* are likely to get into the book she is going to write. Among the stories is one about General Jackson's cheating somebody in a most outrageous manner. She will come out with the story at a very bad time for the success of her book in this country. The prejudices against the old man are very much softened already, and the moment he withdraws from

---

* The Croton Aqueduct was begun this year, but was not available for the great fire.

public life he will be, by general consent, one of the best men that ever lived. She has also a story about a plot formed by Jackson and Benton to steal Texas from the Mexicans, in order to keep up the power of the slave-holding States. Besides these, she has picked up various facts, as she calls them, relating to the abolition question, some of which are exceedingly improbable. While at Boston she fell in with Dr. Follen and his wife. Follen is a German; he came to this country with high expectations; they were disappointed, and he became exceedingly discontented. Miss Martineau has adopted his views about the country, which are quite unfavorable, and, in some instances, grossly mistaken; and when she has once taken up an opinion, which she often does very hastily, there is no reasoning her out of it. At Boston the abolitionists took possession of her. She is now going to Niagara with Dr. Follen and his wife and another lady, a zealous abolitionist, whose name I do not recollect. . . .

"As to my returning to Europe, I can say nothing further, except that I do not see any prospect of it at present. Mr. Leggett's health is improving; he is at New Rochelle, and some time must pass before he is able again to attend to the management of the paper. It is very important that the paper should not again be left in the state in which it has been for the last six months. I thought, when I was on board the Francis I, that I would on no account go to sea again; but now, if it were in my power, I would embark to-morrow and join you again at Heidelberg. I fear, however, that I shall not see Europe again." . . .

Miss Martineau, during her visit to this country, directed a great deal of interest to the subject of copyright for foreign authors, and, on her return to England, got up a petition to Congress, which was largely signed by prominent English writers. She enclosed it to Mr. Bryant, with notes from Wordsworth, Lord Brougham, Miss Edgeworth, and others, adding, "You can help us both as author and editor, and I beseech you to operate with all your might." The request was scarcely needed, for the "Evening Post" had already taken up the question. The book press of the country was pouring forth reprints of English works with astonishing fer-

tility, and few but English authors were read, inasmuch as the
publishers, having nothing to pay them, could afford to sell
their productions at a much cheaper rate than those written
on this side of the Atlantic, even when written with the same
degree of talent and attractiveness.   The "Evening Post,"
however, placed no stress on the scheme for an international copy-right law, which Miss Martineau urged, but,
consistently with its course on all commercial questions, maintained that, if literary property is to be recognized by our
laws, it ought to be recognized without regard to the legislation of other countries; that the author who is not natural-
ized deserves to be protected in the enjoyment of it equally
with the citizen of the republic, and that to possess ourselves
of his books simply because he is a stranger is as gross an
inhospitality as if we denied his right to his baggage or the
wares he might bring from abroad to dispose of in our
market.   The public mind seemed to be prepared for abolish-
ing any unequal distinction in the right of property founded
on birth or citizenship, and the publishers and booksellers,
who had at first been averse to the measure, were at length
brought to give it their assent.   But the members of Congress were not ready.   They did not understand the question; no party purpose was to be served by studying it, or
supporting any measure connected with it; no disadvantage
was likely to accrue to either party from neglecting it, and
for this reason, as Mr. Bryant said, politicians by profession
always yawned when the subject happened to be broached.
Up to this time it has remained untouched by the national
Legislature.

I now continue the extracts from Mr. Bryant's correspondence:

"NEW YORK, MAY 23d: I have made a bargain with the Harpers
for publishing my poems.   They are to do it in a neat manner, and
with a vignette in the title-page.   I have written to Wier to furnish a
design.   They will pay me twenty-five cents a copy; the work is to
be stereotyped, and an impression of twenty-five hundred is to be

struck off at first.   For these I shall be paid six hundred and twenty-
five dollars.*

"Mr. Charles Mason † has assisted me in the management of the
paper till now, but he will leave me in a few days.   It is my intention
to employ some young man to relieve me of a part of the drudgery,
such as looking over the mail papers and getting out the local news,
etc.   Do not give yourself any trouble about me; I am in excellent
health—never better—and am fatter than when I left Europe.   I met
Mr. Halleck the other day; he enquired about you, as he always does.
He says the world is going back; that nothing is talked of but stocks
and lots and speculations; that many of his old acquaintances, who
were formerly rational companions, are now so sordid in their conversation that it is absolutely intolerable, and therefore he has forsworn
society altogether.   I have seen Mr. Cooper several times since my
return; he appears quite discontented, and talks of going back to
Europe.   He has just published a book about Switzerland.   I have
not read it.   Mr. Halleck says it is a good book."

"NEW YORK, MAY 31st : ‡ An apology as usual.   I have been much
engaged in various affairs since my return, and have carried your
letter for a long time in my coat pocket, hoping that the time would
arrive when I could collect my thoughts and answer it in a better
manner than I shall now do.   I had heard before you wrote, and was
glad to hear, that you had found an occupation for the winter in
Boston. §   Why should you dwell upon the ungrateful part of it?
Here am I, who have been chained to the oar these twenty years,
drudging in two wrangling professions one after the other; and it as-
tonishes me to hear a man of your tastes talk of the misery of being
obliged to point out the beauties of the English poets.   As to the
effect of analysis, it is doubtless just as you say, but there is a pleasure
annexed to it—that of the discovery of truth.   I have often wished
that I could tell why I am pleased with this or that fine passage or
poem.   It would have been a 'joy unspeakable' to my wife and me

---

* They were published in a neat one-volume edition.
† Afterward, I think, Chief Justice of Iowa.
‡ To R. H. Dana.
§ Lecturing on the poets.

could it have been in our power to read one of your pleasant letters in the midst of the solitude which surrounded us in the cities of strangers. . . .

"Plans for the future I have none at present, except to work hard, as I am now obliged to do ; I hope, however, the day will come when I may retire without danger of starving, and give myself to occupations that I like better. But who is suffered to shape the course of his own life? I have bargained for printing a third edition of my book. They will stereotype it, and allow me the same compensation that was paid me by Russell, Odiorne & Co. I am to have a vignette for the title-page from a design by Wier, illustrating the little poem called 'Inscription for the Entrance to a Wood.' It is a copy of a little landscape at West Point.

"Cooper, you know, has published a book about Switzerland ; I have not read it, but it seems more likely to take than his last. Verplanck is getting up an edition of one of his public discourses, with illustrations by Wier. I saw the illustrations before I went to Europe. They were a mere outline in pen and ink, in a broad margin of the book, a sort of running pictorial commentary on the text ; a new idea, and in many parts strikingly executed. They are to be published precisely in the same manner." . . .

"NEW YORK, JULY 4th : * I employ the leisure which this day gives me in beginning a letter which must be sent on the 8th of this month. Day before yesterday—Saturday—I went to Orange Spring for the purpose of passing Sunday and the 4th of July. I found the place uncommonly beautiful. The season has been so rainy that the vegetation was exceedingly luxuriant, and the verdure the most brilliant that can be imagined; but the weather was very hot, and you know how sultry Orange is in the summer; the mosquitoes were very numerous and very hungry; my chamber, which was in the third story, just under the roof, was *un volcan de fuego*, as Salazar † used to say, and the house, which is badly kept, was crammed with fashionable company. So the next morning, which was Sunday, I paid my bill, took my umbrella, and a paper containing a clean shirt and a razor, in

* To Mrs. Bryant.
† A Spanish gentleman with whom Mr. Bryant once lodged.

my hand, and walked to Newark.   Arrived at Newark, I found that
no public conveyance was to be had to New York, and, accordingly, I
concluded to finish my journey on foot.   When about three miles from
Hoboken, I was overtaken by a man in a gig, who asked me to ride,
which, being a little tired, I accepted, and got to New York by dinner-
time, and here I am again in my own chambers when I thought to be
rambling the woods on the mountain-side of Orange. . . . Mrs. Coleman's proceedings against Leggett resulted in his making over to her
one entire third part of the establishment of the 'Evening Post,' so
that she comes in as partner, with a voice in the control of the paper.
I had no objection to this, because Leggett sometimes needs a curb.
Dr. Anderson has taken much interest in the paper since my return ;
he has frequently written for it, and his articles are excellent both for
matter, style, and temper.   Mr. Leggett is yet at New Rochelle, improving in health, but not rapidly.   I do not believe he will return to
the paper till cool weather.   In the mean time, I have nobody to as-
sist me except Dr. Anderson, whose assistance is a secret; nor, in
truth, do I feel much need of any assistance.   My health is excellent;
I work harder than I ever did before, but I was never so well able to
work hard before.   I think I should be quite stout if study did not
keep me down; as it is, my digestion is always perfect, my head clear,
and my mind serene.   I only want you and the children back, to be
as contented as I can be while harnessed to the wain of a daily paper.
The 'Evening Post' was a sad, dull thing during the winter, after
Sedgwick * left it, and people were getting tired of it.   I have raised
it a good deal, so that it begins to be talked about and quoted.   It
needed my attention very much. . . . I must now apply myself to
bringing it up to its old standard, after which I shall look for a purchaser.   Dr. Anderson says he will find me one.   I think, from the
attention he pays to politics, visiting frequently, talking much, and
coming to the office to read the papers we receive in exchange, that
he may possibly become a purchaser himself.   But he will not confess
that he has any such thoughts." . . .

---

* Theodore Sedgwick, Jr., a distinguished young lawyer, son of the Theodore
Sedgwick, of Massachusetts, named on p. 178, and a nephew of Miss C. M. Sedgwick, who assumed temporary control of the " Evening Post " during Mr. Leggett's
illness.   He wrote for it, also, several masterly essays on public questions under the
signature of " Veto."

"July 5th: Mrs. Van Polanen is really going to Holland. Mr. Ware thinks she is going to be married. She has offered me her house at the rate of five hundred dollars a year, which is reasonable enough as rents go; but she wants me to take it from next August, which is three months earlier than I want it, as I suppose you will not leave Heidelberg earlier than September, in which case, if you stop a little at Paris or London, you will not arrive here till the 1st of November. She expressed, however, a willingness to make some deduction on that account. I think that, if she will make it equally cheap to me, or nearly so, I will furnish a room in that house, and live there till you return. She wants you to return by way of Holland, and to pass through the Hague, where she will reside." *

"New York, July 20th : Now for myself, and the promise I made you to get somebody to help me in the paper. This promise is literally fulfilled. I have got Dr. Anderson to help me, and a very able helper he is. The varieties from foreign journals which you see in the 'Evening Post' are all compiled by him, and now and then a very able leading article is from his pen. The paper is in better odor than when I returned, but I do not see that the subscribers increase, although everybody praises it. Mr. Leggett is yet in the country. My own health is excellent; I sleep well, eat with a regular appetite, and

---

* The Mrs. Van Polanen here referred to will be remembered by older residents of New York as the wife of Mr. Roger Gerard Van Polanen, who for many years represented his native country, Holland, in the United States, as Consul General in Washington's time, and as Minister in Jefferson's. Before coming here he had held high official stations—in Asia, as the head of the Judiciary in the Dutch Colony of Batavia, in Africa at the Cape of Good Hope, and in South America in Dutch Guiana. His varied experiences in these positions, together with his intimate acquaintance with nearly all the literatures of Europe—German, French, Italian, and English— rendered him a most agreeable companion ; and, as he had been personally acquainted with Voltaire, Gibbon, and Fox, his reminiscences were delightful, particularly his stories of Gibbon's weekly dinners at Lausanne, where he met the most illustrious scholars and statesmen of Europe. Mrs. Van Polanen, his wife, was, like himself, a native of Holland, and almost equally accomplished. She became a Unitarian in the course of her residence in this country, and built a pretty church for that faith at Bridgeport, in Connecticut. They were both of them early attracted to Mr. Bryant, who found the greatest pleasure in their society.

work hard. My book will be out in about a fortnight. The engraving for the title-page is neatly executed. . . .

"I went to-day to see Mr. Van Buren. He looks a little older than when I saw him last; the newspapers say he is about to be married to a literary lady—one paper named Miss Martineau. He laughed. Miss Martineau, you know, has a very bad opinion of him. He said he was told it was Mrs. Willard. I found the little magician at the Astor Hotel. He was in a parlor facing the South; the sun was blazing against the shutters, which were nearly closed, and the room was a furnace of heat. I told (Judge) Oakley, who was with me, that I believed this was a contrivance to shorten the calls of his visitors. These politicians, you know, are politic in everything; they even 'drink tea by stratagem.' The vice-president's son, Major Van Buren, was with him, a handsome, manly looking young man. Matty very familiarly asked how old I was.

"The world is running very much into novels—the literary world, I mean. Here are three in one week. 'Elsawatawa,' I believe that is the name, by a Virginian, said to be no great matter; 'Lafitte,' by Mr. Ingraham, a professor in some institution of learning turned planter, born in Maine, and living at Natchez, with whom I travelled two days in a stage-coach in Virginia, and did not find very agreeable; the book is said to be tolerable; and, finally, my friend Dunlap's novel called the 'Water Drinker,' of which I have heard no opinion. Of course, I have no time to read them. Miss Sedgwick is engaged in publishing a work in continuation of the little book called 'Home.' 'Home' is her most popular production; five or six editions of it have gone off; it was published at Boston; the continuation is published here by the Harpers. I have read Miss Sedgwick's 'The Linwoods' since I came; it is interesting, but not the best of her works in point of talent by any means. Simms * is here for the purpose of publishing a novel." . . .

Mr. Bryant had returned to the distractions of the press with reluctance; and the plan of disposing of his interest in it,

---

* Mr. Gilmore Simms, of South Carolina, writer of a book of poems, and of several popular novels. The people of Charleston, while I write, are erecting a monument to his memory.

alluded to above, was seriously entertained. In September,
1836, he wrote to his brother John in Illinois to look out for a
modest home for him in the West. He said:

"DEAR BROTHER: I think of making some disposition of my interest in the 'Evening Post' and coming out to the western country
with a few thousand dollars to try my fortune. What do you think of
such a plan? What could I do next summer or next fall with a little
capital of from three to five thousand dollars? Will you write me at
large your views of the probability of my success, and of the particular modes of investment which would yield the largest profit? I am
inclined to think that I might make money as fast as I can do it here,
and with much less wear and tear of brains. Write me fully, but do
not go too much into conjecture; speak only of what you *know*, or of
what has actually happened. I have not been much pleased since my
return with New York. The entire thoughts of the inhabitants seem
to be given to the acquisition of wealth; nothing else is talked of.
The city is dirtier and noisier, and more uncomfortable, and dearer to
live in, than it ever was before. I have had my fill of a town life, and
begin to wish to pass a little time in the country. I have been employed long enough with the management of a daily newspaper, and
desire leisure for literary occupations that I love better. It was not
my intention when I went to Europe to return to the business of conducting a newspaper. If I were to come out to Illinois next spring
with the design of passing the year there, what arrangements could be
made for my family? What sort of habitation could I have, and what
would it cost? I hardly think I shall come to Illinois to live; but I
can tell better after I have tried it. You are so distant from all the
large towns, and the means of education are so difficult to come at,
and there is so little literary society, that I am afraid I might wish
to get back to the Atlantic coast. I should like, however, to try the
experiment of a year at the West.

"You ask whether the paper is doing well. I found affairs in
some confusion and embarrassment on my return, in consequence of
there being no responsible and active person to look to the business
part of the establishment, but I retrieved them shortly. The subscription also had diminished somewhat during Mr. Leggett's illness, but
not materially, and we are now going on very well again. Mr. Leg-

gett has recovered, and returned to the office about the beginning of this month. We think here there is no doubt concerning Mr. Van Buren's success—so little doubt, indeed, that we do not fret ourselves much with electioneering. He is certain of the vote of this State.*

"My book is out. It contains some thirty pages more than the last edition, and is better printed. I had a letter from my wife the other day, dated August 2d. She was still at Heidelberg. She had made a little excursion to the Rhine, visited Coblentz and Ems, and some other watering-places.† She was to go to London by way of Paris, and return to America either by the London or the Liverpool packet. It is very likely that she is now on her voyage.

"Mother in her letter to me—her first letter—praised the healthfulness of the situation. It seems to me, however, from what I have learned in one way and another, that bilious fevers are considerably prevalent among you, and this is rather a bad form of fever. Whether your being without physicians is much disadvantage, I doubt. Nature is, I believe, a better physician than most of the physicians whom we call in, in vain reliance on what we suppose to be their superior knowledge. The practice of physic is here undergoing a considerable revolution. Physicians begin to think that a vast many patients have been drugged out of the world within the last fifty years, and the let-alone system is becoming fashionable. I am so far a convert to it that I distrust a physician who is inclined to go to work with large quantities of medicine."‡

---

* As a candidate for the Presidency.

† This was in company with Mr. Longfellow.

‡ He was, in fact, an entire convert to the homœopathic methods, to which he adhered for the rest of his life.

CHAPTER SEVENTEENTH.

THE RISE OF ABOLITIONISM.

A. D. 1836.

IT is not surprising that a man of sensibility should endeavor to get out of the hurly-burly of politics. Jackson's "Experiments upon the Currency," as his efforts to save the Government and the nation from a deluge of paper money were called, infused new acrimony into party passions by transferring discussion to the channels of trade. There can be little doubt that by withholding the public deposits from the federal bank, and scattering them among a multitude of local banks, the Government had encouraged a vast expansion of credit, which, with other causes, produced an extremely florid but factitious prosperity, shown in all sorts of extravagant speculations. "No scheme," said the "Evening Post," "seems too vast to stagger popular credulity. Plans the most impracticable are received as easy of accomplishment, and entered upon with undoubting confidence. The thought obtrudes itself apparently into no man's mind that there is a stopping-place for all this motion, or that the machine, urged to too great a velocity, will at last fall to pieces. No one seems to anticipate that there must come a time when the towering fabric which speculation is building up, grown too huge for its foundations, will topple on the heads of its projectors and bury them in its ruins." To rebuke a frenzy at its height, by predicting a collapse, is always dangerous, and the "Evening Post" incurred no little odium in consequence. But that was not its worst offence. Be-sides denying the utility of the national bank, it questioned whether special banking corporations of any sort were com-patible with the best interests of society. The business of trading in money, it maintained, was like every other busi-ness, and ought to be permitted on the same conditions as any other business. Special charters for such purposes are an invasion of the equal rights of the people, inasmuch as they create a class distinguished from others by peculiar privileges.*

A small number of persons went with the journal in these opinions, but much the larger number, even of its democratic allies, regarded them as an assault upon existing institutions, created by State authority, and they denounced the promul-gators of them as enemies of vested rights and supporters of a disguised agrarianism. This was an exaggeration of igno-

---

* Mr. Bryant and Mr. Leggett confined their editorial opposition to acts of spe-cial incorporation, but they seem, both of them, to have perceived, much in advance of others, the evils likely to flow from the very principle of incorporation for trading purposes. They had no objection to the simple association of men for trading pur-poses, but they were unwilling that such associations should derive any peculiar character or privilege from the law. They saw the old contest between Power and Freedom here revived—but revived, strange to say, in the name of freedom. Shall not men be free, it was asked, to combine their efforts and their resources in joint enterprises for their own good? Certainly, the Locofocos replied—but then they must combine as individuals, without requiring the State to give them any guarantees and immunities in their corporate capacity. The immense advantages to be derived from the organized concentration of wealth, talent, and industry in bank-ing, railroading, manufacturing, etc., they did not deny ; but they held that these combinations should never be allowed to absorb their individual members in the general and abstract whole—which had, in the slang of the day, "no body to be kicked nor soul to be damned." Have not the developments of time justified their fears? Incorporations have conferred prodigious maternal benefits upon the nation ; but are they not the masters of the nation?—the modern Frankensteins which have got the better of their creators? Are not the great railroad, banking, and insurance companies more powerful than the State? Have they not forced upon us the question, whether the State shall assume control of these corporations, thereby dangerously augmenting its powers, or whether the masses of the people shall not interfere in a way not very satisfactory to the best interests of public stability and order.

rance and fear, for in a few years the reasonableness of the "Evening Post's" position was acknowledged, and became so apparent that, in 1838, a general banking law was passed by the Legislature of New York, the principle of which has since been adopted in our national banking system, whose friends extol it as among the best, if not the best, in the world.

Among the minor topics which the "Evening Post" treated in a way to augment its unpopularity were inspection, conspiracy, and usury laws. Enactments requiring the inspection by public authority of products offered for sale—tobacco, flour, beef, pork, salt, etc.—remained on the statute books, which needlessly enlarged the powers of the Government by the creation of swarms of office-holders—political janisaries— who interfered in elections and otherwise controlled the free action of the people. By the decisions of the courts also it had been determined that agreements among workingmen to fix rates of wages were conspiracies against trade, and several persons had been prosecuted and condemned in consequence in different parts of the State. The "Evening Post" regarded such laws as violations of individual rights, and it battled against them with great energy. It had the satisfaction, sooner or later, of seeing them all swept from the codes, with the exception of the usury laws, relics of mediæval ignorance, which, although abolished in Massachusetts and other more enlightened New England States, are still in force in New York.

The dispute in regard to corporations before it was settled occasioned a great division in the Democratic Republican party of New York, which extended to other parts of the Union. Those of its members who held to strict constitutional notions, with the mass of the young men, adopted the doctrines maintained by the "Evening Post," while the older men, and particularly such as were attached by personal interest to the existing system, and the timid, who fear all changes because they do not see the consequences, arranged themselves

on the other side. The strife grew more and more impassioned
every day, despite the anxiety of those who desired to compromise—"to keep the party together," as the phrase went—
by reconciling the extremes. No adjustment could be effected,
the factions fell apart, and the journal which was so largely
instrumental in bringing about the split was visited with the
obloquy that always falls upon instigators of revolt in an organized camp.

The "official gazette" at Washington, speaking for the
general Administration, solemnly excommunicated it as heter-
odox in faith and a worker of mischief in practice. The
organs of the State Administration were no less explicit and
exclusive in their denunciations; and the Tammany Hall Committee, which controlled the political movements of the city,
refused to recognize it any longer as belonging to the true
church. Only a small number adhered to its fortunes, composed chiefly of workingmen, who saw in the great corporations
their active enemies and oppressors, and enthusiastic young
men, ardent doctrinarians, whose generous impulses were not
yet benumbed by contact with the cold business of life.*
The recalcitrants came to be known in the phrase of the day
as Locofocos, because of an attempt they had made to get
possession of Tammany Hall, the Democratic head-quarters.
A public meeting having been called in that place, they packed
the room at an early hour; but their opponents found it out,
and turned off the gas which supplied the building, in the hope
of leaving them in total darkness. But they were prepared
for the emergency, and pulling the recently invented matches,
known as Locofocos, with some candles, out of their pockets,
they continued the proceedings.

These agitations were natural among a people enjoying
full and free political life. Fierce, disturbing, bitter as they
were, they could and would be settled in the end by the

---

* At the election for Mayor in 1836 they gave a vote of 2,712 out of a total vote
of more than 26,000.

ballot-box. But there was another question far more formidable, to which the ballot-box might not be competent; it hovered now as a storm-cloud on the horizon, "its lightnings sheathed, its thunders silent, but gathering with every moment angrier force and more appalling fury"—the question of slavery. The democratic press might have forgiven the vagaries and excesses of the "Evening Post" on subjects of commerce and currency, and condoned its refusal to march to the music of party, if it had stopped there; but it did not. It was lending a more or less eager ear to a new and hateful sect, called "The Abolitionists." "It openly and systematically," screamed the official organ, with horror in its face, "encourages those miscreants."*

Ever since the origin of the Government slavery had been our skeleton in the closet. Some of us tried to persuade ourselves that it was no skeleton, but a form of heavenly beauty; and others, who had their misgivings, were for the most part too cowardly to utter them; or, if they did utter them, it was in secret and with bated breath. At length a set of simple-hearted men arose, who said plainly that it was a skeleton, and a gigantic one, and, what was more, that it ought to be taken from the closet and instantly buried forever out of sight.

In 1832 they formed the New England Anti-Slavery Society; a year later the City Anti-Slavery Society, of New York; and finally the American Anti-Slavery Society. The sentiment embodied in these associations rose like the Afrite of the Eastern tale, which, springing out of a bottle—a small ink-bottle in this case—swelled so rapidly that the whole welkin was filled by its monstrous shape. Of course the South, where slavery existed, took alarm, and the North, commercially allied to the South, was scarcely less terrified. Here were men who, believing in the old religious dogma that all sin is to be repented of at once, asserted that slavery was sin, and ought to be immediately and uncondition-

---

* "Washington Globe," September 18, 1835.

ally abandoned. It is impossible, at this day, to conceive the tempest of indignation and hatred that greeted their first appearance. Their meetings were broken up, their lecturers stoned, their schools dispersed, their homes set on fire, and their more conspicuous leaders hunted from town to town, with a price upon their heads. Not in the great cities alone, with their excitable and turbid populations, but in quiet New England villages, the mob assumed the upper hand, and conceived itself chartered to commit any sort of outrage upon these innovators. The magistrates, sworn defenders of public order, were powerless against it, because they shared its passions and approved its doings. The rights of a free press, of free speech, of free assemblage, went down before its clamors and violence, yet they closed their eyes to the crime, while the respectable classes clapped their hands, and the churches sang *Te deums.*

In the earlier days of this agitation, neither Mr. Bryant nor Mr. Leggett was disposed to take part in it. In common with nearly all the people of the North, and with many of those of the South, as recent debates in the Virginia House of Delegates after the bloody insurrection of slaves under Nat. Turner proved,* they cherished the delusion that slavery, though an unmitigated evil, was in the process of extinction. Human reason and the sense of justice, they thought, would gradually alleviate its abuses, while the rapid material advances of the nation, rendering it unprofitable as a mode of industry, and more and more feeble as a political and social force, would ultimately reduce it to nothingness, as in the Northern States. Besides, as strict constructionists of the power of the general Government, they held that only municipal law could properly deal with what they regarded as an exclusively municipal institution. But they were never perverted by their political tendencies and alliances into that tortuous morality which justified inaction within the States, or which denied to citizens

---

* These were published at length in the " Evening Post."

of the free States the right to subject the system to criticism, remonstrance, and rebuke.

It cannot be denied that the aspects in which emancipation was first presented were not of a kind to allure the co-operation of sober and moderate minds. One speaks with reluctance at this day of the errors of men who, actuated by the most generous sympathies, confronted hatred, contempt, suffering, and death, in a work which time has crowned and consecrated by a glorious consummation. But history declares that a great deal of the obloquy which befel the early Abolitionists was provoked by their own overwrought zeal. In their devotion to the divinest and highest of all truths — human freedom — they sometimes overlooked the lesser truths by which it is best recommended. They did not always cherish the gentleness and sweetness which are the inmost essence of wisdom, and among its most effective weapons. Rightly indignant at the indifference and sordidness of the public conscience, they were too apt to denounce, with intemperate severity, all who did not at once accord with them in sentiment, both as to their objects and their methods—although those objects were not clearly defined by themselves, and their methods but imperfectly apprehended by the people. No institution of Church or State seemed to be sacred in their eyes so long as Church and State tolerated or refused to move in active aggression against a social anomaly so widely pernicious, so flagitiously sustained; and they flung their battle-axes into the ancient structures, little heeding where they fell.

For this reason many persons looked upon them rather as the enemies of order than as the friends of the slave. They might, perhaps, have remained for a long time—what they were in the beginning—an obscure and despised sect, but for the frenzy of the South, which insisted upon their extirpation, not by law only, but by violence; the intrigues of Northern party leaders, eager to conciliate the South by any degrading compliance; and the cowardice of the trading classes, whose tills were menaced by the withdrawal of Southern patronage. All these combined in the demand for the most despotic suppressive legislation and in fomenting the malignant passions of the populace. They, however, over-shot the mark. The North was yielding and it was trucu-lent, but it was not wholly debased. Men of courage and con-viction were still left, who were unwilling to see the rights of citizens trampled in the dust, or extinguished in blood, to save the interests of a class which, at best, but represented an atrocious and cruel wrong. Mr. Bryant and Mr. Leggett were among them. Few as the Abolitionists were in number, feeble in power, offensive as they had made themselves by indiscre-tion and arrogance of speech, they were only using the dearest rights of free men in defence of imperilled humanity, and the " Evening Post " raised its voice in their behalf. It condemned the violence of the mob and the indifference of the authorities, and it opened its columns to an unfettered discussion of the real character and dangerous influences of the so-called " do-mestic institution."

During Mr. Bryant's absence in Europe, Leggett had been unsparing in his denunciations of the action of the Govern-ment in authorizing a violation of the mails by the postmasters on the pretext of discovering incendiary publications. He had been no less earnest in his defence of the rights of free speech and of petition. The country was in the midst of the bitter contest when Mr. Bryant returned. Congress in both branches had decreed that no remonstrance against slavery in the District of Columbia, no demands for its removal, should be received; the venerable John Quincy Adams in the House of Representatives was waging a stubborn, invincible war for the right of the constituent to be heard; and even churches, moved to their depths, were about to be split asunder by a debate which should never have arisen among the disciples of the Son of God. Mr. Bryant, in his treatment of the matter, was more subdued and suasive than Leggett, but none the less decided. His position and tone may be learned from the following remarks on the speech of a Mr. Tallmadge in Congress:

"Mr. Tallmadge has done well in vindicating the right of individuals to address Congress on any matter within its province—a right springing from the nature of our institutions, and never denied till now. For this we thank him. This is something, at a time when the Governor of one State demands of another that free discussion on a particular subject shall be made a crime by law, and when a Senator of the Republic, and a pretended champion of liberty, rises in his place and proposes a censorship of the press more servile, more tyrannical, more arbitrary than subsists in any other country. It is a prudent counsel also that Mr. Tallmadge gives to the South—to beware of increasing the zeal, of swelling the ranks and multiplying the friends, of the Abolitionists by attempting to exclude them from the common rights of citizens. For this counsel he deserves the thanks of the South. Yet it seems to us that Mr. Tallmadge, who, on other occasions, has shown himself not to be wanting in boldness and freedom of speech, might have gone a little further. It seems to us that the occasion demanded that he should have protested with somewhat more energy and zeal against the attempt to shackle the expression of opinion. It is no time to use honeyed words when the liberty of speech is endangered. In vindicating the North from the charge of sharing in the designs of the Abolitionists, he might have deplored and condemned, in the strongest terms, the excesses to which the people of the North have been led by a fanatical hatred of that party. He has shown how the rival parties eagerly sought to clear their skirts from the stain of abolitionism; but, instead of representing this spirit as in all respects laudable, he should have added with what a wolfish rage they fell upon a small association of benevolent and disinterested enthusiasts, and discharged the coarse fury of party spirit upon those whose only fault was to maintain and seek to propagate opinions which thousands of benevolent men had maintained and expressed before them, not only in our own, but in all countries of the globe. He might have added how, in this very city, the law had been violated by a postmaster erecting himself into a censor of the press, and refusing the aid of the mail in conveying publications which he deemed objectionable. He should have condemned those acts of violence and tumult which made the friends of despotism abroad to exult, and which covered with shame the faces of those who were looking to our country as a glorious example of the certainty with which good order and respect for personal rights are the fruits of free political institutions. There should be no compromise with those who deny the freedom of debate within or without the walls of Congress, in conversation, at public meetings, or by means of the press. If the tyrannical doctrines and measures of Mr. Calhoun can be carried into effect, there is an end of liberty in this country; but carried into effect they cannot be. It is too late an age to copy the policy of Henry VIII; we lie too far in the occident to imitate the despotic rule of Austria. The spirit of our people has been too long accustomed to freedom to bear the restraint which is sought to be put upon it. Discussion will be like the Greek fire, which blazed the fiercer for the water thrown to quench it. It will scorn the penalties of tyrannical laws; and if the stake be set and the faggots ready, there will be candidates for martyrdom." *

Thus day after day the "Evening Post" uttered its sentiments, in the face of a hostile public prejudice; but, while it saw its own fortunes crumbling about it, it was only the more fixed in its devotion to what it deemed the highest good of the Republic.

It was during these fierce conflicts, shortly after Mr. Bryant's return from Europe, that chance made me acquainted with him; and this is, perhaps, the best place in which to refer to the incident, as it will explain to my readers how I am able to speak of him henceforth from personal knowledge. A briefless barrister in the great city, I had been led to a modest boarding-house at No. 316 Fourth Street, where for some time I was almost the only inmate. But one evening, on entering the common room, the owner, a native of Great Barrington, introduced me to a gentleman, whose name I did not hear, as

* "Evening Post," April 21, 1836.

about to become a member of our small and select family. He
was of middle age and medium height, spare in figure, with a
clean-shaven face, unusually large head, bright eyes, and a
wearied, severe, almost saturnine expression of countenance.
One, however, remarked at once the exceeding gentleness of his
manner, and a rare sweetness in the tone of his voice, as well
as an extraordinary purity in his selection and pronunciation
of English. His conversation was easy, but not fluent, and he
had a habit of looking the person he addressed so directly in
the eyes that it was not a little embarrassing at first. A certain air of abstractedness in his face made you set him down
as a scholar whose thoughts were wandering away to his
books; and yet the deep lines about the mouth told of struggle
either with himself or with the world. No one would have
supposed that there was any fun in him, but, when a lively
turn was given to some remark, the upper part of his face,
particularly the eyes, gleamed with a singular radiance, and a
short, quick, staccato, but hearty laugh acknowledged the
humorous perception. It was scarcely acknowledged, however, before the face settled down again into its habitual
sternness. Of public affairs this gentleman spoke with
great decision—as one who thoroughly comprehended them,
and had no fear of the ultimate issues. I was not told,
until he had gone, that this was Mr. Bryant, the poet and
journalist.

He was for some weeks in the house before I saw him
again, going very early in the morning to his office, taking
long solitary walks in the afternoon, and confining himself to
his room in the evenings. On Sunday one managed to get a
little talk with him, which, though he was courteous when approached, he neither invited nor repelled. He was always a
patient listener, but seldom initiated any topic. His greeting
of strangers was cold and formal, and he never stopped to
prolong a conversation. As soon as the immediate subject of
remark was despatched he turned away to his own musings.
Once or twice, I think, he asked me of his own accord to stroll

with him in the open fields, now the upper part of the city, but even in these rambles he preserved a singular reticence. The only observation of the time I now recall related to Jones's Wood, on the East River, which, he insisted with much earnestness, should be reserved as a place of recreation and amusement. "In a few years," he said, "the city will have grown up beyond this, and then it will be too late."* His love of trees and flowers was obvious, and, as he looked upon them, he would murmur to himself some appropriate verses, such as John Mason Good's lines to the Daisy,

> "Not worlds on worlds in phalanx deep
> Need we to tell that God is here,"†

or Burns's address to the same flower, or a line or two from Wordsworth.

When his family, consisting of his wife and two young daughters, came back from Europe, in the autumn of 1836, he showed himself more sociable. Mrs. Bryant was a person of such lively sympathies, and so breezy a cheerfulness, that she seemed to inspire him, as she did others, with some of her own animation. He became chatty and playful, but never familiar. Even in telling a story or anecdote he maintained his reserve, which seemed to say, Do not presume upon it if I deign to jest with you. His children, of whom he was fond, he treated with great consideration and tenderness, but he always exacted their obedience. He prattled with them commonly in the foreign language which they happened to be learning, and he amused them and himself very much by turning the old nursery rhymes or the popular songs of the day into the idioms of France, Germany, Spain, or Italy.

Knowing his fame as a poet, I was surprised to observe

---

* He afterward took up this subject in his journal, and persisted in writing about it until public interest was awakened in it, and our fine Central Park was the result.

† He was apparently very fond of these lines, and he repeated them very often to friends with whom he walked.

how few habitual visitors he seemed to have. His acquaintance with the artists he preserved by means of the Sketch
Club, and I learned that Cooper and Halleck, and some of the
more prominent politicians—Dix, Marcy, Wright, Flagg, B. F.
Butler, and a young man named Tilden—paid their respects
to him at the office; but none of them came to the house.
General society he avoided, and, though he had written for
his fellow New-Englanders of the New England Society the
lines on "The Twenty-second of December,"

> "Wild was the day; the wintry sea
>   Moaned sadly on New England's strand,"*

he seldom or never shared in their jollifications, or sought their
companionship. Joseph Curtis, the earnest advocate of free
schools,† Isaac T. Hopper, the Quaker philanthropist, and
George Arnold, the Unitarian Minister to the Poor, occasionally
sought him out, and counselled with him; but otherwise he
lived alone.

This seclusion was due partly to choice and partly to the
exacting nature of his professional labors, but largely also to
the fact that his political opinions involved him in a mist, if
not a cloud, of prejudices and dislikes. The more opulent and
cultivated classes of the city were "Whigs," who detested
Democrats as agrarians and levellers. Even the most charitable among them found it difficult to understand how a gentleman of education and refinement, impelled by no craving for
office or leadership, could take the side of an unkempt and un-
washed multitude, whose popular name of Locofocos was supposed to indicate their inflammatory character. Mr. Bryant
was not, however, very much disturbed by this mild social
ostracism; his sources of happiness lay in himself, and in that
noble companionship of books, "which never come unduly and

---

* For the anniversary dinner of 1829.
† See his Life, by Miss Sedgwick.

never stay too long"; while his estimate of himself was too modest to exact personal homages.*

But he would have been more than man if he had been wholly insensible to the vituperations which the party news-papers showered upon him—a scurrility which our best and purest men have been exposed to and have affected to disre-gard; but to which no man, however conscious of rectitude, is wholly inured. Mr. Bryant never replied to such abuse; he never even complained of it in conversation; but that he felt it is clear from his poem of "The Battle Field," written at this time, which refers to

> " A friendless warfare! lingering long
>   Through weary day and weary year,
> A wild and many-weaponed throng,
>   Hang on thy flank, and front, and rear." †

Our little family in Fourth Street was gradually enlarged by that of the Rev. Dr. Dewey, by Mr. Ferdinand Field, a relative of Charles Lamb's Baron Field, and by others. Call-ers became more frequent; among them were Mrs. Jameson, on her sad voyage to Canada, ‡ and Miss Sedgwick, ever beaming with intelligence and goodness. The latter was

---

* Yet he had too much self-respect to be wholly indifferent to the mode in which he was treated by "good society." I remember in 1842, when Charles Dickens was here, Mr. Bryant was invited by a prominent citizen to meet him at dinner, but de-clined. "That man," he said to me, "has known me for years, without asking me to his house, and I am not now going to be made a stool-pigeon, to attract birds of passage that may be flying about."

† "Democratic Review," October, 1837. The stanza in this poem, beginning, "Truth crushed to earth will rise again," which everybody knows from the frequency with which it has been repeated, was first quoted by the late Benjamin F. Butler, Attorney-General under Jackson and Van Buren, in a speech made in Tammany Hall. As he closed, a voice of unmistakable brogue shouted out, "Hurrah for Shakespeare!" "No," responded Mr. Butler, "not Shakespeare, but a pupil of his in the school of Nature and truth—our own Bryant," when the building rang with cheer on cheer.

‡ See "Memoirs of Anna Jameson."

VOL. I.—23

deeply interested at that time in the Italian prisoners of State recently exiled, and she found in Mr. Bryant a ready coadjutor. He busied himself in getting up a public dinner to the Count Confalonieri, the most notable of the victims of despotism, who was yet too much a sufferer from long incarceration to be able to accept the attention.* The noble old man, Felix Foresti—who, after sixteen years of the dungeon, still carried with him the freshness and simplicity of youth—rejoiced in his friendship ; and others—Piero Maroncelli, the companion of Silvio Pellico,† Albinola, Tenelli, Argenti—shared in his active sympathies. Miss Sedgwick made him acquainted also with Dr. Follen, to whom a slighting allusion occurs in one of his letters,‡ but whose erudition, talent, and disinterestedness he quickly learned to prize. No one of the acquaintances of that time, however, was more endeared to him than Miss Eliza Robbins, an elderly unmarried sister of his father's friends, Mrs. Howe and Mrs. Lyman. She was a person of extraordinary intellectual endowments, engaged in the teaching of young women at their homes or in the public schools, and the writer of several school-books of great utility. Her knowledge was varied and accurate, particularly in the line of old English literature, and her ability to converse surpassed that of any person that I ever heard, reminding me of what I had read of the wonderful powers in that respect of Burke, Madame De Staël, and Coleridge. Her talk, indeed, was a continuous and full stream of narrative, argument, criticism, anecdote, and pathos. "I called to see Miss Robbins," writes Miss Sedgwick, in one of her letters, " on my way home. She lamented her brother's death (Governor Robbins, of Boston) with the eloquence of an old Hebrew. If your eyes were shut, you might fancy that it was a supplemental chapter of Job. I thought I should have remembered some of it, but I might as well have tried to catch a pitcher of water from the Falls of

---

* The correspondence with him I find in the "Evening Post."
† See " Le Mie Priggione."
‡ See *ante*, p. 315..

Niagara." But, like all voluble talkers, she was at times given
to " words of learned length and thundering sound," and it
was an amusement to see the poet taking her vocabulary to
pieces. *

After several months of casual intercourse, I had formed
no real intimacy with him, nor had I reason to suppose that
he took the slightest interest in my affairs; when one day he
surprised me not a little by saying: " My assistant, Mr. Ulshoeffer" (a son of the late Judge Ulshoeffer), " is going to
Cuba for his health; how would you like to take his place?"
I replied that I had never been inside of a newspaper office
in my life, and would make but a sorry fist at the business.
" Well," he replied, in a friendly way, " you can learn; and I
think you the very man for it." He then went on to say that
he had been a lawyer himself, but had found the life of an
editor quite as agreeable, and infinitely more useful. " Come
and try." I went to the office within a few days, and tried,
and the result was, as young Ulshoeffer died in the interval, that I have remained there ever since—now nearly fifty
years. Mr. Leggett came in once or twice after I had joined
the force; but he had already projected a periodical of his
own, to be called " The Plaindealer," to which he soon devoted his entire attention. Unfortunately, the " Evening Post "
was not in a condition to pay for varied or effective services;
and the editorial department was reduced to three persons.†
Mr. Bryant wrote the leading articles and reviews of books;
his first assistant took in hand the exchanges and the theatres;
and the third person acted as a general reporter, with occasional aid from other reporters, while ship news was gathered

* On one occasion, in later years, she was sitting in his library alone, when a
cabinet-maker brought back a rocking-chair he had taken to mend. When Mr.
Bryant came in, Miss Robbins said: " The mechanic has returned your chair, and
expressed the hope that its equilibrium had been properly adjusted." " Did he say
that," replied Mr. Bryant; "he never talked so to me; what did he really say?"
" Well, if you must know," rejoined Miss Robbins, " he said he guessed the rickety
old concern wouldn't joggle any more."

† It now consists of about twenty.

by pilots in the common employ of the several evening journals.   As the staff was so small, the labor was very severe;
but it fell most heavily upon Mr. Bryant, who had taught his
public to expect every day some disquisition worthy to be
read.   I remember with what delight we hailed the arrival of
a foreign packet early in the morning—it was before the days
of steamships—because it enabled us to fill our columns with
European intelligence cut directly from the English papers.
Our hours were from seven o'clock A. M. to about four P. M.;
and promptly every morning Mr. Bryant was at his desk,
working without intermission till the paper had gone to press.
He was then very impatient of interruption, even irascible at
times, but uniformly courteous toward his colleagues and the
printers.   His articles, always prepared in the office, were
written, like Pope's "Homer," on the first scrap of paper that
came to hand—the backs of old letters, or the reverse side of
former articles.   Writing slowly and carefully, with many
erasures and corrections, but in a neat and graceful script,
his proofs required very little rectification.   Often the fore-
man of the printing-room would stand over him, snipping off
line by line as he wrote, in order to be in time for the
" make-up."

Commonly he began his disquisition, whatever it might
be, with an anecdote or story illustrative of the theme, which
caused a witty opponent whom he had castigated to say that
the " Evening Post " always opened with a stale joke and
closed with a fresh lie.   His ready memory of the poets and
essayists helped him to apt quotations wherewith to enliven
or enforce his argument.   He seldom surpassed a half-column
of print in getting his thought well out, in which respect he
differed from Mr. Leggett, who was fond of expatiating
through entire columns.   From Leggett, too, he differed in
other respects, seldom indulging in the discussion of general
principles, but taking up the particular aspects of each question, and cultivating greater suavity of tone.   Delicate irony
or ridicule was his favorite weapon; but, when the occasion

served, he could be excessively sharp and stinging. Readers familiar with his journal only in its later days, when age had tempered its passions, and prosperity invited it to conservatism, know nothing of the aggressive ardor and fiery vehemence it displayed in former times.* The "Evening Post" had gradually come to be the leading defender and representative of the more liberal creed of democracy, and it was compelled to maintain the initiative and bearing of a leader. The country journals looked to it for their cues ; the lesser politicians were guided by it ; and the more prominent statesmen of its party were glad to get its support. Its opponents charged it with an excess of partisanship ; but, however great its zeal, it was always studiously decorous in its modes of expression. Mr. Bryant held that a gentleman would be a gentleman in his public utterances no less than in his private demeanor ; and he endeavored never to write under the influences of passion. "You answer that fellow," he would often say to me, "for I dislike him so much that I might not be courteous or do him justice." As his political convictions were sincere and earnest, he felt it to be his duty to uphold them earnestly ; and, if his likes and his dislikes were strong, passing into obstinacy, if not prejudice, in certain cases, they were never founded upon the relations of the objects of them to himself. In his judgments of men he first disclosed to me what the old Swedish seer Swedenborg means when he says that the better angels see in others not their persons but their human quality. He estimated the people he met with, in private as in public, not by their external advantages, but by their purely inward worth. Always prepared to do full justice to everybody's virtues, or genius, or wit, and very quick to discern merit or excellence of any kind, he was yet principally impressed by manliness and sincerity of character. When these were found, he gave a willing hom-

* It was curious to remark, in the notices of Mr. Bryant that appeared just after his death, how the writers estimated his poetical character by his earliest pieces, and his editorial character by his later writings.

age; when they were not, he turned away—without regard to any social or adventitious distinctions. For this reason he was never in much favor with the little great men of politics, for some of whom—the mere managers of political machinery —he never disguised his dislike; while as to others of more mark—Van Buren, Wright, Marcy, Tilden—or, afterward, Seward, Chase, and Sumner—though he respected and admired them, he seldom gave heed to their notions of policy.

Mr. Leggett, as I have said, soon left us to establish a periodical of his own, " The Plaindealer," of which the first number appeared in December, 1836. It was not long before his independence and ardor embroiled Mr. Bryant unpleasantly with his eminent contemporary, Washington Irving, the only literary controversy, if it may be called such, in which he was ever engaged. Discussing a practice, which obtained among the publishers of the day, of mutilating important passages in foreign works in deference to pro-slavery prejudices, Mr. Leggett departed a little from the strict line of his argument to charge the amiable essayist with " pusillanimity " because he had changed a verse in Mr. Bryant's " Song of Marion's Men,"

" The British soldier trembles," *

in order to conciliate English feeling. This charge naturally gave offence to Mr. Irving, who made a dignified reply, in the course of which—after a full and frank explanation of the motives of his proceeding—he said that, if he had evinced any timidity of spirit, it was wholly in Mr. Bryant's behalf, and that " he was little prepared, after all that he had done, to receive a stab from his (Mr. Bryant's) bosom friend." Leggett appended to this reply a complete exoneration of

---

* Mr. Irving made it read,
" The foeman trembles in his camp."

Mr. Bryant from any complicity in his remarks, directly or indirectly, and acknowledged further that he had " on various occasions heard Mr. Bryant express the kindest sentiments toward Mr. Irving for the interest he had taken in the publication of the poems, and for the complimentary terms in which he had introduced them to the British public." * To leave no doubt in regard to the sincerity of this feeling, Mr. Bryant himself hastened, in the next number of " The Plaindealer," to say that, although he would not have made the alteration, he had never complained of it, having no doubt it was done with the kindest intentions ; but he expressed his surprise at one or two unguarded passages of Mr. Irving's note, which seemed to connect him with the attack.

Mr. Irving rejoined as follows in the "New York American":

"To WILLIAM CULLEN BRYANT, Esq.

"SIR : It was not until this moment that I saw your letter in ' The Plaindealer' of Saturday last. I cannot express to you how much it has shocked and grieved me. Not having read any of the comments of the editor of ' The Plaindealer ' on the letter which I addressed to him, and being in the country, out of the way of hearing the comments of others, I was totally ignorant of the construction put upon the passages of that letter which you have cited. Whatever construction these passages may be susceptible of, I do assure you, sir, I never supposed, nor had the remotest intention to insinuate, that you had the least participation in the attack recently made upon my character by the editor of the above-mentioned paper, or that you entertained feelings which could in any degree be gratified by such an attack. Had I thought you chargeable with such hostility, I should have made the charge directly and explicitly, and not by innuendo.

"The little opportunity that I have had, sir, of judging of your private character, has only tended to confirm the opinion I had formed of you from your poetic writings, which breathe a spirit too pure, amiable, and elevated, to permit me for a moment to think you capable of anything ungenerous and unjust.

---

* "Plaindealer," December 28, 1836.

"As to the alteration of a word in the London edition of your poems, which others have sought to nurture into a root of bitterness between us, I have already stated my motives for it, and the embarrassment in which I was placed. I regret extremely that it should not have met with your approbation, and sincerely apologize to you for the liberty I was persuaded to take—a liberty, I freely acknowledge, the least excusable with writings like yours, in which it is difficult to alter a word without marring a beauty.

"Believe me, sir, with perfect respect and esteem, very truly yours,

"WASHINGTON IRVING.

"THURSDAY MORNING, *February* 16, 1837."

This slight collision left " no root of bitterness " in the heart of either of the parties to it, and, whenever they happened to meet at the houses of common friends, which was not very often, as they both lived out of the city, their intercourse was marked by the greatest affability and kindness.

CHAPTER EIGHTEENTH.

POLITICAL WARFARE.

A. D. 1837, 1838.

MR. BRYANT was too much absorbed in the political discussions of the time to be able to give any attention to personal disputes, even if he had been inclined to that sort of warfare—which he was not. Out of the agitation of abolitionism another question had arisen, in which he took a deep interest. It was that of conferring the right of suffrage on negroes, who in the State of New York were emancipated from bondage, but not yet admitted to the full privileges of citizenship. Of course, it was easily confounded with the more general antislavery movement, and provoked much of the same kind of hostility. Mr. Bryant endeavored to show that they were essentially different questions. He said:

"It appears to us that it is very unwise to connect this question with that of the principal object of the Abolitionists, which is, to do away with slavery in the Southern States. The great objection brought against their course hitherto has been that they were meddling with a matter with which they had no concern, and which their interference might make worse for both master and slave. There is not the least ground for either of these objections in the case of the petition in question. We recognize the blacks as citizens, and we have a perfect right to say how easy we will make the condition of their citizenship. The moment we allow ourselves to be restrained in legislating on this subject by a regard for what is or may be said at the South or anywhere else, we submit to external interference, we allow a power from without to dictate what shall be the qualifications of our voters."

The distinction was gradually recognized by the people; and the negroes, in spite of the fierce opposition they encountered, were qualified at the next revision of the Constitution, in 1845. It was a considerable advance in public opinion, and shows that a wiser and better feeling was beginning to work.

A more general reason for Mr. Bryant's earnest interest in politics was the election of his personal, though not intimate, friend, Mr. Martin Van Buren, to the Presidency. In the partisan journals that leader was universally represented as a crafty and trickish politician, who gained his successes by the low arts of the politician rather than by the liberal methods of the statesman; but Mr. Bryant, who had known him for some years, had always found him to be a gentleman of broad general views, of remarkable sagacity, unstained honor, and winning courtesy of manner. He was cautious in action, and more disposed to rely upon party machinery than Mr. Bryant entirely approved, but he had given him no occasion to suspect the sincerity of his convictions or his disinterested patriotism. Jackson's preference of Van Buren perhaps influenced him somewhat, as he still retained a high admiration for the "old hero." "Faults he had, undoubtedly," Mr. Bryant, when Jackson left office, wrote; "such faults as often belong to an ardent, generous, sincere nature—the weeds that grow in a rich soil. He was hasty in his temper, and, though sagacious generally in his estimate of human character, apt to be led by the warmth of his friendships into great mistakes. He appointed men in several instances to places for which they were quite unfit. Notwithstanding this, he was precisely the man for the period in which he filled the Presidential chair, and well and nobly discharged the duties demanded of him by the times. If he was brought into collision with the mercantile classes, it was more their fault than his own. No man, even the most discreet and prudent, could, under the same circumstances, have done his duty without exasperating them against him. The immediate and apparent interests, though not the permanent and true interests of trade, were involved in the controversy with the national bank; and, as men are apt to look principally to the convenience of the moment, the attack upon it naturally offended the mercantile classes. Artful party leaders exaggerated the cause of offence until they were almost entirely alienated from his administration. This, and not hatred of Jackson, was the true cause. Had Zeno himself been President, the result would have been the same." * . . .

The administration of Van Buren—as the successor, or, as they used to say, the pet of Jackson—inherited all the difficulties of the original Jacksonian policy, to which time had added some of its own. The prosperity of 1836, produced by an infatuated commercial confidence in speculative enterprise, was followed, as many foresaw, and the " Evening Post " predicted it would be, by the inevitable revulsion. Already, at the close of the year 1836, there were many signs of coming distress—but the bubble did not burst till the summer of 1837. A panic began then, which, for its sudden and disastrous arrest of the business of an entire community, has seldom been equalled in a time of peace. Merchant after merchant failed, the most substantial houses going by the board; the banks suspended the payment of specie; credit and money alike disappeared; manufactories were stopped, and large classes of working-men thrown out of employment.

It was in vain that the " Evening Post " and other authorities argued that these catastrophies were the result of a previous state of debauchery; that our foreign credits had been enormously expanded; that a fall in the markets abroad had been followed by an unexampled fall in the domestic markets; and that a deficient harvest at home had for the first time compelled us to resort to an importation of corn and bread-stuffs. Men who suffer seldom reason. They had lost their fortunes,

* " Evening Post," December 3, 1836.

and it was easy to find a scapegoat on which to cast the burden
of their own sin.   Nor were they wholly destitute of plausible
pretexts. Jackson's specie circular, as it was called—a man-
date forbidding the receipt of gold and silver in payment for
purchases of public lands, one of the principal objects of previous speculation—no doubt, aggravated the distress.   It was,
however, an aggravation of symptoms only, and not a source
of disease.   That lay much deeper, but the mercantile community refused to see it.   They raged and howled at the party in
power.   Deputation after deputation from the commercial
centres waited upon Mr. Van Buren to implore a repeal of
the offensive order; clamorous meetings were held all over
the country; great orators, like Clay and Webster, lent the
force of their eloquence to the popular ferment, but Mr. Van
Buren remained firm.   In the face of the remonstrances of
committees, of the denunciations of newspapers, and of the
threats of overheated young men, who wanted to take up arms
to dislodge the Government by force, he not only adhered to
the policy of his predecessors, but he recommended a step forward.   It was the total separation of the finances of the Government from the paper-money banks, which he regarded as a
main source of the prevailing evil.   In the estimation of the
traders this was like giving an additional turn to the screw,
which was already excruciating their bodies, and their outcries
grew into a deafening and terrific roar.

As the proposed change was in a direction which the
"Evening Post" had long advised, of which, in truth, that
journal was, if not the author, the earliest and most strenuous
advocate, it was bound to support the measure with all its
force.   Contending, as it had always done, that the business of
dealing in money, or of lending credit to individual enterprises, was, like every other business, a matter of private concern, which required no further interposition of law than to
prevent fraud, it was delighted to find the federal Government
making an advance in the right direction.   In proposing to
become the custodian of its own funds, it released one of the

most important functions of commerce from its direct super-
vision, and it paved the way to other equally important advances in the sphere of commercial freedom. The defence of
this scheme for an independent treasury, by the "Evening
Post," contributed not a little to its formal acceptance by public opinion, but at the cost of the journal.

Nevertheless, devoted as Mr. Bryant was to the general
policy of the administration, he could not give it an unqualified approval. Antislavery was no longer the voice of one
crying in the wilderness. It was pressing forward, in one
shape or another, into the political arena. Petitions to Congress to put an end to the evil in the District of Columbia,
and in the territories where the general Government was supposed to have a right of control, were multiplying every day,
and they grew by the very means adopted to suppress them
—the refusal to receive them by the national Legislature.

"Must Congress," asked Mr. Bryant, "open its ears to
every private claim for mere pecuniary redress, and yet exclude the petitions of thousands of men directed against what
they deem a most flagrant and crying abuse? Nothing can be
simpler than the course both reason and equity prescribe.
Let the suggestion of the petitioners be candidly investigated
and discussed. If their requests have no foundation in justice
and truth, it is easy enough to establish the point, and dismiss
the plaintiffs with the satisfactory knowledge that their decla-
rations have been at least heard. Or, if they have raised a
question in the face of the Constitution and laws, give them
the evidence of their error, that they may retire from a contest which must be utterly hopeless. Whether right or wrong,
there will be no end to their remonstrances so long as they
shall be treated with cavalier or cold contempt. The very
fact that they are served in this manner can only strengthen
their determination and add fresh zeal to their perseverance.
Will it not excite the suspicion that there are other causes for
this abrupt procedure than the bare impracticability of what
they demand? None shrink from discussion but those who

are afraid of the truth, and none seek to veil their deeds in darkness and silence unless apprehensive that the light will reveal some wickedness." In a few months after these words were spoken (January, 1838), the Democratic young men of New York held a meeting to condemn the gag-resolutions presented to Congress by one Patton, and the Legislature of the State of New York denounced, with all its authority, the rejection by Congress of the popular demands.

The slave-holders were too keen-sighted not to foresee that any discussion of slavery was perilous, and were therefore not satisfied with demanding a suppression of the right of petition. They insisted that abolitionism itself should be silenced by law. Their legislatures called upon the legislatures of northern communities to make it illegal to agitate the subject. Governor Ritter, of Pennsylvania, was the only northern governor who peremptorily refused to communicate their wishes to the legislative body of the State to which he belonged. The others acquiesced, or were silent. But among the masses of the people this acquiescence or silence was less and less approved. It was felt, by increasing numbers of them, that the haughty pretensions of the slave-holders ought to be resisted. Assuredly, in the neutral District of Columbia and in the territories, they had a right to intervene; and they would intervene. This undercurrent of feeling the politicians and statesmen were slow to perceive; and Mr. Van Buren was so ignorant of it that, in his inaugural address, he had pledged the whole power of the Government to an active hostility to the designs of the antislavery agitators.

It was a sore trial to the " Evening Post "—devoted as it was to the financial projects of the administration, and vindicating it warmly, as it did, in many points of moment, such as its controversy with Great Britain on the northeastern boundary, and its efforts to maintain the supremacy of law on our northern frontier, where a wide-spread sympathy with Canadian revolt led to alternate armed invasions from either side—to be obliged to throw itself into opposition on nearly every ques-

tion in which slavery was implicated. But it did not hesitate. That question was assuming a greater magnitude and
more menacing aspects every day, and it would not blind itself to the importance of the struggle.

In spite of the successes of the slave-holders in Congress, in
the press, and in vulgar public sentiment, the party of freedom
had been enlarged and strengthened by recent events. At the
close of the year 1837 a mob, in its blind fury, had murdered
the Rev. Elijah P. Lovejoy, and destroyed his presses, at Alton,
Illinois; and the outrage sent a shudder of indignation throughout the free States. Freedom was now baptized in blood, and
consecrated by its first martyr. Men like Dr. Channing, Wendell Phillips, Salmon P. Chase, William Leggett, and Gerrit
Smith raised the banner of free speech, as the precursor of a
more universal freedom. Mr. Bryant was already committed.
A year before, when Cincinnati was disgraced by a meeting
which resolved to put down the Abolition press of J. G. Birney
by violence, he had said: "There is no tyranny exercised in
any part of the world more absolute or more frightful than
that which they (the Cincinnati meeting) would establish. So
far as we are concerned, we are determined that this despotism
shall neither be submitted to nor encouraged. In whatever
form it makes its appearance, we shall raise our voice against
it. We are resolved that the subject of slavery shall be, as it
ever has been, as free a subject for discussion, and argument,
and declamation, as the differences between whiggism and
democracy, or the differences between Arminians and Calvin-
ists. If the press chooses to be silent on the subject, it should
be the silence of free-will, not the silence of fear." * Now again
its voice was raised, all the more forcibly for the calm determination with which it was uttered. "The right," said the
"Evening Post," "to discuss freely and openly, by speech, by
the pen, by the press, all political questions, and to examine
and animadvert on all political institutions, is a right so clear

---

* "Evening Post," August 8, 1836.

and certain, so interwoven with other liberties, so necessary, in fact, to their existence, that without it we must fall at once into despotism or anarchy. To say that he who holds unpopular opinions must hold them at the peril of his life, and that if he expresses them in public he has only himself to blame if they who disagree with him should rise and put him to death, is to strike at all rights, all liberties, all protection of law, and to justify or extenuate all crimes. We approve, then, we applaud—we would consecrate, if we could, to universal honor—the conduct of those who bled in this gallant defence of the freedom of the press. Whether they erred or not in their opinions, they did not err in the conviction of their right, as citizens of a democratic State, to express them; nor did they err in defending their right with an obstinacy which yielded only to death." *

These words are common words now; but they were golden words when they were written. The spirit of slavery had so infused itself into the minds of even educated men that lawyers of distinction, and clergymen from their pulpits, argued that the fate which had overtaken Lovejoy was deserved; and that every one who shared his opinions, or condemned the manner of his death, ought to be subjected to the same punishment.

Nothing shows more clearly the utter degradation of public feeling, and the manly independence of Mr. Bryant, both of party and opinion, than his course in regard to the case of the Amistad negroes,† which produced at the time a great deal of excitement. This was the case of a small number of poor Africans who had been stolen from their native land and sold as slaves in Cuba, but who, in a voyage from Havana to Principe, on the schooner Amistad, rose upon their purchasers, killed several of the crew, and compelled the others to navigate the vessel, as they supposed, toward their homes.

---

* " Evening Post," November, 1837.

† This was in 1839, but it is convenient to refer to it here.

They were deceived, and she was brought into American waters (Long Island Sound), where she was seized, and the insurgents imprisoned as criminals. Mr. Bryant, after causing the law to be investigated by his friend, Theodore Sedgwick, Jr., who prepared an elaborate argument for the " Evening Post," insisted that they could not be held. They are not slaves, he argued, but freemen; not malefactors, but heroes. Mr. Forsyth, the Secretary of State, and Mr. Grundy, Attorney-General, did what they could, officially and otherwise, to get the miserable creatures delivered up, on claim of the Spanish minister, which meant their surrender to a hopeless bondage; but the courts adopted the view the " Evening Post " had taken, and the captives were at length restored to their friends.

Not unwilling to leave slavery to its fate within the States, in the assurance that it would be ultimately crushed to death by the progress of our democratic civilization, Mr. Bryant was wholly averse to the toleration of it where it could be reached, or to the extension of its boundaries. But this attitude, moderate as it was, was hardly satisfactory to any of the existing parties. It was too moderate to please the more zealous Abolitionists; not moderate enough to meet the wishes of their antagonists; and in every way offensive to professional politicians, who desired to see the subject removed entirely from the field of discussion. Yet his journal held on its way, giving and getting blows on all sides. The fiercest passions were often engendered by these conflicts, and

> ". . . Wrath, that fire of hell,
> Which leaves its frightful scars upon the soul,"

was not an infrequent guest of the bosom of the poet, who would far more willingly have listened to other and more harmonious voices.

Back of the scheme for the seizure of Texas, which the slave-holders began to avow, Mr. Bryant discerned their purpose to establish a great slave-holding empire in the south-

west in the event of their defeat within the Union.   The vigorous blows of Jackson had disposed of nullification for the
nonce; but the spirit of it lived in these sectional projects.
He thought it important to counteract their effects by vigorous appeals to a national sentiment, and in that view he
consented to take part in the proceedings of the New York
Historical Society when it celebrated the fiftieth anniversary
of the inauguration of Washington.   Mr. John Quincy Adams was chosen the orator, and Mr. Bryant the poet, of the
occasion (April, 1838).   Averse as he was to occasional writing, he would not, under the circumstances, allow his repugnance to overcome his sense of duty.   Mr. Adams, it
was understood, was prepared to make a powerful plea in
behalf of the Constitution and the unity of the nation, and,
although he did not wholly agree with Mr. Adams in political sentiment, he was glad to contribute his influence and talent to the general object.   He wrote a poem, in four stanzas,
to be sung by the choir, beginning,

> " Great were the hearts, and strong the minds,
>   Of those who framed in high debate
> The immortal league of Love that binds
>   Our fair, broad empire, State with State,"

which answered its purpose, and was widely published in the
newspapers of the day, but which, owing to certain slight
technical defects, he refused to incorporate in his works.*

Other contributions to patriotic sentiment had already appeared when the Union was threatened, such as " The Green
Mountain Boys," intended to recall the daring of New England heroes; " The Song of Marion's Men," in which we hear
the tramp of the gallant partisan warriors of the South; and
" Seventy-Six," which glowed with the fire of the revolutionary sires.

Allusions to his occupations and interests at this time are

* The repetition, I suspect, of similar rhymes in two different stanzas.

to be found in these extracts from his private letters, with which I close the chapter :

" New York, February 27, 1837 : * You have kindly suggested the true reason of my not writing to you before, or, rather, one of the reasons. My newspaper is really a task which takes up all my time, and the affairs of the republic give me no little trouble. You cannot imagine how difficult it is to make the world go right. The *gains* you talk of I wish I could see. The expenses of printing and conducting a daily paper have vastly increased lately, and there is no increase in the rate of advertisements, etc., to make it up. I should be very glad of an opportunity to attempt something in the way I like best, and am, perhaps, fittest for; but here I am a draught-horse, harnessed to a daily drag. I have so much to do with my legs and hoofs, struggling and pulling and kicking, that, if there is anything of the Pegasus in me, I am too much exhausted to use my wings. I would withdraw from this occupation if I could do so and be certain of a moderate subsistence, for, with my habits and tastes, a very little would suffice. I am growing, I fear, more discontented and impatient than I ought to be at the lot which has fallen to me. The improved health which I enjoy ought to make me contented with almost any occupation. I am sorry to hear that yours is not better. . . .

" For the literary world, I am afraid you know more about it than I do. I see the outside of almost every book that is published, but I read little that is new. I, too, hear a good report of ' Astoria,' and *I*, too, have not read it. ' Ion ' I have read, and think there is justice in the remark you make on reading the extracts. Besides, it is not dramatic in the manner ; I wonder that a man of sense should write a *play* so. It is full of lyrical flights and misplaced rhetoric. Cooper has a book in press relating to some part of Europe—France, I believe. I see Cooper occasionally in his visits to town, for he lives in the country. He is a restless creature, and does not seem well satisfied with his position in this country, though his great reputation, his handsome fortune, his fine health, and his very amiable family, ought to make him so. Verplanck I see occasionally ; he is as entertaining as ever, but is growing fat. Do you read the novels of Simms, Bird,

* To Richard H. Dana.

and Kennedy? Verplanck speaks highly of 'Horse-shoe Robinson.' But what can one do amid such a deluge of new things? Did you see the engraving of Halleck?—a fine likeness. The same engraver is now at work upon a drawing of me, by the same painter, Inman. I have had my portrait taken several times, but owing, I suppose, to the fault of the original, I have never liked any of them. This drawing in water-colors by Inman is, perhaps, as good as any, but it does not please me. I shall see in a few days what the engraver makes of it. . . ."

" NEW YORK, MAY 22, 1837 :* I am glad you are situated so comfortably as you appear to be from your description. I hope you will pass a pleasant summer, and wish, with all my heart, I could be with you. But of that it is idle to think. I have enough to do, both with the business part of the paper and the management of it as editor, to keep me constantly busy. I must see that the 'Evening Post' does not suffer by these hard times, and I must take that position in the great controversies now going which is expected of it. There is much agitation here; the greater part of the merchants are gone over to the Whigs, and, being unfortunate in their enterprises, prefer laying the blame on the Government to laying it on their own want of prudence. Van Buren needs all the management which has been ascribed to him to weather this storm. I say management, but I think firmness is the best management, and of this I must do him the justice to say he shows a good deal. He is not yet driven from his purpose by all their fury and all their threats, and I think will not be. He knows them well enough to know that they must have their fit of unreasonable rage, and when that is over they will be quiet again.

" I had a letter the other day from Dana. He says to me: 'Keep eye and heart upon poetry all that you can amid the bustle and anxiety. As to reforming the world, give all that up. It is not to be done in a day, nor, on your plan, through all time. Human nature is not fitted for such a social condition as your fancy is pleased with.' "

" NEW YORK, MAY 25th :† Specie is not less scarce here than with you; and the merchants have been making a terrible uproar about it. They are ready to bite off the heads of all who do not

* To Mrs. Bryant, in the country.   † To Miss Julia Sands.

choose to think exactly as they do in this matter. Swartwout made a speech at the Merchants' Exchange, and told them that he would take the responsibility of receiving bank notes, on which they voted him thanks and a service of plate. He has since backed out from this in consequence of new orders from Washington. Some of his friends, however, say that he never made the promise, and that the merchants were mistaken. If he gets the plate he will get it for nothing. In the mean time we have had a great deal of wrath and cabbage, as you call it here; hot blood and high words; but people are now becoming soberer. I understand that the clergymen have been taking the people to task for their Union Meetings, as they are called, for their greediness for gain, their gambling speculations, excessive use of credit, and extravagant living. These things have almost persuaded some that the specie circular is not the cause of their misfortunes."

"NEW YORK, MAY 29th:* I cannot allow this opportunity to send you a hurried letter by Mr. Dewey escape me. Even in your philosophic retreat, I suppose you are willing now and then to hear from the noisy, agitated world you have left. A different world it now is from what it was when you quitted it—noisy and agitated still, but with the working of fiercer though not stronger passions. I often envy you your quiet retirement, in which you hear no more of this uproar than you please. Yet, let me tell you that the world has mended in some respects. If it has not grown more amiable, it has grown less luxurious and less ostentatious. Many people have given up the idea of living by their wits, and have undertaken, as the saying is, to live by work. Here are two important instances of amendment.

"My wife and children are gone into the country to Great Barrington. I, in the mean time, am chained so fast here that I do not know when I shall be able to visit them.†

---

* To the Rev. William Ware.

† Mrs. Bryant, writing to Mrs. Ware about that time, says:

"Mr. Bryant has gone to his office. You cannot think how distressed I am about his working so hard. He gets up as soon as it is light, takes a mouthful to eat —it cannot be called a breakfast, for it is often only what the Germans call a 'stick of bread'; occasionally the milkman comes in season for him to get some bread and milk. As yet, his health is good, but I fear that his constitution is not strong enough for such intense labor."

"I suppose you have heard that Mr. Leggett has established a weekly periodical called 'The Plaindealer,' which is much liked here, not that it can be called exactly popular, but it is much sought after, read, and talked of, and, of course, exerts considerable influence. It is thorough on the Abolition question. But I dare say you have met with it. He is now the editor of a daily twopenny paper called 'The Examiner,' which he supplies with the greatest portion of the leaded articles. How he finds time and words to write so much I know not. . . . I am about to read the Palmyrene letters, which I hear are yours. Miss Martineau, I remember, said they formed a 'new era' in American literature, but it was throwing them away to put them into the 'Knickerbocker.'"

"NEW YORK, JUNE 18th :* I am very glad you find something to interest you in the country. I remember when a residence there was to you a perpetual holiday. I hope you will stick to your riding on horseback till you have made yourself mistress of the accomplishment. You have shown a commendable degree of courage, and have now only to acquire ease and dexterity. As to the want of society of which you complain, you must endeavor to make yourself amends for it by passing more of your time in that society of the wise and good of all ages which you will find in your mother's library. You like Mrs. Hemans's 'Life,' you tell me; the extracts from the letters are interesting, but the rest of the work is not written with much grace or discrimination. I have bought you Retzsch's 'Outlines,' illustrative of Hamlet and Macbeth, together with those designed from Schiller's 'Combat with the Dragon.' Your instance of ludicrous translation from Shakespeare I have heard related in another manner: *Il n'y a pas un rat qui trotte.* Certainly the Germans have rendered Shakespeare better than any other people whose language I am acquainted with. . . ."

"NEW YORK, SEPTEMBER 9th :† Your desire for the 'Selections from the German Classics' shows that you are disposed to retain what you have already acquired. You will never, I hope, allow a dislike of exertion or a love of amusement and frivolous occupation

* To his daughter Fanny.   † To the same.

to obtain the ascendency over you. You are now arrived at ' years of discretion,' as they are called—the time of life when your own reason is strong enough, if you will follow it, to show you what you ought to do to form your own character and intellect. You have, as we all have, three enemies to contend with—laziness, selfishness, and ill-temper—and you must master them, or they will master you. Now is the time to put them in chains for the rest of your life. After you have once fairly subdued them, they will give you no further trouble. If allowed to get the upper hand, they become the parents of almost every kind of wickedness and every kind of suffering. I do not speak of them thus because I think you more in danger than many others from these evil propensities. You have your share of them, doubt-less; but I thank God that you have a strength which, if rightly employed, will enable you to overcome them. In this work you will find great support from religious motives, from cultivating a reverence for the Supreme Being and a desire to do what is pleasing to Him, and from studying the beautiful and tender example given in the life of Jesus Christ."

"NEW YORK, AUGUST 21st:* My friends, when they meet me, congratulate me on being yet alive. You will ask what this means. On Saturday last I received a challenge. A good-natured, well-bred man, Reynolds, who formerly lectured on Captain Symmes's ' Theory of the Earth,' and who has been appointed historiographer of the ex-pedition now fitting out for the South Seas, walked into the office on ' unpleasant business,' as he called it, and presented me a written in-vitation to fight a duel, from a man named Holland, one of the editors of the ' Times ' newspaper. Holland had taken offence at something which appeared in the ' Evening Post ' on the subject of the ' Times,' and wrote to me for an explanation. My answer did not satisfy him; he wrote again; I declined giving any other answer, and so he asked me to fight. I told Mr. Reynolds that when Mr. Leggett, a gentleman of strict honor, was associated with me in the conduct of the ' Evening Post,' he wrote Holland word that he was a scoundrel; which he chose to take quietly. I said that Holland must settle that affair first, and that then I would consider whether his note deserved any further

* To Mrs. Bryant, at Great Barrington.

reply. Reynolds was very anxious to persuade me to give some other answer, and said that the affair might easily be adjusted. He would not take back my note to Holland, so I wrote down what I have given above as my answer, and sent it by a boy. When you come down you shall see the correspondence. My friends are much amused at my having got into such a scrape, and laugh heartily at the idea that a popinjay who curls his whiskers should think to engage me in a duel."

What amused them more than his getting into the scrape was his adroit way of getting out of it. Mr. Leggett retained enough of the spirit of the naval officer to be willing, if not somewhat eager, to void his quarrels at the end of the sword, or with the pistol, a fact very well known in society; and Mr. Bryant's reference of his would-be antagonist to one who was not, like himself, a non-combatant, was thought to be a clever piece of strategy.

"New York, October 29th:* I am very happy to hear that you and your mother like the President's Message so well. I always knew that Mrs. Sands judged candidly when both sides of a question were presented to her. I like the political economy of the first of your two last letters very much. It is quite orthodox and clear, but that of the second letter is misty . . . The lines alluded to by the Scotch clergyman I manufactured for Mr. Verplanck. They are a translation from the Æneid, and are found in a note to one of his public discourses, I forget which. Here they are:

> " 'Patriots were there in Freedom's battle slain,
> Priests whose long lives were closed without a stain,
> Bards worthy him who breathed the poet's mind,
> Founders of arts that dignify mankind,
> And lovers of our race, whose labors gave
> Their names a memory that defies the grave.'

"I was at Mr. Verplanck's some ten evenings since, at a meeting of the Sketch Club, and a pleasant time we had of it. The late member was quite entertaining, and there was Mr. Gleddon (is that

---

* To Miss Sands.

his name ?), the Egyptian, and Professor Holland, of Washington College, who wrote the life of Van Buren, a well-informed, agreeable man.
By the by, have you heard of my affair of honor with the other Holland, late editor of the late 'Times'?—

"'Campbell's Letters from the South' I have not read, except
some parts of them in one of the English magazines, where they first
appeared. You are right in entertaining great expectations from the
electro-magnetic machine, but its claims to attention are now eclipsed
by the wonders of animal magnetism and the curiosities of the Fair
of the American Institute. I have a report, lately made to the French
Academy of Medicine, translated partly by myself, which I mean to
publish. I will send it to you. It is a very curious affair. A magnetizer challenged the enemies of the science to witness the proof,
and promised to convince them of its truth. The Academy appointed
a committee of shrewd fellows, who had their eyes open, who saw
through all the tricks of the magnetizer, thwarted all his arrangements, and witnessed the entire failure of every one of his experiments. I have no doubt that animal magnetism is the flam of
flams.

"I heard Mr. Dewey's address, and a noble discourse it was.*
Buckingham, the English traveller in the East, is here, and is to lecture—a most eloquent and interesting man in his particular way, they
say—but a certain English friend of mine does not give him as much
credit for principle as for talent, and he certainly makes too much
parade of his sufferings in his appeal to the American public. His
sufferings consist in being exiled from India by the East India Company, on whose government he had animadverted in the 'Calcutta
Journal,' of which he was proprietor. He lost the property of the
journal in consequence, but he has since been a very successful lecturer in England, and is by no means in a starving condition, as I
hear. His sufferings are equal to those of a prosperous blacksmith
whose landlord turns him out of his shop, and who thereupon becomes
a thriving shoemaker.

"How can you ask whether I have read the 'Letters from Palmyra' when you say in the same breath that I have puffed it? Why
do you not ask whether I have not picked somebody's pocket since I

* On "The Unitarian Belief," probably.

saw you? Read it!—yes—and think it a glorious book. Martineau
—as a lady of my acquaintance calls her—Martineau is a little extravagant in her raptures about it, but certainly the letters are a noble
composition, and do the author infinite honor. The Unitarian clergymen are ready to tear Miss Martineau into rags for treating them so
badly. I do not know how her friend Mr. Ware takes her general
censure of the class to which he belongs."

" NEW YORK, OCTOBER 25th:* I am very much obliged to you for
your kind offer, and if I were at liberty I should like nothing better
than to pass a year in Illinois. But I am fastened here for the present. The 'Evening Post' cannot be disposed of in these times, and,
on account of the difficulty of making collections, its income does not
present an appearance which would enable me to sell it for its real
value, even if I could find a purchaser. I am chained to the oar for
another year at least. The prospects of the journal are, however, improving, though I am personally no better for it at present. I am
very much perplexed by the state of my pecuniary affairs. I have
taken a house in town at as moderate a rent as I could find, and expect my family from the country in a very few days.† I am obliged to
practice the strictest frugality—but that I do not regard as an evil.
The great difficulty lies in meeting the debts in which the purchase of
the paper has involved me."

" NEW YORK, JUNE 28, 1838: ‡ . . . You are so kind as to wish
to be informed about my literary projects. I have no time for such
things. When I went to Europe the 'Evening Post' was producing
a liberal income; Mr. Leggett, who conducted it, espoused very zealously the cause of the Abolitionists, and then was taken ill. The business of the establishment fell into the hands of a drunken and saucy
clerk to manage, and the hard times came on. All these things had a
bad effect on the profits of the paper, and when I returned they were
reduced to little or nothing. In the mean time, Mr. Leggett and myself
had contracted a large debt for the purchase of the 'Evening Post.'
He retired, and the whole was left on my shoulders. I have been

* To his brother John.
† The house was in Carmine Street—a not very fashionable neighborhood.
‡ To R. H. Dana.

laboring very diligently to restore the paper to a prosperous state, and begin to have hopes that I shall retrieve what was lost during my absence in Europe by careful attention to the *business* of the paper, properly so called. I cannot leave the establishment till I have put it in good order. Nobody will buy it of me. With so much to pay, and with a paper so little productive, I have been several times on the point of giving it up, and going out into the world worse than penniless. Nothing but a disposition to look at the hopeful side of things prevented me, and I now see reason to be glad that I persevered.

"I have no leisure for poetry. The labors in which I am engaged would not, perhaps, be great to many people, but they are as great as I can endure with a proper regard to my health. I cannot pursue intellectual labor so long as many of a more robust or less nervous temperament. My constitution requires intervals of mental repose. To keep myself in health I take long walks in the country, for half a day, a day, or two days. I cannot well leave my business for a longer period, and I accustom myself to the greatest simplicity of diet, renouncing tea, coffee, animal food, etc. By this means I enjoy a health scarcely ever interrupted, but when I am fagged I hearken to Nature and allow her to recruit. I find by experience that this must be if I would not kill myself. What you say of living happily on small means I agree to with all my heart. My ideas of competence have not enlarged a single dollar. Indeed, they have rather been moderated and reduced by recent events, and I would be willing to compound for a less amount than I would have done three or four years since. If I had the means of retiring, I would go into the country, where I could adopt a simpler mode of living, and follow the bent of my inclination in certain literary pursuits, but I have a duty to perform to my creditors. . . . Mr. Verplanck I see only now and then; I used to see him almost daily, and if I do not now, it is because he will have it so. He is kind, however, and entertaining when I see him. Sedgwick is at Rockaway, getting better, I am told, rapidly in the sea air. Morse is gone to Europe. Cooper does not live here; he is at Cooperstown; but he calls at the office of the 'Evening Post' when he comes to town."

Mr. Dana's reply was so full of sympathy and good sense that a part of it is worth citing.

" Some portions of your letter have made me feel for you. I had taken it for granted that you had all along been doing well in your paper, and that, if your desires did not enlarge along with your means, you would, in a *very* few years at farthest, go back into the country, and chime song once more with your own Green River. ' Ah,' said Allston to me a few days ago (or, rather, *nights*, for he and I play the owl when we meet), ' I read over " Green River " the other night. That man is a true poet, his *heart* is in it. What he gives you comes from his own spirit.' I don't like thinking of it. It makes me sad whenever it comes into my mind that you are laboring on the broad, dusty, public highway, and your flower-plot all the while lying waste. Yet I do not see how, at present, you can choose but do it. You have energy and perseverance, and these, I trust, will help you back again, sooner than you may now look for, to a situation in which you may live your true life. . . . I am sorry that Verplanck should estrange himself from you.* I hope it is only in appearance so. Surely he would not let politics come in between him and you. It is evil enough that moral differences should sometimes divide us as they do. We might for the most part, in such cases, not only be courteous to one another, but like one another also, without harm to our virtue. And must difference of opinions make the faces of friends strange to one another? It gives one the heartache to think on't. Why, what would poor I do, who, believing in the Triune, and unwounded by those who hold my Divine Master to be nothing but a man, a little more knowing and better than themselves, mayhap? Or who, either earthing themselves in materialism, or pleasing their fancies with a bigger air-bubble called spiritualism, have worked themselves clear of nearly all that gives life to faith, and power and sanctity to the Word of God? What should I do, who, living in a country like this, am head and heart an old-fashioned monarchist, and who, if an Englishman, should, aside from expediency, be in heart a stiff Tory, rather than a yielding Conservative. If there are points in which we can sympathize, why should we not break off the anti-pathetic points, and go along quietly together without goading one another ? "

---

* This estrangement was political, not personal, and grew out of Mr. Verplanck's course in respect to the United States Bank. When he was nominated for office by the friends of that institution, Mr. Bryant felt it to be his duty to oppose him.

CHAPTER NINETEENTH.

A. D. 1839.

MR. BRYANT'S labors, of which he complains, were certainly harder during these years than at any period of his life, before or since; but they were not without reliefs, and even compensations. They did not wear upon him as they might have done otherwise, because of his habit of never carrying the shop with him. The moment he stepped outside the office its cares and anxieties were cast aside. At his home he utterly refused to talk of public affairs, or to hear others talk of them, and any one who persisted in thrusting such topics upon him was silenced. His leisure he regarded as a time sacred to his books, his family, and his friends. In this way he kept his mind fresh and alert; the jaded faculties were relieved by pleasant gambols in the realms of fancy; the imagination was supplied with new materials; and the affections warmed and solaced by the sweet amenities of the home.

A good deal of the leisure that fell to him in these busy days he spent in the study of the German language, with which he had made a beginning at Heidelberg. The lectures given by Dr. Charles Follen on the German poets perhaps quickened his zeal in this direction, but more decidedly the singular enthusiasm of his teacher, the Baron Ludwig von Mandlesloc. This was a simple-hearted, self-sacrificing, noble-minded man, who had abandoned to younger brothers a considerable heritage at home, to share the fortunes of this republic, which he admired.   Pursuing the precarious life of a teacher, he yet gave his scanty gains, his time, his health even, to the poor, the sick, and the ignorant.   His native literature he loved almost as much as he loved his kind, and he found in Mr. Bryant an eager and sympathetic pupil.   Their walks together beyond the suburbs were made vocal with the strains of Goethe, Schiller, Rückert, Heine, which the good baron rolled out at the top of his voice.   But not in the fields alone they walked; their steps often turned to the wharves, where newly arrived emigrants needed his care, or to the thickly peopled tenements of the eastern side, whither he went to carry aid and consolation.   Through him Mr. Bryant was led to that warm concern for the German race which, to the end of his life, he was quick to manifest.   The good baron's privations and labors, however, soon wore him out.   He was sent to Berkshire for his health, where he fell into the kind hands of the Sedgwicks, who ministered to his sufferings till he died.*

Another recreation Mr. Bryant found in the long pedestrian tours to which he devoted his summer vacations.   Every day he spent two or three hours in exploring on foot the immediate vicinity of the city—Westchester, Hoboken, and Long Island; but when he could get a week or more to himself, he extended his excursions to the Palisades, to the Delaware Water Gap, to the Catskills, and to his own beautiful valleys of Berkshire.   He generally went alone, but preferred a companion, if he could procure one.   Mr. Ferdinand E. Field, now of England, speaks of him in a letter to me as the " most indefatigable tramp that he ever grappled with.   A baker's biscuit and a few apples seemed to suffice him for food; and he put up cheerfully with the rude fare of wayside inns and laborers' cottages.   His knowledge of soils and seasons, and his interest in agriculture, and the modes of life and opinions of the farmers, soon got him into pleasant chats with the people we

---

* Miss Sedgwick wrote a long memoir of him for one of the magazines.

encountered." It would be impossible, says Mr. Field, to describe his delight in wild flowers and trees, every one of which
seemed to be an old acquaintance.*

Mr. Bryant used to complain that so many Americans go
to Europe to drive or walk over Wales, Scotland, or Switzerland, who have never taken the trouble to visit scenes of almost unequalled natural beauty and magnificence within sight
of their windows. "The western shore of the Hudson, for
example," he once wrote, "is as worthy of a pilgrimage across
the Atlantic as the Alps themselves. You are kept in perpetual surprise by the bold beauty of the sylvan paths along the
breast of the mountains, and by the perpetually changing combinations of wood, water, rock, and hills; while, from time to
time, an interest of another kind is awakened by numerous
remains of old fortifications, which, in the revolutionary war,
crowned nearly all the prominent points." Mr. Bryant wrote
glowing descriptions of these trips for his journal, which must
have had an effect in exciting a more general appreciation and
love of our own landscape. Certainly the trips themselves
helped to make him that loving and truthful painter of its
beauties that he was in his poetry, justifying the praise of
Emerson, "that he first, and he only, made known to mankind
our northern nature—its summer splendors, its autumn russets,
its wintry lights and glooms." †

Nor was it all hard work within the office, as many distinguished visitors came to relieve its monotony by their talk.
Among them was Cooper, who, as Mr. Bryant says, always

* On one of these tours, Mr. Field narrates, they stopped over night at the inn
of a small village, when the landlord, by some means or other, discovered the name
of one of his guests. Word was soon passed to all his Democratic cronies of the village that the great New York editor, Bryant, was in town, which brought the whole
of them in quick time to the hotel. Then, after a loud hurrah for Bryant, they set up
a shout for a speech, a speech, which annoyed the poet very much. He was doubtful
for a time whether he should fly out upon them in anger or skulk away by the back
door; but his companion was enabled to allay the little storm by explaining that
"the great editor" was tired to death with a long day's work, and had gone to bed.

† Address at the Century celebration, in 1864.

called when he was in town. ʹThe difference between the two men was very striking, and yet their intercourse was singularly côurteous and agreeable. Cooper, burly, brusque, and boisterous, like a bluff sailor, always bringing a breeze of quarrel with him; Mr. Bryant, shy, modest, and delicate as a woman—they seemed little fitted for friendship. Yet Bryant admired not only the genius, but the thorough-paced honesty and sturdy independence of Cooper; and Cooper, while he appreciated the finer vein of the poet, was won by his able and fearless vindication of opinions with which he himself did not always agree. "We others," Cooper once said, "get a little praise now and then, but Bryant is the author of America." In spite of his positive and, at times, overbearing manner, the novelist was a fascinating companion. Having seen much of the world—first, as a naval officer, who had traversed the greater part of its surface, then, as the friend of Lafayette, in Paris, who procured him an entrance to the best French society, and, finally, as somewhat of a literary lion in London—he was able to fill his conversation with pictures and anecdotes of the men and things he had seen. He had a great deal to say of Sir Walter Scott, whom he really admired; but, having been called, according to a silly prevalent fashion, the Scott of America, he seemed to resent it as a reflection upon his originality, and indulged in some sharp criticisms of the great novelist. Lockhart, he averred, had tampered with the diaries of his father-in-law in preparing the "Life of Scott," and fell under his severest animadversions. But the great objects of his dislike were the French romancers, of whom Eugène Sue was then a chief, and whose descriptions of society he pulled to pieces with an unsparing sarcasm and ridicule.

A very different view of French literature was taken by another habitual caller, Major Auguste Davezac—a brother-in-law of Edward Livingston—who had been an *aide-de-camp* of Jackson at New Orleans, and remained an ardent admirer and trusted friend of the old hero to the day of his death. He was a bachelor or widower, with time and means enough to make himself familiar with nearly all the recent products of the French press, and ready to repeat their contents with an exhaustless memory, and a facile and impressive elocution. It was like listening to one of the best of the French romances or memoirs, read aloud, to hear him talk; and, though an intense democrat in his political convictions, his reading had been so wide, and his tastes were so choice, that, whatever his subject, he was invariably delightful. He commonly timed his visits to the exigencies of the office, but, come when he would, all pens were dropped, and all ears opened, to catch some of his sprightly or fervid utterances.*

Another visitor, about that time, whom we were always glad to see, was John L. Stephens, the traveller—a small, sharp, nervous man—full of his adventures in Arabia Petræa, Nubia, and elsewhere in the Old World, and among the buried cities of Central America. His books, now mostly forgotten, had considerable vogue then, and we were permitted to anticipate the public in a considerable part of their contents. But Stephens was suffering from the effects of a fever caught at Chagres, which speedily carried him off, to the great loss of our literature of travel.

More captivating than Stephens was the venerable Audubon, the naturalist, still fresh from his wanderings over the continent, from Labrador to the capes of Florida, and from the Alleghanies to the Rocky Mountains. He was a tall, well-formed, athletic figure, as straight as an Indian, with a face bronzed by exposure, eyes as bright as those of any of his own birds, an eagle beak, and tresses of white hair that fell upon his shoulders. His voice was soft and gentle, but with an accent and vivacity derived from his French blood. He never wearied in telling, nor was the listener wearied in hearing, of his exploits in the solitudes of the forests among wild beasts or wilder Indians, or of his meetings with distinguished men in Europe—Goethe, Cuvier, Champollion, Lucien Bonaparte, Wilson, Louis Philippe and other crowned heads—such as are

* He was afterward our minister at the Hague.

described in the narratives prefixed to his volumes. He got up an exhibition of his original drawings of birds, in the Lyceum rooms, which was wonderfully beautiful; and, old as he was, contemplated new visits to the woods, to paint the quadrupeds, as he had painted the birds, of America. His house, in a small park, beyond the skirts of the city, on the banks of the Hudson, was a delightful place to visit, and strollers of a Sunday morning, who happened in upon the venerable artist, found him at his easel hard at work, but always ready to pour out his descriptions of his long and solitary journeys.

Other literary men were rather occasional than habitual visitors: Bancroft, drawn by the double sympathy of literature and politics; Wm. G. Simms, of South Carolina, a voluble talker, who desired to set us right on the Southern question; Edgar Poe, if I mistake not, once or twice, to utter nothing, but to look his reverence out of wonderful lustrous eyes, besides a host of the lesser lights from the eastward, reflecting the inspirations and affectations of Thomas Carlyle. That luminary had risen only a little before upon the horizon. "Have you read Carlyle's Miscellanies?" wrote Bryant to Miss Sands;* "you will like them better than his History. In Boston they are all agog after him, and they will take up Kant next." Not in Boston only, but everywhere young men sat up of nights to master the fascinating but nebulous philosophy of Teufelsdröckh. Mr. Bryant was not caught by the rage. He read Carlyle attentively, and was not insensible to his Rembrandt-like power of portraiture, or his broad floods of sardonic humor, mingled with tender touches of pathos here and there; but his taste was offended by the too obvious gymnastics of Carlyle's style, and his cynical worship of force of the gunpowder kind. He allowed his younger assistants to ventilate their admiration of the Scotchman as of one destined to explode all shams, and crush out all evil, but with a furtive, in-

---

* July 20, 1838.

credulous smile as he read their proofs. Nor was he at all involved in that contemporary fog of thought called Transcendentalism which pervaded the New England hills. For Emerson the chief, whom he regarded as greatly superior to Carlyle in clearness and depth of insight as in grace of diction, he always expressed strong admiration, but he took no pleasure in his mere metaphysical subtleties.

> "What pleasure lives in heights, the shepherd said,
>   In height and cold, the splendor of the hills."

His interest in Emerson, I think, was rather in the American writer than the philosopher. Nothing likely to exalt our literary rank ever escaped him. "Have you read (he once said to me) the tales of one Hawthorne (almost an unknown writer then) in the 'Democratic Review'? They are wonderful, and the best English written on either side the Atlantic." To the Rev. Mr. Ware, who had just collected his "Letters from Palmyra" into a volume, he wrote (September 19, 1838):

> "MY DEAR WARE: I should have written earlier to thank you for your last beautiful and eloquent work, but you know how to make allowances for one who is daily obliged to write more than he cares for, and has no way of indemnifying himself but by bilking his correspondents. I am glad that you have spoken to the public through the press. Everybody reads and admires your books. You are much better known here than when you lived among us. Your old hearers now plume themselves not a little upon your new reputation, and hold their heads high, I assure you."

A little while before this, when Mr. Prescott's "Ferdinand and Isabella" appeared (April, 1838), having read it with delight, he took great pains to commend it to public favor in a long and elaborate article which anticipated most of the Reviews. Mr. Prescott was a stranger to him, but he saw in the work a new triumph for American letters; and, when his friend Miss Robbins was on a visit to the East, he charged her particularly to tell him all about Prescott. To this injunction we probably owe the following letter from Nahant, August 26th, which shows the historian at home:

"MY DEAR FRIENDS: . . . Last evening (but one) I went to see Mr. Prescott, who is our next neighbor. I have come, from having much curiosity about great people, to regard them with utter distaste; but I must say the historian of ' Ferdinand and Isabella' is an exception. He is made to be loved, so amiable, unaffected, and even youthful, does he appear. I will not say ' childlike,' I have heard that word so often used in mere affectation. Mr. Prescott, though the father of a family, has never left his paternal home. His beautiful wife and pretty children are cherished with the fondest love by the venerable heads of the house. Both, like the good man whose ' Funeral' you have so exquisitely described, are prepared by pure and useful lives for whatever is to come. We fell to talking at Mr. Prescott's of the late Admiral Coffin, who happened to be a relative of both our families, and I—I could not help it—ran into endless genealogies, with which Mr. Prescott helped me, and we were all amused with the pleasant traditionary lore which each furnished. Mr. Prescott spends about ten hours of the twenty-four in his studies, always indebted to other eyes than his own. At early morning he educates his children, and at evening may generally be found with his father and mother. They give no parties, and all live the life of reason." *

* Miss Robbins adds, what I cannot forbear from quoting:
"Yesterday I read Dr. Bowditch's memoir, prefixed to the translation of the ' Méchanique Celeste.' I will tell you how his son has affixed your name to this great work, now in possession, by the gift of the author's family, of the most distinguished persons living. In his library and in his great mind he had a ' poet's corner.' Among the poets of America, Bryant was his favorite. He has often said that he thought ' The Old Man's Funeral' was one of the most beautiful pieces in the English language. Never can it be hereafter perused by us without recalling one of the most interesting and touching scenes at the close of his own life. His love of poetry was such that it entered into his most familiar thoughts. The last draught of water he ever took, he exclaimed, ' Delicious ! I have swallowed a drop—a drop from

' Siloa's brook that flowed
Fast by the oracle of God.'

One of his services to literature at this time was rendered through the son of his friend Dana, who, in the year 1834, had been compelled by an affection of his eyes to abandon his studies at Harvard and undertake a sea voyage. Instead of going to Europe, as most young men would have done, Dana resolved on a trip, by way of the South Seas, to California, then quite unknown. In order to get the full benefit of his expedition, he shipped before the mast, and kept a diary of his experiences which he condensed into a book called " Two Years before the Mast." The elder Dana sent it to Mr. Bryant with a request that he would read it, and get a publisher for it if he approved. Mr. Bryant was so struck by its originality, vigor, and truth, that he at once set about bringing it before the public. But he found that the trade was quite indisposed to take hold of the book, and his letters relating to his efforts are interesting as showing what a parturition good books are sometimes compelled to go through. He wrote to the father, June 24, 1839:

" I will now tell Mrs. Bryant what he said of his wife, to whom the 'Méchanique Celeste' is dedicated. ' This translation and commentary are dedicated, by the author, to the memory of his wife, Mary Bowditch, who devoted herself to her domestic avocations with great judgment, unceasing kindness, and a zeal which could not be surpassed, taking upon herself the whole care of her family, and thus procuring for him the leisure hours to prepare the work, and securing to him, by her prudent management, the means for publication in its present form, which she fully approved ; and without her approbation the work would not have been undertaken.' This lady consented that $12,000 of their small property, with no prospect of reimbursement, should be appropriated to the work in question. Dr. Bowditch particularly honored the female sex. Seventy-five pages of the translation were the work of his accomplished daughter-in-law. I like that women should receive their due, from great men especially. At Cambridge I found Mr. and Mrs. Ware, dwelling in great content among their own people. I wish you were both here. Mr. Bryant is so much admired at Boston, I am afraid he would be worried with homages, but they would be honest. Mr. Grattan (author of ' Highways and By-ways ') is here, and says (he is an Irishman) that he is astonished and delighted with the refinement, cordiality, and apparent happiness of American society. The absence of mendicity and a degraded lower order is a perpetual delight to one from the other side, if he is '*a man and a brother.*'"

" I am sorry that I have no better account to give of my success in the commission with which you intrusted me. I have seen the Harpers, and do not find them disposed to publish the book at all at present. Three of the brothers were together—there are four of them in all—and the one who had the conversation with your friend, Mr. Woods, after saying a few words, went out. The others then told me that James Harper, who had made the offer to Mr. Woods, had never laid the matter before them, that they did not object to the book, that they had no doubt a publisher might be found for it, etc., and that the best way would be for me to write to you and advise that, since two chapters were to be written, the author should finish the work and offer it to them, or to Carey, Lee & Blanchard, of Philadelphia, in the autumn. I told them that the two chapters might be written off-hand, that the book was, in fact, finished already, and that I had come to make final terms. They were engaged with so many publications— some new, but the principal part the old publications which are stereotyped—that really they could not engage to get out your son's work at present; they thought they should be very glad to do so in the autumn, but could not now make any bargain."

He next applied to Appleton, then to Coleman, to Wiley & Putnam, and "they all with one accord made excuse." Finally, he turned to Philadelphia, and October 2d again wrote to the father :

" I have been obliged to give up the idea of effecting the publication of your son's work. I wrote to Lea & Blanchard, of Philadelphia, stating as fully as I was able its merits and its prospects of applause and success. They returned a polite answer, in which they declined publishing it on account of ' the depressed state of the trade of the country.' They were compelled, they said, to ' avoid making new literary engagements unless they were of a nature of the success of which they could not doubt.' Books of voyages and travels, they added, do not often pay the publisher, much less the author. Finally, with an apology for offering their advice, they say that, in their opinion, the best thing Mr. Dana can do is to find some publisher in Boston, where his family connection is so well known, who would undertake its publication, etc."

Repulsed on every side, Mr. Bryant was yet determined not to yield; and he resumed negotiations with the Harper Brothers, who were induced to bring out the book the next year (1840). Mr. Bryant gave it a good send-off in the " Evening Post," and procured one review of it by his friend Theodore Sedgwick, Jr., for the " New York Review," and another, by another hand, for the " Democratic Review." But these friendly services were needless. The book spoke for itself, and the public recognized its merits as soon as it was issued. Old seamen bore witness to its fidelity, the public schools ordered it for their libraries, and preachers even mentioned it from their pulpits as an admirable cure for that form of youthful sea-sickness which consists in a frenzied desire to go to sea. Ten thousand copies were speedily sold in this country; and in England, where it was republished, the sale was quite as great. Since then, edition after edition of it has been printed, and the work may be said to have taken its place among the classics of adventure.*

Just before the receipt of Mr. Dana's first letter, Mr. Bryant was called upon to deplore the loss of his old colleague, Leggett, whose health had been impaired by too assiduous labor while he was in the " Evening Post," and whose attempt to manage a periodical of his own only increased the disorder. It brought on bilious attacks, accompanied by great suffering and an utter prostration of strength. A timely retirement to his country seat in New Rochelle mitigated his pains, and it was thought that he was sufficiently recovered to accept the appointment of *Chargé d'Affaires* to Guatemala, in Central America, which Mr. Van Buren, whom he had often assailed, magnanimously tendered him ; but on the eve of his departure an attack of more than usual malignity supervened, and he died in less than three days, in the thirty-ninth year of his age (May, 1839). Mr. Bryant, besides celebrating his virtues in

* I endeavored to procure from the Messrs. Harper the precise number of copies sold, but, owing to a loss of some of their early accounts by fire, they could not comply with my request.

verse, prepared a brief memoir of him, which was published
in the "Democratic Review," and he assisted Theodore Sedgwick, Jr., in compiling two volumes of his editorial writings,
which were issued the next year.*

The winter of 1839 promised to be more than usually
pleasant for Mr. Bryant, for one of his friends, Dr. Follen,
was completing a highly instructive course of lectures on the
life and poems of Schiller; another, who was staying with
him, Mr. Dana, had come on from Boston to deliver a course
on the dramas of Shakespeare (full, as I recollect them, of profound remark and nice criticism); and a third, Mr. Longfellow,
was delighting brilliant audiences with his graceful delinea-
tions of the characters of Molière. Once, when the two latter
were Mr. Bryant's guests at a dinner, they were joined by
Halleck, and thus the four most famous poets that our literature had yet produced were brought together, and their con-
versations, we may well suppose, if they could have been
reported, would have added a lively chapter to the best
chronicles of table-talk. Dana and Halleck were men of the
past in politics and religion; Bryant and Longfellow men of
the present and future; and, while there was a good deal of

---

* " The Political Writings of William Leggett." New York: Harper & Brothers,
1840. For the Democratic young men who erected a monument to his memory at
New Rochelle he also wrote this inscription:

TO WILLIAM LEGGETT,
THE ELOQUENT JOURNALIST,
WHOSE GENIUS, DISINTERESTEDNESS, AND COURAGE
ENNOBLED HIS PROFESSION;
WHO LOVED TRUTH FOR ITS OWN SAKE,
AND ASSERTED IT WITH MOST ARDOUR
WHEN WEAK MINDS WERE MOST DISMAYED BY OPPOSITION;
WHO COULD ENDURE NO TYRANNY,
AND RAISED HIS VOICE AGAINST ALL INJUSTICE,
AGAINST WHOMSOEVER COMMITTED
AND WHOEVER WERE ITS AUTHORS—
THE DEMOCRATIC YOUNG MEN OF NEW YORK,
SORROWING THAT A CAREER SO GLORIOUS
SHOULD HAVE CLOSED SO PREMATURELY,
HAVE ERECTED THIS MONUMENT.

reciprocal admiration among them, there was contrast and antagonism enough to bring out many a fiery spark. But the intercourse of the poets was suddenly dashed by the melancholy death of Charles Follen, who was known to all, and an esteemed friend of two of them—Bryant and Longfellow. Follen was a passenger on the steamer Lexington, on her voyage from New York to Providence, during a dark, cold, and tempestuous night, when she was burned to the water's edge, and nearly all on board perished in the flames, or by cold, or amid crushing fields of ice (January 13, 1840). Well known in Boston and New York, having formed many friendships among their more distinguished citizens, the shock of the calamity was felt in both cities. Only a little while before the event, Mr. Bryant had written a vigorous article on the want of proper precautions for the safety of passengers on these very steamers, and his words came back to him as prophecies. Follen was a native of Hesse Darmstadt, early distinguished for his learning and liberal sentiments. Connected with the Burschenschaft, and author of several patriotic odes, he fell under the suspicion of the government, and was driven, first from Giessen, then from Jena, and finally from Switzerland, because of his opinions. Coming to the United States, he secured appointments at Harvard, and ultimately married an eminent American lady, Miss Eliza Lee Cabot, by whom his memoirs were written. " He was," says Mr. Bryant, who respected him highly, and became strongly attached to him, " a man of vigorous intellect, much cultivated in the various departments of knowledge, and of calm and solid judgment. His experience of the evils of arbitrary government, joined to a feeling of universal good-will, and the genial spirit of hope, which was ever strong in him, led him to embrace the purest democratic principles. The world had not a firmer, a more ardent, a more consistent friend of human liberty. His passions, naturally energetic, were all so perfectly subjected to the control of the higher qualities of his character, that, although you saw they were not extinct, you saw, also, that they were held in place and overruled by justice and benevolence. No man could have known him, even slightly, without being strongly impressed by the surpassing benignity of his temper. He is taken from us by a mysterious Providence, in the midst of his usefulness.

> " ' It was that fatal and perfidious bark,
>   Built in the eclipse, and rigged with curses dark,
>   That sank so low that sacred head of thine.' "

CHAPTER TWENTIETH.

THE HARD-CIDER CAMPAIGN, ETC.

A. D. 1840, 1841.

MR. VAN BUREN'S administration, though it had been conducted with great dignity and prudence, achieving at home its principal measure, the emancipation of the Government from dependency upon banks,* and maintaining harmony abroad against serious difficulties and complications,† came to an end in a frenzy of disfavor. Coincident with a period of widespread commercial distress, for which it was made responsible, although the same depression of trade and industry prevailed in England and on the continent, it was not credited with the revival when it began. The opposition was sagacious enough to take advantage of the prevalent discontents, and to promise a change. But, to make sure of success, it was necessary to combine the many dissatisfied factions by adopting a policy of non-committalism, both as to its candidates and its cause. Mr. Clay, their traditional and most brilliant leader, was intrigued out of the Presidential nomination,‡ and a new man, a military chief, General Harrison, put in his place. To this rather unmeaning figure-head a Virginia abstractionist, Mr. Tyler, who was but nominally a Whig, was joined as a candidate for the Vice-Presidency. No declaration of prin-

---

* The Independent Treasury Bill was passed July 4, 1840.
† The disturbances on the Canada frontier.
‡ The nominating convention was held at Harrisburg, December 4, 1839, and voted by States, according to their electoral power, and not by popular delegation.

ciples or of purposes was made, and a campaign was begun which, for noise, display, and debauchery, was never before paralleled in the history of the nation. As Harrison had once lived in a log cabin, and was reputed to be a drinker of hard cider, the cabin and the cider-barrel were made the unseemly symbols of political faith. " If you could imagine," says a contemporary writer,* " a whole nation declaring a holiday, or season of rollicking, for six or eight months, giving itself up to the wildest freaks of fun and frolic, caring nothing for business, singing, dancing, carousing, night and day, you might have some notion of the extraordinary scenes of 1840." Mr. Bryant was at first disposed to treat this immoral tomfoolery, which the most respectable classes promoted by a personal participation in it, with serious and indignant argument. But he soon saw that he might as well attempt to reason against the northwest wind or the tides of the sea. The only answer would have been a hurrah and a horse-laugh, and so he took the times in their own spirit, and flung at them the keenest shafts of banter and ridicule. On no other occasion were his humorous powers so frequently called into play ; and his hits at the muzzled candidate, the mouthing orators, the immense parades, and the junketings, though ineffective, were among the best sallies of his pen.

" The enemies of the Democratic party," he said, describing the turn that the controversy had assumed, " threaten to put it down by singing. They have pointed at it the whole artillery of the gamut. We are all to undergo solmization ; we are to be destroyed by ' the sweet and contagious breath,' as Sir Andrew Ague-cheek has it, of our adversaries. . . . The readers of the ' American ' and the readers of the ' Star,' the drawing-room and the tap-room, are united on this point. While the one set trill their Tippecanoe ballads to the air of *di tanti palpiti*, the other thunders them out to the tune of ' Come, let us all be Jolly.' A regular organization has been set on foot for this purpose. Tippecanoe clubs are forming, not only in the various

* N. Sargent, " Public Men and Events," vol. ii, p. 107.

wards of the city, but throughout the country, to drink hard cider and sing songs in praise of Harrison. Stores of ballads have been provided to serve as heavy ordnance for the political campaign; glees and catches are ready to be thrown into our camp like hand-grenades and Congreve rockets; the Whig poets are at work like armorers and gunsmiths fabricating election rhymes, and we scarcely open a Whig newspaper without finding one or two Harrison songs. The plan is to exterminate us chromatically, to cut us to pieces with A sharp, to lay us prostrate with G flat, to hunt us down with fugues, overrun us with choruses, and bring in Harrison by a grand diapason."

In this strain he kept it up for most of the campaign. He was very glad to get out of it, however, when he could, and, as his assistants had increased in number and efficiency,* he was able this year to begin his country trips as early as April. He visited, in the course of the summer, his old home at Cummington, whence the family was now departed; the eastern parts of the State of Pennsylvania, which are remarkably lovely; and the Catskill Mountains, with every cleft and crevice of which he became as familiar as he was with the leafy retreats in the nearer neighborhood of New York. Allusions to some of these trips are contained in the following letters to his friends Field and Dana :

"NEW YORK, MAY 6, 1840:† I regret exceedingly to hear that you have suffered lately from ill health. We must have you out again to America for the benefit of the air. I agree with Mr. Cooper in his last novel, ' The Pathfinder '—which, by the way, I like very much,

---

* His friend J. K. Paulding, who expected to be released from office as Secretary of the Navy by the defeat of Van Buren, wrote to him as follows : " You have fought ably, nobly, and untiringly for the good cause, which is not lost, but only mislaid for a while, I hope and trust. The manner in which the ' Evening Post ' is conducted its staid and sober dignity, and its freedom from the base slang, and still baser falsehood, with which so many newspapers are debauched and disgraced, makes me proud to remember that I have a humble claim to be associated with its honors." When he returned to New York, Mr. Paulding contributed a good deal of editorial matter to the journal.

† To Ferdinand E. Field, who had now returned to England.

particularly the concluding part—that the climate of America, although it is the fashion to find fault with it, is as good as any climate, and better than many.   Another walk on the Palisades would put you to rights again, for a week at least.   Or you might go with me, where I went three weeks since, to Bethlehem, a beautiful little town inhabited by Moravians, twelve miles west of Easton, in Pennsylvania.   Mr. Parker accompanied me.*   You would have been delighted with the place, its appearance of thrift, its neat habitations, its orderly population, even to the boys in the streets, its charming situation on a hill sloping down to the Lehigh, its broad, shallow, rapid river, with firm, dry shores, bordered with forest-trees, and shagged here and there with thickets of the kalmia and rhododendron.   Along the banks are beautiful shaded walks, leading to a great distance, and near the town is a little island covered with ancient trees of immense size, and carpeted with green turf, whither the people of the place repair to celebrate, after the German manner, their birthday festivals.   On our return we walked to Easton along the Lehigh, among rich farms and beautiful hills and groves.   Easton we only saw in the evening, but it appeared to be situated in a very picturesque country.   From the bridge over the Delaware we had one of the most glorious moonlight views I ever beheld.   But I suppose Mr. Parker has written you all about our excursion.

" We have left the house in Carmine Street, after inhabiting it for two years and a half, and have taken a house in Ninth Street, near the Sixth Avenue, not far from Brevoort's house, which you remember, doubtless, a kind of palace in a garden.   Our little dwelling is a comfortable two-story house, quite new and very convenient. . . . In most other respects the world goes on much as it did when you were here. The greatest change that I perceive in New York is the introduction of cabs and mustachios, and in some instances beards as long as those worn by the Dunkers.   As I advance in life the world widens in some respects and contracts in others ; I have more acquaintances and fewer intimates.   But I begin to moralize, and, for fear of being tiresome, as well as because I am at the end of my sheet, I will stop short."

" NEW YORK, JUNE 9, 1840 : † The newspapers say that you are at New Haven delivering your lectures.   I think of coming up, and

* Mr. Reginald Parker, of England.   † To R. H. Dana.

taking this occasion to look at the place in summer, which I have never yet done. If the weather is fair, I shall set out in the Thursday morning's boat; if not, perhaps I shall come on Friday. I shall stay but a night or two. . . . The story you saw or heard of in one of the weekly prints is an old affair of mine, written, I believe, nine years ago, and published by the Harpers, in a volume with some others. I have done with writing tales, for the present at least. . . . My wife and I often talk of you, and recollect your visit to New York as an agreeable interruption to the seclusion of our lives. I met Halleck the other day. He seems to have liked you very much, and spoke of the pleasure he received from your conversation, although at that time his hearing was much more imperfect than usual. When I saw him the other day his deafness was hardly perceptible. . . . If you are with Mr. Hillhouse, or should see him before I come up, please to remember me to him, and to Mrs. Hillhouse."

" NEW YORK, SEPTEMBER 12th : * I have made two journeys into the country. Once I went to New Milford, in Connecticut, by steamboat and railroad, and then walked up along the Housatonic through Kent, Cornwall, Canaan, and Sheffield, to Great Barrington, fifty miles. Here I saw my daughters, and then walked to Pittsfield, from which I wandered over to Hampshire County, to Worthington, where I studied law, and to Cummington, where all that is left of my father rests in a burying-ground, on the summit of one of the broad highlands of that region. Do you know how beautiful the Canaan Falls are? I never saw anything like them in New England. And yet I lived within eighteen miles of them for ten years, without making them a visit. I always thought that they were mere rapids. Yet they are extraordinarily beautiful, the wild Housatonic pouring over the precipice in two broad, irregular sheets of snowy whiteness, with a little island of trees and shrubs hanging from the brow of the rock between them. My next visit was with my wife to Bethlehem, a Moravian settlement in Pennsylvania, nearly ninety years old—a peaceful, industrious, orderly, comfortable little community. It is situated on the Lehigh, a rapid and most beautiful river, with an island in the midst, shaded with old oaks and elms and drooping birches, whose twigs

* To the same.

hang down to the water. This is the pleasure-ground, the place for their little assemblies, their birthday commemorations, coffee-drink-ings, and musical parties—for music is a passion with these people. They announce a death with plaintive music from their church-tower; they accompany a corpse to the grave with music, and they hate the sound of a bell so much that they never allow their church-bell to strike more than a dozen times to call their population to worship. One of the pastors of the congregation was a fellow-passenger with my wife when she came out from Havre.—I am glad you think of republishing your writings. It is time. I see no reason why you should not put in the reviews. Some of them are among your most characteristic compositions; nor do I perceive any reason for leaving out the short ones. Your success at New Haven, I have no doubt, will bring you invitations to lecture at other places, though probably at your own risk, which seems to be the turn the fashion of lecturing is now taking."

The Catskill trip was taken in July, in company with Thomas Cole, the artist, who had removed from the city and fixed his abode on the banks of the Hudson, near the shadows of the great hills. He was a modest, thoughtful, sweet-tem-pered man, whose love of nature was as deep as that of Mr. Bryant, and they took great pleasure in sauntering together among the mountains, scaling their heights, or threading their thickets, from dawn to dark. To some of the less frequented coves—deep chasms between perpendicular precipices, shaggy with rocks and trees, and echoing with the roar of hidden cas-cades—they ventured to give appropriate names, which, it is understood, they still retain. Cole derived from these wan-derings some of the most impressive effects of his pictures, and they enabled Mr. Bryant to commend the attractive re-gion to public admiration in the columns of his journal. In one of his poems—the " Catterskill Falls "—he has endeavored to incorporate the popular belief that they who perish by cold enjoy in their last moments singularly splendid and fan-tastic visions of life.

All through the summer the noise and nonsense of the

political farce continued, until the defeat of Van Buren at the polls in November. Harrison, the successful candidate, was inaugurated the next March (1841) amid salvos of rejoicing, but the poor man had barely a month to enjoy his triumph. He died on the 4th of April. It was the first time that a President had died in office, and there was something pathetic as well as ghastly in such a termination of such a campaign. Mr. Bryant remarked upon it as his view of the circumstances suggested; he was respectful, but not panegyrical, in what he said of the dead chief magistrate; but his coldness of tone gave great offence to the adherents of the new reign. What chiefly provoked their resentments was his refusal to conform to a prevalent practice, by reversing the column-rules of his journal, to put it in the black of mourning. He thought it a piece of "typographical foppery," beneath the dignity of an enlightened press, and refrained. Such a storm of obloquy thereupon broke forth from other journals that, if he had been the "vampire" or the "ghoul" which they called him, it could scarcely have been more violent.

Tyler, who, as Vice-President, succeeded Harrison, and whose political tendencies were not those of the party by which he had been elected, was soon involved in acrimonious squabbles with its leaders. To the Democrats these furnished matters of amusement, and to Mr. Bryant a great relief, as he was now no longer called upon to defend an administration with which he was not in entire accord. He could once more fling his arrows of assault where they could be most effective. He had no great confidence in Tyler, and still less in the opposition to him, and he saw that the rupture was a sure presage of dissolution to the Whig party.

"Mr. Tyler's character and temperament," he said, "unfit him to become the favorite of any one party or of the people at large. He is well-meaning; he would be glad to administer the Government beneficially for the people; but his want of clear notions on many subjects, and of definite information upon others, coupled with a certain credulous readiness to adopt opinions presented to him in a plausible manner, makes him a very uncertain, irresolute, and unsafe politician. He cannot be made the passive tool of any party : for that he has too much candor and too much uprightness of intention ; neither is he a man to be guided by the independent conclusions of his own mind ; for that he has not either sufficient clear-sightedness or sufficient decision. In matters where he has already expressed a positive opinion he is firm—nay, obstinate—for he prides himself on his consistency ; in other matters he is haunted by a perpetual distrust of his own capacity to arrive at a just judgment—a judgment which the people will ratify. He, therefore, asks counsel on all sides, becomes confused by the comparison of conflicting arguments, and pronounces at last an accidental verdict. So it is that in his public acts he is sometimes with one party and sometimes with another ; not exactly because he is a political eclectic, who takes something from each, according to a fixed principle of selection, but because of a certain infirmity of judgment. . . . It was both the duty and the policy of the majority in Congress to make the best of his peculiar character, to give the best play to his virtues, to veil as much as possible his deficiencies, to yield him every proper facility in the management of public affairs, to co-operate with him in making the Whig rule as acceptable to the people as possible, and, at the close of his four years, allow him to pass into an honorable retirement."

But they chose to criticise, to thwart, to bully, and denounce him ; in a word, to engage in president baiting, as Mr. Bryant called it, greatly to Tyler's discomfort, but also at their own cost. Every blow they struck at him seemed to dislocate their own shoulders ; or, as in the case of Hudibras,

> " The gun they aimed at duck or plover
> Was sure to kick the owner over."

In May of this year (1841) Mr. Bryant made a brief visit to Illinois to see his mother and brothers, going by way of Chicago, no longer a little village in a wet marsh, but a noisy and bustling town, giving promise already of its marvellous future. On the prairies the wolves were still howling in solitary places; yet ten years had made a vast difference in the appearances of a frontier settlement.* He found his brothers—four of them now—no longer living in log huts in the midst of unbroken plains, but in handsome brick houses, with orchards and grain-fields about them, and churches, schools, and court-houses filling up the neighborhood. His venerable mother was still active and vigorous, trying for a second time the life of the pioneer, but now rejoicing in a family of stalwart sons, one of whom had achieved a national distinction, while the others were substantial and prosperous citizens, at times the law-makers, of a rapidly growing State.

He did not think it prudent, however, to take his usual rambles this summer. A new party was in power which he thought needed watching. The controversy in regard to the national bank was getting exhausted; Jackson, like another St. George, had given that Dragon of Wantley a fatal wound; and its enemies might exclaim:

> " Thy pomp is in the dust; thy power is laid
> Low in the pit thine avarice hath made."

But extraordinary schemes for new protective legislation were broached, and Mr. Bryant wished to be on hand. The Compromise Tariff of 1832, a strictly revenue tariff, was not satisfactory to the manufacturers, and a more efficient measure was proposed in its place. This was so exorbitant in its provisions that it got the name of the Black Tariff. It was the original pretext of the protectionists that they wanted the aid of the government only while their enterprises were young and precarious, and that, once established, they would dispense with its further fostering care. But experience had shown that the needs of this class grew by what they fed on. The effect of the artificial stimulus given to particular branches of trade had been to augment the domestic competition in them,

* See "Sketches of Travel," vol. v. of collected works.

or to nourish them, not into a stable, vigorous life, but into a spasmodic state of alternate strength and weakness. After thirty years of governmental coddling, here they were again at the doors of Congress, demanding a prodigious increase of privileges and favors. Mr. Bryant fought the project tooth and nail; and he was encouraged in his opposition to it by the brilliant successes already achieved by the great anti-corn-law movement in England over hostile opinions. He thought it a shame that any monarchy should be allowed to outstrip the republic in liberality of action.

" All the tendencies of the times, throughout the civilized world," he said, " are directed toward a condition of larger freedom—not only to freedom of thought and speech, but to freedom of intercourse. Liberty of trade is getting to be a popular rallying cry wherever there is any approach to a free expression of popular opinion. The emancipation of commerce from the shackles of legislation is but a continued manifestation of the same spirit which broke the yoke of the feudal system, and which is leading the masses of every civilized nation to fret under the restraints of partial and aristocratic governments. Free-trade is thus a part of the grand movement of mankind toward a nobler condition of social existence. Humanity is weary of the narrow notions and confined habits which have produced so much of its misery in the past. It looks to the whole world as the proper theatre for its future exertions. Commerce is one of the modes by which man communes with man, and, like the sea over which its products are freighted, it must be broad and boundless. Everywhere are the walls of caste and sect crumbling before the generous enthusiasm of freedom and progress, and it would be idle to expect that the feeble and disgraceful prejudices and jealousies which separate nations can escape the general overthrow."

In these sanguine expectations, however, Mr. Bryant was deceived; selfishness was stronger than logic or sentiment, and he was again compelled to see the old system of injustice revived. Another form of contemporary error, which took the name of Native Americanism, was spreading widely, and he opposed it; but he deemed it only a transient outbreak of bigotry, and not half so pernicious as the schemes of the protectionists.

It was not until September that he was able to get his run in the fields, and he chose for his excursion the charming region in the environs of Lebanon Springs. They were near the birthplace of his young friend Mr. Samuel J. Tilden, already a politician of marked sagacity and comprehensive knowledge, whom he visited, and by whom he was accompanied on a visit to ex-President Van Buren, at his country seat near the village of Kinderhook. A letter to his journal, of September 18th (1841), gives some account of their interview.

"NEW LEBANON, SEPTEMBER 18th: The crowd of summer company which was collected at the Springs has flown, and I have these beautiful valleys to myself, and the woody hills with the glorious views they command. I ramble for hours on the summits, and do not fall in with a living creature. The other day I was led by curiosity to visit Kinderhook, which I had never seen before. It is one of the pleasantest of villages, situated amid a circle of swelling uplands and fresh meadows that skirt the winding streams. On one of these upland swells, just high enough to make the elevation perceptible, stands the village, its broad streets embroidered with elms, and its clean, comfortable dwellings half hidden by fruit-trees and shrubberies. . . . About two miles south of the village is the dwelling of ex-President Van Buren, where he employs himself in the cultivation of his newly purchased acres. Thus far the farm does credit to his skilful administration. The ex-President begins the day with a ride on horseback of ten or fifteen miles; after breakfast he is engaged with his workmen till he is tired, and he then takes himself to his library. In these occupations, and in friendly intercourse with his old friends and neighbors, the farmers of Kinderhook, he passes his time. I suppose he must like now and then,

'—through the loop-holes of retreat,'

to peep at the great Babel of the world, and to speculate on what they are doing at Washington; but he is so absorbed in his agricultural work that he appears to have no more time to think of politics than any other well-informed man not a politician by profession. I was glad to find him so free from the pedantry of party men, and to know that his mind could so readily command resources beyond the occupations in which so large a part of his life has been engaged. When, however, the conversation is directed to political subjects, he expresses himself with frankness and decision, and with that penetration into the minds and motives of men which is one of the most remarkable of his faculties. His style of conversation is lively, idiomatic, and simple, giving much matter in few words—very different from that of most men trained in the forum or in legislative debate, who are apt to fall into a diffuse, speech-making, wearisome manner."

Mr. Bryant was more pleased with the ex-President than he shows in his letter, which was intended for the public. He had known him before only amid the responsibilities of official position, which rendered him cautious and reticent; but here, in the leisure and abandonment of private life, he was unrestrained and communicative. His stores of anecdotes, relating to the distinguished men he had seen on both sides of the Atlantic—Jefferson, Madison, Burr, the Livingstons, and many of the prominent statesmen of Europe—were inexhaustible, and he told them in a piquant way, very much in contrast with his cumbrous written style. Mr. Van Buren corresponded afterward with Mr. Bryant, but his letters are lost.

A month later he was the guest of his friend Dana, whose summer retreat was at Rockport, Cape Ann, a wild and craggy nook on the extreme eastern point of Massachusetts. "Woods and waters, waters and woods," said Dana, describing it in the letter of invitation; "beautiful woods, and mossy, filled with birds all song, and again jagged and lofty rocks, and breakers on the shore, or under the trees of oak, pine, and maple." Mr. Bryant went by the way of Cambridge, where he was glad to renew his acquaintance of the old Review days with the Channings, Allston, and others; to see again the Rev. William Ware in a new home, and possibly to encounter Longfellow and Lowell, if they were then returned from the country. It was this brief sojourn on the shores of the ocean that suggested to him the "Hymn of the Sea," which, with the following letter, he sent some months later to Mr. Ware, editor of the "Christian Examiner":

"NEW YORK, MAY, 1842: As you are making a *bee* to furnish out the first number of your periodical in its new form, I shall contribute my assistance, such as it is, along with the rest of your neighbors. You may rely upon my doing something. I am sorry to hear that the 'Christian Examiner' is not so successful as it ought to be. The cause to which you ascribe it is doubtless the true one—that of its having taken the review form, which is too solemn and didactic for the public taste. It is wonderful what success some of our magazines— the lighter sort—have had. The publishers of the 'Lady's Book' and 'Ladies' Companion' talk, and I believe with truth, of their ten thousand subscribers and more. 'Graham's Magazine' has also a very large circulation. . . . I hope another cause of the falling off in the subscribers of the 'Christian Examiner' is not any decline in the numbers of our denomination. Yet it must be admitted, I believe, that we do not multiply as we did a few years since. Is the increase of the Unitarians at the present time in proportion to the increase of the population? I am not able to judge with much precision. Betwixt the neologists on the one side, and the archaists on the other, I fear that sober and sensible notions of religion are not making much progress just now; at least, not in the shape in which they are received by us." *

* When the Hymn was published, it was found to contain a curious error of transcription, which Mr. Bryant thus corrected in writing to Mr. Ware, long afterward:

"NEW YORK, SEPTEMBER 27, 1842: I made a blunder in the 'Hymn of the Sea' which surprised me when I perceived it.

"'The long wave rolling from the *Arctic* pole
 To break upon Japan—'

is not what I meant; it does not give space enough for my wave, nor does it place my new continent or new islands in the widest and loneliest part of the ocean. I meant the Southern or Antarctic pole, and by what strange inattention to the meaning of the word I came to write Arctic I am sure I cannot tell. I corrected the error and published the poem in the 'Evening Post,' as extracted from the 'Christian Examiner.' It has been in most of the newspapers since, but I perceive they copied from my copy."

CHAPTER TWENTY-FIRST.

NEW POEMS.

A. D. 1842.

AMONG Mr. Bryant's more intimate personal friends in New York was the Rev. Orville Dewey, his pastor, second as a divine to Dr. Channing only in his denomination, and a preacher of profound thoughtfulness, culture, and eloquence. It was to him that the following letter was addressed, which, as it gives a lively account of what was going on in the city at the time, is worth copying.*

"NEW YORK, JANUARY 11, 1842: I fully meant to have seen you off on your sailing for Europe, but I arrived at the wharf just in time, as the saying is, to be too late. The steamboat had left the wharf a few minutes before, and I had nothing to do but to go back again, feeling, as you may suppose, very silly. No less, I am glad to hear such good accounts of you and your family; for your acquaintances here gather up and repeat to each other all the particulars that are told in the letters that any of you write. You are now, I suppose, immersed in the amusements of Paris—such of them, at least, as you have a taste for; wearying yourself, and your wife and daughter, with running after sights, with a comfortable and cheerful home awaiting you when you are fairly tired out. New York, in the mean time, is by no means dull, I can assure you. You are in Paris to be sure, but you must not suppose that everything worth taking an interest in is to be found at Paris. You shall judge.

"*Firstly*. There is animal magnetism, which, since the publication

---

* Mr. Dewey had sailed for Europe in the latter part of 1841.

of the Rev. Mr. Townsend's book, has made great progress in America, in New York and elsewhere. It is quite the fashion for people to paw each other into a magnetic sleep. Physicians somnambulize their patients and extract teeth literally without pain.

"A Dr. Buchanan, at Louisville, mixes up phrenology and animal magnetism, puts certain faculties to sleep and excites others, operates upon alimentiveness and makes people hungry, upon destructiveness and makes them choleric, upon ideality and makes them talk poetic-ally, upon mirthfulness and makes them pleasant, upon love of appro-bation and makes them put on airs; or paralyzes one of those organs after the other, and makes the choleric man imperturbably good-nat-ured, the funny man as stupid as an oyster, etc.

"*Secondly.* There is Lord Morpeth, the Irish Secretary in the late Whig ministry. Dinners and parties to Lord Morpeth have been all the rage till within a few days, but they have now become impossible by reason of his going to Washington. Proud and happy is the man who can boast to have entertained a live lord. Lord Morpeth is a quiet, well-bred, unassuming man, with an awkward person, sensible, extremely cautious in his opinions, and not much given to talk.

"*Thirdly.* There are politics, which are particularly interesting just now; your good old Whig party breaking up like the ice in March; the political world taking a short turn and darting off into the empyrean of democracy as if it never meant to come back; but all this you will read in the newspapers.*

"*Fourthly.* There is homœopathy, which is carrying all before it. Conversions are making every day. Within a twelvemonth the num-ber of persons who employ homœopathic physicians has doubled; a homœopathic society has been established, and I have delivered an inaugural lecture before it—a defence of the system, which I am to repeat next week. The heathen rage terribly, but their rage availeth nothing.†

---

* Of seven States that voted for Harrison the year before, five had reverted to the Democrats.

† Mr. Bryant was by hereditary right interested in medicine ; and, when a friend put in his hands a work upon the Hahnemannic theory, he was greatly impressed by its simplicity, and its apparent scientific basis. He applied the system in a great many cases of the smaller ailments that fell under his own observation, and became in time thoroughly convinced of the efficacy of its remedial provisions. He ever after-

"*Fifthly*. There is literature, which is just now bursting into an abundance of blossoms—poetic blossoms, you understand. Mrs. Sigourney has published a volume of poems, Miss Gould another, Mrs. S. B. Dana another, Flaccus—I do not know his real name—another, and there are five or six poets besides whose verses have appeared since you left America, but whose names I do not recollect. I hope their verses are all good; I have not had time to read any of them. Longfellow has published 'Ballads and other Poems'—some of his best things. Add to these the verses in the 'Lady's Book' and the 'Ladies' Companion,' periodicals with a vast circulation; in the 'Ladies' Wreath,' and in Mrs. Griffith's 'Family Companion'; in half a score of annuals and other miscellanies, and you will allow that our poetic literature is marvellously productive. The hedges are full of clover-blossoms, and you cannot set your foot down without crushing a buttercup.

"*Sixthly*. We have lectures. Public lectures were never so much in vogue as this winter. The theatres are deserted for Mr. Eames and for Mr. Sparks, and for Dr. Lardner and the steam-engine. . . . I could tell you of many other matters of equal importance here. Our club (the Sketch Club) flourishes, meeting regularly, and entertaining itself more agreeably than ever—how? You know that already. But the end of my sheet is near, and I must stop. Now, what have you in Paris to set off against all these things? . . . If that iron hand is unclenched that used to take such cruel hold of your head, write me a line. Run off a few words at the end of your pen as you would do from the end of your tongue if you should meet me in the street."

If Mr. Bryant had withheld his letter for a month, he might have added to his catalogue of sensational things a more prodigious sensation than Morpeth or animal magnetism—the arrival of the great Boz. Dickens was then at the height of his popularity, both at home and abroad. In this country his earlier books had been read by everybody that reads at all. "Pickwick" was regarded as such a magazine of fun that you

ward resorted to it in the indispositions of his family, and of his working people, when he retired to the country. His name and his lecture helped to commend it to a more universal attention than it had yet received either in the faculty or with the public at large.

had only to open the covers, in any society, to produce an ex-
plosion of laughter. Its principal characters—Pickwick himself, Snodgrass and Tupman, old Weller, Mrs. Weller and Sam,
old Wardle and the Fat Boy, the Rev. Mr. Stiggins and the
weeping Trotter—were as well known to the most of us as any
oddities on Broadway, or on the boards of the Park and the
Bowery. The newspapers overflowed with the peculiar
forms of wit known as Wellerisms, and I am not sure that some
of them were not better than the originals. With this sort of
introduction, a spontaneous movement of welcome received
Dickens on his arrival in Boston. It was reported that his first
question on landing was, " Where is Bryant? " as if he thought
the poet must of necessity be an inhabitant of Boston. Mr.
Bryant seems to have been touched by the popular excitement, for he called upon the novelist as soon as he reached
New York; and, not finding him in, called a second time.
Dickens acknowledged these attentions in the following characteristic note:

"CARLTON HOUSE, *February* 14, 1842.

"MY DEAR SIR: With one exception (and that's Irving) you are
the man I most wanted to see in America. You have been here twice,
and I have not seen you. The fault was not mine; for on the evening of my arrival committee-gentlemen were coming in and out until
long after I had your card put into my hands. As I lost what I most
eagerly longed for, I ask you for your sympathy, and not for your for-
giveness. Now, I want to know when you will come and breakfast
with me: and I don't call to leave a card at your door before asking
you, because I love you too well to be ceremonious with you. I have
a thumbed book at home, so well worn that it has nothing upon the
back but one gilt ' B,' and the remotest possible traces of a ' y.' My
credentials are in my earnest admiration of its beautiful contents.
Any day but next Monday or next Sunday. Time, half-past ten.
Just say in writing, ' My dear Dickens, such a day. Yours ever.'
Will you? Your faithful friend,

"CHARLES DICKENS."

They breakfasted together at a time appointed, Halleck
and Professor Charles Felton, of Cambridge, being of the

party, and a lively time they had of it.   Felton, writing to Mr.
Bryant afterward, says: " A breakfast with Bryant, Halleck,
and Dickens, is a thing to remember forever."   The story-
teller's exuberant animal spirits and frank boyishness of manner, to say nothing of his wit and nice observation of men and
things, took direct hold of Mr. Bryant's quieter temperament,
in spite of an unmitigated Cockneyism of dress.*. Subsequently he entertained Dickens at his own home, was of the
number of those who invited him to a public dinner at the
Astor House, and he even attended the ball given to him by
the fashion and wealth of the city at the Park Theatre.†   More
than that, when a French contemporary journal‡ made a little
fun of these extraordinary demonstrations, assigning as the
motive of them a desire to escape the imputation of money-
loving, and to get a good report from the visitor, he put a
more rational construction on the outbreak.

"We do not think our French critic," he said, " has gone to the
bottom of the matter.   The main cause is the merit of the individual,
and an honest desire on the part of the community to testify their
appreciation of it.   Many who take a more active part are, no doubt,
prompted by a vain curiosity, or by a paltry ambition to render themselves conspicuous.   But the great majority of them are sincere admirers of the man and his writings.   His more obvious excellences
are of the kind which are easily understood by all classes—by the
stable-boy as well as the statesman.   His intimate knowledge of character, his familiarity with the language and experience of low life, his
genuine humor, his narrative power, and the cheerfulness of his philosophy, are traits that impress themselves on minds of every descrip-

---

* Dickens wore flashy waistcoats and a great deal of jewellery.

† Writing to Dana, April 19th, he said: " You were right in what you said of
Dickens.   I liked him hugely, though he was so besieged while he was here that I
saw little of him—little in comparison with what I could have wished.   It was a
constant levee with him ; he was obliged to keep an amanuensis to answer notes and
letters.   I breakfasted with him one morning, and the number of despatches that
came and went made me almost think that I was breakfasting with a minister of state.

‡ The " Courrier des États-Unis."

tion. But, besides these, he has many characteristics to interest the higher orders of mind. They are such as to recommend him peculiarly to Americans. His sympathies seek out that class with which American institutions and laws sympathize most strongly. He has found subjects of thrilling interest in the passions, sufferings, and virtues of the mass. As Dr. Channing has said, 'he shows that life in its rudest form may wear a tragic grandeur, that, amid follies or excesses provoking laughter or scorn, the moral feelings do not wholly die, and that the haunts of the blackest crime are sometimes lighted up by the presence and influence of the noblest souls.' Here we have the secret of the attentions that have been showered upon Mr. Dickens. That they may have been carried too far is possible; yet we are disposed to regard them, even in their excess, with favor. We have so long been accustomed to seeing the homage of the multitude paid to men of mere titles, or military chieftains, that we have grown tired of it. We are glad to see the mind asserting its supremacy, to find its rights more generally recognized. We rejoice that a young man, without birth, wealth, title, or a sword, whose only claims to distinction are in his intellect and heart, is received with a feeling that was formerly rendered only to kings and conquerors. The author, by his genius, has contributed happy moments to the lives of thousands, and it is right that the thousands should recompense him for the gift." *

After Mr. Dickens had left the city, and reached Niagara Falls, he entrusted to Mr. Bryant an address to the people of the United States, urging the passage of an international copyright law. With it he enclosed letters from Carlyle, Bulwer, Tennyson, Campbell, Talfourd, Hallem, Hunt, Milman, Sidney Smith, Rogers, Foster, and Barry Cornwall, all of whom seconded his appeal. Mr. Bryant, in publishing the address, commended the object of it; but he founded his argument not on the ground simply of justice due to foreign authors, but on the fact that American literature itself had reached a state of development in which our native authors required protection from foreign pillage. He referred to recent works of Irving, Cooper, Dana, Longfellow, Hawthorne, Sparks, Ban-

---

* "Evening Post," February 18, 1842.

croft, and Ware, as having lifted us to a higher place in the republic of letters, of which we were no longer strangers at the gate, but active denizens, and bound to its other members by all the laws of justice, honor, and hospitality.

When Dickens returned to England and wrote his caricatures of American life, Mr. Bryant thought it a shabby return for the public hospitality he had consented to accept; but he did not share in the revulsion of feeling with which they were greeted by the press. Of the famous "American Notes," he simply remarked:

"Mr. Dickens was but four months in the United States, and, allowing him to make the best use of his opportunity, must have gone back without knowing much of the country or its people. He reprehends many things, it is true, very properly, and satirizes others amusingly. Of the latter, what he says about the national abomination of tobacco chewing and spitting is an example; of the former, his remarks on the ferocity and malignity of party spirit, and the liccntiousness of the press. In regard to the newspaper press, however, though its character is bad enough, he has overcharged his censures. The journals of several of our principal cities—Boston, Philadelphia, and Charleston—are quite as decorous, for aught we see, as the best of the English journals. In this city the newspaper press is worse than anywhere else in the United States; but the example of two or three presses in New York does not prove the general profligacy with which all the newspapers in the Union are conducted. It is true that the best of us, probably, have something to amend, and it is true, also, that the standard, both of morality and decorum, is not sufficiently high among the greater number of those who manage our newspapers. Without attempting to justify them by the example of the London journals, which, perhaps, would not be difficult, if comparison were a fair mode of justification, we have no objection to see the scourge of reproof well laid on, and let those wince who feel the smart.*

Mr. Bryant was engaged the while in getting out a new volume of his poems. The Harpers had printed a fifth edition

---

* "Evening Post," November 9, 1842.

of the earlier volume, and to this he added another small volume containing the crop of later growth.* Surprise has often been expressed that he should have written so little poetry, but the real wonder is that he should have written any at all. Considering the nature of his daily occupation, its absorbing toils, its incessant and harassing distractions, the wide diversity of thought it exacted, and the inharmonious passions it often aroused, we are astonished that he should have been able to gather so many as twenty new poems in his new collection. These we doubtless owe to his persistent banishment of the anxieties of the desk from his hours of leisure, and to those long pedestrian tours which racked off the lees of newspaper conflicts, and allowed his poetic emotions to effervesce. It is remarkable, indeed, how few traces of the agitations and sharp collisions of his life are left on his poems.

Since his return from Europe, in 1836, he had written, " The Living Lost," " Catterskill Falls," " The Strange Lady," " Earth's Children Cleave to Earth," " The Hunter's Vision," " A Presentiment," " The Child's Funeral," " The Battle-Field," " The Future Life," " The Death of Schiller," " The Fountain," " The Winds," " The Old Man's Counsel," " An Evening Revery," " The Painted Cup," " A Dream," " The Antiquity of

---

* Of this volume Mr. Dana wrote, December 2, 1842 : ". . . I have been *greatly* pleased with your ' Return of Youth.' It has not only your usual sentiment, truth, and beauty of description and language, but more of strictly poetic *fancy* than many of your later pieces. The first stanza, as a whole, serves very well for the opening, at least with the exception of one line, which is to me a little too much after the order of the manufacture which was carried on some half century ago—' and prompt the tongue the generous thought to speak.' The whole piece is most beautiful, and I want you to substitute a line for this which shall be more in unison with the rest. Should it require a change of one or two of its neighboring lines, no harm would come of it. You can bear the toil of emendation, and, depend upon it, the whole thing is worthy of it. ' Noon' is beautiful, though not equal to ' Evening Revery.' Have you a poem with some few passages of more stir and passion (I don't mean, of convulsions) than these ? If your poem is long, it will need to have here and there a peak thrown up out of the level. Don't think me impertinent, and don't let me bother you. After all, every man must work on according to his natural workings at the time, or he will hurt what is good by *attempts*. It will be beautifully serene and meditative, though it should be without what I speak of."

Freedom," "The Maiden's Sorrow," "The Return of Youth," and "A Hymn of the Sea," and it would be difficult to find in any of these any loss of strength or delicacy in his poetic fibre. In "The Fountain," "The Old Man's Counsel," "An Evening Revery," and "The Antiquity of Freedom," the blank verse of "Thanatopsis" and "The Forest Hymn" reappears in all its solemn and stately beauty; and in "The Battle-Field," "The Future Life," "The Maiden's Sorrow," "The Child's Funeral," and "A Dream," his favorite quatrains exhibit all the old seriousness and sweetness of thought, with perhaps an added music and deeper human sympathies; while "The Winds" and "Catterskill Falls" disclose before unnoticed or unsuspected varieties of power. When the new volume appeared,* the critics acknowledged its unabated charms. Professor C. C. Felton, of Cambridge, in the "North American," said: †

"Mr. Bryant, during a long career of authorship, has written comparatively little; but that little is of untold price—ὀλίγον τε φίλον τε —little, but precious and dear. What exquisite taste! what a delicate ear for the music of poetical language! what fine and piercing sense of the beauties of nature, down to the minutest and most evanescent things! He walks forth in the fields and forests, and not a green or rosy tint, not a flower or herb or tree, not a strange or familiar plant, escapes his vigilant glance. The naturalist is not keener in searching out the science of nature than he in detecting all its poetical aspects, effects, analogies, and contrasts. To him the landscape is a speaking and teaching page. He sees its pregnant meaning and all its hidden relations to the life of man—"

Then, after praising his technical excellences, which are put on a level with the lofty thought and sentiment, Professor Felton added this:

"What a beautiful gift is this! Here is a man whose life is cast among the stern realities of the world, who has thrown himself into

* "The Fountain and Other Poems." New York: Wiley & Putnam, 1842.
† "North American Review," October, 1842.

the foremost line of what he deems the battle for human rights, who wages a fierce war with political principles opposed to his own, who deals with wrath and dips his pen daily in bitterness and hate, who pours out from a mind, fertile in thought and glowing with passion, torrents of invective, in language eloquent with the deepest convictions of the heart and keen as the blade of Damascus; yet able to turn at will from this storm and strife and agony to the smiling fields of poetry, where not a sound of the furious din with which he was but just now surrounded strikes upon the ear; yet delighting to still the tumult of daily conflict, and for a time to cherish those broad and mighty sympathies which bind man to man and nation to nation in one universal brotherhood of hearts. We gaze with wonder on the change, and can scarce believe the poet and the politician to be the same man. But so it is, and happy is it that the scorching stream of lava passion which the central fires of politics pour over the fields of life may be fringed by luxuriant verdure, gemmed with flowers of exquisite hues and richest fragrance; and every man who loves the muse, and longs to see the grace and charities of letters and refinement shedding their delights far and wide over the rugged scenes of American life, may thank the poet-politician for teaching the often-forgotten lesson that there is even in the republic something better than the passions that fret their little hour in the columns of a newspaper, and then pass from the minds of men forever."

All this was meant to be, and was, complimentary, but it shows how little Mr. Bryant was understood even by gentlemen of position and learning who admired his abilities. Setting aside the exaggerations of Professor Felton's phrases in regard to "torrents of invective," "bitterness and hate," and "scorching streams of lava," it is evident that he did not see that Mr. Bryant's political activity was animated by the same broad and mighty sympathies that inspired his poetry. He was, doubtless, deeply in earnest, and sometimes spoke of those who perverted public trusts to ignoble ends with burning indignation; but the prevailing tone of his discussions was calm, dispassionate, and dignified, and as impartial in their judgments as those of a man who adopts a party can be. The general truth of those judgments was amply vindicated by the progress of time.

No one was more keenly aware than Mr. Bryant himself of the incongruity of his daily occupation with his finer faculty; and we have seen, by his letters, how he endeavored to get away from it; but he was by use and wont accustomed to the fetters, and he found in his editorial life many compensations. He had been taught from his youth up that every citizen is bound to interest himself in public affairs, and the interest he took, he had reason to believe, was of great and lasting benefit to the community.* Not only had he raised the character of the newspaper press, but he had by its agency reformed many abuses, and prevented others. On one great evil—that of slavery—his voice was a voice of power all over the land. Letters came to him from good men and women, in every part of the country, testifying their approval of his course; and among these he valued none more highly than those of Dr. Channing, who frequently, by spoken messages or by writing,† encouraged his efforts. Mr. Bryant had enjoyed few opportunities of personal intercourse with the great moralist; he made his acquaintance, in 1821, in Boston, saw him several times afterward, and always called upon him when he visited New

---

* To a friend, who adverted to this subject once, Mr. Bryant smilingly recalled that fine passage of Milton: " It is manifest with what small willingness I endure," "to leave calm and pleasing solitariness, to embark upon a troubled sea of noises and harsh disputes ; put from beholding the bright countenance of Truth, in the quiet of delightful studies; but, were it the meanest underservice, if God by his secretary, conscience, enjoin it, it were sad for me if I should draw back."

† I remember reading these letters, but they are not now recoverable. One of them related to Mr. Bryant's habit of excluding reports of certain crimes from his journal. In the beginning of his editorship he refused to publish any of the details of these crimes, thinking that the tendency of it was to corrupt the public mind; but, at a later day, he took another view of the morality of the case, arguing that the best way of convincing society of the need of reform was to let it know of the hideous ulcers that were generated in its bosom. I do not think that he would ever have justified the realism, in which certain French romancers have since indulged, although he had strong faith in publicity as a means of cleansing polluted nooks. Let in the light, he used to say, if you would drive away the bats, and owls, and other obscene birds.

York. For Channing's abilities and character he cherished the highest admiration; often defended him in the journal, and, when he died (October, 1842), deplored his loss as a great public bereavement. A heart-felt notice of his career concluded thus:

"   It is not, however, the theological opinions of Dr. Channing that we have at present to consider; our concern is principally with his character as a political moralist, in which he has left behind him a reputation that will not die while our language exists. In most of the eloquent writings which he has given to the world within the last fifteen years, his aim has been to recall the practice of government and legislation to the strictest conformity with the highest standard of right; to banish from it whatever was inconsistent with justice, benevolence, and the most reverential regard for the natural equality of the human race. It was in 1828, we think, that his essay on the American Union appeared in an eastern periodical. In that essay he pointed out, with great clearness, the true objects of government, and in particular of the American government, insisting strongly upon a rigorous simplicity of legislation, and tracing a multitude of abuses to a departure from that great and essential principle. Much of the language of that essay has since been familiar to those who are not aware of the source from which it has been derived, and many of its views have become incorporated with the public opinion of the day. Since that time he has published tract after tract upon public questions and public measures, all of them having in view the same great object of bringing the national policy into a more perfect agreement with the principles of benevolence and justice, and all of them instinct with a fervid eloquence which seemed to grow more and more earnest and intense with every successive publication. In several of them the question of American slavery was discussed—discussed with the perfect freedom of one who poured out his thoughts without fear or reserve, yet with a moderation and fairness which those who differed with him did not always appreciate. It may be that, in his desire to reach a great object, he did not always sufficiently estimate the practical difficulties which were to be surmounted, but it were better to err on that side than to abate anything of an essential principle. He never belonged to any of the antislavery associations, and often rebuked the Abolitionists for their ferocity, intolerance, and party spirit, while he vindicated their right to the most perfect liberty of discussion, and agreed with them in maintaining the right of all men to personal freedom.

"The eloquence of Dr. Channing's writings is of a peculiar and original caste. It is fluent, clear and impassioned, enchaining, and persuading the reader with all the power of the finest-spoken eloquence. It is remarkably unadorned with figures, illustrations, and comparisons; it is bare of those ornaments which make what is sometimes called fine writing, and yet it is as far as can be imagined from dry, jejune, and apothegmatic. Truths are stated, and reasonings are urged in the most lucid and choice phrases of the language, and with the most harmonious collocation of words; to every idea the fullest development is given, and view after view of the same thought is presented to the mind, until the mind becomes familiar with all its aspects, and filled with the impression that it is fitted to produce. So admirable is his use of language that phraseology, which, when analyzed, seems to have no character but that of simple propriety, has in his hands a poetic effect, and an irresistible power of kindling emotion in the reader." *

A few days after the death of Channing, when the Unitarians of New York held a meeting in the Church of the Messiah, to commemorate the life and character of their great chief, Mr. Bryant contributed the hymn which was sung on the occasion:

> "While yet the harvest-fields are white,
> And few the toiling reapers stand,
> Called from his task, before the night
> We miss the mightiest of the band."

* "Evening Post," October 5, 1842.

CHAPTER TWENTY-SECOND.

A POLITICAL EMBARRASSMENT.

A. D. 1843, 1844.

IT was an evidence of growing change in public opinion that the " Evening Post " was increasing in circulation. The merchants had abandoned it because of its financial opinions,* and the " dough-faces " † denounced it for its outspoken antislavery sentiments; yet, instead of sinking under the adverse gales, it was spreading a broader canvas to the wind, ‡ and meeting the angry seas with a more contemptuous boldness. Although it refused to fall in with what was deemed the patriotic view of the Right of Visitation and Search asserted by England and the other powers in the quintuple treaty for the suppression of the slave-trade; although it condemned the shameless treatment of Adams by the House of Representatives for his indomitable defence of the freedom of debate, and of Geddings for his manly vindication of the freedom of the high seas, § it found itself actually getting into wider favor. The calmer judgment of the North had been awakened; men began to ask themselves if the constitutional convictions of Northern constituents were to be held only by the consent of slave barons and slave bailiffs. Northern sentiment was, moreover, revolted by the increasing severity of slave-holding laws, made under

---

* At one time it was so low that its publishers were obliged to borrow money of private friends to pay its current expenses.

† A name given to the timid and pliant adherents of party, who allowed their opinions to be kneaded into shape by the pro-slavery leaders.

‡ It was greatly enlarged in size.

§ In the Creole case.

a pretence of resisting the aggressions of abolitionism.   Manu-
missions by will or bequest were forbidden in many Southern States; free negroes might be sold into slavery for the
slightest offences, and the penalties against attempted revolts
were multiplied and aggravated.   Is such the system, it was
asked, that we are to uphold or connive at?   Even Northern
governors were emboldened by the growth of the free sentiment to refuse the surrender of fugitive slaves; and Northern
Legislatures demanded the repeal of the gag-law of Congress
(the 20th Rule), which shut out antislavery petitions.

Mr. Bryant rejoiced in this return of prosperity, not only
as a sign of reviving confidence in the principles of his
journal, but privately also, as it enabled him to gratify a hope
which he had long nourished of getting a home in the country.   Writing to his brother John (February 5, 1843), he says:
"Congratulate me! there is a probability of my becoming a
landholder in New York! I have made a bargain for about
forty acres of solid earth at Hempstead Harbor, on the north
side of Long Island.   There, when I get money enough, I
mean to build a house."   Meanwhile, he thought it no waste
of these expected means to make a brief visit to the Southern
country, where he had never yet been.   Some time before, his
friend Simms, of Charleston, had invited him thither, presenting, perhaps, the most tempting allurement that could be
offered him—the picture of a semi-tropical spring.   "We
have some refreshing novelties at that season," wrote Mr.
Simms, "which will bring you singular renovation and delight
after a long winter of cold.   Our country lies too level for
much that is imposing in scenery, but the delicate varieties of
forest green, the richness of the woods, their deep and early
bloom, and the fragrance with which they fill the atmosphere,
will awaken you to a more encouraging memory of youthful
hopes and dreams than any contemplation of the old, familiar
objects.   There are no irregularities of rock and valley such
as your native hills everywhere present, but mystery clothes
the dense and tangled forests that lie sleeping around us.

You will see the brown deer emerging from the thickets, and fancy in the flitting of some sudden shadow that the red Indian is still taking his rounds in the groves which hide the bones of his family."

In March, 1843, Mr. Bryant went South. Some of his acquaintances were doubtful of his reception there, in the agitated state of public feeling, with his known and pronounced opinions on the subject of slavery, but they knew little of the openness and warmth of Southern hospitality. He went by way of Washington, where he had not been for twelve years, and then to Richmond, which he greatly admired, and afterward to Charleston, where he hoped to get an opportunity to inspect the cotton plantations and the workings of slavery in the seat of its power. He spent about a month among the planters, hearing their defences of "the institution," and witnessing the festivals and frolics of the negroes, when he passed over into Florida to breathe the fragrance of the orange-blossoms and enjoy the delights of summer, while his own home had scarcely yet escaped from the snows. The terrible Indian war being over, travelling was everywhere unobstructed and without danger.* The splendor and luxuriance of the vegetation, the abundance and variety of the flowers, the grassy lakes of the everglades, the time-stained towns, which seemed as if, like the chapel of Loretto, they had travelled from an older continent, and the languages spoken, mainly those of Minorca or Spain—transplanted him into a new world. Every day brought some surprise to the eyes; and the people he encountered seemed to be unable to do enough to render his residence pleasurable.† Throughout the South, instead of the coldness and repulsion which had been predicted for him, he met only with kindliest greetings. " Our visit to the South," he wrote to Mr. Dana after his return, May 26th, "was extremely agreeable. New modes of life and a new climate could not fail to make it interesting, and the frank, courteous,

---

* See "Sketches of Travel," vol. ii.   † Ibid.

hospitable manner of the Southerners made it pleasant. Whatever may be the comparison in other respects, the South certainly has the advantage over us in point of manners." In the
account of his journey written for his newspaper, Mr. Bryant
indulged in no criticisms of slavery. He regarded himself as
the guest of the kind people who had opened their houses
for his entertainment and comfort, and his sense of propriety
would not allow him to return their good-will with unfriendly
disclosures of what he had seen or heard. He was not, however, as we shall soon see, beguiled by these generous attentions out of his settled judgments on the real character of
slavery.

Soon after his return, Mr. Bryant completed the purchase
he had bargained for on Long Island. It was near a little village
afterward called Roslyn, overlooking an estuary of the Sound—
such a nook, indeed, as a poet might well choose, both for
its shady seclusion and its beautiful prospects; embowered
in woods that covered a row of gentle hills, and catching
glimpses of a vast expanse of water, enlivened in the distance
by the sails of a metropolitan commerce. The estate was at
first confined to a few acres only, on which he proposed erecting a house according to his own taste; but he was soon en-
amored of a house already erected on it, and the next year
made it his own. It was an old-fashioned mansion, built by a
plain Quaker in 1787, containing many spacious rooms, surrounded by shrubberies and grand trees, and communicating
by a shelving lawn with one of the prettiest of small fresh-
water lakes. It promised him not only a snug retirement, but
a retreat for the cultivation and nourishment of his friendships.
Curiously enough, he began to feel more and more the need of
intimate associations. The decided individuality of his character and the untoward circumstances of his early life had kept
him from mingling much with men; but he appears to have felt
the isolation. Writing to Mr. Dana, who was still one of his
very few correspondents, he indulges in a lament on this
score:

"You speak of the solitude in which you find yourself since All-ston is gone.* Dr. Johnson said that we must keep our friendships in repair; but there are some losses in friendships which can never be made up. For my part, it has been my fate to live so long among people with whom I have what Charles Lamb calls imperfect sympa-thies, that I have learned to be content with those respects in which we can understand each other. I have never, however, had such an associate as Allston. . . . At last, I have house and lands on Long Island—a little place in a most healthful neighborhood, just upon the sea-water—a long inlet of the Sound overlooked by woody hills, and near a village skirting several clear sheets of fresh water, fed by abun-dant springs which gush from the earth at the head of the valley. I cannot come to you at Cape Ann, but you can come to me at Hemp-stead Harbor, as you must. You shall have fruits of all kinds in their seasons; and sea-bathing, if you like it. I found it of great benefit to me last summer ; but the water, I am sorry to say, is as still as a mill-pond; and you shall sleep a' mornings till the sun is half-way on his journey to noon."

In the interim, while preparing for his change of domicile, he remembered that he was still a stranger to the northern parts of his own New England, in one of the remotest hamlets of which, moreover, lived a solitary relative. He passed two or three weeks of July, accordingly, on the borders of Lake Cham-plain, which for picturesque grandeur have, perhaps, few supe-riors on this continent. The spurs of the mountains from which the State of Vermont is named are outlying rivals of the White Mountains of New Hampshire, and possess many of the same characteristics: vast silvery lakes reposing in the bosom of wooded hills, and large fertile valleys running up to the wildest of rocky passes on the heights. It was in the depths of one of these valleys that he sought out the home of an aunt, of whom he gives this account :

"If I were permitted to draw the veil of private life, I would briefly give you the singular, and to me most interesting, history of

* He died July 8, 1843.

two maiden ladies who dwell in this valley. I would tell you how, in their youthful days, they took each other as companions for life, and how this union, no less sacred to them than the tie of marriage, has subsisted, in uninterrupted harmony, for forty years, during which they have shared each other's occupations and pleasures and works of charity while in health, and watched over each other tenderly in sickness; for sickness has made long and frequent visits to their dwelling. I could tell you how they slept on the same pillow and had a common purse, and adopted each other's relations, and how one of them, more enterprising and spirited than the other, might be said to represent the male head of the family, and took upon herself their transactions with the world without, until at length her health failed, and she was tended by her gentle companion, as a fond wife attends her invalid husband. I would tell you of their dwelling, encircled with roses, which now, in the days of their broken health, bloom wild without their tendance; and I would speak of the friendly attentions which their neighbors, people of kind hearts and simple manners, seem to take pleasure in bestowing upon them; but I have already said more than I fear they will forgive me for if this should ever meet their eyes, and I must leave the subject."

These ladies, whose deaths long since removed the restraints which Mr. Bryant felt, were Miss Charity Bryant, his father's youngest sister, and a Miss Sylvia Drake. Meeting one another at Bridgewater when they were about twenty years of age each, and forming the attachment spoken of in the extract, they removed to Waybridge, where they set up the romantic mode of life which was continued for more than fifty years. Miss Charity died at the age of seventy-three, and the other did not long survive her loss.

The years 1843–'44 were among the most important in our political annals, because they were those in which the conscience of the North was made to feel the true character of slavery more vividly than ever before. The immediate cause of this awakening was the series of intrigues by which the province of Texas was wrested from the dominion of Mexico. An invasion of it by emigrants from the United States was afterward followed by a struggle for independence, which, when independence was achieved through the assistance of sympathizers in the United States, led to a project for its admission into the Union. In every one of these steps slavery was the leading motive. Although at the outset it was ostensibly in possession of the field, controlling all departments of the Government, and mastering both the great political parties, yet, as it was a battle against the moral sense of mankind, it could never feel itself wholly secure. The supremacy of the slaveholders was threatened by the rapid progress of the North in population and wealth. This progress was only to be counterbalanced and overcome by the conquest of new regions in which slavery could be introduced. Texas comprised a territory equal to that of six of the larger States, and, once in the grasp of the slave-holders, might be used as a means of political control for the future. The scheme was a stupendous one, and it was carried out with equal cunning, fearlessness, and energy.

Mr. Bryant had opposed it from its very inception, many years before; he continued his hostility at every new development of the plot, and, in fact, became so active and prominent in his antagonism that his efforts require to be described in more detail than we shall be able to give to other parts of his political career.

He was not opposed to annexation in itself: on the contrary, his confidence in the federative system was so strong that he believed in the practicability of its indefinite extension; but that extension, to be entirely safe, required some sort of assimilation or affinity between the parts to be federated. The Democratic party was, he thought, right in its general adherence to the gradual absorption by the republic of neighboring peoples, but it was wrong in favoring that absorption at the expense of a great war, of an enormous debt, and of a consolidation of slavery. How clearly he saw the evils of the scheme may be illustrated by one or two extracts from his paper:

"THE ANNEXATION SCHEME.—If there was no other objection to the scheme for annexing Texas to the territory of the United States, the unprecedented haste with which it has been urged upon the action of the Senate should be reason enough for its rejection. It is admitted on all sides that a measure of greater importance, either for good or evil, has seldom claimed the attention of the country. Its very importance, then, demanded that it should be dispassionately considered before any decided step was taken.

"The annexation of Texas would change essentially the political constitution of two separate nations. It would convert Texas itself from an independent power, with a distinct and thoroughly organized government, into the mere province of another nation, with a derived and secondary government only, besides modifying in many ways its commercial relations with the world. And as to the United States, it would introduce a new member into the confederacy, materially affecting the present rights and relations of the older members, and probably controlling their federal legislation for the future.

"Now, it is obvious to our minds that changes so important should not be made without the deliberate sanction and consent of the people of both the nations which are interested. Several years have passed since the formal assent of the Texans was given to the project of annexation to the United States. This assent, in the first place, was expressed through the Legislature of the nation, and not by an organic act, as the case seemed to require, and it has not since been confirmed. Whether the majority of the people are still in favor of the project, we are left to infer from the silence, rather than the decided action, of their authorities. But this is a question of little practical importance.

"The real issue to be decided is, whether the people of the United States, whose rights are deeply involved, whose cherished sentiments are likely to be violated, whose civil liberty and peace are endangered, have been properly consulted in this matter. Has it not been sprung upon them with the suddenness of surprise? Have they had the time to investigate the bearings of the question, or to ascertain the precise nature of that new relation which they are to be forced to assume? Are they not called upon to enter into vast and momentous responsibilities, without being allowed the time which is requisite to weigh and understand the tendencies of their untried position? Surely, in an affair of such wide-reaching influence, there is needed all the wisdom and prudence which the collective intellect of the nation could bring to bear upon the determination of it.

"We are the more surprised that the haste which has marked these proceedings should have come from persons professing to be friendly to the rights of the States. If we understand the doctrine of State rights, it is that the different States are only members of a general partnership, and not the elements of a consolidated government. According to this theory, it is manifest, certainly, that no new partner should be admitted into the firm until the older members had been regularly consulted."*

As the treaty for the annexation of Texas was rejected by the Senate, it was forced into popular controversy at the next ensuing presidential election. Mr. Van Buren, the choice of the Northern Democrats, because he had taken ground against the project, was, notwithstanding his habitual deference to the opinions of the South, defeated of a nomination in the National Democratic Convention by Southern intrigues. An old rule, requiring a two-thirds majority to effect a nomination, was revived, and, in consequence, Mr. Polk, a comparatively unknown man, but a slave-holder, was nominated in Mr. Van Buren's stead. The New York delegation opposed the proceedings throughout, with great ability and earnestness, but it was both out-generaled and out-voted. Mr. Bryant was inclined, for a time, to withhold his approval of the nomination. But what was he to do? It was impossible for him to ally himself with the whig opposition, whose fundamental measures of policy he had always been foremost in denouncing; and yet his own party was on the eve of surrendering itself into the hands of leaders whom he depicted in this wise :

"The annexation of Texas means nothing more nor less than the extension and perpetuation of slavery at the risk of war, and with war if it cannot be got without. It is the pure Southern Upshur-Tyler scheme. It is the pill without the gilding, the dose without the sugar.

* "Evening Post," May 6, 1844.

It is plain enough to see that, if this question had been committed at the outset to men of mind large enough to take in all the interests of this great nation, Mexico would have been satisfied, the question of slavery avoided, and Texas annexed with honor and satisfaction to the whole people. But, for our shame and misfortune, the matter fell into the hands of a few fanatics, as crazy on the subject of ' domestic institutions' as the maddest Abolitionists in the Union—men who believe, or affect to believe, that the *summum bonum* of Republican freedom lies in the possessing of a few hundred slaves—and by these slave-holding fanatics was the question of Texas, a great question of extension of empire, dwarfed into one of enlarging the influence of that pernicious institution which defaces and disgraces our otherwise glorious country.

"This abortion, rejected with contempt and disgust by the whole country, a few Northern Democrats are swaddling and nursing and trying to coax into life. Now, we say it with mere reference to the interests of the party—interests which no wise person can overlook— that any Northern Democrat who seeks to identify the party with the extension of slavery, and to make that the rallying question, is only fit for bedlam; and no greater political insanity can be imagined. Slavery is an old, decrepit, worn-out, feudal institution. Shall the young Democracy, in its heroic youth, stifle its ardent nature by so unnatural an alliance? Where slavery and slave representation exist under the Constitution, let them exist. It is the bargain, it is the bond. But to extend these evils to another portion of the Western hemisphere, and, above all, to make this the rallying cry of the party, is evidently suicidal."

A choice of evils was thrust upon Mr. Bryant, but a choice of extreme perplexity and embarrassment. In the end he concluded that it would be more practicable to guide his own party into a better direction than it would be easy to reconcile his life-long aims to a junction with his adversaries. He was, of course, taunted with inconsistency; but he justified his position in this way, which, at this time, will seem more ingenious than satisfactory:

"In supporting Mr. Polk we resist the pernicious project of a National Bank, which will most certainly be carried into effect if the

Whigs obtain the ascendency in the Government. In supporting Mr. Polk we withstand the project of distributing the proceeds of the public lands—a most corrupting and demoralizing project in its effect, to say nothing of the constitutional objections to which it is exposed. In supporting Mr. Polk we take the only method of procuring a repeal of the present unjust tariff, though the Whigs declare their determination of maintaining it as it is, with all its oppressions and abominations. In supporting Mr. Polk we support the scheme of a treasury independent of banks and corporations, which all experience has shown to be a measure of vital importance. In an election involving such great issues, no man, no public press, taking the views of them which we take, can with a safe conscience remain neutral, and allow a national bank to be built up, the proceeds of the public lands to be distributed among the States and scrambled for by speculators and jobbers, and an iniquitous tariff, which crushes American industry, to remain in force, without using his best exertions to defeat the party which comes forward with all these projects of mischief.

"But, it is said, do you regard the question of the annexation of Texas as of no importance? and will you support a candidate with whom you disagree on that question? We certainly consider the Texas question as one of great moment; but, if those who are unfriendly to immediate and unconditional annexation do their duty, we need fear no danger from that quarter. The imminence of the peril is already over, and, if we stand to the ground we have taken, every hour diminishes it. There are enemies to the annexation scheme in Texas itself, among whom we believe we may count its president (Sam Houston); there are enemies to it in the South, even in South Carolina, and the factitious zeal which has been awakened in its favor elsewhere is already beginning to grow cool. We have only to act conscientiously in this matter, to meet the question frankly whenever it comes up, cause it to be well understood that we submit to no attempt to force the annexation upon us as a party measure, and to wait for the honest and unprejudiced formation of public opinion, and the day of this scheme, we are fully assured, will soon be over. . The establishment of a national bank and the consummation of the other mischiefs contemplated by the Whigs are dangers of another kind. If the Whigs succeed in the approaching election, these mischiefs will certainly be inflicted.

" These considerations left us no alternative, when the subject first presented itself to our minds, but the support of the Democratic nominations. We are not in the habit of taking our ground lightly in such cases, nor can we be easily driven from it." *

A great many of the New York Democrats coincided with Mr. Bryant in this view. They were unwilling to abandon their own party for another, to no one of whose principles they could assent; and yet they were equally unwilling to give countenance to their own party in the false attitude it had been led to assume. They endeavored to extricate themselves from the difficulty by organizing a movement within the party to resist its fatal error. In order to ascertain how far this was practicable, Mr. Bryant, in connection with six of his friends, issued a private circular to such persons as they supposed might be in agreement with them, soliciting information, and proposing, in certain events, a concerted mode of action.

" [*Confidential.*]

" Sir : You will doubtless agree with us that the late Baltimore Convention placed the Democratic party of the North in a position of great difficulty. We are constantly reminded that it rejected Mr. Van Buren and nominated Mr. Polk, for reasons connected with the immediate annexation of Texas—reasons which had no relation to the principles of the party. Nor was that all. The Convention went beyond the authority delegated to its members, and adopted a resolution on the subject of Texas (a subject not before the country when they were elected ; upon which, therefore, they were not instructed) which seeks to interpolate into the party code a new doctrine hitherto unknown among us—at war with some of our established principles, and abhorrent to the opinions and feelings of a great majority of Northern freemen. In this position, what were the party at the North to do? Was it to reject the nominations and abandon the contest ? or should it support the nominations, rejecting the untenable doctrines interpolated at the Convention, and taking care that the support should be

* " Evening Post," July 26th.

accompanied with such an expression of their opinion as to prevent its being misinterpreted? The latter alternative has been preferred, and we think wisely; for we conceive that a proper expression of their opinions will save their votes from misconstruction; and that proper efforts will secure the nomination of such members of Congress as will reject the unwarrantable scheme now pressed upon the country.

"With these views, assuming that you feel on this subject as we do, we have been desired to address you, and to invite the co-operation of yourself and other friends throughout the State:

"1. In the publication of a Joint Letter, declaring our purpose to support the nominations, rejecting the resolutions respecting Texas.

"2. In promoting and supporting at the next election the nomination for Congress of such persons as concur in these opinions.

"If your views in this matter coincide with ours, please write to some one of us, and a draft of the proposed letter will be forwarded for examination."

This circular was signed by William C. Bryant, George P. Barker, John W. Edmonds, David Dudley Field, Theodore Sedgwick, Thomas W. Tucker, and Isaac Townsend. Of course, when it found its way into print, it put the mere partymen into a rage. They characterized the act "as treason—foul Abolition treason—under the mask of philanthropy, federalism under the guise of Democracy, falsehood under the covering of truth," and they had no names for its authors more mild than contemptible, wily, insidious, black-hearted plotters of unimaginable mischief.

In reply to these denunciations, Mr. Bryant said:

"The confidential circular, which has made so much noise, was only a preliminary to an immediate public declaration of opinion. It was written to ascertain the opinion of the individuals to whom it was addressed. Such of them as were favorable to the views expressed in the circular were, as will be seen on reading it, to be invited to give their signatures in a public declaration of the same views, to be published as soon as possible. Of course, an inquiry in regard to the opinions of individuals must be private. Such things are not pub-

lished in the newspapers. But, on the other hand, no part of the actual proceedings in resistance of the attempt to force the annexation
scheme down the throats of the Democracy was to be secret, or could
in its nature be secret. Their effect will be to make the Texas question an open question in the Democratic party of this State, and present to those who are unfriendly to annexation a ground on which
they can conscientiously vote for the Democratic nominations."

The proposed Joint Letter appeared in due time, and it is
here given in full, with the introduction of the " Evening Post "
(August 20, 1844), as an interesting part of the history of the
time :

"We publish to-day, as we promised, the Joint Letter which was to
have been sent to the persons answering the circular. By its positions we are willing to abide. They have been carefully considered. Taken with deliberate judgment, they will not be hastily
abandoned.

" We ask the Democratic electors of this State to read this letter.
We believe it contains unanswerable truth, and points out the only
course consistent with their integrity as Democrats and citizens. We
quarrel not with those who differ from us. They may be good men
and sincere Democrats. We give our own views with the same freedom we yield to them. But, so far as we are concerned, or our counsel can have any influence, we advise our fellow-Democrats to support
the Baltimore nominations with all fidelity, with an energy and earnestness that know no rest, and at the same time set their faces like
flint against the 'reannexation of Texas at the earliest practicable
period,' or the mixing of that question with the struggles of party.

" *To the Democratic-Republican Electors of the State of New York :*

" FELLOW-CITIZENS : The present circumstances of the Democratic
party induce us to address you. It has been placed by the late Baltimore Convention in a position of difficulty, from which nothing can
extricate it but prudence, firmness, and a recurrence to its original
principles.

" The Convention rejected Mr. Van Buren, to whose nomination
a great majority had been pledged, and nominated Mr. Polk, for reasons connected with the immediate annexation of Texas, and then

passed a resolution, the purpose of which was to pledge the whole party to the *annexation at the earliest practicable period.* This signifies neither more nor less than the annexation as soon as it can receive the forms of law, and pays no regard to our relations with other nations, to the debts of Texas, or to its slave institutions.

"In this position, ought the Democratic party at the North to reject the nominations and abandon the contest, or support them, rejecting the resolution respecting Texas, and taking measures to counteract its tendency? The latter alternative has been wisely preferred. But it ought not to be done silently. On the contrary, there is every reason that upon a subject of such magnitude, where apparent acquiescence might be drawn into precedent, the voice of the whole party should be made known. That we may do our part toward this object, we have united in this address, not merely to make known our own views, but to ask the co-operation of our fellow-electors in measures to counteract the tendency toward immediate annexation.

"We protest against the resolution, because

"It was an unauthorized act of the Convention. The members had received from their constituents no instructions upon the subject. They were elected before the question had been presented to the country. They were elected for a definite and limited purpose. If they had authority to pass any resolutions, they had none to go further than to reiterate the old-established, well-known principles of the party. They were elected to select candidates for office, not to promulge new creeds or annex provinces.

"But, if the members of the Convention had had the authority of a majority of their constituents for its resolution, it would not have bound the minority, because it was not an exposition of any principle of the party, or of any measure which those principles require.

"The authority of party is as limited as its purpose. Men having the same views of the principles of their government unite for the purpose of putting those principles into practice. That union is a party. It is founded on certain general principles, and is limited to them. To adhere to them, and to concur in such measures as they require, is the whole duty of party men. In other respects, each may act and vote as he judges right, without complaint from his associates.

"The Democratic party has been in existence from the foundation of the Constitution. Its principles are as old as the Government, and have since been constantly repeated. They are 'equality and freedom; equal rights to all; no distinction of persons; no special privileges, and no restraint of the individual, except so far as may be necessary to protect the rights of others. We regard every man as a brother, having equal rights with ourselves. We are for the strictest construction of all grants of power, and the strictest accountability of and those only, which these principles require. So far, we hold ourselves bound as party men—but no farther.

"The greatest danger to our institutions arises from the tendency of party to engross every public question. This comes of the selfishness of mere partisans, who seek to turn everything to their own ends. We see no more reason for submitting all our actions to its control than to the control of fashion or sects.

"When, therefore, a convention of party men seek to pledge the party to a measure not within these limits, we look upon the act as of no greater force than the act of any other equal number of equally respectable persons. As an opinion, we adopt or reject it as we think it sound or otherwise; as authority, we disregard it.

"For these reasons, though firmly attached to the Democratic party, we hold ourselves not bound as party men by the resolutions of the Convention. The resolution itself we consider unwise and unjust. We condemn it, not because we are opposed to the extension of our territory, or the admission into our Union of new communities—not that we would not resist the interference of any European power in the affairs of the New World—a policy to which this whole people is devoted—but because

"1. We have a treaty with Mexico, binding us to 'inviolable peace and sincere friendship.' Texas is now engaged in war with Mexico, and taking her, we take that with her, breaking our pledge of inviolable peace. It is not an act of sincere friendship to take to ourselves a country which once belonged to her, which she has never surrendered, and is now struggling to regain. Our recognition of the independence of Texas admitted that her forces had actual possession of the government of that country, but it admitted no more. It neither admitted nor denied that Mexico had claims and rights in respect to Texas.

" 2. Texas has an enormous public debt, which she is unable to pay, the amount of which is unknown, and which must either be assumed by us, or left, as it now is, a dishonored claim upon an insolvent State. In the latter case, we add another to the list, already too great, of insolvent or repudiating American States. In the former, we assume for the Union a debt not contracted by it or for it—an act of doubtful power and evil tendency.

" 3. Texas is a slave country, and, if received with its institutions, all magistrates and officers of what class soever.' This is the Democratic creed, and the whole of it. The measures of the party are those, will claim admission into the Union with its slavery, its unequal representation, and its requisition upon the free States. We are not Abolitionists, and have no sympathy with them. We are willing to abide by the compromise of our fathers. We will not obliterate a line of it. We will not stop short of it, but we will not go a step beyond it. No threats, no reproaches, shall force us beyond it. We stand by the Constitution of our country. But when it is proposed to extend that Constitution and compromise to foreign countries, we take leave to inquire what sort of countries they are, and by whom inhabited.

" It is said that the annexation of Texas will not increase the number of slaves. If it were so, it would not remove our objection, for the annexation would still increase our connection with slavery. Why should we multiply our relations with it, even if the sum total remains the same? If we were proposed to bring under the American flag all the slave communities in the world, would it overcome your repugnance to it to tell you that the number of slaves would not be increased?

" We are unwilling to give to any foreign slave-holding nation those extraordinary and unequal privileges greater than our own, which our forefathers gave to their brethren and companions in arms. A citizen of Mississippi with five slaves has virtually as many votes as four citizens of New York. If Texas ever comes into this Union, no one of its citizens shall have, with our consent, more power than a citizen of our own State.

" But they err who think that the annexation of Texas will not increase slavery and the number of slaves. The annexation is pressed upon us by a portion of the South as a new source of prosperity for slave industry, and a new guarantee to their institutions. Do they not know their own interests better than we? Political economy and our own experience both teach us a different lesson. Slavery has increased in Virginia and the Carolinas since the annexation of Louisiana. Slave breeding is always commensurate with slave markets. Population expands with the means of its subsistence and the demand for its industry. To increase the market and the value of labor is to increase the population. No law of political economy is more certain.

"For these reasons we are firmly and unalterably opposed to the annexation of Texas, in any shape in which it has yet been offered to the American people. But we cannot consent to see Whig candidates elected, and Whig policy prevail in the general Government. Nor shall that ever happen if any effort of ours can prevent it. The great principles of our party were never more firmly rooted in the hearts of a majority of the American people than at this moment, and, if the election can be made to rest on them, we shall assuredly prevail. How shall we separate the true issues from the false? How to reconcile the conflicting wishes and duties which the error of the Baltimore Convention has created, is the question we have anxiously considered. We see no means of doing so but to support the nominations made at Baltimore, and, at the same time, promote the nomination of members of Congress opposed to this annexation. The President can do nothing of himself if the two Houses are of a different opinion. To this point, then, we invite your particular attention. You can, if you choose, effectually counteract the tendency to annexation by electing members of Congress opposed to it. You are about to elect thirty-four members of the Lower House of Congress, and a State Legislature that will elect one member of the Senate. If we might be allowed to counsel you at this crisis, we would do so, and earnestly entreat you not to falter in your support of the Baltimore nominations, but, at the same time, to nominate for those elections no man who is committed to this scheme—this unwise, unjust, un-American scheme of adding Texas to our dominions, without even a plausible pretext, with indecent haste, regardless of treaties and consequences, with its war, its debt, its slave institutions, and their preponderating political power.

"*July* 15, 1844."

This was an unsuccessful battle in its immediate effects. It did not arrest the tendencies of the Democratic leaders.

On the contrary, Mr. Calhoun, Secretary of State, acting in conjunction with President Tyler, on the very last day of their tenure of office (March 3, 1845), procured authority, by a joint resolution of Congress, to incorporate a foreign power into the Union, without a single constitutional sanction, and with the certain prospect of war.   But the battle, though unsuccessful, was not fruitless.   It aroused an opposition to slavery which was no longer confined to the moral convictions of a few individuals, or of a small class.   The contest passed into national politics, where it became more and more dominant. At the next presidential election the antagonists of slavery were strong enough to make independent nominations, and, within ten years thereafter, were able to rally to their side a formidable array of intelligent and manly voters.

END OF VOLUME FIRST.

Milton Keynes UK
Ingram Content Group UK Ltd.
UKHW012136080124
435706UK00003B/121